TOUGH TALKING COWBOY

By Jennifer Ryan

Stand-Alone Novels
THE ME I USED TO BE

Wild Rose Ranch Series
TOUGH TALKING COWBOY
RESTLESS RANCHER
DIRTY LITTLE SECRET

Montana Heat Series
TEMPTED BY LOVE
TRUE TO YOU
ESCAPE TO YOU
PROTECTED BY LOVE (novella)

Montana Men Series
HIS COWBOY HEART
HER RENEGADE RANCHER
STONE COLD COWBOY
HER LUCKY COWBOY
WHEN IT'S RIGHT
AT WOLF RANCH

The McBrides Series
DYLAN'S REDEMPTION
FALLING FOR OWEN
THE RETURN OF BRODY MCBRIDE

The Hunted Series
EVERYTHING SHE WANTED
CHASING MORGAN
THE RIGHT BRIDE
LUCKY LIKE US
SAVED BY THE RANCHER

Short Stories
CLOSE TO PERFECT
(appears in SNOWBOUND AT CHRISTMAS)
CAN'T WAIT
(appears in ALL I WANT FOR CHRISTMAS IS A COWBOY)
WAITING FOR YOU
(appears in CONFESSIONS OF A SECRET ADMIRER)

JENNIFER RYAN

TOUGH TALKING COWBOY

Wild Rose Ranch

AVONBOOKS

An Imprint of HarperCollins*Publishers*

Excerpt from *Waiting on a Cowboy* copyright © 2020 by Jennifer Ryan.

TOUGH TALKING COWBOY. Copyright © 2020 by Jennifer Ryan. All rights reserved. Printed in the United States of America. No part of this book may be used or reproduced in any manner whatsoever without written permission except in the case of brief quotations embodied in critical articles and reviews. For information, address HarperCollins Publishers, 195 Broadway, New York, NY 10007.

First Avon Books mass market printing: April 2020
First Avon Books hardcover printing: March 2020

Print Edition ISBN: 978-0-06-297508-9
Digital Edition ISBN: 978-0-06-285185-7

Avon, Avon & logo, and Avon Books & logo are registered trademarks of HarperCollins Publishers in the United States of America and other countries.

HarperCollins is a registered trademark of HarperCollins Publishers in the United States of America and other countries.

FIRST EDITION

20 21 22 23 24 LSC 10 9 8 7 6 5 4 3 2 1

*For all of you facing challenges—whether it's addiction, trauma,
physical or mental illness, abandonment, loneliness—I hope Drake
and Adria's happy-ever-after inspires you to find your own.
You deserve it.*

TOUGH
TALKING
COWBOY

Chapter One

Adria unlocked the front door and stood in the opening, feeling the stillness as intensely as the prickle of awareness that something was wrong. Without thought, her hand dipped into her purse and her fingers closed over her phone and the bag she pulled out. Her purse slid off her shoulder and dropped to the floor.

She felt her sister's need in every fiber of her being. She "heard" her sister's cry for help. With their connection, sometimes they didn't need words to communicate.

Adria's heart raced as the quiet coming from the bathroom seemed to thicken the air until she could barely draw a breath. Every step toward the door felt like it took forever. Her mind shouted *Hurry*, but her heart warned of heartbreak beyond the closed door. She pushed it open against the barrier on the other side, found her identical twin lying motionless on the floor, her lips tinged blue.

Adria's stomach pitched, sour bile rising to her throat.

She swallowed hard and tried to think through the dizzying shock.

Nothing, not even her resigned heart, could prepare her for this.

She dropped to her knees and shook Juliana. "Wake up!"

No response. Not even a flutter of her eyes.

Adria's heart pounded. Her mind skittered from one scary thought to the next. She warned herself not to believe what was so obviously true.

She leaned down, tilted her sister's head back, pressed her lips to Juliana's, and gave her mouth-to-mouth. They'd breathed as one in utero, but she never expected she'd have to take over for her beautiful, broken sister like this. "Come on, Jules, I can't live without you. Don't do this to me."

She gave her three more breaths, then had to use drastic measures to bring her back.

She flipped her phone over, dialed 911, put the phone on speaker, and left it on the floor next to her dying sister.

"Nine-one-one, what is the emergency?"

"My sister overdosed. Heroin. I'm administering naloxone." Adria unzipped the bag she'd instinctively pulled from her purse, found the syringe, and unwrapped it. She broke open the glass ampoule, used her teeth to pull the cap off the needle, and filled the syringe despite how much her hands shook.

"What is the address of the emergency?"

She rattled off the house number and street for Wild Rose Ranch as she jabbed the needle into her sister's bare thigh and pushed the plunger.

Waiting for a response stopped Adria's heart. She held her breath. The world around her paused.

And nothing happened.

Fear squeezed her heart. Hope made her send up another prayer.

Juliana didn't miraculously wake up, but her barely there breaths deepened and evened out.

"Paramedics are three minutes out. Have you administered the naloxone?"

"Yes. She's breathing. Shallow, but even."

The terrifying blue in Juliana's lips faded as they turned pink once again.

"Roll her to her side if she's not already in that position."

Adria turned her sister and brushed the blond hair from her face, relieved but still worried sick. "Why, Jules?" Of the two of them, it was Adria who had reason to want to escape and numb her emotions and drown out her nightmares.

Yes, their childhood sucked. They'd grown up with a drug-addicted mother who prostituted herself out for drugs, and money to buy more drugs.

She always needed more.

She'd done a lot worse than sell herself to get them.

Mom, Christie, now Crystal since she started working at the Wild Rose Ranch, had done so many drugs she'd short-circuited her reasoning, judgment, and empathy. She only cared about herself and proved it to her young twins too many times to count.

Adria hated seeing her sister do the same thing she'd watched their mother do their whole lives—self-destruct.

It broke her heart to pieces.

"I'm not going to let you do this to yourself." She combed her fingers through Juliana's hair and tried to breathe through the fear and heartache.

"Paramedics and police have arrived." Focused on Juliana and making sure she kept breathing, she'd forgotten about the dispatcher on the phone.

"The door is open. We're in the bathroom." She checked the urge to hide Juliana's drug paraphernalia. Even though her stomach knotted at the thought of the police seeing the evidence and possibly arresting Juliana, she didn't stop them. Juliana needed help. And Adria would make sure she got it.

She reminded herself they weren't alone in the world. They had their sisters Roxy and Sonya. Without them, without the Wild Rose Ranch, they'd probably both be dead by now.

"Miss, we're here to help. Please step back."

Adria leaned down and kissed her sister on the forehead. "Hold on. You're going to be okay now. I love you."

The paramedic held his hand out to help her up off the floor. She appreciated the gesture, because even though he was there for her sister, he took the time to help her, too. His presence eased her mind.

But her heart still clenched when he put his dark hand on her sister's deathly pale wrist to check her pulse. The wild rose tattoo that started at her sister's shoulder and wrapped around her arm stood out dark green and pink against her translucent white skin. Four roses. Juliana, Adria, Roxy, and Sonya.

Her imagination had one of those roses shriveling and dying. She pushed the nightmare image out of her mind. She couldn't even conceive of her sister leaving her.

An officer's radio squawked behind her, the dispatcher relaying information about a burglary in progress. All Adria wanted was for these guys to care about her sister more than anything else, because right now, nothing mattered more than saving Juliana's life.

"Miss, can you answer some questions for me?"

She didn't turn to the officer, but watched the paramedic check her sister's blood pressure. "What do you want to know?"

"Let's start with your name."

"Adria Holloway. That's my sister Juliana."

"Twins?"

Usually that was so obvious, but Juliana had lost weight the last many months she'd been partying away her days and nights instead of attending school. Adria had just graduated. But as far as Adria knew, Juliana had dropped out. She hadn't attended classes since the first week of the semester. And it pissed Adria off to see her sister waste the opportunity to do and be something better than this: a drug addict, looking for her next score instead of living the life they'd been given here on the Ranch.

A second chance Adria tried hard every day to embrace instead of her own demons.

"Identical," she confirmed, though not in every way.

"Can you tell me what happened tonight?"

Adria wished she knew what possessed her sister to think getting high and putting her life at risk was a good idea. Or that it solved anything.

"I'm not sure. I was on a blind date." *From hell.*

More than a year after her last dating debacle, she'd wanted to try again. Another chance to see if she could get past her hang-ups and connect with a man and not see him as the monster from her nightmares.

Lonely, she'd wanted to connect with someone. She wanted some physical contact, to feel a man's hands run over her skin and feel the pleasure in his touch.

She'd never use one of those stupid apps again. "I ended the date early and came home."

Not because her date talked about sports for nearly an hour, didn't have any cash or even a credit card—really?—to pay for dinner, and then had the nerve to ask her to his place afterward. But because she'd had a bad feeling.

Like she'd go to his place after swiping on his picture and messaging him twice to set up the date. She knew nothing about him, except for his favorite football team and that he wanted her to give him head before they had sex.

He preferred it that way.

She left him with a big "Fuck you," and hauled ass home, her mind on her sister and not the Raiders' biggest fan.

"I walked in the door and knew something was wrong." She'd felt Juliana slipping away. Like a piece of her that Adria carried in her soul evaporated. The echo of fear and desolation swamped her system again. She wrapped her arms around her middle, wishing her sister would wake up and hug her. "I grabbed the naloxone and ran to her."

"Has she overdosed before?"

"Once." She never wanted to receive that call from the hospital again. Another shot of pure terror raced through her. For a split second that time, she'd thought her sister had died. Just like tonight when she saw her passed out on the floor, her face gray, lips blue, and barely an ounce of life left in her.

"Looks like she was getting ready for bed." The officer pointed his pen at Juliana's state of undress.

In her red lace bra and a black leather skirt that barely covered her ass, maybe it looked like she'd been undressing. But Adria knew better. "She was getting ready to go out."

"It's awfully late."

Not for Juliana, who had taken to coming home after dawn, sleeping the day away, and spending her nights out partying.

Because of Juliana's unpredictable schedule, Adria had started sleeping in Roxy's room, which was usually unoccupied since she inherited a ranch in Montana and lived there now with her new family. Roxy was raising her adopted stepsister, Annabelle, and got engaged to Noah Cordero.

She'd found her home. Love. Family.

Adria was working on finding her own happiness, while Juliana played Russian roulette with her life.

"She likes the nightlife." Juliana liked driving an hour or so into Vegas. So many strangers looking for a good time. Fun. Frivolous. No strings. No expectations. Just go with it.

What happens in Vegas stays in Vegas.

Juliana thought that suited her. She thought she could escape whatever drove her.

All it did was make her worse because when you're that high and out of it, you can't feel. Not really.

And when you wake up, you still have the same problems and that just bums you out more.

You still can't escape yourself, because in the end it's just you and your thoughts and your past and the decision you have to make every day to either leave it behind and move on, or stay in that dark place.

The fact that Big Mama and security at the Wild Rose Ranch brothel caught Juliana selling herself with the other prostitutes who worked at the legal whorehouse only showed how far off the rails Juliana had gone these last few months. They'd sworn to each other that they'd never end up like their mother. But Juliana spent more time with Crystal these days than she did with Adria.

Some form of self-punishment? Adria didn't know. She'd begged Juliana to talk to her. But Juliana shut her down and pushed her out of her life.

She missed the closeness they'd always shared.

The closer Adria got to graduation, the more self-destructive Juliana became.

It felt like her fault. They were slowly going in different directions. At some point, they needed to separate, didn't they? They couldn't always do everything together and the same.

Didn't she deserve her own life and successes?

It hurt Adria's heart to think they'd soon travel down different roads, when they'd spent their whole lives not just going down the same path but holding hands as one. But Adria couldn't follow her sister down the path of destruction Juliana continued to take despite the risks and how miserable it made her. Juliana's behavior tore them apart a little at a time.

Adria could only hope that what happened tonight would wake her sister up and make her want to change her ways before things got worse. Because, yes, Adria knew from experience, things can always get worse.

"Do you guys work up at the Wild Rose Ranch?" The officer held her gaze, a look of interest in his eyes.

"No. Our mother does."

That raised a few eyebrows among the three men there to take care of her sister, but they didn't say anything.

The paramedics did their job, efficiently stabilizing her sister, putting in an IV line, and getting her settled on the gurney. They covered her with a blanket and strapped her in. Seeing her covered somehow warmed Adria as well.

After the paramedics rolled Juliana down the hallway, the officer took pictures of the bathroom, including the mirror sitting precariously on the edge of the counter, the remnants of powder on it, and the cut straw her sister used to snort the heroin.

Adria stood on the porch while they loaded her sister into the back of the ambulance.

Just then, Big Mama, Madam of the Wild Rose Ranch, pulled into the driveway in her Cadillac. She'd driven over from the mansion across the wide pasture. Someone up at the brothel must have seen the flashing lights. She slipped out of the front seat dressed in a black skirt, black bustier, red stilettos, her red hair curled in waves, and her black-lined eyes glassed over with sadness and filled with fear. "Is she . . ."

Adria shook her head, unable to speak for fear her sister would prove her wrong and die on the spot.

"What happened?"

Adria ran into the Madam's arms and ample breasts and hugged her close, relieved she'd come and Adria wasn't alone.

Big Mama had been the only real mother figure she'd had since the older woman had rescued her mother, Crystal, from a shelter. Big Mama had given them a home and made sure they went to school, preventing Child Protective Services from taking her and Juliana to a foster home.

Big Mama took care of them. She cared about them. She kept Crystal from ruining their lives anymore.

"She overdosed. I gave her the naloxone just like the doctor showed us after the last time."

Big Mama squeezed her tight. "Good girl. You saved her."

"I can't do this again." The tears clogging her throat burst free on a ragged sob and her sadness and anger poured out.

"I hope you don't have to."

Adria stepped back and tried to rein in her wild emotions. "I won't, because whether she likes it or not, I'm getting her the help she needs."

Big Mama nodded. "Call Roxy. Tell her to call Sonya. It's time to intervene." Big Mama swept her gaze over Adria. "Change into something more comfortable. I'll drive you to the hospital."

The ambulance pulled out. Big Mama went to talk to the officer who walked out of the house. Adria's mind caught up to the fact that she was standing in the too-tight, low-cut, electric-blue tank dress and four-inch strappy heels Juliana insisted she wear on her date. Adria never wore things like this, but Juliana coaxed her to be bold, telling her to "give your date a reason to come back for more." There was nothing "wrong" about dressing sexy for a date, but she hated that the guy thought it was an invitation to hook up. Based on the way she was dressed, even the officer and paramedics thought she worked at the Ranch.

Not the image she wanted.

She needed to stop doing what people told her to do and just be herself and focus on her future.

Something broke inside her when that man . . . Well, that was in the distant past. It happened. She didn't know how to make it go away, but dating random men wasn't the solution.

But God, how she dreamed of a real relationship with a guy who knew how to be kind and made her burn.

She left her nonexistent love life on the back burner. She ignored the heavy, sour ball of dread in her gut and the whisper in her heart that spoke her worst fear, *You will always be alone.*

She ran into the house, peeled off the too-sexy-for-her dress, tossed the uncomfortable heels, pulled on a pair of jeans, a tank top, and a comfy shrug. She slipped her feet into a pair of Keds and left her hair in wild disarray as she grabbed her cell from the bathroom floor and her purse off the tile entry and met Big Mama at her car.

She dialed Roxy as Big Mama drove and followed the ambulance to the hospital.

Roxy picked up on the first ring. "What's wrong?"

This late at night, of course Roxy expected trouble. "Juliana overdosed again. She's in an ambulance on the way to the hospital. I need you to make that call."

"On it. Want Sonya and me to meet you in Vegas?" They'd come running the last time, too.

"No. I want her to see us all supporting her at the rehab. I don't care what it takes, but I'm getting her on the plane and to the rehab center whether she likes it or not."

"I'll make it happen."

Adria sighed out her relief. "Roxy."

"Yeah, honey."

"Thank you."

"What are sisters for?"

In this case, to pick up the pieces when everything fell apart. And to pick up the tab. When Roxy found out she owned the Wild Rose Ranch, she'd made it clear that she meant to use the enormous amount of money she earned to help her sisters. She'd paid for Adria and Juliana to finish school and eliminated all their debt. Now Adria needed Roxy to pay for the astronomically expensive rehab her sister needed to save her life.

"I love you, Adria. You're not alone. Sonya and I will be there."

"Thank you." The simple but heartfelt words didn't seem enough to convey to Roxy how much she appreciated what she was about to do. Because saving Juliana meant saving Adria.

She could live without a man, but she couldn't live without her twin.

Chapter Two

Drake rubbed his hand up and down his battered left leg. His other hand, with the raw, bloody scrapes on his knuckles, held the steering wheel in a death grip. He sat in the driveway and stared out the windshield at the woman he lusted after, hated, was happy to see, and wanted out of his sight for good.

What was she doing here? Why come back when she'd made it clear she couldn't stand the sight of him?

He'd made a fool of himself over Melanie. He believed she loved him. She had once said so. But was it ever real?

She promised she'd be his wife. But that was then. Now she didn't want him or the future they talked about but couldn't make happen. All because she wasn't who he thought she was and he'd changed.

He'd never forget the expression on her face when he'd been medically cleared to come home from the military and he saw her for the first time in months. Her face paled. Her eyes locked on the stupid cane he had to use—he couldn't get by without it. The severe damage to his leg left him with a limp, limited mobility, and even worse, the inability to stand on his own two feet for more than an hour at a time.

The many months he spent in the hospital and at rehab meant his only connection to Melanie came from phone calls that got shorter and text messages that dwindled to a few words when she got around to reading them. Oh, she'd encouraged him to work hard and get better, all the while making excuses for why she couldn't fly out to see him.

Stupid him, he'd held out hope that once they were back together everything would work out fine. But his anger, resentments, and feelings of inadequacy, coupled with her impatience, reticence, and inability to hide the fact she thought less of him now, coalesced into a stunningly awkward attempt to find what they used to have when he was whole and she thought she loved him.

One look at the damage to his face and body, and his embarrassing attempt to seduce her without being able to perform, only ended with him feeling completely useless and her picking that moment to tell him she couldn't do it anymore. Looking at him hurt too much and made her grieve for what might have been if only he'd come home exactly the same as he left.

But war leaves a mark on your soul, just like the bullets and bombs did on his body.

He wasn't the man she remembered.

He barely remembered that guy.

He wasn't really a man at all anymore.

He'd become an empty shell of a body that didn't work the way it used to.

If that wasn't bad enough, the nightmares took over his mind sometimes and made him do things he wasn't proud of and scared him and his family.

He'd scared Melanie. He'd made her afraid of him.

He had a lot of regrets, but that one cut deep and left him with one thought, *I will be alone the rest of my dismal life because of it.*

He'd never do that to another woman.

Which made him wonder what the hell Melanie was doing here now.

And why the hell were his sister and two brothers loading his horse into the trailer?

The unruly side of him flared to life. The anger he couldn't control sometimes raged inside him. Why couldn't they all leave him the hell alone?

His sister, Trinity, walked to Melanie's side and stood next to her. She said something to Melanie, but the glare she directed right at him demanded he get out of the truck and stop being rude.

That had become his default setting these days and he didn't really give a damn. They had no idea what he'd been through, what he'd done, or how fucked-up his mind had become because of it.

PTSD.

Four little letters for something huge. Something that slowly destroyed what was left of his life.

Nothing but the term they gave him to express how fucked-up-crazy he'd become and an excuse for his out-of-control emotions and behavior.

Sometimes, he blacked out and did things he didn't even remember.

He didn't want to think about those times. They scared him.

So he tried to pull his shit together, mentally prepare himself for whatever Melanie and his family had in store for him, and got out of the truck. At the last second, his left leg gave out. He caught himself on the door, cursed, and grabbed his cane to stabilize his stance.

The puppy he didn't want but was his all the same barked and whined, happy to see him, and tried to escape Tate's hold.

Melanie took a hesitant step toward him, then stopped. She looked good in tight jeans, a purple T that hugged her curves, and brown ankle boots. Her honey-colored wavy hair hung to her shoulders, bright and shiny. Too bad he couldn't say the same about the look in her eyes.

Sympathy.

Pity.

The first he didn't need. The second punched him in the gut with what a failure he turned out to be.

"What are you doing here?" The words came out harsher than he intended. He certainly didn't want to make her take a step back. But hell, she'd walked out of his damn life two months ago. He wished she'd stay the hell out so he didn't have to think about all he'd lost, what was missing from his life, and what he'd never have with her—or any woman—ever again.

"Drake, whether you believe it or not, I still care about you."

Right. She could barely look him in the eye because she didn't want to see the ugly scars on his face.

He pinned her in his gaze, hoping she saw the anger roiling inside him and not the hurt she'd caused. "You've got a hell of a way of showing it."

"I know you're hurting . . ."

"You don't know anything!"

Frustration lit her blue eyes. "Only because you refused to talk to me about what happened. At the end, you barely spoke to me at all."

You don't want to hear about the things I did. The terrible things that happened.

He found himself stumbling to come up with anything to say, to explain, to get her to see that he wanted to be who he used to be, but he just couldn't find that guy inside him anymore. Being home didn't feel right. He didn't know where he fit in his family or with her. He tried to go through the motions, but they could all see he struggled to stay grounded and find his footing in what felt like someone else's life. He had become so engrossed in his team and their missions, he didn't know how to switch gears and settle back into civilian society when the war still raged in his head.

"You gave up on rehab."

What's the point? My leg is fucked and so am I.

"You keep your appointments with Dr. Porter but you barely speak to him."

Talking about it only makes the nightmares worse. Don't you get that? Doesn't anyone see that?

Drake glared daggers at his sister for gossiping with his ex about him. "Stay out of my business."

Trinity planted her hands on her hips. "No. We gave you space. We tried to be nice and understanding. We tried to bully you into helping yourself. We let you have your way. You barely leave your room, let alone the house. Declan needs help running this place, but you won't even try."

Drake pointedly looked down at his busted-up leg, knowing that, though all his sister saw was denim, *he* saw the scars underneath.

Melanie got one look at them and tapped out. He wished he could do the same.

A couple times, he'd come close to ending it, but he'd pulled himself back from the brink. He didn't know if he could do it again the next time he sank that low. And he crept ever closer to that point even though he tried to hold it back.

They had no idea how hard he struggled to get through every hour, let alone a day.

You don't need me. "Declan needs someone who can do the job."

"You're not useless." Melanie saying that to him nearly made him laugh, and not in a good way.

Bitterness and rage swept through him, because he'd shown her how useless he was to her and any other woman unfortunate enough to come into his life.

Declan and Tate flanked their sister and eyed him. Tate set the puppy on the ground so he could finally reach Drake. The pup attacked Drake's boots. Drake ignored him, even though he was meant to help Drake connect with something and give him a purpose, something to care about. Drake didn't care much about anything these days.

"What the hell are you doing with my horse?"

"Get in the truck and you'll find out," Declan dared him.

This time Melanie closed the distance between them, though she stayed just out of his reach. "They're worried about you. They love you. Please, Drake, you can't live like this."

Sometimes I don't want to live at all.

He wondered what she'd say about that, but didn't dare voice that echoing thought. His brothers and sister just might go all in and have him committed. They'd threatened it enough times over the last two months.

He made his psychiatrist think that all was well and good at home, but it wasn't, because he was neither of those things.

"What I do or don't do has nothing to do with you anymore."

Her pink lips pressed in a tight line. Defeat filled her eyes. He hated that she gave up so easily. He wanted her to push. He wanted her to fight for him the way he'd fought his way back to her.

But she didn't want him.

She didn't love him.

And maybe he never loved her either. Not enough to put her first.

Add another item to the *I'm a dick* list.

Maybe he'd convinced himself he loved her because he'd needed to hold on to something and someone from home to give him a reason to fight that hard to live. Now that he didn't have anything, anyone, or even the possibility of the life he'd dreamed of having with her, what was the fucking point?

She reached out, grabbed his hand, pressed something into his palm, gave him one last sad frown and pitying look, and rushed to her car.

He looked down at the diamond ring in his hand. "What the hell is this?" Dumping him once wasn't enough; she had to come back and make the point one more time.

"I can't keep it."

You don't want to keep me.

He didn't think his battered heart could take another hit, but this pain was like a wrecking ball, demolishing every last bit of anything good left inside him. He'd known pain, but this left him numb. And furious.

"What the hell am I supposed to do with it?" He barely got the words out before she slid into the front seat of her car.

She gave him another sad frown but couldn't meet his eyes. "I'm sorry."

No, he was sorry. Sorry he believed she'd wait for him to come home from his tour of duty.

Sorry he believed love blurred flaws.

Sorry love wasn't enough to hold them together.

His sister stepped in front of him before he could go up to his room, before the rage building inside him exploded. "Where have you been?"

"None of your fucking business."

Trinity checked her urge to take a step back from him, which only doubled the guilt he felt for snapping at her. He wasn't angry at her. He was furious with himself because Melanie walking out on him made him feel like a failure.

And he didn't fail at anything. Ever.

He fought.

He won.

He survived.

But these last few months didn't feel like living.

It felt like another battle.

And his family got caught in the crossfire of his volatile temper.

The more out of control it got, the worse he felt, which made him even worse to be around.

He didn't even want to be with himself, so how could anyone else want to be around him?

He wanted off the merry-go-round, but it was spinning too fast for him to jump off and he had no idea how to slow it down.

He shifted his weight off his bad leg and tried to ignore the pain. But it throbbed with insistence that he pay attention and do something about it.

He'd just gotten home from the pharmacy with his meds, but was reluctant to take them. Not after seeing his buddy Chase Wilde spiral out of control on pills and land in rehab.

Drake had enough problems.

The last thing he wanted to do was give his family even more reason to worry about him.

Trinity picked up the puppy and snuggled him close, accepting a faceful of dog licks. "Jamie is expecting you. You promised you'd go."

Yeah, and they were driving him to make sure he went. For his own good.

He met Jamie Keller—and her overprotective fiancé, Ford Kendrick—last week when his family dragged him to Rambling Range Ranch to meet her—a fellow soldier who'd come home wounded in body and mind and who could relate to him. She'd worked through her PTSD with their mutual psychiatrist, Dr. Porter, and wanted to help him do the same.

He didn't think he'd be that lucky. But what he wouldn't give for a normal day.

His brain had taken a trip to Crazy Town and didn't know the way back to normal.

Jamie foisted the damn puppy on him, said the tiny beast of an Australian shepherd would help him get out of his head. He grudgingly admitted the puppy helped. But he could barely take care of himself, let alone a pet.

Jamie wanted him to believe his kind of damage could be fixed.

Broken couldn't be fixed. And he was broken.

Melanie could attest to that. She got an up-close and very humiliating look at just how broken he came home.

Ford stuck it out with Jamie all through the worst of her PTSD. Ford put a ring on that, and they were great together. Jamie found her happiness again.

Drake wouldn't mind having a woman like her. Tough. Strong. Someone who was like him and understood the trauma he suffered and still endured.

Never going to happen.

"I changed my mind." After seeing Melanie, he wasn't in the mood to be around anyone. He gimped his way back to his truck to get the bag of meds. The ring smashed in his fist bit into his palm but he didn't care.

"Get in the truck." Trinity's voice sounded like anything but the way his sweet sister usually talked to him. "I'm not fooling around here, Drake. You are going to do this one thing we asked."

He went around the open truck door, grabbed his meds, then slammed the door. He stared down the drive, where Melanie practically peeled away and drove out of his life for good. He hoped. Because every time he saw her, his sense of falling deeper into that dark pit in his mind intensified.

"Drake!"

He spun around too fast and sent a bolt of pain down his thigh and up his hip and almost lost his footing, but caught himself at the last second. Sometimes, he didn't think and moved like he wasn't injured. "What?"

"Let's go."

He hated to disappoint them, but he was in no mood for equine therapy and Jamie pushing him to open up about his feelings. His family wanted to push him to try to do the things he used to love. They didn't understand his limitations. He knew them all too well, because everything he couldn't do anymore took another piece of him. Some of those things took chunks that left even more holes in him than the three bullets that had ripped through him.

Tate plucked the puppy out of Trinity's arms and put him in the backseat and held the truck door open. "We're going to be late."

Declan already sat behind the wheel, his face set in a mask of barely contained impatience.

Why the hell did all of them need to take him? He could drive himself.

But he already knew the answer: because they knew he'd just drive off somewhere and hide out for a few hours if they didn't gang up on him now.

If he stalled any longer, Declan and Tate would probably lose it and wrangle him into the truck against his will. He hated to admit it, but though they'd never been able to overpower him in the past, he was no match for them now.

Trinity walked over to him and put her hand on his chest. He flinched away. She took a step closer and closed her hand over his arm and held tight. "I'm sorry she gave you back the ring and changed her mind about marrying you. You've been through so much. You don't need her adding insult to injury. If she can't accept and support you, then you don't need her."

That gaping hole of emptiness inside him widened with a swamping sense of loneliness.

He needed something because he felt himself free-falling into that dark pit.

"I need you to hold it together and get in the truck. Please, Drake. For me. For Declan and Tate. We're trying to help. But you need to work with us."

He didn't say a word. He stuffed the damn ring in his pocket instead of throwing it into the nearest pile of horse shit, leaned heavily on his cane, ignored the pain in his leg, and limped to the truck. Surly, he shoved Tate to get into the backseat with Trinity. It took some maneuvering, but he got his ass up into the front passenger seat, his leg stretched out, the cane beside him.

For a split second, the sound of the truck door slamming sounded like a gunshot. His muddled mind took him back to the ping and pang of bullets ricocheting off his armored vehicle.

Declan slammed his hand down on Drake's shoulder, shocking him out of the memory.

Trinity leaned forward and brushed her hand over the back of his head. "This is going to be good for you."

He didn't believe her.

For months he'd lived with everyone telling him, "It'll be good to . . ." Fill in the blank.

Nothing felt good anymore.

He rubbed the heel of his hand over the ever-present ache in his chest.

God, how he wanted something, someone, to make him feel good again.

Chapter Three

Adria stood between Roxy and Sonya, wishing she could make Juliana understand that leaving her here at the rehab facility was the only way they knew how to save her life. It killed Adria to see her sister so gaunt, fragile, and pissed off.

"You can't make me do this." Defiant as always, Juliana dug in her heels, even though she'd agreed to come just five hours ago.

Adria held firm and checked the need to hug her sister close and console her. Juliana didn't need to be coddled. She needed a heaping dose of reality and tough love. Even if it made Adria's heart ache. "If you don't stay, you're on your own from now on."

Juliana immediately looked to Roxy.

Adria didn't give her a chance to guilt Roxy into giving her money. That would only give her a way out of doing what she needed to do to survive. "She's agreed to pay for your stay here. It's a steep price, but worth your life. You said you'd do this. You promised me you'd get clean." The tremble in Adria's voice softened Juliana's grim face and defiant eyes. "I almost lost you." The thought clogged Adria's throat. "I can't live without you." This time Adria did reach out for Juliana and held her shoulders. "You're my other half. If I could do this for you, I would." Adria would do anything for her sister.

"Like you did before."

Those harsh words sent Adria back a step. The shock that Juliana would bring up what happened to them as children brought back a flood of nightmarish memories.

Juliana leaned in. "You can't always save me. Maybe I don't want to be saved." Juliana fisted her hands and held her arms rigid at her sides. "Did you ever think about that?" She took a menacing step closer. "Did you ever once think that you made things worse, not better?"

Rage, pure and unrelenting, swept through Adria that Juliana would throw their horrendous past in her face. "I would save you from every second of pain and shame I suffered because I love you. I would do anything for you." And she did. Horrible, unimaginable things that haunted her even now.

Knowing what Adria had done to save her sister tormented Juliana. That was clear now. It's why she needed help. "Won't you do this for me?"

Every muscle in Juliana's body went rigid with the intensity of staring down Adria, but Adria didn't back down. She couldn't. Juliana needed this. If Juliana couldn't make the right decision, Adria would make it for her.

"I don't need this. I'm fine." Denial only made the problem worse. Juliana couldn't admit she had a problem and needed help. "But I'll stay. For you."

Adria shook her head, disheartened that Juliana balked at this chance to get better and find some joy in life. "Not for me, Jules. Do this for you. Make peace with what happened. Purge it from your system along with the drugs. Find a way to be happy."

"Like you?" Juliana asked that rhetorical question just to push back. She went out with her friends and flitted from one man to the next, enjoying their company and just living life. Juliana repeated the pattern their mother had set: masking the pain and trauma of their lives with booze and drugs and the illusion of happiness.

But both mother and daughter were really miserable deep down.

Hurt people do hurtful things.

Adria understood how her past had affected her. A piece of her was broken. She accepted that. She lived with it.

But Juliana didn't have to suffer because of what happened to Adria.

As twins, they shared nearly everything.

This was for Adria to carry.

Because the burden was obviously too much for Juliana to bear.

So it was left to Adria to try to fix Juliana. Because that's what she did for her sister. All the way back to when they were little girls and their mom used them to get what she wanted. Booze. Drugs. Men. Anything that would make her feel good. Or not feel at all.

And most of the time she forgot that she should love her little girls, not hurt them.

Adria had nominated herself the protector. And she'd tried real hard to fulfill that role for Juliana, but she couldn't protect her from herself. She couldn't make Juliana want to stay clean.

"What's it going to be? Are you staying? Or are you on your own?" This time she managed to keep the tremble and emotion out of her voice because Juliana needed this push.

"I'll just go back to Wild Rose Ranch. I like it there." Juliana always challenged others.

"Roxy already spoke to security. You will not be let in ever again. That will not be your life." The thought of her sister ending up a prostitute, falling deeper into this hole, left Adria scared and disappointed. Juliana could do and be anything. She wanted her to choose a better life than the one they had growing up.

Juliana looked to Roxy.

"I will not see my sister turn her back on every opportunity available to her to be a prostitute. Anything you want, you stay clean and I'll make it happen, but you will not work at the Wild Rose Ranch."

"Fine. I'll go back to college."

Roxy nodded. "Great. I'll pay for it. As soon as you finish rehab."

"Now you're blackmailing me?"

Adria rolled her eyes. "Your choices have consequences. If you want to continue doing drugs, you'll do it without our support or enabling you. You get clean, we will continue to be your biggest cheerleaders."

Sonya cocked her head. "Are the drugs more important than anything else in your life?"

Adria asked her own question. "Do you need them more than you need your sisters?"

Juliana deflated and her shoulders slumped. "No. I just can't believe you dragged me all the way up here for this."

"Roxy and Sonya found a new life up here in Montana. Maybe you'll do the same."

"I guess you're going back to the Ranch." Disappointment and fear tinged those words. Juliana didn't want her to leave. She couldn't stand for Adria to be that far away, because deep down she needed to know Adria would be there to catch her if she fell.

"No. I'm staying nearby. You won't be allowed visitors for a little while but I'll be here the second they say I can see you again."

"Promise?" The desperation in that single word broke Adria's heart.

She hooked her hand at the back of Juliana's neck and pulled her forehead to hers. "I swear it. I'm not leaving you. Ever."

Tears welled in Juliana's eyes. "I'm sorry."

"I know you are. It's forgotten." Because that's how they did things.

"I don't want to die." The whispered words were barely audible, but Adria heard her and it tore at her soul to hear those words come out of her sister's mouth.

"Then save yourself this time," she whispered back.

"Juliana Holloway? We're ready for you." The admissions lady stood behind them.

Adria fisted a handful of Juliana's hair. "You can do this. I believe in you."

Juliana nodded, then stepped back.

Adria put her hand over her heart, showing Juliana the tattoo on the back of her hand that read simply, I Love You. Three words Adria sometimes needed to remind herself that she was loved. She needed to love herself. Right now, Juliana needed to know Adria loved her. It would always be. It was as permanent as the ink on her hand.

Roxy and Sonya hooked their arms around Adria's shoulders and hugged her to their sides as the admissions lady escorted Juliana down a hallway to her room.

"She's going to be okay." Sonya kissed her on the side of the head.

"I know she needs to be here—I just hate that she thinks I'm punishing her."

"She deserves to be punished for that callous remark about you saving her." Roxy was the toughest of all of them, but she had such a big heart. "It took guts and a strength I don't know if I possess to do what you did at nine years old."

"I don't know how I did it. I just didn't want anyone to hurt her." *Not my beautiful sister.*

"Well, she's hurting now. I hope she'll take advantage of this program, talk about what happened and how it makes her feel, and release it." Roxy turned to her. "Maybe you need to do the same thing."

"I'm fine. I graduated with two degrees and Trinity and I are opening our own business. What more do you think I can do?"

"Be happy," Sonya suggested.

"I'm happy."

"How about dating?"

Adria rolled her eyes. "Oh, I get it—you two are engaged, so I need to be, too."

Roxy shook her head. "I'd settle for you giving up this notion that something is wrong with you because the two boyfriends you had couldn't accept that for you some things are uncomfortable."

Adria walked to the door, Sonya and Roxy following. "Sex. Sex is uncomfortable for me."

"If they'd just given you time to let go of your past and . . ."

Adria put her fingers over Roxy's mouth. "Stop. The sex was fine. It was me who wasn't. I get that. I also know that being with them was more an experiment than my actually falling for them."

"Maybe you'll find someone better, more open and understanding."

She shook her head. "It wasn't them, it was me. They weren't the problem. I don't know what I want. Right now, I'm okay on my own." Without the complications of some man wanting to get to know her better only to discover her horrible past and realizing that the reason she took things slow, didn't trust easily, and couldn't seem to let go during sex was because she'd been used and abused.

She fought to erase the images from her mind and not let them over-take her with flashbacks to that time.

She hated what happened to her, but she raged inside that her mother had been the one to make it happen.

Roxy held her face in her hand. "Hey. I'm sorry. I didn't mean to bring it all up again."

Adria held Roxy's arms. "I know. Just let it go. We need to focus on Juliana and her recovery."

Sonya brushed her hand down Adria's hair. "She agreed to stay. That's a step in the right direction."

Adria hoped her sister walked the whole path and found what she needed at the end of it.

Roxy brushed her thumbs over Adria's cheeks. "Are you sure you don't want to come and stay with me or Sonya?"

"Trinity has a cabin on her property for me." Adria looked around the beautiful ranch-style building, gorgeous gardens, and wide-open pastures. "You know, Juliana will do well here if she tries." Adria hugged Roxy close. "Thank you for paying for this. I know it's a lot and it's not guaranteed that she won't relapse. We've seen it with our mothers. They do well for a long stretch of time, but then . . . they don't." And that was the sad truth about what they grew up with and how they lived their lives waiting for the next time their mothers self-destructed.

Adria didn't know if she could take seeing her sister live her life like that, too.

"Stop. Juliana's got some stuff to work out. She'll do it here. We'll all be there for her when she needs us." Roxy leaned back. "Sonya and I are here for you when you need us."

Adria nodded, but her heart grew heavy. "I know you're busy with your ranches and your cowboys . . ."

Roxy hugged her again. "We are never too busy for you, little sister. Noah and Austin wanted to be here, but they didn't want to make it look like we brought in the muscle to get Juliana to stay."

"I know what you mean. I hope we'll all get together soon. Go." She stepped back and shooed her sisters away. "Go home to your guys."

"Are you headed to the McGraths' place?"

She nodded to Sonya. "I'll get settled in there before Trinity and I check out the retail spaces tomorrow." Tears welled in her eyes. "I don't know how to thank you for backing me in the business."

"The money was a graduation gift."

Roxy shared her newfound wealth with a generosity that astounded Adria. She never even blinked about how much Adria needed for her business and the cost of Juliana's rehab.

She was so lucky to have such amazing sisters.

And Roxy and Sonya had found two wonderful men who loved them the way they deserved to be loved.

Maybe Adria didn't see that in her future, but it'd be nice to find someone who made her feel as good as Noah and Austin made her sisters feel.

Maybe one day. If she allowed herself to get that close to someone. For the right guy, she might risk her heart, but after all she'd suffered, and seeing her sister a breath from death, she didn't know if she could take another blow to her soul.

Chapter Four

Confined in the truck, Drake felt his skin crawl with the need to escape. He didn't like having his sister and brother behind him. The hairs on the back of his neck prickled with the threat of an ambush. One part of his brain knew that was ridiculous. While Trinity and Tate loved to sneak up on him as kids, they weren't about to do that as adults. Especially since he returned from the Army Rangers and was more likely to lose his shit and try to kill them than play along. Still, that other part of his brain felt threatened.

He hated that he'd had some seriously questionable moments since coming home. He'd pushed Declan away and even shoved Trinity aside, when all she'd done was walk up beside him to put her dish in the sink. They hadn't done anything to warrant his extreme reactions.

If he could control himself, he would. Because the last thing he wanted to do was hurt someone he loved.

And he did love them, even if he couldn't feel it the way he used to.

Everything good inside him got washed under the waves of unrelenting images of death and destruction he couldn't erase from his mind.

"I don't see why this is necessary."

All of them sighed. He caught Declan's eye roll and bet Trinity and Tate did the same in the backseat.

Declan pulled into Rambling Range Ranch and headed down the drive to the massive practice ring.

"There's Jamie." Trinity hopped out of the truck the second Declan hit the brakes and ran over to the woman who thought she could help him.

Declan turned to him. "Your life sucks right now, Drake. We all get it. You don't talk to us or Dr. Porter. You hide in your room for days on end. Something has to change. So get out of the fucking truck and do this. Not for us, but for yourself." Declan forcibly opened up the driver's door and got out, slamming it shut on him and any further conversation.

Since he took the keys with him, Drake was stuck.

He got Declan's anger. He'd stepped up when their mom and dad packed up the RV and headed out on their multistate national park tour. At the time, Declan and Tate took over the ranch, hoping that when Drake returned he'd join them. They'd be the team they were as kids and teens—working together again, but this time without their dad.

But he couldn't stand to be out in the open on the ranch, irrationally looking for snipers in the trees and fearing an IED would go off at his next step in the pasture.

Those kinds of fucked-up thoughts, and even worse, his actions, like taking cover behind the tractor for no reason, or absolutely refusing to leave the relative safety of the barn to feed the cattle, only made it clear he was more a hindrance than a help.

The truck grew too hot for the puppy, so he sucked it up and got out.

Declan and Tate unloaded Drake's favorite horse and saddled him. Thor stood waiting, tied to the fence. These days, he talked more to his horse than the people around him.

He barely spoke to Jamie last week but listening to her story and what happened to her—seeing her well—helped.

The puppy brushed his head against Drake's chin. Drake set him down to run and play.

Drake eyed Jamie coming his way and immediately turned so she only saw the side of his face that hadn't been sliced open by shrapnel and stitched back together.

She walked right up to him. "Why haven't you named that puppy?"

The Australian shepherd left Tate to attack Drake's boots. *Again.* He shrugged. He hadn't gotten around to it.

"He needs a name."

Drake ignored her and the furball at his feet.

Jamie pushed like she always did. "Let's mount up. We'll ride and talk."

The last thing he wanted to do was give voice to the horrible things in his head and prove to her and everyone else how fucked-up he was inside and out. "I told you I don't want to talk about it."

"It's your turn to share. I know you want to forget, and the harder you try, the worse things get. So tell me something. Anything. Fight to be better."

Each and every day he felt the fight going out of him. Some days, he didn't know why he tried at all to make it through the day. "Is this where you tell me that everything is going to be all right?" Cynicism filled those words because he didn't believe anything would be all right ever again.

This was his life now. This was his reality. And it sucked.

"Remember what I told you last week."

You have seen terrible things. You have done terrible things. Terrible things have been done to you. But you are not the terrible thing.

Those words had hit hard and went deep. He wasn't sure he believed them.

"So get your ass up on that horse. We're going for a ride, and we are going to talk."

He glanced at his family, sucked it up, and did what they'd brought him here to do. "Can I get a leg up?" He bit the words out through his locked jaw. He asked, but he didn't have to like it or the need for him to have assistance to get on his damn horse.

Without a word, she waved Trinity over to take the puppy. Jamie dropped into a lunge. He reluctantly put his foot on her thigh, much lower than the stirrup he couldn't reach with the injuries to his hip and leg. She grabbed hold of his ankle and calf to stabilize him. He dropped his cane, grabbed the pommel and saddle, and hoisted himself up, swinging his other leg over the saddle as she lifted him by his leg.

Pain lanced up and down his thigh, up his hip, and into his lower back. He grimaced and let loose a muffled curse and groan. Every little movement hurt, but getting up on Thor was excruciating.

He settled into the saddle and stuffed his feet into the stirrups, hoping the pain would subside, but knowing it would remain unrelenting.

"Better than last week?"

"Sure," he bit out.

"You need to get back to regular physical therapy."

"Uh-huh."

She walked over to her fiancé, Ford, and kissed him for a long moment, their connection and love evident. It seemed so easy between them.

Drake had hoped he and Melanie would be like that again. He accepted her initial shock to his scars. The damage was a lot to take in, but he thought she'd sympathize, then see the guy she loved no matter what had happened to him.

He expected too much.

He wasn't that guy anymore. And what she saw in him now wasn't what she wanted.

He wanted to blame her, but he hadn't made it easy for her to stay. Her reaction made him mad. He didn't hide his disappointment. And when he tried to make up with her and couldn't, he got even angrier.

She walked away without really trying to understand all he couldn't put into words. She gave up on him, and them, without ever trying to prove to him what they shared mattered more than the changes in him.

Jamie gave Ford a blinding smile and mounted her horse. "We're out of here." Jamie kicked her mount to walk down the lane.

Drake followed, mostly because Thor wanted to follow her mare. He tried to block out the pain and overwhelming feeling of danger that wasn't there and concentrate on the ride and the beautiful landscape around him. He used to love being outside in the sun and wind and open space and tried to find that feeling inside him.

Jamie gave him a good twenty minutes to settle into the ride before she came at him again. "So, if you don't want to talk about what happened in Afghanistan, then tell me about Melanie."

Of course Trinity spilled that piece of his past to Jamie. His sister, and his brothers for that matter, should stay the hell out of his life.

Jamie narrowed her gaze. "We're not going back until you talk about something."

Like he couldn't turn Thor around and head back to the ranch anytime he wanted. Even though riding hurt like hell, and he'd pay for it all night and days to come, he liked being on horseback, seeing the land and feeling the wind on his face.

Jamie ignored the fact he remained on high alert. He tried to fight the urge to head for cover.

"When's the wedding?" Women liked to talk about such things. Better to let her talk about that than him trying to explain something he couldn't come to terms with or articulate. He hurt. He raged. He wanted to know why all those good men had to die. He wanted to know why he'd been spared only to live in agony.

It was worse than hell.

Jamie ignored his question and asked one of her own. "Did you love her?"

He had no idea anymore. He liked knowing she was home waiting for him, that when he walked in the door she'd smile and his heart would feel light and he could focus on her and not what he'd done. What he'd seen. What haunted him.

Jamie shared a little more of her life. "When I came home, I couldn't wait to see the people I left behind. But at the same time, I didn't want them to see me."

That about summed it up. He wanted Melanie to see only the man she fell in love with. He wanted things to be exactly the same as before a bomb blew up his life. "I'm not the person they remember. They don't want to know me now."

"It took me a long time to figure out that once I accepted what happened, grieved for all I'd lost, and found a way to live again, I'm not that different."

"I am that different." He didn't recognize anything about himself anymore. He used to be so laid-back, focused but fun to be around. He never used his size or strength to intimidate or hurt anyone. Now he couldn't control himself.

"I lashed out. I shot Ford in the arm. Tried to kill him twice. Well, not him, but what I saw in my mind."

Drake shifted in the saddle and looked at her. The truth was in her eyes. She'd been that out of control. And lost.

He sometimes couldn't find his way out of his head.

"And he stayed with you?" Obviously. But Drake couldn't imagine the person he loved trying to kill him—twice—and sticking around for more.

Melanie got out before any of his real mental problems touched her.

He was oddly happy about that.

Jamie brought her horse up close to his. "He saw the pain inside me. He saw how much I was suffering. He wanted to fix me. Your family wants to fix you. But the only person who can fix you is you."

"I'm not damaged, Jamie. I'm broken. I can't be what they want anymore." He couldn't be the man Melanie, or any woman, deserved. The life he'd dreamed of having after his military career would forever remain a fantasy.

"Ford believed in me. He supported me even in the worst of times. Your family wants to do that for you."

Melanie bowed out before things got really bad.

"I know." His family had his back no matter what. But he also knew their bringing him here two weeks in a row meant their patience was wearing thin.

How long before they gave up on him, too?

"You will find someone who sees the pain, the suffering, and the man buried beneath all that."

Was it crazy to think that sounded like a prophecy?

Wishful thinking. That's all.

He was grasping at smoke.

But God, what he wouldn't give to hold a woman in his arms and feel her wrapped around him and let the smell of her, the feel of her, and the well of pleasure fill him up and push out the bad.

That's what he'd hoped would happen with Melanie. That somehow her love would eradicate the nightmares.

But that was too easy. Too much to ask of one person.

Chapter Five

Exhausted, finally numbed out on the pain meds he took the second he got back to Rambling Range after his ride with Jamie, Drake barely kept his eyes open in the front seat of the truck on the drive home.

Jamie got him to open up and tell her about Melanie. Mostly because it was the only thing in his head. He never wanted to think about her again.

He regretted the way he acted. He'd given her reason, and then some, to stop trying and walk away. He wasn't the man he used to be, and he'd given her little reason to love, let alone like, the new him.

It made him think about something Ford's Grandpa Sammy said during his and Jamie's engagement announcement last week. The words echoed in his head.

Love is too precious to waste, too good to let go, and too wonderful not to enjoy.

Sometimes, though, love wasn't enough and it walked right out of your life.

Or walked right in.

That stray thought popped into his mind the second a beautiful woman walked out of the stables headed straight for him.

Them.

His heart stopped, and for a second he couldn't breathe.

"I call dibs," Tate said from the backseat.

Declan stopped the truck, threw it in Park, and shut off the engine. "I'm older. I get her."

Trinity smacked both of them. "Keep your hands to yourselves. She's my new business partner and I won't have you drooling over her."

Brown cowboy boots, faded blue jeans, a simple V-neck white T, soft curves, clean face, and long golden hair all made for one hell of a package, but her blue eyes held Drake spellbound. In their depths he caught a deep sadness, hurt, shyness, and compassion. Trinity practically tackled her in a hug that made her take a step back before she held on to Trinity. Two golden heads together in a hug that showed how close they were to each other.

He wanted that moment for himself.

He wanted that woman to hug him like that. Like it mattered.

"Let's go say hi to Adria." Tate jumped out to do that, but Declan stayed put. "Trinity hasn't stopped talking about her, but she never said anything about her being that pretty."

Pretty?

Her heart-stopping beauty punched him in the chest. Adria was nothing short of knockout gorgeous.

And not for him.

Drake grabbed the door handle, but didn't even get the door open before the puppy his brothers and sister refused to take off his hands woke up beside him and pounced on his chest and Declan went on about Adria.

Pretty name.

"She's staying here for a while. You okay with that?"

"Whatever." Drake didn't remember Trinity talking about her coming. He blanked on a lot of what happened these days. He used to be so on top of everything. Now he felt like he was losing time along with his mind.

"She's had it rough lately. Her sister OD'd a couple days ago. Adria brought her here to the rehab you got Chase Wilde into last month."

He didn't want to think that he'd wind up like Chase, popping pain pills to get through the day. Even the next minute. He needed his meds, but he didn't use them to escape. But he was getting worried that he'd need them the rest of his life if this unrelenting pain didn't subside.

"She and Trinity are going to set up shop in town."

What shop? "What are you talking about?" How did he not know about this?

Declan rolled his eyes. "Get your head out of your ass and start participating in our lives instead of expecting us to be solely caught up in yours." Declan turned his back, dropped out of the truck, and slammed the door.

Drake pushed aside his immediate denial and anger that his brother would say such a thing and admitted Declan spoke the truth.

Declan shook Adria's hand, said something that made her smile and nod, and held on to her hand just a few seconds too long for Drake's comfort. Why? He didn't know. At least, he didn't want to think about it.

Adria suddenly glanced at him. Their eyes locked. Her lips turned up in a slight smile.

And all of a sudden it hurt to look at her and remember that he wasn't someone she needed or wanted to know.

He slid out of the truck. Even that small movement hurt like hell. Even worse, he needed the damn cane to balance his weight and not fall over. At the last second, he remembered the puppy, plucked him off the seat, pushed the door closed, and carried the wiggling little thing as he left his family at his back. He didn't greet Adria, who should stay well away from him, and headed for the cabin and solitude.

His family didn't know he went there all the time. Or maybe they did. But right now, he needed to escape them, his past, his thoughts, the pain . . . Everything.

The long walk only increased his simmering anger and amplified the pain in his hip and back.

Frustrated by it all, he climbed the steps and walked into the cabin, bypassed the open living room and kitchen, and headed for the bedroom and some peace and quiet. But when he walked in and spotted the open duffel bag, a white negligee hanging out of it, reminding him of what he'd never have again, rational thought escaped him, and he went ballistic.

He dropped the puppy on the bed, grabbed the offending piece of satin and lace, and ripped it in two, tossing it left and right, then sent the duffel flying off the bed with one swipe of his hand. It crashed into the dresser, sending the lotion, perfume bottle, and makeup bag scattering in a hail of eye shadows, lipsticks, and pencils raining onto the floor.

The sound of them hitting the hardwood like bullets and the puppy's incessant yapping sent him into a blind rage and into the nightmare he couldn't keep at bay any longer.

Chapter Six

Come up to the house for a beer." A spark of interest lit Tate's eyes.

Adria already turned down saddling a horse and going for a sunset ride. She liked Tate, appreciated the flirtatious grin and his attempts to get to know her better, but right now she needed to focus on getting *Almost Homemade* up and running and her sister well.

She'd skip whatever this thing was that Tate was trying to initiate.

After her disaster date a few days ago, she put men and finding Mr. Right in the things-that-will-never-happen-to-me column along with being able to belt out a tune like Adele.

She just didn't have it in her to try again right now and see it fall apart before it ever really got started because she didn't respond to men the way other women did.

Exposing her issues to one of Trinity's brothers would only make things difficult for her and her new business partner before they ever got the store off the ground.

Trinity smacked Tate in the gut with the back of her hand. "She's had a hell of a day. Let her get settled in the cabin before you show her what a pest you can be."

Adria appreciated her friend stepping in to make this a bit less awkward. Or more. Adria really couldn't tell at this point. All she wanted to do was grab something to eat and spend a quiet night in, watching TV or just sleeping. Anything to take her mind off Juliana and the emptiness in her heart. She missed her sister terribly and it had only been a few hours.

"Thank you for the invitation, but Trinity and I are going to look at the storefront spaces early in the morning."

Tate nodded. "Sorry to hear about your sister. Another time."

She didn't respond to that one way or the other. "Thanks for understanding." She gave Trinity a hug. "You and me. Tomorrow. We will find an amazing space for our store."

Trinity beamed with happiness. "I can't wait. Your sister is so generous for giving you the money. I can't believe we're really going to open our own business."

"Roxy believes in us." And right now, Adria needed something to take her mind off Juliana. She needed to focus on something other than whether her sister would leave the rehab before she ever really gave it a chance.

Adria waved goodbye to Trinity and Tate and headed over to the cabin. She rolled her shoulders, easing the ache from feeding and watering all the horses in the stables before the family got home. In exchange for a place to stay, she'd promised to help out on the ranch.

Roxy taught her well how to care for the horses at Wild Rose Ranch, so she had that covered. She'd leave the cattle to Declan and Tate. Both capable and cute.

Drake intrigued her. Especially because he came with a warning. All three siblings ordered her to steer clear of the ex–Army Ranger. She wondered if he had a tattoo that said, Do Not Engage. Because his family made it clear his volatile temper could explode unexpectedly like an erupting volcano.

That thought evaporated when something thudded and crashed against the wall in the cabin. The barking puppy had her running up the steps, straight through the door, and into her bedroom. A lamp flew past her, inches from her head, and crashed against the door frame.

"What the actual fuck!"

Just as she got a glimpse of the destruction in the room—her torn clothes scattered everywhere and the bed in shambles, the mattress off-kilter—Drake came after her, diving and knocking her to the floor. His big body slammed into hers as they slid across the hardwood.

"Stay down."

She tried to get free, but he outweighed her. By a lot.

Just like that, she was nine years old in a dingy apartment with a man she didn't like, who wanted her to do things she didn't understand.

Pinned beneath Drake, terrified and unable to move, her nightmare came back full force. Ice-cold fear raced through her veins and froze her.

And just like then, she recognized the only way to save herself was to go along because he could overpower her.

Drake rose up, hooked his arm around her waist, drew her to his chest, and dragged her back into the room, slamming the door. "I've got you, Chappie. Hold on."

Chappie?

The past took over his mind, just like it had hers at odd moments. She knew how trauma could drag you back into the nightmares of what had happened, sink you in depression, make living hard, and force you to fight to find even one good thing in yourself and life again.

The flashback showed Drake a world only he could see. What set him off? She didn't know. But he was lost in a reality where she couldn't reach him.

Drake acted like something threw him off balance and he fell on his side, taking her with him. Drake screamed, but protected her head. Or in his mind, Chappie's.

That protective instinct and the care he took with her—Chappie— helped ease her mind. He was trying to save his friend.

She breathed a little easier and the intensity of her fear washed away, but she remained cautious and alert.

Drake grabbed his left leg and moaned. "I'll get you out of here. Don't you die on me, Chappie." Desperation filled those words.

He dragged her across the floor, shoving everything out of their way: clothes, a drawer he'd pulled from the dresser and tossed, the sheets and pillows. They reached the corner. He slid himself up and into it, pull- ing her up between his legs and holding her against his chest. One arm banded around her waist. The other lay on her chest as he wrapped his big hand around her throat and squeezed. "I won't let you die. Hold on.

They're coming for us, Chappie." Drake leaned his head against hers and tightened his hold on her neck. "Come on, Chappie, don't do this to me. They're all gone. Not you, too!"

In the next ragged breath, Drake's whole body went lax behind her. Every part of him went loose, except his grip on her neck.

Adria didn't want to, but she imagined Chappie suffered a severe injury to his throat. Despite Drake's own injuries, he'd tried to keep pressure on the wound and save his friend.

He truly meant to keep Chappie safe and protected, but she had a very bad feeling Chappie bled out and died in his arms. Drake just couldn't take it. So he relived it, trying and failing to save his friend over and over again. What a torment to have to live with.

She tried to pull away, but Drake held on tighter.

She feared struggling too much. It might trigger another flashback. One where he thought he was fighting someone, not saving them.

Shaking and fighting off her own demons, she prayed he would come back to himself soon. Heart hammering in her ears, her breathing erratic, she fought the instinct to thrash against him and try to escape, knowing he'd probably subdue and hurt her if she did.

With that disturbing thought, she focused on what she could do to calm herself and get through this without making it worse. For either of them.

She started with the basics she'd learned in therapy and sucked in a big breath, held it for the count of five, then let it out for the count of five. She did it again. And again.

Feeling steadier, she kept up the breathing and forced herself to relax, starting at her toes and working her way up to her head until she settled into Drake's big body.

She turned the dark thoughts in her mind to happier memories. Riding with her sisters at Wild Rose Ranch. The feel of the horse under her and the sun warming her skin. The wind blowing across her face and through her hair.

The sound of Juliana's laughter.

The smiles on her sisters' faces.

Ten minutes later, she was calm and ready to wait out Drake, who had really lost his shit and destroyed her room. To keep her mind busy, she made a mental list of what she needed to replace.

Drake suddenly shifted behind her and pulled her up his body, pushing one particularly hard part of him right up against her rump.

And just like that, fear shot through her again. Tense, shaking, she held her breath and waited with anxious anticipation and trepidation about what he'd do next.

Overwhelmed, she fought to stay focused on reality, the here and now, not the past, assess what was really going on, and not let her mind spin truth into nightmare.

I'm okay. He's not hurting me. He's not that disgusting man. I'm okay.

While Drake held her, he didn't do anything sexual. He didn't hurt her. His hold remained snug, but not painful.

I'm okay.

She took a deep, calming breath, letting the fear wash away a little at a time. One breath. Two. Three. She thought about petting the horses in the barn and the welcoming hug Trinity gave her.

Drake settled along with her.

She'd kept her hands braced on the arm he had wrapped over her middle. She brushed her fingers over his skin in soothing sweeps, hoping he loosened his hold.

His big hand contracted on her hip. The fingers wrapped around her throat went loose. He pressed his face into her hair and kind of hugged her before settling again.

She had a weird feeling his mind had shifted from saving Chappie to realizing he had a woman in his arms. Maybe he was thinking of better times with the ex Trinity told her about when she'd called to let Trinity know she'd made it to the ranch.

Better to be cuddled than killed.

That seemed wholly unfair. He hadn't hurt her. Not really. Scared her, yes, but everything else had been meant to protect his friend.

It still took her a beat to not let panic overtake her again for something Drake didn't intend. Yes, he wouldn't let her go. That's it.

He simply held her.

I'm okay.

And she was. Now that the initial shock wore off, she let herself feel him surrounding her and pressed against her.

It wasn't terrible, even though it wasn't a good situation.

It had been a long time since she'd been this close to a man, especially one as big and strong as Drake. She expected his size to scare her more. But the longer nothing bad happened, the more she was able to separate her past from the man holding her while he slept peacefully with her in his arms.

Trinity had shared her worries about Drake's downward spiral and debilitating injuries. The scar on his face marked him as a man who'd seen some terrible shit. Adria really couldn't conceive of Drake having a war raging in his head, his trying to save the world and being unable to save his friends.

And so she settled in to wait him out because if he needed her to keep the nightmares away for a little while, why not pay him back for all he'd given his country?

She didn't want to disturb him, but she needed something to do. Very slowly, she shifted and slipped her phone from her back pocket.

Drake held her closer, his hand contracting on her neck. Even in sleep, he tried to save Chappie.

She went still. He held her snug against him. She breathed out and relaxed. He did the same, brushed his nose against her head and hair, then he was out again.

She pulled up a game on her phone, trying not to make any sudden movements.

A soft cry sounded from under the bed. She'd completely forgotten about the barking puppy that drew her into the house in the first place.

She made kissing noises to draw the dog out. He slinked to the edge of the bed and stuck his light brown muzzle out. Light blue eyes locked on her. The Australian shepherd yapped once and pounced out from under the bed onto a pair of her panties, where he promptly peed.

"Come on," she whispered. "Add insult to injury, why don't you."

The puppy ran toward her, white-, black-, and gray-speckled ears flopping up and down. His two tan front paws pounced on her thigh, black tail wagging.

"You're just full of mottled colors."

Talking only made Drake press harder on her neck, so she stopped.

The puppy climbed up her middle, licked Drake's hand on her hip, then bounded up and flopped on her chest next to Drake's arm. She looked down at the puppy, accepted her lick on the chin, then smiled when the pup settled in and fell asleep on her.

"Everybody wants to sleep with me."

Feeling like Drake and the pup's favorite cuddle buddy, she accepted her fate. She tapped on her game, turned off the sound on her phone so she didn't set Drake off on another flashback, and played one round after the next.

After an hour on the floor and pressed intimately against Drake, she immediately sensed the change in him. A split second after he woke up, he splayed his fingers wide and raised his hand an inch off her throat.

The puppy lying against his arm felt the movement, woke up, crawled up her chest a few more inches, and licked his face over her shoulder.

"My witch has two more bubbles. I'll be done in a sec, then I'll get off you." She glanced sideways at his very close face and met his shocked eyes. "If you're ready to let me go."

He released the hold he had around her waist and held his hands out wide. Without his hold, she slipped off his lap and landed with a thump on the floor between his legs. She held the pup with her free hand against her chest. He yapped and barked at Drake, who bent his knees, pushed himself up the wall behind them, stepped over her, and shot across the room. He turned to her, eyes wide and watchful.

She sighed. Not wanting to upset Drake further, and reminding herself he hadn't known what he was doing, she tried to keep things normal.

She shot the next bubble on her game and remained sitting on the floor. "So I don't know what you and the puppy have against my underwear, but you tore it all up and he peed on it." She glanced up and gave him a lopsided smile, because yeah, now it kind of seemed funny. "He seems to take your side. What's his name?"

Drake opened his mouth, slammed it closed, locked his jaw, and stared at her like she'd lost her mind.

Maybe she had.

The puppy ran over to him, sat between his widespread feet, and barked at her.

She leered at the puppy. "You lay on my boobs for half an hour and still you take his side." She glanced up at Drake. "I'm Adria, by the way."

He didn't move a muscle, except for the one ticking along his jaw.

"Just thought you'd like to know the name of the woman you slept with."

His head whipped back like she'd smacked him across the face.

"Not in the joking mood. Got it." She finished her game and held up her phone. "Won another level." The cute witch jumped up and down on the screen.

Ass flat and her body stiff from Drake tackling her earlier, she planted her hand on the floor and pushed herself up.

Drake took two steps back and came up short against the window, where the blinds hung by one hinge. "Did I h-hurt you?" His voice shook and his eyes scanned her from head to foot and back up again.

She put some false cheer into her voice. "I think you wanted to hug me more than hurt me." She shifted her weight from one foot to the other and looked at the destruction in the room. "Are you angry I'm staying here?"

He drew back even more. "No." He glanced around, his gaze landing on her torn nightgown. "It had nothing to do with you. I never meant . . . I didn't want . . . I'm sorry."

"Trust me, Drake, this is not the worst thing that's ever happened to me."

His eyes went wide at that bold declaration.

She waved it away. "I'm not mad at you." She could replace her clothes. She couldn't take away his pain, no matter how much she wanted to because she knew what it was like to hurt that much. "You don't need to apologize or be embarrassed or anything. No one got hurt. That's all that matters."

His mouth scrunched and his eyes filled with regret and apology.

Her stomach rumbled for like the twentieth time. "It's late. I'm starving. You hungry? I'm going to get something to eat. Take your time, then join me if you want to." She sucked in a ragged breath and clenched her hands to stop them from trembling. The crisis seemed over, but the tension had grown so thick in the bedroom, it flowed from him to her. She couldn't get out of there and to the kitchen fast enough.

She opened the fridge and pulled out the roast chicken, bagged salad, and dressing she'd picked up at the grocery store in town before Roxy dropped her off here because Sonya insisted on returning the rental car. Trinity would drive them around until Adria bought her own car. She set everything on the counter and popped off the plastic lid on the chicken just as the puppy ran in and jumped on her legs.

"You smell food and all of a sudden, I'm your favorite." The pup jumped again and yapped at her. "Okay, sweetheart. I get it. You're hungry, too." She picked up the speckled puppy and held him close, accepting the puppy kisses on the cheek as she pulled off bits of meat. She held them out to the pup, who devoured his share in seconds.

The big man in her room remained silent.

She took several bits of chicken, shared more with the pup, then listened intently as sounds of movement came from the bedroom. If she wasn't mistaken, he was putting the mattress and bed back to rights.

"Just leave it, Drake. I'll clean it up later." All sound stopped again.

The puppy barked for more chicken. She handed over another few pieces and waited Drake out.

He finally appeared in the living room and headed for the door.

"Did you forget something?"

He stopped, turned to her, and tried to hide the scars on his face. "I'm sorry."

She shook her head. "Nothing to be sorry about."

He couldn't control what happened. She understood PTSD enough to know that. But seeing how it affected him only made her realize how traumatized he actually was. He couldn't control the past taking over his reality.

She gave the pup another bite of chicken. "I meant your little friend."

"Keep him."

She scrunched her mouth into a half frown and eyed the pup. "Rude. He's just going to give you away after all you did for him." She turned to Drake. "He protected you. He stood up for you. He's yours whether you like it or not." She set the pup on the floor. His little legs carried him right to the big man he so obviously adored. He plopped on Drake's boot and chewed at the lace sticking out the bottom of Drake's frayed jeans. "See."

"Are you sure you're okay?"

She raked her fingers through her hair. "Well, it's been kind of a shit day."

"I'm sorry." He swept his hand over his hair and gripped his neck in a tight squeeze.

She tried not to notice the muscles clenched in his massive arms, but damn, they were hard to miss. She could appreciate a good-looking man from a distance.

She thought about those arms locked around her. He hadn't used that strength to crush her even though he could.

It helped her to think about that and the way he held her in order to banish the thought that he, and every man, was like the monster in her mind.

Drake hadn't come after *her*. The second he woke up she saw the concern he had for her.

"I meant because I had to leave my twin sister at the rehab center. I feel a little lost without her." She stepped out from behind the counter. "Which is why I get that you feel lost without your squad, or whatever you call them." She walked toward him, seeing for the first time that he held his broken cane in one hand and stood mostly on his right leg.

Dark, disturbing things lurked in his narrowed eyes and drew her in even more. She'd been a little girl with all those dark nightmares tucked inside her with no way of letting them out. She had to learn to live with them. He wanted to push them away, but what he really needed to do was accept them as part of who he was now.

She didn't want him leaving here feeling like he'd done something wrong and needed to atone for more than he already carried with him.

She slowly approached him. This time he didn't step away but stood there eyeing her like she was a lion on the prowl.

She stopped right in front of him and looked him in the eye. She wanted him to see he didn't scare her. "I'm sorry about your brother-in-arms. You fought hard to protect Chappie. You almost died trying to save him. I'm trying so hard to save my sister, but she's slipping away."

It took a good ten seconds, but Drake relaxed his jaw and shoulders and his eyes filled with compassion.

For a long moment, they stared at each other. She felt his strength, his understanding, and gave herself another reminder that he wasn't a monster but a broken man in need of caring and comfort just like she'd been as a child. She'd had Juliana. He didn't allow anyone near him, except when his subconscious made him hold on to her in the bedroom, and now when she offered him something he needed and it didn't come with all the baggage and expectations of his family or friends and loved ones.

"I couldn't save Chappie. Any of them." The gruff words sounded like a forced confession and were filled with such deep regret her heart ached with them.

He'd been through so much.

She reached out and placed her hand on his arm. "You tried. That's all they asked of you. They knew what they signed up for. They knew you had their back. They had yours. They died so all of us back home could live free and happy. They did that for you, too. It may not be easy right now, but you need to find a way to do that—*to live*—for them."

He didn't exactly shove her away so much as he took her shoulders and held her at arm's length before he let her go and stepped back again. "I just want to be left alone."

"Judging by the way you held on to me in there for over an hour, I'd say that's the last thing you want."

"I didn't mean to do that."

"Yes, you did. Every time I tried to slip free, you held on tighter."

"I'm sorry," he bit out, his whole body going tense.

She tilted her head and studied his face. He turned his head so she couldn't see the scars. He didn't know her. He didn't know that her nature compelled her to try to help, that everything inside her wanted to somehow pull all the bad out of him and take it on herself to spare him.

She'd done what she could for her sister when they were little and she'd volunteered to do the bad things, but she couldn't do it for Juliana's drug problem. She couldn't do it for Drake.

The sense of helplessness she'd felt since leaving Juliana at the rehab center—throughout Juliana's downward spiral really—intensified, because she didn't know what to do for Drake, except to be kind and understanding.

"Trinity must have forgotten to tell you I was staying here for a little while."

"She probably told me and I didn't listen or can't remember."

Adria acknowledged what he didn't say with a nod. His mind wasn't all there these days. Trinity had warned her about his volatile temper, but she hadn't said anything about his inability to focus and his need to constantly be on alert, checking every door and window, looking for an attack that wasn't coming. He did it even now, while still keeping her at a safe distance and in front of him. She had no doubt he was aware of the puppy attacking his boot and every breath Adria took and movement she made.

"I'm guessing you use this place to get away for some peace and quiet and to work out your shit without all of them watching you."

Drake's eyes widened. "They stare. They hover."

"Blessing and a curse to have a big family. I wouldn't really know— I've just got my sisters, and even that can get intense. Anyway, you want to come here and chill, be my guest. It's your place. I'm just visiting. Trinity and I will be busy with opening our shop, so I'll probably only be here to sleep. The rest of the time, it's yours. Just don't tear up any more of my clothes, or I'll be running around here naked." She gave him a smile to let him know she was joking. His frown deepened. "Deal?"

"I'll leave you alone."

"I really don't mind if you want to hang out. Without my sisters, it's kind of quiet here." *And lonely.* "Since I'm not family, it might be easier . . . If you want to talk to someone, I'm a good listener."

He picked up the puppy and held him to his chest. "I don't want to talk about it. I don't even remember telling you about Chappie."

"You didn't. That was more my interpretation of what happened in there and how you tried to save me. Well, Chappie in your mind."

"Exactly. My fucked-up mind. Stay away from me. I'll stay away from you." He turned for the door, but without his cane, he nearly lost his balance and toppled over before he righted himself at the last second.

She slipped under his left arm, wrapped her arm around his waist, and propped him up. "I'll walk you back to your place."

"I don't need your help."

She turned the doorknob with her free hand and swung the door wide. "We just met. Let's not lie to each other. It's just a bad way to start."

He looked down at her. "Start what?"

Her whole body went hot at the way he looked deep into her eyes. With his strong, lean body pressed along hers, she had to check the need to snuggle closer. He smelled like hay and horses, dirt and grass, and the wind. He smelled clean, like Montana. She'd only been in the state for little more than a day, but she loved it here.

Despite how close she held him, he still held himself back. That momentary glimpse of something didn't override the fact he wanted to get away from her because of his physical and mental condition.

She tried not to take it personally. "Well, you did sleep with me, so that at least makes us friends."

His eyes narrowed. "I don't get you."

She nudged him to walk out the door with her. "I think you don't like that *I* get *you*. You're not the only one who had a bad flashback in that room."

"What?"

She left the door open and helped him down the porch steps, taking his weight when he needed to lean on her. "I take it Trinity didn't tell you anything about me."

"Not that I can remember."

They walked together toward the main house, the puppy happily enjoying the ride in Drake's arm. "Let's just say, I had a crappy childhood. I know what it feels like to think you deserve to be punished for what you did. You want me to rage and yell at you. Well, sorry. It'll take more than one temper tantrum to piss me off, because I know what you did is born of deep hurt and guilt. The hurt is real. The guilt is of your own making. Let it go."

"You have no idea what I've done."

She stopped with him in the front yard of his house and stood tucked under his arm at the bottom of the steps leading up to the wide porch and front door.

She tilted her head back and stared up at him and gave him a truth it had taken her a long time to come to terms with herself. "You survived. When you give yourself permission to believe that you did what you did because you had to, you'll finally be able to put it in the past where it belongs. Believe that it's okay to survive and live and move on and want something better than that."

"I deserve everything I got and then some. I'll be alone the rest of my life because of it." He pulled his arm free of her and stepped back again.

The door opened behind her. "You're wrong about that. You have people who love you and won't let you be alone no matter how hard you push them away."

"Where the hell have you been, Drake?"

She turned to Trinity just as Declan and Tate stepped out behind her. "He went for a walk to exercise his bad leg and somehow broke his cane. He was gimping it home when I spotted him and lent him a shoulder to lean on." She caught the stunned surprise in Drake's eyes when she turned back, and he put on that indifferent mask he wore to hide how he really felt.

She should probably tell his family what really happened, but the last thing Drake needed was them overreacting and piling onto him. He harbored enough guilt and recriminations for his actions. Those he'd done on purpose and the ones he couldn't control.

She'd had to learn to give herself a break. She gave him the one he needed now.

She took the wiggling puppy from his hands and set him in the grass to do his business.

Trinity came down the stairs and looked from Drake to her and back. "Is everything okay?"

"Great," she said, letting Drake off the hook again. "Thanks for the hug. I needed it." She waved to Trinity and the guys on the porch, then turned and walked back to her cabin, calling over her shoulder to Trinity, "See you in the morning."

She needed to eat, clean up her place, and stop thinking about a man who made it clear he didn't want her help. Why would he? She couldn't help her sister.

What was she going to do for him?

She needed to focus on supporting her sister's recovery and getting her business up and running. Trinity warned her away from Drake for good reason. The last thing she needed to do was get involved with her business partner and friend's big brother.

She mentally patted herself on the back for getting through what happened and not falling to pieces, but finding her calm and understanding Drake's situation.

Sympathy and empathy made her want to help him with his soul-deep need to find his way back to connecting with people. She got that. Pushing people away didn't make you feel better. It made you lonely. And being alone sucked.

Drake thought he was better off alone, but one day he'd discover having someone on your side willing to help and stick it out through the hard times was so much better.

She'd had Juliana.

She wished her sister would let her be there for her now.

But just like Drake, she'd pushed Adria away when all she wanted to do was help.

She stopped in the yard outside the cabin and looked up at the amazing Montana sky filled with a billion stars and felt as alone as she'd ever been.

She wrapped her arms around her chest, hands on her shoulders, and felt the echo of Drake's embrace.

She'd been warned to stay away from Drake. She usually played things safe, but not this time. Because her heart was still in that room, locked in his arms, willing to give him what he needed and she craved: companionship, understanding, compassion, and someone to hold when life got scary and hard.

Chapter Seven

Drake stood outside the kitchen entrance, eavesdropping on his brothers and sister, who were sitting at the breakfast table with Adria.

"How did you two meet?" Declan asked.

"Baking class. Trinity's mixer wasn't working. She leaned over it to check the beaters right as I plugged it in and a cloud of flour poofed up into the air and covered her whole face and part of her hair."

"You did it on purpose." Nothing about the friendly, teasing way those words came out said Trinity actually blamed Adria for the unfortunate mishap.

Adria laughed. "I did not."

The light sound tightened Drake's gut. He'd spent the whole night tossing and turning, trying to remember what he'd done to her last night only to keep coming back to the feel of her in his arms when he woke up. With his hand wrapped around her throat. And her soft body pressed down the length of his. The citrus and flower scent of her shampoo in his nose and working its way into his system. Even now, he could smell her.

"I was just trying to help you." Adria had helped him last night. More than she knew. He'd spent months silent about what happened with everyone—his family and shrink included—demanding he talk about it, which only meant he'd have to relive it. He didn't want their sympathy. He didn't want them to know how badly he failed.

But that's not how Adria made him feel. She simply got it.

Whatever glimpse she'd gotten into his twisted, messed-up mind hadn't sent her running. Despite shaking like a leaf and her initial hesitation to make any sudden moves when he came to, she hadn't seen him as a threat.

The last thing he wanted to do was hurt her. Or anyone.

After last night—he didn't know how to explain it—but he wanted to keep her safe. He wanted to be close to her because she made it so easy to be around her. Protecting her and being with her, in his mind, conflicted with each other. He couldn't guarantee he wouldn't lose his shit and do something like he did last night. Or something worse.

And that scared him.

"You did help. You made that amazing peach buttercream frosting to go with my vanilla bean cake."

"Everyone in the class voted yours the best."

"Because of you." Trinity reached out and put her hand over Adria's. "We got to talking and you told me about your *Almost Homemade* concept."

Drake walked into the kitchen, drawn by the amazing smells filling the room, and wanting to know more about Adria. "That's your new business?"

His family looked up at him, stunned that he spoke. Usually he came in, grabbed a coffee, and left without saying anything.

Trinity stood and took the puppy from him. "I'll take him out."

Drake took his seat at the head of the table next to Adria. He didn't much like how close Declan sat on Adria's left. "Morning."

Adria studied his face. "You didn't sleep?" Since she was on his left, she got an up-close view of the scars crisscrossing his cheek and jaw.

She barely looked at them, instead focusing on his eyes and the dark circles that gave him a haggard look he was getting used to seeing in the mirror even if he couldn't get used to the scars.

"I got a couple hours. Seems the nap I took yesterday was all I needed."

She frowned along with his brothers.

Declan leaned forward, closer to Adria. "I thought you were out for a walk. When did you take a nap?"

"I had to stop and rest after I broke my cane. I fell asleep against a tree." Lies. He hated telling them to his family. Or at all. But he didn't want them to know what happened. Not when he didn't really know what he'd done. But the devastation he'd left in Adria's room said whatever he'd done wasn't good.

He could only imagine how she felt being in his arms, unsure if he'd hurt her. *Trapped.* The thought sickened him.

He didn't know how she managed to sit next to him. But he remembered her compassion. She didn't pity him. Somehow, after whatever he'd done to her, she looked deeper than his bad behavior and found some kind of understanding.

And that seemingly small thing made a huge difference in his dark world.

He took a sip of the coffee Trinity set in front of him on her way out the door with the pup. He snagged a slice of coffee cake off the platter on the table. The smell made his stomach rumble. The amazing taste and soft texture had him taking another bite.

His brothers stared at him because these days he barely ate anything.

To get them to stop focusing on him and to find out more about Adria, he asked, "What exactly is *Almost Homemade*?"

Trinity had probably told him about it. More than once. But these days he was lucky to keep one thought in his head at a time.

Adria scooped a pile of fluffy scrambled eggs with melted cheese and chives onto his plate from the covered pan. They steamed on his plate. Then she spooned salsa over the top and dropped a dollop of sour cream on the whole thing. "People these days don't cook. They order in. They eat out. They buy prepackaged and frozen food. They pay out the nose for meal delivery services. I think there's a market for that middle ground where you've got some basic cooking skills, can shop for fresh ingredients from our grocery lists, and the recipe is easy."

"What kind of food are we talking about?" Tate stuffed the last of his cinnamon-caramel-drizzled cake into his mouth. "Because this is amazing."

"Soups. Pastas. Sides. Main dishes. Desserts. Everything in one package." Adria pointed to the empty coffee cake platter. "For example, all the ingredients for this cake are included in the package except for the eggs, butter, and milk you'd need to add to the mix."

Drake took the first bite of eggs and moaned. "These are really good."

"Eggs don't have to be boring."

Drake took another bite. "Aren't there lots of places, even the grocery store, that sell boxed mixes?"

"Like the coffee cake, yes. But where we'll be different is the meals. What's your favorite dinner?"

"Pizza."

"Okay, in the refrigerated case we'll have fresh-made dough and a kit with sauce, cheese, and toppings. Take it home, roll out the dough, add the sauce, cheese, toppings, pop it in the oven. Fresh, hot pizza that is made with the best ingredients." Adria scrunched her tempting rosy lips. "Pizza is easy. It's not that people can't cook—they want it to be fast and simple. Chili. The kit will have all the spices measured in one packet. Canned beans. Add the precooked ground beef and pork and water, simmer for an hour. You're set. Same thing with chicken broccoli Alfredo. One kit. Fresh fettucine pasta, sauce, precooked chicken, chopped fresh broccoli. Simple instructions. Everything you need in one bag."

"So it's kind of like a grocery store, but the food is all packaged together in one bag for whatever the meal is?"

"Exactly. All good, quality ingredients in a convenient package that you can take home and quickly cook without having to measure and prep."

Trinity joined them and dumped the puppy into his lap. "Let's say you guys actually wanted to cook something, say like . . ."

"Meat loaf," Declan chimed in.

Trinity rolled her eyes. "We have a bag of spices with directions for that. You supply the beef, mix in the spices, put it in a baking dish, and cook it in the oven."

"Some things will be like that, others we'll make in the shop that you can pick up and with minimal effort put it on the table and enjoy with your family." Adria reached over and petted the pup. "Did you name him yet?"

He'd relented because he couldn't ignore his little shadow and he'd needed to fill the hours he didn't sleep last night with something to do. "Sunny."

Adria beamed him a smile. "That's a sweet name. Bright. Cheerful. Like him."

Drake was none of those things. "I named him after the bomb-sniffing dog who saved my life."

His brothers and sister went still and stared at him, holding their breath.

Adria put her hand on his arm. "It's a wonderful tribute to your fellow soldier. Was the dog assigned to your team?"

He didn't expect the question. Mostly because when he said stuff like that his family shut up, too afraid to set him off. "Uh, yeah. Sometimes."

"I can't imagine being the handler. You get attached to the dog, and then you have to put him in harm's way, knowing he could die. I can't imagine how devastating it is to lose one of the dogs."

"It sucks for everyone."

Her hand contracted on his arm.

He didn't like to think about how they lost Sunny. She wasn't sniffing out a bomb, but protecting her handler when she got shot. Losing her hurt just as much, maybe more, as losing a fellow soldier. They knew what they were getting into, but the dogs were trained to do a job they didn't ask to do. They didn't know the risk. They didn't have a way out.

Before he got lost in another nightmare, Adria pressed her hand to his face, covering the scars with her warm palm. "Having Sunny around probably gave you a sense of home in the midst of something that shouldn't have become normal."

His heart thrashed in his chest. He didn't know what to say or do with her words and understanding.

Sunny planted his front paws on Drake's chest and licked his chin, taking him out of his head. The exact reason Jamie gave Sunny to him, so he focused on the dog, not his dark thoughts.

Adria removed her hand from his face and petted the dog. "You're a good boy." She locked eyes with him. "He could save your life, too, if you gave him a chance and stopped acting like you don't want him."

Was she talking about the dog, or how much he wanted her, a woman, and a future he thought he'd have one day with a wife and kids? He didn't know. But he did know that life wasn't possible. And her making him want it pissed him off.

He stood, dumping Sunny off his lap and onto the floor with a yelp before he found his feet and leaped at Drake's boots, attacking the laces with his sharp little teeth.

"Nothing and no one can save me. Just leave me the hell alone." He spun on his heel and left all of them at his back. His limp and the pain radiating through him followed. They would always be with him. The rest of them, her, any other woman who might come into his life would leave. He couldn't be who he used to be, or even what they wanted him to try to be.

If Adria didn't get that last night when she got an up-close view of his crazy, then he'd have to prove it to her another way.

None of them got it. He'd accepted it. His injuries were permanent. This was him now.

Chapter Eight

Adria sat back in her seat feeling like she'd pushed too hard. Drake seemed so relaxed and present this morning.

"You touched him." Trinity fell into the seat across from her. "I can't believe he let you touch him."

She usually kept her hands to herself, except with her sisters. With them, she could be affectionate. It surprised her how easy it was for her to give the physical contact Drake so obviously craved despite how hard he pushed everyone away.

"He ate his entire breakfast." Declan stared at Drake's empty plate.

"He spoke." Amazement filled Tate's voice. "He carried on an entire conversation without a single grunt or glare or simply ignoring everyone."

Adria perked up. She'd made a difference. She'd helped.

After failing her sister so badly, she needed this little boost.

"What is going on with you two?" Trinity eyed her.

She didn't know how to answer. Yes, she was drawn to Drake, his pain, his need to connect with someone. It's how she felt when the bad things happened and she'd turned to Juliana for comfort. But was that all there was? Nope. It felt like something more. But how could she explain something she hadn't quite figured out herself?

She couldn't tell them what happened last night, not without making them worry even more. Or making them think Drake didn't want to really live, instead of just survive and hide every day.

She didn't believe that.

This morning proved he wanted to be a part of things. He wanted to connect. At least with her.

And that made sense to her. "I'm not you."

"What does that mean?" Declan took her plate and Tate's and stacked them.

"There's no history between us. I don't expect anything from him. I'm not looking for who he used to be. I only know him as the man he is right now. I know something about being traumatized and feeling like the person you used to be died and you don't want to be the new you."

Trinity reached across the table and held out her hand.

Adria leaned forward and clasped it.

Trinity knew her story. Not the details, but the basics. Enough to know that Adria sympathized with Drake.

"What happened to you?" Declan leaned in, ready to listen to her sad tale.

She kept that part of her life in the past. At least, she tried to. Dating was still hard. Being with a man even more difficult. "Let's just say, I know what it's like to have to do things to survive. Things you don't want to do." Trinity squeezed her hand. "Drake needs time to grieve who he used to be. It'll take time to figure out who he is now and what he wants to be."

"He's been home for months," Tate pointed out.

"And in that time he's lost even more. His fiancée walked out on him. His physical injuries have healed but they left him permanently altered. His mind won't let go of the past. He thinks he'll never be free of the chaos in his mind. But you saw it this morning. He found a way to quiet it. For a little while at least."

"I'll take it." Trinity smiled softly. "Maybe he'll have more quiet moments."

"If that's the best we can hope for, then I hope so, too." Declan took the plates to the sink. He turned back to her. "Are you going to tell us what really happened last night? Because we don't believe the bullshit story he told us about going for a walk."

Drake reappeared in the kitchen doorway. "Bullshit or not, it's none of your fucking business."

Declan leaned back against the counter and eyed Drake. "You are our business. We're trying to help you."

"Help me what?"

Declan took a step forward. "Not be such a dick all the time. How about that?"

Drake took a step and came up a foot away from Declan. "Get off my back and I won't be such a dick all the time. How about that?"

Adria didn't want to see them come to blows. Drake's powder keg of rage seemed likely to blow any second. She was beside them before she remembered moving.

She put a hand on Drake's arm and Declan's. "Relax, Drake. Declan's just worried about you."

Declan put his hand on her shoulder, but before he said anything, Drake planted his hand on Declan's chest and pushed him back a step. Declan's hand fell back to his side. "Don't fucking touch her."

Declan's eyes went wide with surprise and fear, but oddly enough he smiled and held his hands out wide. "Got it."

Drake glared daggers at Declan.

Trinity pleaded from the table. "Come on, you guys. Stop this."

Adria put her hand on Drake's rock-hard bicep. "Let it go."

He looked down at her, then back at his brother. And just like that, he backed off, grabbed the bag of puppy kibble off the counter, and walked out without looking at anyone.

Adria didn't dare say anything.

Drake intrigued her. She felt a connection to him because of the pain she recognized in him. Even if she wanted to help, to be there for him, Drake didn't want her interfering in his life.

He wasn't ready to put the past behind him.

He wasn't ready to be with anyone.

As for her, she didn't know if she could ever be with any man, especially someone as broken as Drake, without her past ruining it.

Chapter Nine

"I cannot believe my brothers." Trinity planted her hands on her hips and hung her head, her voice echoing off the brick walls of the large, empty commercial building. "I am so embarrassed. They act like they're five sometimes."

Adria thought of how she and her sisters got into it when they were teens, fighting over makeup and bathroom time. "It's okay. Drake is in protection mode 24-7." Though Declan had only given her a friendly pat, she appreciated that after what Drake did to her, he thought maybe she didn't want to be touched without her consent.

"He's stuck in smoldering rage mode."

Adria agreed and disagreed with that. "He pushes you guys away because he's trying to protect you from himself. He can't deal with his emotions. He's aggressive. But do you really think he'd hurt one of you?"

Trinity frowned. "Not intentionally. But he reacts to things he perceives as a threat, even when they're not. Instinct. Some kind of protection thing, like you said. He's never done anything on purpose."

That had been Adria's experience with Drake in the cabin. "He can't deal with you guys wanting him to flip a switch and be better. So he avoids you so he doesn't disappoint you and protects you from his wild mood swings."

Trinity's forehead crinkled as she thought about it. "The doctor did say it would take a lot of patience and understanding and that he'd initially push us away because we remind him of what life used to be like. But it's been months and nothing has changed. In fact, he's gotten worse. This morning was the first time I saw before-the-war Drake. He didn't even flinch when you touched him. He didn't yell at you when you stepped in to help Declan."

"I'm nobody to him. I don't know before-the-war Drake. I don't expect him to act or be like someone he doesn't know anymore." She wrapped her arm around Trinity's shoulder and hugged her to her side. "He still loves you. He's trying to learn to love himself again."

Trinity softened her voice. "Do you know that because of what happened to you?"

"Yes. We both faced the possibility we wouldn't survive, but what Drake went through is different than my experience. He looked death in the face. People he fought beside, was friends with, loved even, died by his side, Trinity. Right in front of him. He couldn't stop it. He couldn't protect them. He couldn't keep them safe. So he tries to do that for you and your brothers."

"We're all fine. We just want him to find some peace."

"How can he when he relives what happened over and over again in his mind? One thing I've learned from my experience—he has to accept that he can't change it. Living and being happy doesn't mean that he's taking what those who didn't make it should have had. In fact, it honors their sacrifice. Until Drake realizes that, he's stuck."

Trinity tipped her head to Adria's. "How do I unstick him?"

"Love him. Listen to him. Try to understand that even his silence and outbursts are an expression of the enormous pain inside him."

"It probably doesn't help that Melanie dumped him."

"Probably not." She probably shouldn't ask—none of her business—but she did anyway. "Why did she break up with him? She couldn't deal with the PTSD?"

"To tell you the truth, I'm not sure what happened. They spoke all the time. Texted. Sent pictures to each other. She hung on through both deployments. I thought they'd make it through anything. But he got shot a month into his second deployment. Through his thigh. Nothing major hit. He came home for a couple weeks to recover before he went back to base and shipped out again. I'd never heard them argue. They argued a lot the last few days he was home."

"She didn't want him to go back." Adria would have felt the same way about someone she loved after they'd already been hurt.

"The reality of being with him hit her hard. It hit all of us, seeing him bandaged up and on crutches, knowing that if he went back it meant people would be shooting at him again."

That was the job.

It took guts and courage for Drake to go back and face it again.

"The few phone calls we got during the rest of the deployment were off. We could tell from what little he said that things over there were getting more dangerous. The enemy was more brazen. And he hinted that things with him and Melanie were strained. He asked all of us to check on her from time to time. Which we did. She asked us to talk Drake out of signing up for another tour. She knew we worried and wanted him home."

Adria guessed what happened next. "Then Drake got hurt and his tour was over and they're sending him home permanently."

"Melanie seemed happy." Trinity lost herself in thought. "Drake hated that he couldn't go back. He had this need to return and do his job. We all found it outrageous, given what he'd been through."

"He needed to save his buddies who were still over there." Her heart ached for him so much she wanted to find him and give him a hug—and hope that simple gesture eased some of the pain.

Trinity pressed her hand to her chest. "Oh man, that makes sense. We just called him crazy and told him how lucky he was to be home." Trinity sighed. "Which probably made him feel worse because his friends were still there putting their lives on the line or didn't make it back at all."

Adria put her hand on Trinity's shoulder. "Keep trying to put yourself in his place, understand where he's coming from. You'll get him to come around more and more."

"I hope so. I'm going to try harder. You really helped me see that we were trying to help but going about it the wrong way." Trinity faced her. "The first few days Drake was home, we expected Melanie to stay with him. She had in the past. None of us thought it was a big deal. But she'd come by after work, stay a couple of hours, then leave. I didn't want to say anything or ask Drake about it, but it felt odd. They didn't seem connected anymore. Melanie could barely look at him. She'd pat his arm or knee and say that everything would be okay, but she didn't hold him. He had to peel me off him when I first saw him. I wanted to hug him and never let him go."

"He was injured—maybe she was afraid of hurting him or expecting too much when he needed time to heal?"

Trinity shook her head through all those words. "It was more like she'd already distanced herself from him. We tried to draw him out. She let him be quiet and alone. He wasn't supposed to drive, but one night he said he needed to see her and took the truck. He came back less than two hours later in a rage. He trashed his room, punched holes in the walls, and just went crazy. Declan and Tate finally went in and stopped him. We were afraid he'd hurt himself more. He never said Melanie's name again. We didn't ask what happened. Two months, maybe more, went by without the two of them seeing each other or talking. Then all of a sudden she showed up the day you came to stay with us and gave him back his ring."

"That had to be a hard day." And she got why he'd lost his shit that night in her room.

"He didn't try to change her mind. He just looked resigned to the fact it was over and he'd be alone forever." The pain and sadness in Trinity's eyes made Adria's heart ache for her and Drake. "After all he'd been through she left him when he needed her most."

"Not everyone is equipped to deal with trauma." She had two failed relationships to prove it.

"But she said she loved him."

"People say things they think they mean all the time." Her exes swore they understood that intimacy was difficult for her. They didn't. Not when frustration set in and she couldn't be what they wanted her to be. "Whatever happened between them, love wasn't enough. Or simply wasn't there. Maybe it wasn't her, but Drake. Maybe he pushed her away one too many times and so she left him alone like he demanded."

"You can see he doesn't mean that. Why couldn't she?"

"We could speculate for hours, but only they know what really happened. Maybe it was for the best. You never know . . . they could get back together."

"I hope not."

"Why would you say that?"

"Because I want him to be happy with someone who isn't just there for the good times. He needs someone who will protect him, even if it's from himself. If she loved him, how could she leave him, or let him leave her when he needed her so badly?"

Adria didn't have an answer. She pulled Trinity into another hug and held her close. "He has you," she reminded her friend.

"Juliana has you to stand by her."

And yet Juliana had pushed her away time and time again.

And just like Drake, her sister needed to fix her problems. And Adria had to accept she couldn't change Juliana. Or Drake.

"You never give up." Trinity held her at arm's length. "You won't let her fall without being there to catch her."

"I can't stand for her to be away from me, but I know she's where she needs to be, getting the help she needs." But Adria's heart still ached.

Trinity rubbed her hands up and down Adria's arms. "And we are in this dismal and dreary building talking about our problems instead of celebrating. This is our place!" Trinity jumped up and down on her toes.

Adria couldn't hide her smile as she glanced around the wide, empty room. "It needs a lot of work, but it's ours. Or at least it will be when the Realtor finalizes the transaction."

They'd looked at six commercial spaces but this one had everything they needed. It was downtown on a busy main street, had lots of parking in the back, and they could move in right away and start the repairs and renovation to make it their space.

"We're in business!" Trinity beamed with happiness.

"Almost." Adria wished Juliana was here to share this moment. They'd shared everything else in their lives. It kind of felt wrong to do this without her input and being here.

But they were getting older and would inevitably have lives that took them away from each other. She just didn't see it happening this way.

She hoped Juliana was getting better, that soon they'd be together and Juliana would want to be a part of the new shop and Adria's life again.

Like Drake, Juliana was angry and dealing with some things she couldn't accept and put in her rearview.

Adria hadn't given up. Not by a long shot. She never would. But Juliana saw the rehab as a punishment and a betrayal by Adria.

She hoped with a clear head and open heart, Juliana would forgive, and they could go back to being sisters and loving each other.

Maybe Drake hoped the same thing would happen between him and Melanie.

The thought made her feel like she'd miss him if that happened.

Chapter Ten

Drake thought he might explode. He hadn't seen Adria in three days. *Correction.* He'd stayed the hell away from her.

For good reason.

Somehow when Adria showed up, she looked through a crack in his fortress walls, and something changed.

He didn't like it.

He didn't know what to do with it.

"This only works if you actually talk to me." Dr. Porter had said that at least ten times during the last twenty minutes of their video chat. His concerned face stared at Drake from the laptop on the coffee table. The veteran and PTSD specialist's office was too far away to do these appointments in person, but Dr. Porter had the military experience and education to handle and understand someone with Drake's mental health issues.

Drake crossed his arms over his chest and glared at the man who refused to give up helping him, despite how many times Drake told him he couldn't be helped.

"Come on, Drake. Something is going on with you."

That got his attention. "Why do you say that?"

"You're not calling me from the usual place. You're emotional, not apathetic. You look like you're facing a firing squad instead of your usual indifference to our calls."

Drake opened his mouth, but nothing came out. He couldn't confess what he'd done to Adria. He'd scared her.

What the hell was wrong with him?

Someone like her—smart, strong, confident, so aware of others around her—yet she had no idea how on the edge he felt. Or maybe she did. "She pities me." It had to be that, because he couldn't let himself believe she actually liked him. He didn't like himself. At all. Especially after what he'd put her through.

"Is it Melanie who pities you?"

Shit. He didn't mean to speak out loud.

But something compelled him to answer, because he didn't want the doc thinking he was pining away for a woman who turned her back on him without even a fight. Nope, she'd wanted him to be something he wasn't anymore and finally said, "I'm out."

"Screw Melanie. She wanted a nice, safe, normal life. I'm not nice. It's not safe to be around me. And I'll never be normal again."

"Why isn't it safe to be around you?"

Adria walked into the cabin—finally!—and slammed the door, then stopped short when she spotted him. "Uh, sorry. I'll come back later if you want to be alone."

"Come here." He didn't mean to bark the order, but if he was going to do this, it needed to be done now. He may not be able to confess what he'd done, but Adria deserved to hold him accountable. This was the only way he could think of to allow her to do that. Dr. Porter would hear about what he'd done and his fate and punishment would be decided.

She approached the back of the leather sofa and stared over his shoulder. "Hey, if you're in the middle of a call or something, I'll leave."

He grabbed her hand, cutting off whatever she was about to say, and pulled her around the couch and down to sit beside him. "Tell him about this." He picked up the nightgown he'd torn and showed it to Dr. Porter.

She turned to him. "Did you pull that out of the trash?"

He'd gone through the bag she left on the floor in her room to see what he'd done and what he owed her. "Tell him!"

Her face contorted with pure frustration, then she turned to the screen. "Hi. I'm Adria. And you are?"

"Dr. Porter. My psychiatrist. Now tell him." Drake felt the edges of his mind turning red with fury and tried to hold back the tide of anger and frustration.

She glanced over, glared at him, then turned back to Dr. Porter, leaned over his leg so the doc could see her better, and said the completely unexpected. "Drake doesn't really know me. He doesn't know what that nightgown means to me. You see, my sister put it in my bag as a way to tell me to get out of my head and have some fun. I like pretty things, but sometimes—okay most times—they remind me of what happened when I was nine. Back then, my mother owed a drug dealer money. He thought he could earn his money back by dressing me up, taking pictures, and selling them on this kiddie porn site he ran for pedophiles. Nice, right? My mother was so messed up on drugs she completely checked out on her kids and left us vulnerable to that sick bastard."

"What the fuck?" Drake didn't know any of this.

She turned to him. "Do you really think you're the only one bad things happened to?"

"No."

"But you think living in your own shit, wallowing in it, means you're tough. You can take it. You survived. You can survive feeling like this the rest of your life."

"No."

"Then what the fuck are you doing? You hold all those nightmares inside and they mix like a chemical reaction until you can't hold them inside anymore and you explode. You lash out at the people around you. And when that happens, well, we get things like this nightgown, and worse."

"I don't mean to."

"Then do something about it. Stop pretending like you don't hurt and grieve and wish things were different."

"I'm not."

"You are. You punish yourself. You scare everyone around you. You avoid your family like you avoid feeling. You love to ride, but you never do. You used to work with your brothers but you won't even go down to the stables or ride with them out in the pastures to feed the cattle. You pretend you can't do anything instead of testing your limits and figuring out what you *can* do."

"I've tried to get you to talk about all of this, Drake," Dr. Porter chimed in, agreeing with Adria's brutal honesty.

"I don't want to do any of that stuff anymore."

"You don't want to live."

Adria's blunt words hit so close to home he stopped breathing.

"When we talked about Chappie, didn't it make you feel better to share how much you miss him, how hard you tried to save him, the pain that consumes you because you couldn't? Didn't it feel better to have someone listen and understand and acknowledge that what you went through sucked? It was terrible, Drake. The worst thing that can happen. I'm sorry. You're sorry. No one could ask more than that from you."

He didn't know what to say or do, so he fought back. "I lost nearly my whole damn team."

She put her hand on his chest and gave him sympathy instead of the anger and hate he deserved. "Friends. Brothers. They were your family over there. You would have done anything for them. You'd have traded places with them."

"In a heartbeat."

"Would they have done the same for you?"

"No doubt."

"Then find a way to dig past all the guilt and regret and do them the honor of being grateful for their sacrifice and the second chance at life you've been given."

"I am grateful."

"Then act like it," she snapped. "Do something to get better. Talk to your doctor. Do your physical therapy. Go riding with your brothers. Do the things you love to do and enjoy them."

"It's not that easy. Look what I did to you." He held up the ruined nightgown.

She barely glanced at it. "You weren't in your right mind. Your PTSD made you lose control. Luckily, I knew how to remain calm and not push you over the edge." She pointed to the tattered garment. "You weren't angry at *me*. That wasn't about the war but something else. So confess. Why did you tear up my clothes?"

"I flashed back to being overrun by insurgents and the firefight with my team and Chappie."

She shook her head. "No. You didn't flash back to that until I came into the room. Why were you tearing up *my* stuff? Your fiancée—"

"She's not my fiancée anymore." His jaw clenched so hard it ached.

"Why not? What happened?"

"None of your fucking business."

"Really?" She snatched the satin and lace shreds from his hand. "You made it my business when you did this. What was it? Trinity thinks Melanie couldn't deal with your bad attitude and you pushing her away all the time and that you couldn't let go of the hope that you could go back to the Army."

"She got her wish. They won't take me back."

"So if she got to have you home with her where she wanted you, why aren't you planning a wedding?"

"Why do you care?"

She held up the torn outfit again. "I put this on and it takes me back to my nightmare. You look at it and you need to destroy it. Why?"

"Leave it alone."

"No. I think this"—she shook the dangling shreds—"has more to do with what is really messing with your mind than what happened over-seas."

"Really?" She didn't know anything, but his heart jackhammered be-cause he didn't want his secret exposed. He didn't want *her* to know.

She didn't relent and taunted him again. "It's pretty. I bet Melanie would look great in it."

He looked away, unable to meet her eyes and reveal what he really thought.

Her head tilted to the side, her golden hair falling over one shoulder. "Or maybe you pictured me in it. You'd just seen me in the driveway be-fore you came up here."

The damn woman didn't know when to stop reading his mind and shut up.

"You were pissed at her, but took it out on me."

Frustrated, he grunted. "I was mad at me."

"Trinity said Melanie could barely look at you when you came home. You went to her house one night and came back and it was all over. You got worse after that."

"We broke up."

"Why?"

"You said it. She couldn't look at me." He didn't mean to, but his hand went to the scars on his face before he dropped it to his leg and rubbed his aching muscles.

Her gaze followed his every move and studied his every tell. "You went there to make things right. You wanted to show her that you still loved her."

He looked away.

"She didn't want to sleep with you. Because of the way you look?" Shock filled her words but all he heard was her pity.

He rolled up, nearly toppling her off his leg and the sofa. He'd barely realized she was still pressed against him. He walked around the couch and paced the too-small space between the kitchen and living room.

He wanted Adria to let it go and shut up. But she didn't.

"We saw each other in the driveway. I smiled at you. I wanted to meet you. You stared at me. You didn't want your brother to touch me even in a friendly way." Her eyes went wide. "You want me."

Feeling surly, he lashed out. "Conceited much?"

"Oh, I think I'm right on the money. You wanted me and came up here and destroyed my stuff because you didn't think I'd want you because of a few scars and a bad temper."

He raked his fingers over his head. "That's not it."

"Yes, it is. Melanie didn't want you, so you think no one will."

He tried to hold it together, but his anger flashed. "She tried. I tried. But I couldn't. I can't. Not anymore. So what good was I to her? I'm no use to any woman now."

Adria shook her head. "You're kidding, right?"

He held his hands out wide. "Does it look like I'm kidding?"

She braced her hands on the back of the sofa, leaned in, locked eyes with him, and said the unexpected again. "There is nothing, and I mean nothing, wrong with you."

"How the hell would you know?"

"Because I'm the one you held wrapped in your arms with your thick, rigid, I-want-to-fuck-her dick pressed against my ass for nearly an hour."

He went still. "You're lying."

"Why would I lie about something like that?"

Dr. Porter chimed in again. "Maybe one of you should explain what really happened."

Adria ignored the doctor, just like he did. She got up from the couch and walked around it to face him.

He stared down at her, everything inside him wanting her to be right, for it to be true.

Hope rose up inside him.

"I don't know what happened between you and Melanie. Maybe the way she looked at you, or didn't look at you with a longing and need to be with you, turned you off."

He started thinking out loud. "I thought because she loved me, she wouldn't care about the scars and that I couldn't move the way I used to. We'd figure it out."

"But she hesitated. The moment felt like you needed to show her that you could be the man she remembered. But overwhelmed by what happened to you and trying to fix something in your life and make it work, you couldn't. Too much pressure. Too much riding on it. Her not showing you the compassion and patience you needed to quiet the nightmares and fall into her. She couldn't see past the damage to the man she loved. You took her rejection and turned it into every woman rejecting you. You convinced yourself you couldn't be with any woman, that every woman would only ever see the bad, the damage. You let your insecurity, guilt, and anger win."

"I don't know why you need me," Dr. Porter interjected, startling both of them as they stared at each other. "Sounds like she's got you pegged. Listen to her, Drake."

"Just because it worked once doesn't mean it will work again."

"You'll never know unless you try," she challenged.

His mind went blank for a second. She didn't mean with her. She meant for him to give it a go by himself. Well, he'd tried. And failed. And gotten more pissed and despondent about it, because without sex, what the fuck was the point of surviving all he had if he couldn't be with a woman, make a life and have a family with her?

That's what he'd always wanted. But right now, he'd take a willing woman who'd give him a chance to see if he could get it up again.

"Juliana once said that my sisters and I carry around our baggage like an apology we owe the world. I've been thinking about that lately. I was with a couple of guys, but I could never really get past my own inhibitions and remembering what happened to me.

"My mother is a prostitute. She loves sex and doesn't care who knows it. I'd like to stop thinking men will believe I'm like her if I just have fun and enjoy it."

"Uh . . ." He really didn't know what to say to that, except, "Shouldn't everyone enjoy sex?"

"Exactly. But I get hung up on her past, my past, and get it all in my head that I'm doing something wrong because that despicable man made me do things that made me feel icky. I knew it was wrong and I did it anyway because I needed to protect my sister." She rubbed her hands up and down her arms. "We have that in common—trying to protect everyone around us and scarring ourselves in the process. So if you're willing to try, so am I."

His fucked-up brain did not compute. "What are you saying?"

"Maybe we can face down our demons together. No strings attached. No expectations. Judgment-free sex. I'll show you you're not impotent, and maybe you can help me let go and enjoy myself."

The idea appealed a lot, but they didn't know each other well, and the last thing he wanted to do was hurt her feelings or disappoint her. "You're serious?"

"How long do you want to go without knowing if you really can or can't have sex? How long will you deny yourself that pleasure? How many women will you let get away because you think you can't be with them?"

He tried to find a rational reason why this was a bad idea when everything inside him wanted to try. But he didn't want to use her like that. "You're my sister's friend and business partner."

"You guys, this might not be such a good idea." They'd completely forgotten about Dr. Porter.

Drake wished he'd shut up because the more Drake thought about it, the more he wanted to do it. Or at least try. And he had to admit, he felt a stirring inside him he hadn't felt in a long time.

Anticipation. Need. Hunger. They all started to wake up inside him.

Adria walked back to the coffee table and held up the laptop and stared at Dr. Porter. "Talk therapy is good and all, but I think what we both need is a little sex therapy. And you're not invited." She closed the laptop lid on whatever Dr. Porter's reply might have been.

Adria held Drake's gaze. Mind made up, she didn't back down. "How long should I go without knowing if I can let go, feel like a whole woman, and find satisfaction with a man? I deserve to feel wanted and needed and be okay with that, don't I?"

He nodded because he'd always made sure the woman he was with enjoyed it as much as he did.

"Whatever and whoever we are outside this cabin makes no difference. In here, you and me, we'll give each other what we've both been missing."

Drake still hesitated. "Don't get me wrong, I want to, but I'm not sure how this will go between us. We barely know each other."

That seemed like it should have been her line.

"I don't need you to love me, Drake. I just want you to want me. It seems like something about me appealed to you, enough that when you held me, your body responded."

Everything about her appealed to him from her silky blond hair, intelligent and compassionate blue eyes, round breasts that were the way he liked them—just enough to fill his hands and mouth—slim hips, and toned legs that would wrap around him and hold him close. "You're not the problem."

Her gaze locked with his. "Nothing about you is a problem for me."

He wanted to doubt that, but the fierce truth in her eyes and words made him believe her.

Why else would she make this deal with him?

He answered that for both of them: she needed to prove something to herself, just like he did.

But she hadn't seen him naked and tallied up all the scars she couldn't see that added up to an unappealing sight he could barely stand.

"You know I mean it. Maybe we met at the right time to give each other what the other needs."

Maybe part of him couldn't stand up to the challenge, but the rest of him was willing to do other things. His need to touch her soft skin intensified. What he wouldn't give to have a woman in his arms again, to feel her move against him, to kiss and stroke her. God, that would be heaven.

He understood what she thought she could do for him, but he needed to know what she wanted from him. "What do you need?"

"I'd like to shut out the world and my past and just let go. I'd like to know what it feels like to lose control. I don't think it's the case, but if you can't . . . perform, I bet you can still make a woman . . . feel good." Her pretty blush endeared her to him.

"I prefer when it's mutual, but yes, I can get you off. I will." He wanted to watch her fall apart.

"And I will do whatever it takes to prove to you, you are not broken. And maybe I'll convince myself that I'm not either."

He saw it then. This meant more to her than proving a point. She really wanted to help him. And herself. "You just can't help helping others."

She looked him dead in the eye. "My other attempts failed miserably. I . . . hurt the guys because I wasn't . . . right."

"There's nothing wrong with you," he assured her and let his gaze roam down her body. That cute blush intensified and made him want her even more.

"They thought it was their fault. I think you know that if I can't . . . well, we both need someone willing to try with no expectations that it will end the way we hope it will and no reproach if it doesn't."

He agreed with that and it eased his mind that this was a mutual exchange.

She sucked in a breath and looked him in the eye again. "When you were holding me, something deep inside you . . . I don't know . . . wanted me, this, to happen. Even though I was scared, I still knew you wouldn't hurt me. I know that right now, too. I hope you feel that way about me."

Meaning if this didn't work out, she wouldn't hurt him by making him feel inadequate.

Drawn to her, he went with his gut, closed the distance between them because his body wanted hers pressed to his, and hooked his hand around her waist and slowly drew her close. He wrapped his other arm around her and increased his hold so she was tight against him. Her softness to his hard body felt right, though one part of him remained unwilling to commit to the images and desires running through his mind.

"I don't remember what I did to you, but I bet having you in my arms like this made me remember how long it's been since I had a beautiful woman in my arms. How much I craved touching her—you—until we were both lost in each other." He brushed a kiss to her hair and spoke as openly and honestly as she'd done with him. "I want to feel like all I've done, all I've sacrificed and lost, everything that happened to me doesn't matter because you just want me so damn bad. As bad as I want you." He hadn't wanted a woman this intensely in he didn't know how long.

It took every ounce of patience and strength he had to wait for her response, because he might have made the first move, but the next one was up to her, because if they were going to do this, it had to be her choice.

So he held his breath and waited.

Chapter Eleven

For a split second, Adria wondered how she wound up in Drake's strong arms. But his words melted her heart and touched her deeply. He meant it. He wanted her.

And she felt it.

A wave of need swept through her.

She placed her hand on his face over his scars, managed to slide up his body under his tight hold as she went on tiptoe, and pressed a soft kiss to his lips. One wasn't enough. She did it again. And one more time.

Her heart pounded against his and she settled into him.

His heated gaze remained locked on hers. "That's sweet, Adria, but I think someone who's bold enough to propose sex with no strings and says she's willing to do anything to prove I'm not broken would kiss me like she means it."

Adria accepted the challenge she needed to get past her nerves with a smile that made his eyes widen. She pressed her lips to his again, swept her tongue along his bottom lip, then dived in and stroked her tongue along his.

His arms tightened around her and a deep groan rumbled his chest against hers.

Her whole body instinctively stilled, unsure what came next. Her past came back in a wave of fear that made her tremble.

Drake slid his hand up her neck to the back of her head, broke the kiss, and stared into her eyes. "You say stop, I let you go." He didn't mean it as a threat, but deep down she took it that way, because she needed him to hold on to her.

"Don't let go. Please."

His eyes darkened with possession, his arms contracted, and he kissed her like his next breath depended on it.

She gave herself over to him and the overwhelming sensations rippling through her. She stopped thinking about what she was doing, how she kissed him, what it meant or didn't mean, and her insecurities that maybe she wasn't enough and let her body do what it naturally wanted to do.

She rocked her hips into his. One big hand slid down her spine. He palmed her ass and pressed her closer.

She expected to feel his hard length or at least his swelling flesh rise between them. Undeterred by his lack of response in that area, she latched on to the fact the rest of him seemed willing and able and desperate for more of her. So she slid her hand down his hard chest, flat, rippled abs, and over his fly to his flaccid but thick cock. He pressed into her palm and she stroked him.

He kissed his way down her neck, then let out a breath. "More."

She squeezed him in her palm and rubbed her fingers along the length of him, hoping the different sensations would help him rise to the occasion. She took her time, stroking and rubbing, not worried in the least, hoping, given time to settle in, he'd get out of his head and respond.

While she tempted him, he cupped her breasts in his palms and swept his thumbs over her hard nipples. The sensation set off fireworks of tingles through her breasts and made them grow heavy in his big hands. She stroked him again and again with one hand and slipped the other up under his shirt and along his side, her fingers sliding over his warm skin.

He pushed her away and raked both hands over his head and held it between his palms, his breaths coming in uneven pants. "It's not working." Frustration and shame lit his gray-blue eyes when he dropped his hands and stared at her, then looked away.

"We just got started."

"I knew this was a bad idea. It's not going to work."

She stepped close and put her hand on his chest and felt his thrashing heart pounding against her palm. "Did I do something wrong?"

He put his hand over hers and pressed it harder against his chest. "No. It's not you. It's me."

It was hard for her to ask because it reminded her of that despicable man. His voice rang in her head. *It's not bad. You're so beautiful. You want to make me feel good, don't you?*

NO!

But she did want to make Drake feel as good as he made her feel. This wasn't her past but a chance to turn her twisted thoughts and memories into something that was real and meaningful and intimate in a way that was mutual, not self-serving and vile.

Drake read something in her, cupped her face, and made her look at him. "You make me feel so good. All I want to do is be able to show you that, but the longer it takes, the more I fear it won't happen, and I don't want to disappoint you."

She hooked her hands on his wrists as he held her face and gently brushed his thumbs over her cheeks. The soft caress made her want to rub her face into his warm hands so he wouldn't stop.

"I'm only disappointed you stopped touching me. I'm disappointed you won't let me keep touching you."

"I want you to, it's just . . . I can't make it work. And I want it to because I want to be deep inside you." He pressed the heel of his hand into his eye. "My fucking head is all messed up. I want to just be with you, but the thoughts are going round and round in my mind."

She didn't know how to quiet them. She wanted him focused on her, not . . . Inspiration struck. "I think I know what to do."

Skepticism darkened his eyes.

"This is going to take a level of trust for both of us that we normally resist. But I'm willing to try if you are."

He reluctantly nodded.

She stepped back and took his hand. She tugged to get him to follow her the few steps to the sofa. "Sit."

He eyed her but reluctantly took a seat and stared up at her.

"Don't move. I'll be right back."

"Adria."

She pressed her fingers to his lips. "You're reluctant. I'm nervous. But I think I can give you what you need and you can give me what I want. Just give me a sec and I'll make it worth your while."

Drake kissed her fingers and nodded without a word.

She rushed into her bedroom and stopped in front of the dresser. *You can do this.* Because if she gave up now, she feared neither of them would try again for a long time.

She grabbed the hem of her shirt and pulled it up and over her head. She tossed it on the dresser, unhooked her bra, pulled it down her arms, and laid it on top of her shirt. She didn't meet her image in the mirror, afraid she'd chicken out.

She undid the button on her jeans, slid the zipper down, leaned over, and removed her boots and socks, then hooked her thumbs in the waistband of her jeans and panties and pushed them down her legs and kicked them off. Naked, nervous, but her mind set, she went to the bedside table and peeled off one of the condoms from the roll her sister had stuffed in her bag as a dare.

If he can try, I can, too.

She hid the foil packet in her hand, took a deep breath, and reminded herself that this was a chance to be with a man who understood in some way what this meant to her. Like him, she didn't want to spend the rest of her life without having a satisfying physical relationship.

I want to feel the way other women feel in a man's arms.

She took another deep breath to calm her nerves.

I can do this. With Drake.

Because it was him, she believed that.

She walked back into the living room, if not confident, then determined.

Drake turned to her. His eyes widened the second he saw her walking toward him, not a stitch of clothing on.

She didn't say a word when she closed the distance, stood between his widespread feet with her back to him, sat on his lap, settled back into his chest, discreetly dropped the condom beside his thigh, took one of his hands and pulled it across her body and placed it on her hip. She took the other and pulled it up her chest and settled it on her neck. She pressed her cheek to his and softly spoke her wishes. "Let's start where we began. While you slept, you wanted a willing woman in your arms." His hands contracted on her skin. "Here I am, Drake. Right here, right now, I'm yours. Touch me."

Body stiff, she jumped when he hugged her close and whispered in her ear, "Put your feet on the table." He pulled the coffee table closer with his booted feet.

She put both feet on the table and settled into him and his warmth and strength wrapped around her.

His lips brushed her cheek in a soft caress. "I'm a military man. I understand orders. You say go. You say stop. I'm at your command."

And just like that, she relaxed into him. And he didn't move his hands one inch. She sucked in a breath and let it out, loosening the last of her apprehension. "Go."

She expected him to move his hands and reach for whatever tempted him first, but he didn't loosen his hold or move a single finger. He raised his shoulder so she'd turn her head toward him and kissed her. Long and deep, it spun out for several seconds. She lost herself in the taste of him, the sweep of his tongue, the soft groan he couldn't contain. Only then did he brush his fingers from her throat down to her breast. His big, warm hand covered and molded it to his palm.

This is where she normally got nervous and unraveled. But with Drake, she melted and arched her back, pressing her breast into his hand, wanting—no needing—more.

Drake kissed her one last time. He wanted to look at her draped down his body, naked and beautiful. All that creamy white skin. An unexpected vine and roses tattoo twining from her shoulder down her arm. Her hands rested on her thighs, on either side of the blond triangle that pointed him to heaven.

He hadn't missed the embarrassment or timid way she walked out of the room, trying to be so confident and take charge so she could prove to him he wasn't broken. To prove to herself what happened to her as a child didn't taint what she wanted from him now.

He couldn't allow himself to think about what happened to her, because it made him want to rage, and all he wanted to do right now was make her forget. He wanted to show her that not all men used and hurt women.

He could find the last shreds of kindness inside him, pull them together, and give her an experience that was just for her.

He'd promised to get her off, but what he really wanted to do was show her that it was okay to enjoy sex. With a prostitute for a mother, he imagined she thought sex was some dirty deed.

She'd been used. Maybe he was using her to see if his problem was all in his head. God, he hoped so. And judging by the need gnawing at him and the heat building inside him, maybe she was right about that. But his need to use her also sparked a deep, primal necessity to please her.

He wanted to hear her moan his name and lose herself in all the pleasure he could give her, even if he couldn't complete the act himself.

And so he set his mind to what she wanted, what made her lose herself in his touch, and what made her lose control.

She liked kissing him, but he wanted her free to feel every touch, every sensation.

He swept his other hand up her belly to her other breast. He squeezed both in his hands and plucked both of her hard nipples, tugging softly, eliciting a sweet moan from her lips.

Her body moved against his as she arched and sought more of his touch.

He shifted beneath her, positioning his dick along the seam of her soft rump. She rocked her hips back into him and for a second he felt something stir, but dismissed it and refocused on her.

She rubbed her hands down the sides of his thighs and back up and over his arms and up to cover his hands at her breasts.

He brushed his lips against her ear. "You like that?"

"Your hands are so big."

He swept them down her body, the tops of her thighs, and back up to her stomach. "You are so soft." He nuzzled his nose into her hair, cupped one breast in his hand, and sent the other down her belly. He swept his fingers over her mound and dipped them low. He started slow and easy, brushing one finger between her soft folds, stoking the fire.

She kept her feet plastered to the table, her knees bent and only a few inches apart. He wanted her to relax and fall apart in his arms.

It didn't take long for his efforts to be rewarded with her sweet sighs. With each stroke and dip of his finger into her wet core, she lost herself in the rhythm and found a way to drive him to the heights of need. She not only rocked into his hand between her legs but planted her hands on his hips and rubbed her rump against his hardening cock. It was like a lap dance where you got to touch the woman. And God, he liked touching her and feeling her move against him.

He sank one finger deep, then slid it out and softly rubbed it over her sweet little nub in gentle strokes that made her writhe.

"Drake."

"I'm right here with you. I won't let you go." He nuzzled his face against her head, squeezed her breast, and sank two fingers deep inside her. Her knees fell apart as her hips rocked forward, then back as he pulled free. Her ass rubbed his thick cock and he nearly lost it, but he held back and waited her out because she was close. She just needed to let herself ride the tide of pleasure. So he sank two fingers deep, rubbed his aching erection against her ass, and whispered in her ear, "You feel so damn good." He thrust his fingers deep again and rubbed his palm against her mound, creating the friction she needed against her clit, and she shattered in his arms. Her body gripped his fingers tight and contracted around them. With his hand over her breast, her heart thrashed against his palm.

He held her, his own body throbbing with the need for release. As much as he reveled in the fact he wasn't permanently out of commission, it thrilled him even more that he'd pleased Adria.

Something in him shifted with the thought that she'd been able to let down her walls, trust in him, and just let herself enjoy the moment free of any outside or inner apprehensions.

He slid his hand up her belly and wrapped both his arms around her and hugged her close. "That was amazing." He meant it.

He'd always wanted his partner to get as much as he got out of a sexual encounter, but this was another level. Maybe because he got that she needed his help in her own space and time to find what she needed. Because he needed that, too. In pleasuring her, he'd had the freedom and time he needed to let his body do what he wanted it to do without him thinking and focusing solely on whether or not it did.

Adria slowly sat up on his lap, glanced over her shoulder, and held up a condom. "We're not done yet."

"Are you sure?" He didn't want to push.

She rubbed her ass against him again. "I want you to feel as good as you made me feel."

"I was right there with you." He wanted her to know that he'd gotten just as much out of it as she did.

She stood, turned to him, set the condom on his stomach, and went after his button and zipper. She hooked her fingers in the waistband of his jeans and boxer briefs.

He grabbed her hands and stilled them.

Her questioning gaze met his.

"My hip . . . It's kind of messed up."

She leaned in and kissed him softly. With her face an inch from his and eyes locked on him she said, "It doesn't matter to me." She tugged down his clothes and freed his not-so-hard dick. Without hesitation, she wrapped her hand around him and stroked from base to tip and back down. His flesh jumped and hardened at her sweet touch. He laid his head back, closed his eyes, and sighed, thankful his body responded the way he wanted. He glanced at her to see if the scars and burns bothered her. He held perfectly still when she traced her fingers over them in a soft caress while her other hand clamped around his dick and stroked him up and down.

She didn't stop touching him. In fact, she took her time, looking her fill, sweeping her hands over him to see how he responded. So he let go of his worries that he repulsed her and focused on the feel of her hands on him. His eyes closed again, then flew open when her tongue licked the head of his dick and her lips closed over him. She sank to her knees and sucked him deep into her mouth, then back up. Timid at first, she found what worked for her and him, because the second he groaned when he liked something, she did it again. He felt the rising tide of pleasure rush through him, but he wanted to be buried deep inside her when he came.

He tore open the condom, brushed his fingers through her hair to get her to release him, rolled the condom on, hooked his hands under her arms, dragged her up his body, and took her mouth in a deep kiss as she settled on his lap again. With her knees straddling his hips, she took him into her hot, wet core in a slow slide of her body over his until he was locked deep inside her. And then she moved and he followed, their bodies rocking and him thrusting in and out of her.

He broke the kiss to take one of her sweet, hard nipples in his mouth. She slid her fingers through his hair and held him close. He rubbed his hands over her hips to her ass and squeezed, pushing her down on him and grinding his hips against hers. She sighed and rocked against him, her body contracting around his. He thrust harder and deeper, his tongue sweeping over her breast until he had to let her go and let loose the moan deep in his throat as she set his body on fire.

He tried to hold back and make it last.

With her hands on his shoulders, she leaned close, slid her hand over his head, and whispered in his ear, "Go." The same order she gave him to start.

He thrust deep once, twice, and let himself go. And she went with him, amplifying his orgasm until he was spent and panting out his breaths like he'd run a sprint.

He still had her ass gripped in both hands. She leaned against him, her head on his shoulder, face in his neck. She breathed as hard as him and didn't seem inclined to leave him anytime soon. Not that she could with him holding her locked down on his lap.

He liked the feel of her against him, surrounding him.

"Did I hurt you?"

His hip ached, but the pain got lost in the background, because all he could think about was how good it felt to make love to a woman again. Not just any woman, but this amazing one, who took her time, didn't flinch at the sight of him, or hesitate to show just how into him and what they were doing she was, all while doing her best to figure out what he liked and how to move with him. The second he flinched when she pushed down too hard on his left side, she shifted her weight. When she reached back and grabbed his thigh to support herself and pressed too hard on his old bullet wound and he pulled her back forward, she rubbed her hand over the spot to soothe the momentary pain, then went right back to riding him. His injuries didn't make her give up. She found a better way.

He hated to think about the past and Melanie in this moment, but he did and settled why they would have never worked for the long haul. Melanie didn't know how to stick it out and find a better way. She gave up. She saw the scars and wounds and his limitations and didn't look past them to find all the things that he could still do. She didn't see his strengths and that he was still a man who needed the comfort and joy of being with a woman.

He ran his hands up Adria's back and wrapped them around her in a tight hug. "No, sweetheart, you didn't hurt me. You brought me back to life." He tightened his hold. "Thank you."

She slipped her hands over his sides to his back and held him close. "Thank you for showing me what it should be like."

"My pleasure. Anytime." He meant it, even if he didn't know what this meant for the two of them.

They'd made a deal. Sex. No strings. He didn't know if he had anything else to give her, because though he was happy to discover his body wasn't a total loss—as far as he was concerned—his mind was still a fucked-up place that he didn't want to inflict on anyone. Especially her.

"Next time, I'm not the only one who's naked."

He chuckled and smiled like it was the most natural thing, even though he couldn't remember the last time he did either. "You shocked the hell out of me when you walked out. But damn, if anything was going to get me to stand at attention, it was you, gorgeous."

She laughed, then sat up on him. His hands slid down her back to her hips. She shyly smiled, then brushed her fingers down his face and the scars he believed she didn't really see. Not in the way that made others cringe.

"I know I don't have a right to ask you to do anything for me . . ."

He traced his fingers down the center of her chest. "What is it?"

"Will you please take what happened today between us and stop telling yourself you can't do things? Take that voice in your head that tells you, you can't and tell it to shut the fuck up."

He smiled and laughed again. "I'll try."

"Do it. Just like you did this." She rocked her hips against him, stirring his interest all over again.

If he could do it once and felt the need building again, he had no reason to doubt he could perform whenever he wanted to from now on.

If he was wrong about this, maybe he was wrong about other things he thought he'd never be able to do again.

She was right: his issues, though numerous, weren't as much in the forefront for him as thinking he'd never have sex again and that it meant he'd never have a relationship with a woman. At least not the kind of relationship he wanted.

And he could have a family.

That thought opened up his future.

She really had changed things for him.

"I'll work on it."

She slipped off his lap and stood before him. Her gaze drifted to his hip, then met his again. "I know your military service was a big part of your life. Don't let it be your whole life. There's so much more about you than that. You showed me that you can be patient and kind and giving to someone who really needed it."

"I only gave you everything I needed, too. Everything you showed me the other night when I attacked you." He raked his hand over his head. "I'm really sorry about that. The last thing I ever want to do is scare you."

"I see you, Drake. You don't scare me." The hint of unease he sensed in her bloomed pink in her cheeks. "Um, I'm gonna go find some clothes. You can clean up in the bathroom."

He waited for her to slip into her room before he attempted to get his ass off the couch. His leg hurt, but in a good way. He hadn't felt this kind of tight pain since he stopped doing his physical therapy. Yeah, he'd convinced himself he didn't need it, that it wasn't doing him any good. The truth was, he got tired of measuring his progress in the tiniest of ways. He wanted results like he got today. But the issues with his leg weren't rooted in his brain. They were real injuries, and he needed to give them time to heal. He needed to put the work in to get his strength back.

Maybe he'd never be as strong as he was and he'd always limp, but if he could walk without the damn cane, that would be something.

He wanted to mount his horse without assistance. He set that as his next goal.

As promised to Adria, he'd work on it.

He stood from the sofa and stretched his leg, made sure he had his balance, and gimped his way to the bathroom to clean up.

By the time he came out, Adria stood in the kitchen, hair tied up in a ponytail, her cheeks still pink, her eyes unsure. She looked good in a red tank top and jeans. "I forgot I promised Tate I'd take a look at a horse he's been training to barrel race."

That was news to him. "You barrel race?"

She smiled. "Yes, I do. If not for my sister Roxy, I'd be a champion."

"Is that so?"

She smiled and his chest went tight. "It is. She's just that good."

"Sounds like you admire her."

"I do. If not for her, I don't know what would have happened to me and Juliana. She took us into her home and kept us safe. She taught us to ride. Up on a horse, I found a freedom I'd never felt in my life. I thought I could race away from all my problems."

He got that. He often tried to do the same thing. "You can't outrun what's in your head."

She nodded. "No, you can't. So you have to find a way to make peace with it."

"About what happened to you . . ."

"You don't have to go there, Drake. I've made peace with it. I just hadn't quite found a way to turn it off when I wanted to . . . you know, be with someone. It always got in the way. Today, you showed me it doesn't have to, that I can shut it off and lose myself with someone."

He ran his hand over his head and tried not to feel like an awkward teen asking a girl for a date for the first time. "I'm, uh, happy to show you again sometime."

"I could prove to you today wasn't a fluke." Her shy smile didn't detract from her bold words.

"Deal." He didn't know how to leave things with her, but he wanted her to know he'd like to do this again. "I'll walk you down to the stables."

"You don't have to. I'm sure you need to get back to Sunny."

"Shit." He'd forgotten about the puppy. "I left him locked in my room."

"Better get back and let him out then." She didn't move to the door with him. "I'll let you go out first. Just so your family doesn't jump to conclusions."

He nodded and headed for the door, but stopped when she called him back.

"Don't forget your laptop. I imagine Dr. Porter is on pins and needles waiting to hear if I cured you." Her sweet smile teased but also tempted him to kiss her again.

He didn't. But he chuckled under his breath and felt even lighter. He hoped it lasted. "I don't kiss and tell." But he would have to let Dr. Porter know he'd worked out one of his many issues.

"I'd like it if we kept this between us as far as your family is concerned. Trinity and I work together. I don't want things to get complicated."

He took her lead and kept things simple. "No one will hear it from me." He picked up the laptop and went back to the door, where he retrieved his new metal cane. He opened the door, but didn't step out. "How do you want to do this?"

"Well, I can't exactly come to you, so I guess I'll see you the next time you show up here."

"Do you care when that is?"

"No. I enjoyed today. I hope to enjoy it again soon." The shy smile on her lips said she meant it. He liked her honesty and directness. It took guts to say and do the things she'd done today after what happened to her.

He should take a page from her book and do the same.

They'd put a lot of faith in each other.

He appreciated that she kept things light and easy. So he left her knowing he'd be back soon, because he needed something good and uncomplicated in his life. Their dirty deal gave him exactly what he wanted without all the complications of a relationship he wasn't ready to have with her or anyone.

Chapter Twelve

Adria hesitated on the porch of the big house. She didn't know how to do this. Juliana didn't mind no-strings-attached sex, but Adria wasn't like that. She couldn't stop thinking about Drake, what they'd shared, and what it meant.

Why did it have to mean anything more than a good time shared by two people who wanted the same thing? *Done. End of story.* Or at least the chapter, because they planned to do it again.

And why not? No one got hurt. In fact, she felt damn good. She *wanted* to do it again.

And the nerves fluttering in her belly were more anticipation for the next time than dreading some awkward moment they might have when they saw each other again.

Get out of your head.

You made the deal because you didn't want it to mean anything more than fun.

She wanted to simply enjoy what they shared physically, but her heart wondered if maybe there was something more there.

Stick to the deal.

Leave it to her to find a way to play it safe while stepping way out of her comfort zone. But she reminded herself that if she expected Juliana and Drake to do the hard work to heal, she couldn't expect anything less from herself. While Drake had certainly helped her take a huge leap toward differentiating what happened in the past and what she could have with a man now, she still wondered if she'd have to go through the same process of learning to let go and trust with someone else.

She and Drake worked because they'd both been thinking sex wouldn't work for them.

She'd needed a man who would stop if that's what she wanted and not take it as a rejection or failure on his part. It wasn't about him. It was about her. And Drake got that, so she'd been able to go with it and not worry about hurting his feelings.

He'd needed that from her.

Drake's problem was solved. He'd overcome the head games he'd been playing with himself by simply getting turned on. Her issues were more complicated and complex.

She needed to stop thinking about having sex with Drake and focus on the fact that Drake was Trinity's brother, not boyfriend material.

He had his demons to slay.

She had a business to open, a sister to help through her recovery, and . . . What about her? What did she want?

Roxy and Sonya had found happiness here in Montana.

Maybe she and Drake weren't headed in the lifelong-partners direction, but she had found something she needed in his arms.

Why shouldn't she enjoy it? She didn't need to map out how this would go. She took a cutout from her straight and narrow path because something about Drake called to her. Some of his pain resembled hers. She wanted to feel better. So did he.

Why not help each other feel better?

The great feeling he left her with last night still felt good this morning.

"Is there a reason you're standing out here and not coming in?"

She stared up at Drake, surprised by the change she saw in him. "You slept last night." The dark smudges under his eyes had disappeared. So had the hard edge in his eyes and the stiffness in his shoulders. He looked relaxed and maybe not happy, but less intensely angry.

"The credit goes to you. Again."

She walked up the steps and stood in front of him. "Happy to help."

"You look good." His eyes shuttered and swept down her body, then back up in a blaze of heat that left her warm and tingling.

She felt good. And sexy, thanks to Drake's blazing gaze. She swept her hair back over her shoulder. It hit her the second he took a step closer that she was flirting with him. She didn't normally do that.

And she didn't want him to think it meant she wanted more than . . . Well, he did look damn good. Thoughts of his hands on her body, the way he made her come apart . . . Yeah, she wanted more.

She noted the sweatpants and tennis shoes replacing his usual jeans and work boots. "What are you doing today?"

"Physical therapy."

"I thought you quit?"

His eyes narrowed on that last word. Quitting wasn't his style, but he'd been knocked down harder than most. "Just a pause." He stepped past her, leaning on his cane to take the steps down. He didn't look back. "I can't expect you to do all the work." Her mind went to her astride his lap, rocking and rolling her hips against his as pleasure ripped through both of them. Something both of them needed, but they had been surprised by the intensity of it all.

He opened his truck door and looked at her then. "I'll see you tonight."

"You can show me your new moves."

"The pressure's on." He climbed into the front seat.

She rushed down the steps and grabbed the door before he closed it and stood between him and the open door.

He didn't like her staring at him, especially since his scarred cheek faced her as he stared out the front window. "What?"

"Look at me."

He sighed out his frustration and turned to stare down at her. The earlier heat in his eyes turned cool with agitation.

"With me, there's no pressure. You want to see me, great. You don't, I'm not going to guilt you or have hurt feelings. That's not what this is between us. That's what we agreed to. When we're together, there's no failure if you try and it doesn't work out the way you think it should. We can simply try things a different way, a way that works better for you, because as you proved to me last night, you won't leave me hanging."

She put her hand on his thigh. "This is about us healing each other, not hurting each other. I would never use your physical and emotional trauma against you. I want to help, not hurt you more." She moved her hand to his arm. "I'm glad you're giving physical therapy a try again. I hope that what happened between us showed you that things can be different if you try."

"I'm ready to work on it."

"Talk to Dr. Porter. He helps you more than you're willing to admit. Do your physical therapy. Sleep. You *will* feel better."

He reached out and brushed her hair. "You made me feel damn good."

"Good, huh? Imagine how I could make you feel if I actually got *your* clothes off."

She tried to step back and end this because it felt way too intimate for what they really shared, but he caught her hand and stopped her. "I saw the embarrassment and fear in your eyes when you walked out of your bedroom. After hearing what happened to you, I know that was a huge step. Asking me to give you something you want in your life took guts you didn't think you had, but you proved you did with that brave act. I'm going today because if you can be that brave, why the hell can't I face a little more pain and get my ass to physical therapy?" He squeezed her hand, held her wide-eyed, amazed gaze, then let her go. "See you tonight."

Unable to move, she watched him drive away, thinking about what he'd said. She'd set out to prove to him that he wasn't impotent, but she'd accomplished so much more than that. It floored her.

"What's going on with you and Drake?" Trinity walked down the steps, her gaze narrowed and direct.

Sunny rushed down the steps and ran around the grass like something was chasing him. Turned out to be his tail. He spun in circles trying to catch it.

"I just wanted him to know I'm happy he's trying to get better and going to physical therapy."

Trinity's gaze shot to the end of the drive, where Drake's truck turned onto the main road. "I wonder what prompted him to go back. We've been after him for weeks to try again."

He thought she was brave. The man had faced down guns and bombs and who knew how many near-death experiences. Men tried to kill him.

He fought back. For their country. For his family. For her. For everyone. He had her beat on the bravery scale. "You had to know he'd eventually find his courage buried under all that pain."

"We thought he'd given up."

"He needed time to come to terms with his new reality. I'm not saying he's done that exactly, or that this is a turning point, but if nothing else, it's a good day for him."

"I'll take it." Trinity held up her car keys. "Ready to go to work?"

She nodded, but her mind was still on Drake. She hoped his good days started outnumbering his bad ones.

Which made her wonder about Juliana. She hoped Juliana had made some progress, even one small step forward toward better health the way Drake had done today.

The way she did last night in Drake's arms.

She had to admit, there was something quite freeing in embracing and nurturing her sexuality.

She felt different. Less guarded. More free.

She couldn't wait to explore her newfound daring side. While she credited Drake for bringing it out in her, she hesitated to think too deeply into the connection between them that made her feel comfortable enough to make the bold deal *and* follow through with it.

He'd been right—it took every ounce of bravery she could muster to walk out and face him naked and wanting to tempt him, because as a child it felt so wrong to be subjected to doing just that for men—for strangers.

But something about Drake felt familiar and safe.

In his condition and after what he'd put her through during his flashback, that's the last thing she should feel. But she did.

She couldn't explain it.

And she couldn't dismiss it either.

She'd tapped into his kindness, empathy, and generosity. He gave to her yesterday with an open heart.

And she wanted more.

Chapter Thirteen

Drake rubbed his hand over his hip, trying to ease the pain and loosen his tight muscles. He'd taken his pain meds. At times, he resented the pain. Other times, he thought it his due. Today, he welcomed it.

The physical therapist had worked him out good. This time, he hadn't resisted, but pushed himself hard. He didn't expect immediate results, but he felt good that he'd made progress.

One step at a time.

He'd get more mobility and strength. God willing, he'd walk without the cane again. He'd stand on his own two feet. He wouldn't worry that he'd stumble, fall, and make a fool of himself.

He'd be able to do a hell of a lot more than sit there and hold on to a woman while she rode him. Not that he minded. In fact, he'd gotten so lost in Adria, the triumph of being able to make love to her evaporated under the overwhelming pleasure he found in her.

Pleasure and joy like he'd never experienced.

He'd longed to feel even one tenth as good as she made him feel last night.

But the point was, the physical therapy would allow him to move the way he wanted.

He could actually help his brothers on the ranch.

He wouldn't feel useless.

"Are you going to tell me what happened between you and Adria?"

Drake shook off his thoughts and stared at Dr. Porter, who came up on his screen and demanded an answer without a hello or any other benign conversation to start things off.

They spoke three times a week, but Drake asked for this call, knowing Dr. Porter hadn't supported what he and Adria agreed to do for each other. He wanted Dr. Porter to know the unconventional "therapy" worked. He didn't want Dr. Porter to think he'd used Adria, because it had been the most intimate and mutual exchange he'd ever experienced.

Drake opened his mouth, but closed it before any words came out.

"Did you hear what she revealed about her past? I admit her tactic for making you see that others have suffered and survived and moved on was a great way to shock you out of your head and make you take a look at yourself in a new way. But, Drake, you have to know that what she proposed could be detrimental to both of you."

"Why? She was right. I thought the bomb took more than a chunk out of my leg. I thought the nerve and muscle damage had made it impossible for me to get it up. Melanie and I tried and failed miserably and that was the end of us. I thought I'd never be with a woman again. Never have a family. A life without sex and that kind of connection with a woman . . . What was the point? But I can."

Dr. Porter sat back in his seat. "That's more words than you've said to me in weeks. I'm glad you're ready to talk and open up about what is going on in your life. So let's unpack the thing with Melanie first. Do you really believe she left you because you couldn't have sex with her?"

"It was a hell of a lot more than that. She wanted me to be me before my tours of duty. She couldn't understand my drive to get back there and my feeling useless that I couldn't go back and help what was left of my team. She didn't understand my anger and why I didn't try to get better. The more things didn't go the way she wanted them, and I didn't act the way she wanted, the more she backed away. When she did, I pushed her away. Our inevitable breakup began long before I got hurt. I was away for a long time, barely kept in touch, and didn't include her in . . . most everything in my life." He saw things better now. "She wanted a say. She wanted me to leave the past behind and move on like that." He snapped his fingers. "When she realized it wasn't going to happen and

I was completely different . . . that was it for her. She didn't want to give me a shot to make things better. She gave up without really trying and that just made me even angrier."

"After what you've been through, it takes time."

"She didn't give me time to do anything. She didn't want to hear promises she didn't think I'd keep. She didn't want to try. I don't blame her. Anymore." Which surprised him, but the hostility and anger he usually felt when he even thought about Melanie didn't rise up inside him.

She didn't give him a chance. She didn't challenge him to rise to the occasion. Figuratively, or literally.

Not the way Adria pushed and didn't accept his say-so.

She provoked him.

Why he found that so appealing, he didn't know, but it was like a dare he couldn't ignore.

As far as Melanie was concerned . . . "I wanted Melanie to be the same as she was before I left, too, but we were both different. Maybe I just didn't see her for who she really was until I needed her to be something she wasn't."

Now that he said it, it made the most sense.

"So, it's really over between you? Even though you now know you're not impotent."

That word made him cringe. "Sex wasn't the only problem. She's not a match for me. I'm not one for her. I see that now." It felt good to acknowledge that and let it go.

"Do you think you and Adria are a better match?"

He didn't know about that. "We shared something deeper than sex. It was . . . healing. For both of us. I barely know her." What he did know intrigued him. Her strength and resilience and fight drew him in, but the empathy without pity she showed had touched him. She got him, because she understood her own pain and the limitations she put on herself because of the trauma she suffered. She wanted to help him. She wanted to help her sister. It was her nature. And that endeared her to him even more because, although he didn't want to admit he needed help, he needed her kind of prodding and understanding to get him to act. "She's my sister's friend and business partner."

"That's two excuses you've made not to have a real relationship with her."

"She made it clear that's not what she wants either. I'm not even close to being good for someone else. I can only say I woke up this morning feeling different."

Dr. Porter's interest was piqued. "How so?"

"For the first time in a long time, I don't feel stuck. I feel like I can do something and things will be different. I went to physical therapy this morning." He'd called right when they opened and practically begged for an appointment. Now he had a standing three-day-a-week regime and a plan to work on his mobility issues.

"That's a good start."

"Because she made me think. I was so sure I couldn't get it up anymore. I made myself believe it."

"Did it ever cross your mind that you thought you deserved that kind of punishment?"

"Yes. But that didn't make it any easier to accept. It pissed me off. It made the rest of my life look like a fucking lonely existence not worth living."

"Drake . . ."

He held up his hand to stop the doc. "You knew I'd gone to that dark place more than once. It's why you sent me to Jamie. But Adria made me confront something I thought was true and couldn't be changed. So I spent some time before falling asleep last night thinking if I was wrong about that, maybe I'm wrong about what else I think I can't do. Maybe I can, if only I'd work on getting better like everyone keeps pushing me to do. I've resisted because I'm a stubborn jackass and I didn't want to try and fail."

"Because you felt like you failed with Melanie and you didn't want to fail at anything else?"

Damn, Doc, don't sugarcoat it.

"It goes deeper. I thought I failed my team, her, my family."

"Yourself?"

"Everyone. My whole life suddenly felt like a colossal fuckup." He rubbed his hands over his face and sank deeper into the couch. "Adria saved her sister's life, like a week ago. She brought her here to go to rehab. She's starting a business. She lives with her past. And still she smiles and engages people. She keeps living her life, moving forward, and still finds it within herself to reach out to someone like me."

"Someone hurting the way she's hurting."

"She's got it all inside her and still . . . I don't know . . . she survives."

"You admire her."

Melanie caved when things got hard.

Adria braced herself for the worst and pushed on and found a way. "Yeah, I admire the hell out of her. After what she's been through, she still found the courage to not only help me, but to open herself to experiencing in a new way something that frightens and brings up horrible memories for her."

"Proving to you that you weren't impotent had to be a lot easier for her than letting go of her dark memories and allowing herself to enjoy being with a man."

"I wanted her to have that. I wanted to erase her past and show her something different and better. She deserves that."

"Why did you want to give her that?" Doc really wanted to know if there was something more between him and Adria.

"She gave me back something very important in my life." He couldn't imagine going the rest of his life without sex and intimacy with a woman. It truly made him feel empty. And he didn't want Adria to feel that way the rest of her life. "I wanted to show her that a man can be kind and generous and not use her. I went into it thinking I'd get nothing but having her close to me." He'd never really held a woman and given to her without expecting it to lead to sex. But with her, he'd been all in for making it all about her.

"After what I imagine you experienced with Melanie, I can see how sharing a closeness with a woman would appeal to you."

The feel of Adria, her smell, the push, pull, and slide of her body against his made him ache for her even now. He liked having her in his arms and pressed against his body. He'd been loath to let her go last night.

"She appeals to me on all kinds of levels. But I'm happy with the agreement we made. Right now, simple is better. I have a lot of work ahead of me. I want to focus on getting well. A relationship takes work and time and I need to dedicate myself to fixing me."

"I take it that means you and Adria will take what you learned last night and move on."

"While my problem seems to be fixed, I'm not so sure about hers." Just because he got her off once didn't mean all her problems were fixed. He imagined her nightmare would come back to haunt her. She needed more time to truly see the difference between what happened to her then and being with a man now. She'd need time to really accept that she enjoyed being with him because it felt good.

"That's just it, Drake, her issues run deep. What happened to her left emotional scars. She needs help to resolve what happened to her."

"I agree. Right now, she wants to try to resolve her issue with sex and intimacy by being with someone she feels she can trust—someone who is willing to make it about what she needs and giving it to her in her own time." He didn't literally mean sex when he said, "giving it to her." Yes, that was part of it, but there was more. She needed patience and understanding. She needed openness and space to explore what she liked and what felt right without judgment or reprisals. She needed a willing partner, ready to act on her demands and desires, or simply stop if that's what she needed.

"Relationships built strictly on sex never last. Do you know why?" Doc didn't wait for his answer. "Because people have feelings and form attachments. I'm not saying men and women can't have sex without love, but more often than not they need more. Adria's idea of sex is something that is exploitive and bad. Having a purely sexual relationship with you without a true commitment outside of that could do more harm than good for her."

"Look, Doc, I'm going with what she said she wants. It's not like I don't like her *and* find her attractive. I do. But she came to me with this. Lord knows there's not a lot about me that could appeal to her."

He turned his head to show off the scars on his face. She'd barely gotten a glimpse of the rest of him under his clothes. Add in his shit personality and anger issues and he wasn't anyone's idea of a hot date. "But she gave me something and asked for something in return. So long as we both accept that's all it is, I don't see a problem." So long as no one else found out about it.

"I can't tell you what to do. I can only warn you that rarely does *just sex* work outside of a one-night stand."

Drake defaulted to rude behavior and slammed the laptop shut, cutting off anything more Dr. Porter wanted to discuss. Or advise him on. He didn't want to talk about him and Adria anymore. He didn't want to justify his behavior or choices.

Adria had a choice and she'd made it this morning when he gave her a chance to say no to seeing him again tonight. He was happy to let her lead. She could put a stop to this whenever she wanted. No harm. No foul. She'd go her way and he'd go his. Until then, why shouldn't he enjoy himself?

It was the only part of his life working for him right now.

Chapter Fourteen

Adria opened the door and stared at Drake standing in front of her, deep lines across his forehead and bracketing his narrowed eyes.

"What's wrong with you?"

"Lots of things. Right now, living with my siblings. I tried to leave the house twice and got stopped first by Trinity and then Declan wanting to know where I was going."

"So?"

"What am I supposed to tell them? 'I'm going to fuck Adria'?"

She leaned her shoulder against the door frame and glared back at him.

It didn't take him but a second to figure out how callous that sounded. "Sorry." He sucked in a breath and let out his frustration. "I didn't know when you thought I'd stop by and I didn't want to make it too late because I figure you're tired after a long day and . . . I don't know, I thought you'd tell me to fuck off. Maybe that's what I deserve. Dr. Porter said this was a bad idea. He thinks you're going to fall in love with me or something, but let's face it, that's not likely to happen." He swept his hand from his face down the length of him like that made any kind of sense.

She narrowed her disapproving blue eyes. "So you've moved on from not thinking you can ever have sex with a woman to no woman will ever love you because of the way you look?"

His head snapped back. "What? No. I don't know. That's not what this is. I'm not looking for . . . that."

Neither was she, but she also didn't want him thinking that his flawed appearance meant someone wouldn't find him attractive and fall in love with him. "Drake. We need to talk."

He shook his head and stepped back on his good leg to leave. "All it takes is a no."

She reached out and gripped his shirt in her fist and pulled him forward.

Off balance, he took the step over the threshold, caught his balance with his cane, and moved the next two steps in as she tugged him inside enough to slam the door. "You said the words were *stop* and *go*."

He raised an eyebrow, his gaze filled with confusion and a little hope.

"But first, let me set you straight. Yes, you have scars."

He turned his head to hide his left cheek.

She reached up, took his chin, and moved his head so he looked down at her again. "But they do not make you any less than drop-dead gorgeous."

"Are you high?"

"That's Juliana's favorite pastime. I get a kick out of blowing your mind." She put her hand on his cheek. "The scars aren't as bad as you think. They make you look dangerous. Girls like that. I love your eyes. The blue-gray is like a brewing storm. And when you saw me naked last night, the look in your eyes, so filled with want and desire . . . well, I needed that look. Badly."

"I did want you. Then. Now." He dropped the shopping bag he carried inside, leaned the cane against the door, and put his hands on her hips, drawing her close.

She swept her hands up his arms to his biceps. "You're a wall of muscles." She ran her hands up over his shoulders and down his hard chest. "All this strength, yet you touch me with such care."

He swept his hands over the swell of her bottom and pulled her up until her hips met his.

She rocked her belly against his growing erection. "My desire and need aren't dampened by the scars. The second I opened the door and saw your scowling, gorgeous face, all those muscles tensed along your big frame, and damn, I wanted your arms around me, your lips and tongue sliding over my skin, and you inside me, making me come apart."

Drake let out a ragged breath at the bold erotic words she used on purpose to tempt him, leaned forward, and pressed his forehead to hers to look deep into her eyes. "Say it." The words came out as a plea.

And she answered. "Go."

He didn't dive in like she expected. No, he cupped her face and kissed her softly, then took the kiss deeper, sweeping his tongue along hers. His arms came around her shoulders and waist and pulled her close, encircling her in all his strength. She sank into him and let go, kissing him back until they were desperate for each other.

She slipped her hands up under his dark blue T and swept her fingers up his back. She felt a couple other scars, but they didn't stop her exploration of all those hard muscles, taut under his warm skin. She ran her fingers down his spine, gripped the edge of his shirt, and pulled it up his back.

She broke the kiss to slip the shirt over his head, but he hesitated and didn't lean over so she could drag it off.

She went with orders. "Give it to me."

He dipped his head and bent at the waist so she could remove it.

She didn't take her eyes off him, but dipped them to his wide chest and ripped abs. "Damn. No man should look that good." Her need to touch him overtook her again. She splayed her fingers wide on his chest and brushed them over his pecs and down his taut belly. She leaned in close, felt him holding his breath, and pressed a kiss on his chest. She let her fingers roam over the dips and curves, not stopping or hesitating when she skimmed over the bullet wounds.

She rubbed her cheek against his warm skin and inhaled his woodsy scent. "Touch me, Drake. I need to feel you."

His arms had fallen to his sides. At her words, he buried his hands in her long hair as she laid a trail of kisses over his chest, bracing herself on his wide shoulders. He sent those big hands down her back and up, along with her shirt. She shook out her hair the second he tossed her shirt aside. His fingers nimbly unhooked her bra and drew it down her arms. He'd seen her naked last night, but the need and awe in his eyes hadn't dissipated. He stared down at her like he couldn't wait to lick her. In the next breath, he did. From her throat, down her chest, to her tight nipple.

She cried out with the sheer pleasure every sweep of his tongue and nip of his teeth evoked.

She arched her back and offered up her breasts to his attention. And he gave them equal affection as she clutched his shoulders and held him close.

He hooked his hands over her ass and down lower until he lifted her against him and she wrapped her legs around his waist. He pivoted and pressed her back up against the wall. He lifted her higher and took her breast in his mouth, suckling deep.

The heat pooling low in her belly flashed and spread through her entire system like a wildfire. She held his head to her breast and let her head fall back against the wall as he suckled and drove her crazy.

"Drake. Please." She needed more.

He unlatched from her breast and pulled her close. Her breasts smashed against his hard chest. His heat spread through her and she rubbed her breasts against his skin. He growled at her ear and limped to her bedroom and tossed her down on the bed. He followed her, kissing her belly down to the button on her jeans. He stared up at her as he undid her jeans, hooked his fingers in the waistband of both her pants and panties, and dragged them down her legs. She usually went barefoot at home, so he didn't have to waste time removing her shoes or socks. Good thing, because she throbbed with need and wanted his hands on her.

He didn't disappoint and swept his big hands from her ankles all the way up to the top of her thighs and hips where he gripped her tight, gave her one last look and a chance to stop him before his head dipped between her thighs and his flat tongue licked her seam, the tip stopping at her most sensitive place and circling slowly.

She melted into the bed on a groan and rocked her hips forward and into his mouth and that roaming tongue that set her on fire.

Drake hooked his hands under her thighs, spread her legs wide, bared her most sensitive flesh to him, and dived in for more, his tongue thrusting deep inside her. She writhed beneath him. Every sigh and moan only drove him to make her do it again, until she was right on the edge.

"Let go, sweetheart." He circled her clit again and plunged one finger deep into her slick core. She shattered, her body clenched around his finger as he swept his tongue over that sweet spot one more time as her body convulsed.

He slipped his finger free and licked her again, setting off aftershocks that rippled through her. "So sweet." He kissed his way up her belly to her breast, flicked his tongue over her nipple, teasing it to attention, then smiled down at her. "You good?"

"Fantastic." She palmed his shoulder and shoved him over so he landed on his back beside her. She rose up and stared down at him. "My turn."

She straddled his lap, planted her hands on his pecs, leaned down, and kissed him. She pressed up, smiled, and slid back just enough to undo his jeans.

He covered her hands with his before he let her drag his pants and boxer briefs down his legs. "My hip . . . you don't have to take them all the way off."

She tilted her head and held his gaze. "You need to do this. You need to know that scars or not, I want you. You can see it, right?"

He nodded, acknowledging the desire she felt running all through her. "A few scars won't change that."

"You haven't seen my leg."

She tried again. Instead of trying to rid him of the barriers, she traced her fingers down his chest and over his left side where red lines rose out of his waistband like tendrils. She didn't stop, but ran her hand over the side of his hip and down his thigh. Because her legs straddled his knees, she felt him tense at her touch. She leaned over and planted kisses over his flat, hard stomach and continued to rub her hands over him until he relaxed.

"Do you trust me?" she whispered, still kissing his stomach.

"About as far as I can throw you."

She smiled against his skin and swept her hands up over his strong arms. "I bet that's a fair distance." She traced her hands over his shoulders, down his pecs and abs, hooked her fingers in his pants and boxers, lifted them up and over his thick erection, and pulled them down as her mouth enclosed his length as she exposed it. He groaned, long and deep. His fingers swept over her head and tangled in her hair.

She kept his mind on her mouth, licking and sucking, while she pushed his clothes down his legs, past his knees. She leaned over him on all fours, her mouth working up and down his swollen flesh, while she planted her foot and pushed his jeans and underwear down to his ankles.

"Fuck, Adria." His fingers tightened in her hair but he never hurt her.

She slid her mouth off him, licked his tip, stared up at him, and smiled. "Not yet." She slid her mouth over him again. He swore and groaned all at the same time. She tried not to smile, but it came anyway before she got back to making him moan.

She loved pleasing him, making him lose himself in the feel of her and the pleasure she aroused in him. It made her feel powerful and wanted and needed.

How could the nightmare come back with all these good and amazing feelings rushing through her?

This wasn't wrong. It couldn't be when it felt so right. And perfect.

"Adria," he called, and it was music to her ears.

She released his pulsing cock, kissed her way up his chest, and planted a long kiss on his lips.

"Condom. Pocket. Now." He reached sideways down to his ankle but couldn't quite reach with her straddling his hips, rubbing her slick center over his hard flesh.

She reached back, pulled the condom from his pocket, tore it open, and sheathed him while he kicked free of his pants, the movement only creating a sweet friction between them.

She rose up on her knees and sank down on him.

He swore and groaned again, clamping his hands on her hips and moving her back and forth over him. She let him control the speed and motion. He didn't seem to want to let her go on her own. She didn't mind. He'd lost himself again in the feel of her body working over his, and she lost herself in the demand of his will for both of them to find the pinnacle of pleasure they were driving toward with every push and pull of their bodies.

It came on like a freight train and bucked her body as he drove into her one last time and let go along with her. Spent and shaking with the aftermath, she collapsed on his heaving chest.

She'd barely gotten settled when he shoved his left leg up into her bottom and nearly toppled her off him.

He moaned in a very bad way and grabbed his thigh.

She moved off him, sat up, and stared down at the crisscross of scars and gnarled skin covering his hip and thigh. He gripped his leg and the corded muscle. He tried to rub at the cramp, but his whole body had gone rigid, making it worse.

She pushed his hand away and took over, rubbing in long, slow sweeps. "Shh. Relax."

He tried to push her hands away. "I've got it."

"Shut up and do what I said. Relax." She rubbed her hand over the scars and knotted muscle. She gently moved his foot down, lengthening out his leg a little at a time as she rubbed with her other hand. "There you go. It's going away." She kept up the massage even after he settled into the bed again. "That's it. You're okay."

His big hand settled over hers. "You can stop."

She leaned down and kissed his hand over hers, then sat up and stared at him. "Is it better?"

"Yeah." His gaze landed on the scars on his chest, then swept down to the ones covering his side, hip, and thigh. "It's not pretty."

"Just because you can't see my scars doesn't make them any prettier. They're a part of me. They're evidence I survived." She flexed her hand under his. "These are a part of you now, Drake. They are proof of what you've been through, your strength, your resilience." She slipped her hand free from his leg and reached up to his face. She looked him in the eye and said what needed to be said. "I'm sorry you got hurt. I'm sorry you lost your friends. But I am so glad you survived and I got to meet you. *You* have changed my life. I am better for knowing you."

He came up, wrapped both arms around her, fell back into the bed, pulling her down with him, and fiercely hugged her. "I don't deserve you."

"We are exactly what the other needs right now." Something in her wanted to take back those last two words. But she didn't want to be selfish and ask for more than he was willing to give, or she had time to provide. *Right now.*

He kissed her on the head. "You are unexpected in so many ways."

"Thanks." She drew the word out, unsure if he'd paid her a compliment or not. "You should know something."

"You're ready to kick me out already."

"Um, I'm not holding you here against your will or anything, but if you want to stay a while longer I might make it worth your while."

"I think you're trying to kill me."

She chuckled, snuggling into his chest and the embrace he hadn't let up on. "You're stronger than you think."

He flexed his arms, squeezing her closer to his rock-hard chest.

She giggled again, then looked up at him. "Not that, tough guy. You carried me in here. Without your cane."

"I didn't think about it. I just wanted you naked and in a bed."

She rubbed herself against his side. "Mission accomplished."

They settled into the quiet for a long stretch that wasn't awkward or strange, given that they didn't really know each other outside of what they shared in these intimate but not revealing moments.

"Adria?"

"Yeah?"

It took him a second, but his deep voice finally came again. "Do the scars bother you?" He really wanted to know if they put her off.

"They make me sad because it must have been a devastating and brutal way you got them. I would never wish a moment of pain on you. But no, Drake, they don't make me want you any less than I did before I got you naked." She turned her head to his and planted her chin on his chest. "I wish I could take them away. I wish you saw yourself the way I see you. Strong. Resilient. And so sexy that every time I see you, I want to climb all over you."

He smiled. A real, full-on smile.

Stunned, she smiled back. "You keep smiling at me like that, and I won't be held responsible for what I do."

"Oh yeah," he challenged. "Prove it." The smile didn't dim. It grew wider when she rose up, covered his body with hers, and kissed the smile right off his tempting lips.

She thought she'd be the one to show him how much she wanted him, but he rolled her to her back and took over. Their lovemaking up until now had a desperate need that drove them. Not this time. He took things slow and easy and drew out every kiss and touch, push and pull of his body over and in hers, until their breaths mingled, hearts beat as one, and the pleasure they shared burst through them.

Rocked by the force and depth of what happened between them, she stared up at the ceiling, trying to center her world again, but it felt completely off when he rolled over, sat on the edge of the bed, and pulled on his clothes. He stared down at her for a moment, then walked out.

She wanted to call him back, but didn't because that wasn't the deal.

She heard the front door close a few moments later.

He's not for you. You can't keep him.

The reminder didn't stop her heart from asking, *Why not?*

Because. It wasn't meant to be that way between them. She couldn't explain it, but it just wasn't.

What they shared was always meant to end. But it didn't have to end now. They could enjoy each other a while longer. She'd back out if things got too personal.

Her heart spoke up again. *Too late.*

No, it wasn't. Lust wasn't love. And that's all they had. She was sure of it.

Mostly. Definitely. Maybe.

Damn.

When she woke up in the morning, found the paper bag he dropped inside the door, and saw the pretty nightgown and sexy lace panties he'd bought to replace what he'd wrecked, her heart melted. Thinking about Drake buying her lingerie made her smile.

Thinking about him period made her happy.

Damn.

Then she saw the note he scrawled on the back of the gift receipt.

I like you wearing nothing but your tattoo, but I owe you these. Looking forward to taking them off you.

Her heart flipped over. *Oh no.*

Chapter Fifteen

Drake rode Thor with Sunny on his lap into the stable yard and stopped ten feet from Declan and Tate. His brothers stared up at him. Sunny barked a happy hello. He gave the fast-growing pup a scratch behind the ears. While Sunny continued to live up to his name, neither of his brothers smiled. He'd avoided them the last ten days, taking the time he needed to work on his physical therapy and settle into his . . . relationship—whatever it was between him and Adria.

The night she first saw his scars—the words she'd said to him that sank deep into his soul—he didn't know what to do with how it made him feel or how he'd changed because of them. He walked out that night with a desire to stay with her so strong it scared him.

She had to know he fled that night without a word because what he'd wanted to say wasn't something they'd agreed to or wanted. Right? But what he'd found in her arms, he'd never thought possible.

So he told himself to remember that he'd promised to give her what she needed and not expect more than she was so generously willing to give. And she was generous with her affection, but they'd shared few words since that night.

He regretted pausing the easy conversation between them and squelching the closeness they shared that night, but it had to be done, even if he sometimes allowed himself to ask why.

Declan folded his arms over his chest. "What are you doing?"

"I'm going to brush down my horse, feed him, and put him out in the pasture. Why?"

Declan turned to Tate. "That was like twenty words or something, right?"

"I expected a *fuck off* at most." Tate smiled like an idiot up at Drake.

He obliged him. "Fuck off." He handed the pup down to Tate, swung his leg over Thor's back, and dismounted. His leg ached, but not as bad as it used to. He rubbed his hand over the tight muscles, then pulled the reins over Thor's tall head.

Physical therapy sucked, but it worked. Slowly. But steadily. His mobility improved and the excruciating pain turned to something that felt more healing.

He worked with Dr. Porter on his mind. Talking about what happened, how he felt, the thoughts he couldn't let go of, eased his anger and resentments, helped him put things into perspective, dulled the flashbacks and nightmares, and allowed him to sleep better.

Generally, he'd found some calm in the storm he'd thought he'd be lost in forever.

"Did you just come from the south pasture?" Declan petted Thor down his long nose while Tate cuddled Sunny.

"Yeah." He'd cut his ride short when he spotted one of their ranch hands. "Brent was out there fixing fences. I helped him out. We got it done in no time."

Declan and Tate exchanged a look. Declan spoke for the two of them. "You cleaned out the stalls this morning while we were out feeding the cows."

"It needed to be done." And he'd needed the distraction from what he really wanted to do, which was going to Adria's cabin, stripping off whatever sexy pair of panties he'd bought her, and making love to her in the morning light.

Tate eyed him. "The last few days, you've worked on fixing up your room."

He'd wanted to do it for a long time. He hated looking at the evidence of his out-of-control rage. "I repaired the walls I busted up, got rid of the broken furniture, and bought some new stuff." For some stupid reason, he wanted decent, solid furniture and a nice platform bed made out of thick beams just in case Adria saw his room. Like she ever would. "I painted. Put it back to rights." The space felt welcoming now and not like a cell. It didn't remind him of the past anymore.

He'd needed a fresh start and the room was a good beginning.

Fix the room. Fix his injuries. Fix his head.

"Why?"

Tate touched Declan's shoulder. "Let me handle this." Tate turned to Drake. "What the fuck?"

Drake eyed them through his narrowed gaze. He wanted to tell them to back off, but they'd been patiently waiting for him to get his head out of his ass and do something around here. He'd slowly worked his way into doing one thing or another, making sure he didn't overdo it and set his rehab back. He felt better. Productive. Useful.

His confidence built with each new success. Big or small.

Working on the fence had been hard, but he'd managed with only a brief stab of panic when he glanced at the nearby tree line and for a moment thought of snipers and an impending attack that would never come.

Just the thought made him breathe harder and tenser. He refocused on his brothers and Sunny wiggling in Tate's arms to be set free to run around the yard. "Don't make a big deal about it."

"It is a big deal." Declan put his hand on Drake's shoulder. "We're happy to see you out of your room, calm, and working on getting better. That's all."

"Fine. Now back off and give me some space to do it without you watching my every move and looking over my shoulder."

"Are you still seeing Jamie for your rides and talking to Dr. Porter?" Tate asked, concerned he was trying to go it alone.

"Jamie once a week. Dr. Porter and physical therapy three times a week." He sucked in a breath and let out another truth. "I saw a surgeon about my leg. Physical therapy will only get me so far, but he thinks he can help improve my mobility by cleaning up some of the scar tissue. He's got an opening next week."

Declan recovered from his shock first. "Okay. Yeah. We'll take you. How many days will you be in the hospital?"

He'd refused any more surgeries because he hated the hospital and feeling helpless lying in a bed. He feared coming out worse, not better. But he wanted to do this. He needed to do it for his own peace of mind.

What he didn't tell his brothers was that the doctor would also bring in a plastic surgeon to clean up his scars. They couldn't make them disappear, but they could make them look less gruesome.

Adria swore they didn't bother her. He never saw even a hint that she lied about that. But another woman might not feel the same way. So he was going for it, despite the fact it meant more pain.

The operation meant he'd lose several nights in Adria's bed. He regretted that because he hoarded away memories of their nights together like they'd end and that's all he'd have left.

He ignored the anxiety that rose up from his belly to his throat at the thought of a day when he wouldn't have Adria.

He shoved that thought out of his mind, and all the others like it, and focused on his brothers.

"Surgery is early in the morning. Two days in the hospital if all goes well, then home and more rehab."

"Okay. We've got your back. We'll get you there and home. No problem." Tate released Sunny. He immediately attacked the laces on Drake's boots.

Tate took off his ball cap and scratched at his sweaty blond head. "What's going on with you and Adria? Did you two have a fight or something?"

That came out of left field and punched him in the gut. "What the hell are you talking about?" They'd been very careful not to get caught. They kept their conversations to more or less hello and goodbye when they saw each other during the day. He'd become adept at sneaking in and out of the house without his siblings any the wiser.

"You two act like you can't stand to be in the same room together for more than two minutes."

Not true, he spent a couple of hours with her every night, though they didn't do a lot of talking. But he liked their comfortable silences, lying in the dark together, her in his arms, her fingers brushing soft strokes wherever they landed on him.

She never showed any sign of being anxious to be rid of him after they had sex.

"Nothing's going on. She's busy with renovating the shop and getting it ready to open. I've been doing my thing, trying to focus on getting better."

"Trinity asked Tate and me to bring a load of wood to the shop tomorrow and put up some shelves." Declan notched his chin up. "Have you seen the building?"

"No."

"Come with us."

He'd like to see what Trinity talked about each night over dinner. She painted a picture of her and Adria's days and the progress they'd made on the old building. "I've got physical therapy in the morning."

"After then." Declan wasn't letting him off the hook.

He wanted to see what Trinity and Adria had been working so hard on, but he and Adria had this unspoken rule that they kept their daily lives separate.

Trinity was his sister. He wanted to support her. "If you can wait until I get back, I'm in." He tried to tamp down how much he looked forward to seeing the place and Adria doing what made her happy.

"Great. We'll get everything loaded and be ready when you get back."

"Sounds good." Drake took Thor's reins and walked him into the stables to brush him down, thinking about the deal with Adria and whether or not he wanted more.

Was it fair to want more when she'd made her wishes clear?

Did she want more?

She'd never given him any indication that she did.

He needed to stop thinking about it.

A car drove into the driveway behind him. He turned, hoping to catch a daytime glimpse of Adria. Instead, two other women climbed out of a truck, both dark haired. One was supermodel gorgeous. The other not as stunningly pretty, but still drew his eye and held his attention.

He wondered if they were here to see Tate and Declan. Where had his brothers gone? And how did those two lump-heads attract these beautiful women?

The women spotted him and walked into the stables. He stopped brushing Thor, tried to decide if he could duck into a stall, but they'd already seen him. And that was stupid. Didn't mean he wanted them to get a close-up look at his face.

"Hey, Drake, I'm Sonya. This is Roxy. Is Adria around?"

First, how did they know him? Second, who were they to Adria? And why did it sound like he should know the answer to that question?

"Uh, I think she's still at the shop with Trinity."

Roxy walked right up to Thor and brushed her hand down his neck. "He's gorgeous."

Sonya scooped up Sunny and accepted the wild licks on her cheek. "He's as sweet as Adria told us."

"Who are you guys?" He blurted out the question, making both of them stare at him.

Roxy recovered first. "Sorry. I thought you knew. We're Adria's sisters."

He raised an eyebrow. "I thought she only had a twin."

"And us," Sonya added. "We're not blood. We grew up together at Wild Rose Ranch."

That sounded familiar. "Where her mom works?"

Roxy's turn to raise an eyebrow. "She told you about her mom?"

"That and what happened to her when she was a kid," he confirmed.

Sonya and Roxy exchanged surprised looks. "She never talks about that."

He shrugged. "She told me."

"Interesting." Sonya dragged out the word by several syllables.

"Not so much. I acted like an asshole and she put me in my place. She wanted me to know bad things happen to everyone."

Roxy nodded. "They do. That's how we all became sisters."

Sonya let Sunny gnaw on her fingers with his sharp little puppy teeth. "I can't believe she opened up to you about her past."

Roxy turned to Sonya. "Maybe she's finally making peace with it."

Drake wanted them to know it was more than that. "If Juliana can face her demons, Adria can face hers."

"The way Adria told us you've faced yours."

She talked about him. He tried not to make too much out of that, but it made him feel good. "I'm working on it."

"That's good. She likes you." Roxy's statement held truth but didn't seem to have a deeper, more personal reason attached to it.

Drake didn't think the sisters knew about their relationship. "I owe her a lot."

Sonya nodded, getting what he didn't say. "She sees the hurt people try to hide."

He stared out the barn doors and felt Adria seconds before Trinity pulled into the drive and Adria jumped out and ran for her sisters. "She's got a way about her."

He didn't think he said it out loud.

Roxy walked up and stood right next to him. "She's special. Anyone who can't see that and treat her that way doesn't deserve her."

He wanted to say he knew and treated her special, but how could he when their relationship was so strange and purely physical now?

You're lying to yourself.

Maybe. But that was reality.

A sad reality.

Adria ran into Sonya's open arms and hugged her fiercely.

Roxy nudged his arm. "She doesn't do anything without putting her whole heart in it."

His chest lit up with something he didn't want to name or acknowledge because no matter how close they'd become, she still wasn't for him. He wasn't what she needed. Not when it came to life and love and family. The better he got, the more he wanted those things.

Adria released Sonya and stared at Roxy, her eyes watery. "I missed you."

Roxy closed the distance to Adria and wrapped her in a hug that looked more maternal than friendly. Roxy was obviously the leader of their pack. "Phone calls and texts just don't cut it. I needed to see you."

Adria held a handful of Roxy's long dark hair and gave it a tug. "I'm so glad you convinced me to come to Montana instead of putting Juliana in a Nevada facility."

"You needed something new. So did she. And it means we can come see you whenever we want."

"How was the drive?"

"Lovely." Sonya rubbed her hand up and down Adria's back.

"And you met Drake?"

Roxy smiled over her shoulder at him. "You said he was gorgeous, but you didn't add that he's built."

Drake tried not to listen to their conversation, but voices echoed in the alleyway down the long stables. He tried to focus on brushing Thor and keeping Sunny from ending up below his feet instead of on them eating his laces. Which reminded him, he needed to buy a few more pairs. He'd already switched them out twice thanks to the toothy little beast who wanted nothing to do with a chew toy.

"I was keeping that to myself so you didn't tell Juliana."

"She likes them big, strong, and tough looking."

"I have to say, Juliana's onto something." Pure feminine appreciation filled those words.

He glanced up at Adria, caught her pretty blush and the sexy smile she shot him before she grabbed both her sisters' arms and pulled them toward the door. "Did you bring the dresses for me to try on?"

He lost whatever her sisters said back, thought he'd like to see Adria in a sexy dress, and tried to keep from thinking about all that girl talk he overheard. But he couldn't dismiss the easy way they talked about him. Not a single mention about the scar marring his face. Trinity had told him a dozen times he didn't look that bad. He disagreed every time he looked in the mirror, but maybe it was just another way he'd been punishing himself.

Yes, Melanie had a hard time looking at him, but maybe that had more to do with the fact it hurt her to see him injured. She didn't want to think about how he'd gotten those scars.

For the first time, he wondered if her reaction had more to do with her hating him leaving her for a job she thought too dangerous than it did with how he looked. Her reasons for leaving him had been numerous, but she'd never come out and said the scars were part of the reason.

He'd put that on her and himself. He wanted a reason that didn't have to do with the fact he'd failed to hold on to her because he'd done as he pleased without considering her feelings and how it would affect their relationship.

She begged him not to take another tour of duty, that she wanted them to start their lives together. He'd gone anyway, expecting her to wait for him.

He'd been a class-A jerk.

To her and himself.

Dr. Porter constantly told him he was too hard on himself. In this instance, he got it.

Didn't mean he was going to cancel the reconstructive surgery. He needed it for his peace of mind. But Adria and her sisters had opened his eyes and bolstered his ego.

Another thing he should thank Adria for one of these days.

Another reason he couldn't wait to see her tonight.

Chapter Sixteen

Adria knew what was coming, dreaded having to say anything, but felt a little relieved to be able to talk to her sisters about her and Drake. As much as she and Drake shared, and as close as they'd become, they now held back from each other to the point they barely spoke.

But the way they came together each night said so much.

At least to her.

Which made her feelings so confusing.

She missed their open, honest talks.

Her sisters waited, saying hello to Trinity on the way to the cabin. But once they were through the door, they didn't hold back.

Roxy went first. "Spill it, little sister. What is going on with you and that hunky cowboy who can't take his eyes off you?"

"He barely spared me a look." Denying it seemed silly, but she went with it anyway.

Sonya rolled her eyes. "Drake is a trained soldier. He doesn't have to look directly at you to track your every move." Sonya softened. "I saw the way you looked at him. Half-afraid to be caught and desperate to check to see if he was okay."

"I worry about him." The confession didn't surprise them.

Roxy tilted her head and studied Adria. "You told him about your past."

"He was so lost in his pain and what happened to him, he couldn't see past it. He couldn't see a way out of it. So I told him what happened, so he could look at me and see that I'd found a way to still live my life." Adria raked her fingers through her hair. "It worked. He's getting better every day. He goes to physical therapy. He talks to his therapist. He even talks to a fellow soldier, who can relate to his experience. I see all the little changes in him adding up to him being able to live a little bit more each day."

Sonya put her hand on Adria's shoulder. "You can't fix him. You can't fix Juliana. You can't take away their pain and make it your own."

"I'm not doing that. I'm happy for Drake and his family. They have him back." And she had something special with him that she needed.

Roxy moved in and hugged her. "And you want Juliana back."

Adria held her close. "Yes. I haven't spoken to her in weeks. That's never happened in our whole lives." Tears stung her eyes and spilled over. "It's like part of me is missing."

Sonya put her hand on Adria's head. "You can't replace her or fill that empty space with Drake and his problems, honey."

Adria stepped back and glared at her sisters. "Did you ever think I'm using him to fix me?"

Roxy and Sonya both eyed her.

Roxy asked the hard question. "What does that mean?"

Adria raised her hands and let them fall. She didn't know how to make them understand. "My heart pounds every time I try to be with a man because I think it's going to turn ugly. The couple of guys I've been with, I tried to be open to their affection, but only ended up enduring it. They thought I was cold or just a bitch because I didn't like it and never . . . you know."

Sonya put her hand to her chest. "Oh, Adria."

Roxy leaped to the right conclusion. "It's not like that with Drake. You, ah, enjoy his company."

Adria tried to lighten things up. "You mean I like having sex with him."

"Do you?" Leave it to Roxy to stay on point and make sure Drake wasn't using or mistreating her.

The grin gave her away. "Probably more than I should."

Sonya knocked Adria's arm with her elbow. "Then you're doing it right."

Adria crossed her arms over her chest. "That's not true. I made another mistake."

Roxy put her hands over Adria's and held her still. "What mistake?"

"Not to get into Drake's story, it's his to tell, but he needed something and I needed something. They turned out to be the same thing, but in different ways."

"You both needed sex?" Sonya's earlier exuberance dimmed.

"Yes. And no." She didn't know how to explain it. "We needed someone to give us a chance to explore sex again without judgment or expectations or even the guarantee it would work out to the other person's advantage."

Roxy stepped back and thought about that. "Sounds like you two connected because you wanted the same thing. That's how relationships start, honey. You deserve someone who understands you and knows what you need and is willing to give it to you."

She scrunched her mouth and tried to hold back the disappointment and regret over what she'd done. "That's where I made the mistake. I made it clear the only thing I wanted was sex and turned something that started out from the get-go on a deep level into something that now feels . . . I don't know . . . not enough."

Sonya's mouth dropped open. "You, *you*, are having no-strings-attached sex."

Adria couldn't believe it either, because that wasn't her. But she'd thought it would break down her walls and allow her to open herself to having a real relationship with a man. Someday. But she soon realized what she shared with Drake didn't mean it would translate to someone else. Because that other person wouldn't be Drake. And finding someone like him, someone who understood her needs and how her past affected her now, well, that seemed a long shot.

She answered Sonya, even though she hadn't really asked a question. "I don't think sex comes without strings. At least for me."

Roxy touched her arm. "How does Drake feel about your arrangement?"

"I have no idea. We barely speak to each other." She bit her lip and thought about their nights. "And yet, I feel so close to him. I don't have to tell him how I'm feeling or how I want the night to go. He reads me and I read him and we give each other what the other needs. It's deep and profound and fulfilling and yet I . . ." She couldn't say it out loud because it seemed selfish.

Roxy finished for her. "You want more."

"I feel guilty for wanting more. I made the deal and set the terms of the arrangement. I feel like what we have is special. I don't want to lose it. In bed, we work great. But beyond that, I have no idea, because both of us have stopped talking about our lives."

Sonya leaned back against the couch. "You flipped the script. Before you were friends with guys. You had similar interests and enjoyed each other's company. You thought they were safe, but you had no chemistry. Now you have real chemistry, but whatever personal connection you share you clipped. You've tried to cut your heart off from being hurt. Maybe for good reason. You said he's not quite right in the head."

Anger flashed. "I never said that. He's a good man."

"With a lot of baggage to unpack," Roxy added, though her voice gentled. "Trinity warned you away from him because he's unstable."

"That was then. He's working on recovering from his injuries and the trauma he's suffered."

"Which is why you thought it a good idea to keep things simple between you in the beginning, I take it." Sonya guessed right.

Adria tilted her head and raked her fingers through her hair again. "You know what? I don't know what I want anymore. The contractor said the new roof on the building would take two days. It's been four. The building inspector dinged us on four infractions in the kitchen area. That cost us another five grand to fix. The chairs I ordered for the tables I picked out arrived and they're the wrong color. I wanted black with rustic wood seats. They're turquoise with black painted seats. I had to send them back and the right ones won't arrive until the day before we open, which means I'll be scrambling at the last minute to put them all together. Juliana won't take my calls even though they're allowing her calls this week. Finally. But no, she doesn't want to talk to *me*. She thinks I betrayed her when all I wanted to do was help. I'm lying to my friend every second of the long days we work together about sleeping with her brother. And I just want something to work out for once."

Roxy cupped her face. "Take a breath."

Adria did as she was told and felt stupid for the outburst and letting her emotions get the better of her.

"You need to give yourself a break," Roxy demanded in her I-know-what's-best-for-you voice. "You have never had trouble analyzing yourself and your life and figuring out what you want and need. It's something I admire about you. You see yourself and life the way it is. Good. Bad. Ugly. Wonderful. Whatever. But you sometimes have a hard time asking for what you want or accepting help."

"I don't need help with the contractors. I'm pretty sure they're afraid of me now after I gave them a piece of my mind and told them to get it done or I'd find someone who could."

Roxy shook her head. "I'm not talking about work or lying to Trinity. I'm talking about you and Drake. You made the original deal. Renegotiate if you're not happy with the current terms."

Adria shook her head. "You don't get it. I am happy with the way things are. I don't want to mess it up."

Sonya stepped up close. "You're afraid he'll turn you down if you ask for more."

Yes! Because she wasn't sure she'd have anything this amazing with anyone else. "I don't want to lose what I have for something I know he doesn't want."

Roxy dropped her hands. "Are you sure? Have you asked him?"

"I don't need to ask. Our relationship is the way it is because he's the one who took a giant step back when things got too personal."

"What happened?" Sonya asked, but Roxy looked just as eager for the answer.

She thought about the night they made love like their lives would end if they didn't make it perfect. And it was that night.

Every night since, they came close but they both held that something more back from each other.

Which made her think of the night all the more. She wanted that back. She wanted it to be that way for them every night.

But Drake didn't want that, or he'd show her that he did.

"Never mind. Seeing you guys makes me miss Juliana all the more and I'm being emotional and unrealistic. You came so I could try on the bridesmaid dresses. Let's do that before it gets too late and your guys start missing you."

No one missed her these days.

Even her twin didn't want to speak to her.

You're being dramatic. Maybe. But damnit, keeping things simple turned out to be hard.

Sonya tried to make a joke. "You just want us out of here so you can have hot sex with Drake."

He wouldn't come until he knew the coast was clear and no one would catch him. Because he didn't want anyone to know about them. Because they weren't a couple. They weren't even really friends, despite how things started out in that direction. So she stated the facts. "That's what we're good at." That's all they shared now.

She got exactly what she wanted.

And she felt lonelier by the minute.

She counted down the days to Juliana getting out of rehab. Things would go back to normal. She'd have her sister back. Her other half.

Sonya unzipped the first garment bag they'd retrieved from the truck after leaving Drake in the barn and walking up to the cabin.

Adria switched gears and stared at the beautiful somewhere-between-purple-and-pink dress. The color was bright and cheerful and so her with its tank straps, tapered waist, and layered full skirt. Juliana would want a darker color, but Adria loved it. "It's beautiful."

Sonya pulled out the same dress in a deep plum. "Do you think it goes with this color?"

She rubbed the soft material through her fingers. "Juliana will love it."

Sonya smiled. "Juliana will be my maid of honor. You'll be Roxy's. Is that okay?"

"Whatever you want." Adria meant it. She wanted her sisters to have the perfect day and everything they dreamed it would be.

Roxy and Sonya planned a double wedding but they'd have separate ceremonies back-to-back. Adria and Juliana would change their dresses in between and take separate pictures with the brides. Roxy and Sonya would share the day but get their own time to shine.

Adria loved the idea and thought that if she and Juliana were lucky enough to find love and get married together, they'd someday do the same thing. Maybe they'd even get pregnant at the same time. Their children would grow up together.

They'd dreamed such things when they were young, hoping for happier times and lives that were forever intertwined.

Roxy unzipped the other garment bag. "You and Juliana can decide which shade of blue you'd like to wear."

The two dresses Roxy picked out were much more elegant than the ones Sonya chose, but no more pretty. It just showed their two separate personalities.

"The navy is gorgeous. But I love the lighter blue, too." Both dresses were strapless with a sparkly silver gem-encrusted belt at the waist, again with full short skirts because this was a country wedding on Roxy's ranch after all.

"They'll look great on you with your golden hair and pale skin. We thought both colors would bring out your gorgeous blue eyes." Roxy handed her the navy dress to start trying them on.

"Drake's eyes will pop out of his head when he sees you in those."

Adria stopped on her way to the bedroom to change and glanced over her shoulder at Sonya. "I'm not bringing him to the weddings."

"Why not? If you want more, inviting him to a family wedding is a great way to let him know," Sonya pointed out.

And open the door for him to turn her down, or worse, end things altogether. "Leave it alone," Adria warned. She shouldn't have told them about her deal with Drake and her mixed-up feelings. She needed to sort them out herself. She couldn't keep relying on her sisters. They had their lives with their future husbands. She appreciated Roxy's and Sonya's support, and even their gentle prodding, but she needed to stand on her own and decide what she wanted herself.

They weren't kids anymore.

She'd made her choices and had to learn to live with them.

The good ones. The bad. The benefits. And the consequences.

Chapter Seventeen

Drake sneaked out the kitchen door and headed straight over to Adria's cabin. He didn't know when he began thinking of it as "hers" but it felt to him that she'd always be there. Still, he had to wonder if she planned to get her own place once the business opened and her sister finished rehab.

Trinity had dumped a bunch of paint samples and furniture magazines on the table, saying simply that Adria forgot them in the truck when they got home. He should have stopped himself from asking why Adria needed them if she lived in the cabin, but he asked anyway.

Trinity stared at him for a good ten seconds before she said the building they bought had an apartment upstairs and Adria planned to move there with Juliana if she decided to stay instead of going back to Nevada.

Why that sent a bolt of panic through him, he didn't want to even acknowledge, let alone examine it. They weren't permanent. They weren't even dating. They both stuck to the agreement. They shared their bodies and not much else.

While it worked for them, he still felt the strain in their odd relationship.

Maybe they'd let it go too far, or hadn't taken it far enough. Something felt off.

He thought about the smile she'd given him in the stables. Sweet. Open. Sexy as hell. Just for him. He'd felt the impact of it hit him right in the chest.

But that didn't mean anything.

Just like the sex didn't mean anything.

He wondered how long he could tell himself that lie before he had to accept that this thing was going to blow up in his face. Because that was the only outcome he could see. She'd made it clear she didn't want anything more with him. She'd gone out of her way to keep their other interactions to a minimum.

Admittedly, he had, too.

Were they both afraid to try for something more?

Or did they both know this was all they'd have and they needed to accept it?

Truthfully, he didn't know what she wanted.

He was better. He'd had a good couple weeks. Things were looking up for him, mentally speaking. He had his emotions and anger under control. He didn't feel like he wanted to punch everyone in his path or have a full-on rage. He'd tempered his paranoia and vigilance when it came to walking in the open and being around people.

The last few days, he actually felt more like his old self. Talking through things with Dr. Porter and Jamie left him feeling more at ease with himself and the past.

His nightmares had abated. Mostly because after being with Adria he felt calm and sated and slept like he did before he'd gotten on the merry-go-round of flashbacks that stole his sleep, sanity, and well-being.

He'd put in the work to make himself better, but being with Adria helped more than anything to mask the pain, turn off the nightmares, and dull his wild emotions. Just thinking about her and what they shared made him feel better.

He needed her.

So damn bad.

Maybe that's exactly why he should turn around and go home. It wasn't fair to need her so much.

Still, his boots led him right to her.

Before he reached the porch steps, she walked out the door and met him as he stood one step below her. She didn't say a word, just hooked her hand at the back of his neck and kissed him hard. Her hunger in full force rocked him and cleared every thought from his head, except the one that seemed tattooed on his mind: *I want her.*

Adria jumped into his arms and wrapped her legs around his waist. He loved that she never treated him like he was disabled or fragile. He'd shown her he wasn't and she accepted what she saw and felt in him.

He stepped up onto the porch and headed for the door. She kissed a trail down his neck and held him tight. He couldn't wait to lay her out on the bed and have his way with her. All he had to do was get her through the door. He stepped inside and turned to push the door closed, but he caught sight of Trinity standing in the distance staring at them.

His heart pounded with dread.

He should say something. Explain.

But Adria took his face, stared into his eyes, and said, "Take me to bed."

He'd sworn to follow her orders. Without the promise, he'd have followed through because he wanted the same thing.

He hated to leave Trinity questioning what was going on, but it was none of her damn business, so he slammed the door shut and did exactly as Adria ordered.

He didn't owe Trinity an explanation or feel the need to defend himself. Not to her.

He and Adria were grown adults with a bargain that worked for both of them.

"I want you now."

See. He had no reason to feel guilty about the woman pulling his shirt off or the one outside who looked up to him.

At least she used to.

He stood at the end of the bed, shirtless, his arms full of a willing woman, who all of a sudden stopped her all-out assault on his senses with her hands sliding over his shoulders, her sweet floral scent filling his nose, and her pretty blue eyes staring at him, her lips tilted into a soft pout. "What's wrong?"

If he told her about Trinity, this night ended right here, right now. Deep down, he suspected it would be the end of their deal for good.

"You've got too many clothes on."

Her shirt disappeared, revealing her bare breasts. The pink tips begged for his lips and he dived in and sucked one into his mouth.

Yep. He was a bastard. But if this was the last time he'd get to be with her, he'd make it worth it. One more sweet, hot memory.

He'd tell her before he left.

But right now, she was his.

They didn't exchange another word or waste any time stripping away their clothes. Desperate need hummed between them, but they still took their time, touching, tempting, kissing, drawing out every sigh and moan.

Though he'd committed every inch of her to memory, he mapped her body with his hands and mouth until she panted and writhed beneath him. He wanted his mark to seep into every cell so she'd never forget him. His touch. His taste. The way he lit her whole body on fire and sent her up in a wild explosion of sparks.

He took his time getting her there, drawing out every stroke of his body over hers until she was wild, desperate, and clutching his ass, pulling him in deeper. Harder.

Lost in her, and her in him, time stopped, and the night slipped away. Everything went away and it was just the two of them entwined in a sensual bliss that went on and on until they were swept away by pure pleasure.

It rocked through him. And just like every other time he was with her, he felt changed. He didn't know how, but she altered him in a way that made him feel better and more whole each and every time.

He rolled to his back and stared at the ceiling. For a brief second he missed her closeness, but then she slipped up to his side, draped her leg over his thigh, laid her arm on his belly, and traced her fingers up and down his chest, her head tucked against his shoulder. He absently trailed his fingers over her tattooed arm.

They didn't speak.

What was there to say after sharing something like that?

He should tell her about Trinity seeing them together.

Nothing, not one word from him or her broke the quiet calm he loved sharing with her.

Selfish to his very marrow, he held her close and savored the feel of her, the memories they shared, and her generous heart for the way she gave herself over to him every night.

Something this good couldn't last.

He wouldn't allow himself to do anything to ruin it.

But he knew eventually he'd mess up; a flashback or unmanageable outburst would end them.

He feared one day she'd wake up, ask herself what she was doing with a man who didn't want to keep her, and move on.

The middle part of that didn't exactly ring true. Not like it did in the beginning.

Maybe they did need to have a talk about what happened next.

Still, no words left his mouth.

He'd never considered himself a coward. He'd faced down insurgents and bullets and cleared buildings where death could be waiting behind the next door he kicked in. Yet he couldn't ask the woman half-asleep beside him in bed if she wanted more from him.

She probably didn't ask because she thought him incapable of giving it to her. Or she wanted him to stick to the deal because she simply didn't want more.

Dr. Porter told him to take things slow, that it would take time for him to really heal and put the past behind him.

He wanted to move forward. He wanted to be like he used to be.

He wanted life to be easier.

He wanted this thing that seemed so easy in the beginning to be easy again.

In his mind, it seemed to have gotten complicated.

Maybe he was making it that way.

"Drake."

"Yeah."

She propped herself up on her arm beside him. "You're thinking too much." She leaned down and kissed him, sliding her body over his, so she lay down the length of him and everything disappeared from his mind again.

Making love to her was his pleasure and torment.

Leaving her an hour later took a lot more effort than the night before. And the one before that.

He spotted the lights on in the house long before he got there. He resigned himself to the inevitable and walked right up the porch steps and went in through the front door like he didn't have a thing in the world to hide.

Trinity, Declan, and Tate all sat on the sofa watching an old Jackie Chan movie. All three of them turned to him and stared.

He didn't say a word. He didn't owe them an explanation.

Trinity's eyes were filled with hurt when she asked, "How long have you been seeing Adria?"

"I'm fucking her, not seeing her." He thought he'd make that clear. For them. For himself.

Declan and Tate exchanged judgmental frowns.

"I don't need your opinions or disapproval. We're adults. We can do what we want."

Trinity shook her head, not believing him. "She's not like that. Her mother . . ."

"I know all about her past."

"She told you." The disbelief in Trinity's words stung, just like it did when Roxy and Sonya were amazed Adria shared what happened to her with him.

Instead of revealing how much they'd shared with each other, and defending himself as not being some callous asshole who didn't care about Adria's feelings and history, he went with his anger. "Let's get this straight. What Adria and I do or don't do is none of your fucking business!" The last he hadn't meant to shout, but he couldn't believe they'd been sitting here waiting for him to come home so they could tell him what an asshole he was for sleeping with Adria behind their backs. It wasn't about them.

He wanted something good in his life. She was it.

If they ruined it for him . . . Well, if they thought he was a ball of roiling rage before, they'd know that was nothing compared to what he'd feel if he lost her.

Fuck!

He'd tried so hard not to have thoughts like that one.

It hit him hard and deep.

Along with the realization that he might have already ruined him and Adria by not being as stealthy as he had in the past and letting Trinity see them together.

Maybe part of him wanted to get caught.

"She's not like that. I can't believe she'd want this." Trinity's words cut.

"What you mean is you can't believe she'd want *me*." With the scars, his bad attitude, and a long road to getting back to anything resembling his normal self, he worried all the time that Adria agreed.

Trinity stood and took a step toward him. "I never said that. I don't mean *that*."

"You all think it. I'm not good enough for someone as beautiful and perfect as her."

Declan leaned forward with his elbows on his knees. "Is that what you tell yourself? I think that IED fucked up your head worse than your leg."

"If you two are together, then why not say so? Why hide it?" Tate asked on a yawn.

"We are not together."

"So this is a rebound thing?" Trinity asked. "You're using her to get over Melanie?"

It took everything in him not to explode with rage that Trinity would accuse him of that. "Adria got exactly what she asked for. She came to me. But thanks for thinking I'm a fucking asshole because I took her up on her offer." He walked out and up the stairs to the room he'd redone and Adria would never see, because after tonight his family would be sure to end whatever the hell he had with her.

They'd embarrass her.

They'd tell her she deserved more.

And she did.

He should just get out of her way and let her get on with finding out now that he'd well and truly fixed her inhibitions about sex.

With that thought came a dozen unwelcome ones of her with other men that sent his fist through the wall the second he walked into his room. He welcomed the stinging pain and fell on his bed on his back and spent the rest of the night staring at the dark ceiling, seething at himself for thinking even for a second that he and Adria could ever be more.

Chapter Eighteen

Chills raced up Adria's arms. She stepped out onto the porch with Noah and stared down at the brand-new white-and-black Jeep Grand Cherokee again. She screamed earlier when they arrived and surprised her with the amazing gift.

Roxy was too generous.

Adria told her she couldn't accept it. But just like the graduation gift that helped her open her business, Roxy wouldn't take no for an answer. Not when they'd both grown up the way they had, only having each other to rely on with mothers like theirs.

As much as they all hated what their mothers did, the Wild Rose Ranch money made it possible to get Juliana the help she needed.

It bought Adria a new vehicle, so she didn't have to rely on Trinity to cart her back and forth to the shop. She'd intended to buy a new car when the store opened and she had a steady income. Roxy took care of it, just like she'd taken care of her and Juliana when they arrived at the Ranch when they were ten.

She missed Juliana more each day, but she was so happy to have Roxy and Sonya in her life.

Noah stepped down one of the porch steps and smiled at her. "Roxy's been worried about you. I'm glad the Jeep made you happy."

She hugged Noah and held on. "I love it. Roxy is the best. And I'm so happy she found love with you."

Drake's pissed-off face came into view a second before he grabbed

Noah's shoulders, pulled him away from Adria, spun him around, grabbed him by the shirt, and got right in his face. "Don't ever fucking touch her again."

The deadly tone chilled Adria. "Drake, let him go."

"Tell him you don't want to sleep with him because you're with me."

Adria sucked in a surprised gasp, tried not to smile, despite how angry she was, and took the few steps down toward Noah and Drake and looked Noah in the eyes. "I don't want to sleep with you."

Noah gave her a lopsided frown. "I feel oddly rejected." Merriment danced in his eyes.

Adria smacked him on the arm. "You're sleeping with my sister. I think you'll get over it."

Noah smiled. "I am so in love with that woman."

Roxy walked out of the cabin, took in the scene, walked down the two steps, stayed on the one above Noah, and wrapped her arms around Noah's neck and stared over at Drake, who still looked ready to kill. "Let him go. He's mine." She flashed the diamond ring on her finger.

Adria had enough. She touched Drake's arm. "Look at me."

Drake's breath billowed in and out in hard gasps. Black smudges marred the underside of his tired and furious eyes. "No one touches you."

She let her anger fly. "I decide who touches me and who doesn't. You don't have a say in who I'm with."

Drake let go of Noah, but not without a little angry shove.

Thank God, Noah took it in stride. The last thing she needed was a brawl in her front yard.

Drake took a menacing step toward her, but it didn't intimidate her. "What if I want a say?"

"You made it clear you weren't looking for anything more than what we agreed to."

"Fuck that damn deal we made." He raked his hand over his head. "I've been up all night thinking about you, that deal, what I want, what you want. You know what keeps repeating in my head? Roxy's words."

"Mine?" Roxy raised a brow, still holding Noah's back to her chest. Both of them an avid audience.

Drake ignored Roxy and stayed laser focused on Adria. "'She doesn't do anything without putting her whole heart in it.' I've seen that. I've felt it every night I'm with you. I don't want that for just a couple hours every night. I want it every hour of the day."

Adria didn't know what to say. Her feelings had grown these last weeks. The connection they shared in the night had been unexpected and surprising and wonderful. And she had no idea what to do with all that, so she'd ignored it and focused on what they did have, not what she didn't think he wanted to give her.

"You made it clear that after Melanie broke your engagement, you didn't want a relationship."

"This isn't some rebound. This isn't about proving that IED didn't permanently break me. I wouldn't have almost killed Roxy's fiancé—"

"There's not a scratch on me," Noah pointed out.

Drake glared hard at him, his shoulders tense, hands fisted. "Trust me, it was a near miss." He focused on her again. Frustrated and agitated, he rocked from one foot to the other. "The point is, I wouldn't be standing here in front of your family completely fumbling over some meaningless fling. Losing you matters more to me than Melanie ever did."

Her eyes went wide. "You asked her to marry you."

"Yeah. Take that in, because it's causing all kinds of havoc inside me."

He loves me.

No one had ever loved her. Well, not no one. Juliana loved her. Her sisters loved her. Maybe her mother loved her once, but now it felt like a lie, because her mother only cared about herself.

But no man had ever loved her.

No man had ever wanted her like this.

Drake took a step closer. "Say something."

She truly didn't know what to say.

Frustrated by her silence, Drake's eyes narrowed a split second before he reached out, grabbed the back of her neck, stepped close, and crushed his mouth to hers. He kissed her long and deep. His fingers softened on her neck and caressed her skin. He broke the kiss and touched his forehead to hers.

He didn't open his eyes as she watched him, but his deep voice sank into her. "Tell me you don't feel that. Tell me you don't kiss me with everything inside you. Tell me you're satisfied pretending we don't exist in the day and only having my hands on you for a couple hours at night." He opened his eyes and stared into hers. "Is that enough for you? Because it sure as hell isn't enough for me. Not anymore." He leaned back and stared down at her. "If it's the scars, I'm having surgery next week. They won't be gone, but they'll be better."

She slapped her hand against his mouth, to shut him up. "No."

If she'd bashed him in the chest with a wrecking ball he'd have had no less of a reaction than the giant step back he took as his body took the blow from that single word. He turned away, his face a mask of pain and loss.

"It's not enough," she called to him. "That's what you asked me."

He turned and stared at her, desperate hope filling his eyes.

"The answer is no, Drake. Even with all we pack into those few short hours, it's not enough. Sneaking peeks of you out in the stables with your brothers isn't enough. Watching you ride off into the pastures alone when I want to be with you sucks. Not knowing how your day went or if you're okay makes me worry."

Drake gave her back the truth. "I spend my whole damn day counting down to when I can sneak over here and see you. It's been forever since I ordered my siblings to bed, but every night I want to lock them in their rooms so I can see you."

She laughed, because she could imagine how hard it was for him to hold back those orders.

"So you want to be my boyfriend?"

He smiled and it was filled with all kinds of boyish charm. "Yeah. Whatever you want, because all I want is for you to be mine."

She already was, so she gave him the order that started it all. "Go." She leaped off the steps and launched herself into his arms.

He caught her against his chest, held her close, and kissed her again.

"It's your lucky day, sis. You get a new car and a boyfriend." Adria heard the smile in Roxy's voice.

Drake ended the kiss and held her tight, looking over at Roxy and Noah. "Sorry I lost it."

Noah, her sweet soon-to-be brother-in-law, defended her. "Keep working on your shit. Because you leave a mark on her, I leave you in a hole."

Adria released Drake and stared up at Noah. "I've never had a brother. It's kind of fun."

Noah notched his chin toward her. "If you're happy, Roxy's happy, and that means I'm happy. So keep us all happy, Drake." Noah eyed the big man behind her, who hadn't taken his hands off her hips even though they could see.

It would take some getting used to, this not having to hide the way they felt in front of others.

"Believe me, if she's not happy, she'll let me know about it. It's one of the things I admire about her. She tells it like it is even when it's hard to say. And hear." He gave her hips a little squeeze.

She snuggled back into his chest. "Get used to it."

Roxy released Noah's shoulders and gave him a little push toward their truck. "Let's go, cowboy. We've got horses to feed."

Drake glanced at the Speckled Horse Ranch logo on the truck. "I bid on one of your horses at auction a couple years back. It went for a pretty penny."

"They all do," Noah boasted. "If you're interested in buying anytime soon, come on by. I'll make you a good deal."

Roxy hugged Adria goodbye and whispered in her ear, "You picked a tough one."

"I can handle him."

Drake overheard and smiled at her again. It seemed to come easier since they'd opened themselves to the possibilities they'd kept to themselves and couldn't wait to share with each other now that they'd admitted what they really wanted.

"Get out of here so she can handle me in private."

Roxy's lips tilted in a cheeky grin. "Dirty and naughty." She glanced back at Adria. "Have fun." Roxy made it an order to remind Adria it was okay to let go of her past and enjoy what she had right now.

Roxy and Noah climbed into their truck and took off with one last wave goodbye.

Drake took her hand and pulled her up the steps to sit with him on the top one. He held her hand, fingers entwined, and stared out at the horses grazing in the pasture. "I'm sorry I leaped to the wrong conclusion and shoved Noah."

"He's a big boy. He can take it."

"It shouldn't have happened. I need to get a grip on my anger and not fly off the handle all the time."

"You don't fly off the handle all the time."

He eyed her.

"Okay, not anymore. No harm, no foul. You saw me with him and wanted me back. Is that about it?"

Drake pressed the heel of his hand into his eye socket. "Yes. The thought of someone else touching you, being with you . . ." He shook his head. "No. I can't."

She leaned into his side. "Good. I feel the same way about you."

"Look at me. I don't think you have anything to worry about."

She punched him in the arm.

"Ow! What was that for?"

"Being stupid." She took his face in her hands, then traced her fingers over the scars on his cheek and jaw. "These don't make you less than. If my sisters weren't engaged, I'm pretty sure I'd have to fight them to the death to keep them away from you."

"Right."

"Yes. Right. Don't you think I'm attracted to you? Don't you feel it when I look at you and touch you?"

He pressed a kiss to her lips, softening in his beliefs, she hoped. "Yes, sweetheart. I feel everything you pour into me."

"Do you think I'd lie to you?"

"No."

"Then believe me when I say the scars don't matter. They don't detract from how sexy and gorgeous I think you are."

"I want to erase them because they remind me of what happened."

"Are you having this surgery because of that or because you think *I* want you to?"

He wrapped his arm around her shoulders and pulled her close. "I know you don't care. I believe that. I really do. But physical therapy isn't enough to restore my mobility. I'm stronger, but I still can't move my hip very well. It hurts. But yes, having the scars cleaned up will make me feel better, too."

"Okay then. I'll come with you."

"You don't have to. I know how close you and Trinity are to opening the store."

She shook her head. "Nothing matters more than being with you." She meant that. If she'd learned anything from her life and being with her sisters it was that the people who care about you and you care about make your life. Not a car, a business—nothing was more important than the relationships that enriched your life.

He kissed the side of her head, pressed his lips to her hair, and whispered, "I want you with me."

"As long as you do, I'm there." She settled into him. She hadn't thought a real relationship would ever happen for her, but then Drake came into her life. He taught her to trust in him and herself.

Who knew what they could have now? But if it was as good as what they already shared, it was worth the risk to her heart that had ached for more with him these last weeks.

She hoped Juliana got better and found something special, too. She deserved that. They both did.

It took being with Drake for her to finally believe it.

Drake leaned back and stared down at her. "There's something else we need to talk about."

She gave him her full attention, interested in what else he wanted to discuss with her. "What's that?"

"Trinity saw us last night?"

She remembered all too well the way she'd practically jumped him on the porch and kissed him. "Not the way I would have wanted to tell her, but okay, she knows. Is she mad that I kept it from her?"

"I think she's pissed I'm using you for sex."

She scrunched her lips and hated that's how he put it and how it made him look bad while it sounded like she was naive and unaware. "First, that's not true. I'm the one who proposed the deal."

"When I told them that, they didn't exactly believe me. Especially Trinity, who said something about you not being like that because of your background."

"Because my mother's a prostitute, you mean?"

He winced. "It's not the same thing."

"I never said it was, but is that what Trinity thinks?"

"No. Hell no. She thought I was using you and didn't know that I could damage you by not knowing about your past. She doesn't want me to hurt you." Drake rubbed his fingers in his close-cropped hair. "Seriously, sweetheart, I don't know how this is going to go. I'm still not anywhere near a hundred percent in the head. The last thing I'd ever want to do is hurt you. I hope you know that."

"I know your intentions are good and honest. I understand your condition and that you're working on it. That's good enough for me."

"And you'll let me know when I'm being a dick."

"Even when you don't want me to." She bumped her shoulder into his, not having the same apprehensions he did. He was too hard on himself. If she kept things easy, maybe he'd lighten up. "Just go with it, Drake. Let yourself be happy. No one, not even the friends you lost, would begrudge you that."

He turned his head, set his chin on his shoulder, and stared at her. "You make me happy."

"Then let's be happy together."

"Will you tell my sister and brothers that I'm not holding you hostage?"

She laughed. "Of course. In fact, I need to get to work. Weren't you supposed to help Declan and Tate put up the shelves today?"

"I blew them off after they gave me the third degree when I got home last night and went for a ride this morning to clear my head."

"I guess that didn't work out so well for you. You were still pissed off when you saw me with Noah."

"I was pissed off because all I could think was that I could have saved myself the grief and stayed with you last night."

"Well, you know how much I enjoy you in my bed. I'd certainly never kick you out."

"I hope you mean that, because I plan on staying with you tonight. After I take you out to dinner."

She raised an eyebrow. "Really? A date?"

"We may have done this a little backward, but that doesn't mean I can't make up for it and do a few things better."

She gave him a cheeky smile. "Oh, honey, you are good at so many things."

He finally smiled again. "Like this." He leaned in and kissed her, taking his time, teasing and tempting her to take the kiss deeper. When he did, she leaned into him, wanting more.

With him, she suspected she'd always want more.

Chapter Nineteen

Drake had no problem sitting in the passenger seat in Adria's new Jeep. She smiled like a kid at Christmas with her new toy. He had to admit, Roxy giving her the car was a pretty outstanding gift. Generous. And loving.

Drake wished he'd done it for her.

He'd been so self-absorbed, he hadn't even noticed she didn't have her own car.

"Is it true you plan to move into the apartment over the shop once it's all done?"

Adria had to sit up straighter to look at him over Sunny's head between them. He sat on the center console, tongue lolling in and out as the fan vent blew on his face.

"That's the plan, why? Too far for you to go to see me?"

"I'm pretty sure there isn't a place far enough on the planet to keep me from coming to see you."

Her smile grew even wider. "I like this."

He sighed and settled back into the seat. "It took up so damn much energy pretending we weren't together. I'm glad it's all out in the open now."

"I hated having to be careful about how much I talked about you with Trinity."

"I did not have that problem. She walked in the door each night and told us every detail about your day. I hung on every word. You'd think that would have told me something."

"You fought it. I did, too. I told myself you weren't ready for a relationship. I had work and my sister to worry about. I didn't need more. I should be happy with what we shared."

"Were you?"

She turned her gaze from the road to him. "I like us this way better."

He settled even deeper into the brand-new leather seat. "Me, too."

She pulled into the lot on the side of the building and parked next to Trinity's truck. Both of them spotted the woman standing in front of the building looking at the brand-new sign that had gone up that morning. *Almost Homemade*. The big black letters matched the new black metal awnings over the wide windows and stood out against the white painted brick.

"The place looks great on the outside."

Adria stared at the woman loitering out front. "Who is that?"

"I was hoping I was hallucinating."

She turned to him and cocked up one eyebrow. "Do you hallucinate beautiful women a lot?"

"Not when I've got the most beautiful one in my life."

Her lips tilted into a half frown, half smile. "Drake?"

He hated that tone. "That's my ex."

Both eyes went wide. "What is she doing here?"

He shrugged. "Hell if I know."

Her glance bounced from him to Melanie and back. "Do you need me for this?"

He didn't much like it, but he'd take care of this one on his own. "I've got it."

"Good. Because I don't know if I can be as nice as you were with Noah this morning."

He laughed because Adria didn't have a mean bone in her body.

They both got out of the Jeep, Sunny jumping out behind them. The puppy ran circles around Adria's legs while she tapped him on the butt to make him run again. Except this time, Sunny ran right through her legs and knocked her off balance. Drake grabbed her around the waist, her back to his chest, and swung her around in a circle, then set her down on her feet. Sunny barked, but it wasn't as loud as Adria's giggles.

He laughed with her, then held his hand up to Sunny. "Enough."

Sunny sat at the hand signal and stopped barking.

Adria petted his head. "Good boy."

Melanie walked up, her gaze sweeping over him. "Drake. You look fantastic. You're walking without the cane. You look so strong."

Adria looked up at him. "Told you." She pressed her hand to his chest, then snapped her fingers at Sunny. "Come on, boy." She disappeared inside the building, leaving him with his surprised ex.

Melanie looked good. Curious. A little apprehensive. And he didn't miss her at all. Not when he had Adria in his life and she made him feel like he could do anything.

"What are you doing here?" He couldn't help his curiosity.

She kept looking him up and down like she couldn't believe it was him. "Everyone is talking about Trinity and her partner opening this place. I thought I'd come by and see for myself and catch up with Trinity."

"I didn't think you two were that close."

"We had you in common." Her eyes dipped to the ground, then back up. "The truth is, I wanted to find out how you're doing."

He tilted his head and studied the changing emotions in her eyes. Surprise. Disbelief. Interest. "Why?"

"Do you really have to ask? We were engaged to be married."

"You made it clear you didn't want to see me ever again."

"You didn't want anyone near you," she shot back.

"You're right. I didn't. But I did." Deep down, he'd needed all of them to stand by him no matter what he said or did to push them away.

He'd needed someone to give him the right kind of push. Adria saw that and had no trouble bulldozing her way past his temper and grabbing hold of his attention. "At first, I was pissed at you for leaving me. It felt like a huge failure. Now I'm glad I found out that you couldn't hold up to the 'for better or worse, in sickness and health' part of the vows."

Anger filled her eyes. "That's not fair."

"You're right. You never made that vow. I pushed you away, and you gave up without a fight." He wanted her to know how much that hurt.

Her whole body went rigid. "You made it impossible to stay."

"I was hurting and lashed out. I wanted you to push past all the barriers I threw up between us. But you're not made that way. I expected too much. I came home hoping I could just pick up my life again, but it wasn't that easy. Everything, including me and you, was different. I didn't know how to be this version of myself. I'm still working on it. You didn't give me a chance. You made it clear you couldn't stand the sight of me." It still stung.

Indignation and anger flashed in her eyes. "I hated seeing you in so much pain." Her eyes dropped to his leg and back up. "But you look so much better now." Yeah, she liked him at his best. Or at least looking it.

He couldn't blame her for wanting a simple, easy life. It hurt that she'd walked away from him, but he understood that it had been the best decision for her.

Maybe she'd seen what he'd had a hard time admitting: they were never really good for each other.

"I am better. It took time and work. But mostly I'm better because of her." He notched his chin toward the window where Adria stood beside Trinity watching them.

Melanie looked at Adria, then back at him. "Who is she?"

"Trinity's business partner. My girlfriend. The woman who saw the man beneath all the pain and anger and scars and saw someone worth taking a chance on. She saw someone who needed a huge wake-up call but couldn't hear it. Not until she came along and cared enough to blast through all the noise in my head and make me listen."

She wrapped her arms across her chest. "I tried to get through to you." She'd earned that defensive tone.

He hadn't made things easy on her. "You and everyone else didn't get it. She does. That's all. I'm not mad at you anymore. I'm not sorry we ended. You knew it was best for you. Turns out, it was best for me, too, because it led me to her." One look at Adria and he felt better. His world felt right.

"And you two are . . ."

It didn't take a rocket scientist to figure out what she meant. She wanted to know if he could be with Adria the way he hadn't been able to be with her. "We're together. In every way. I sure as hell don't deserve her, but she came into my life like it was meant to be. I hope you find someone you're meant to be with, too. I really do." Drake didn't have anything else to say, so he turned for the door.

"Drake?"

He turned back.

She stood perfectly still, staring at him like she'd never seen him. Maybe she hadn't. Not really. Not the way Adria saw him.

"I don't know what to say."

He held his hands out wide and let them drop. "There's nothing more to say. I'm trying to put my past behind me. You should, too." He pointed to the women who had been joined by his brothers in the window. "That's my future in there. Have a good life, Melanie. I mean that." Because he planned to have a very good life with the feisty woman with you-better-have-ended-that-for-good in her eyes and a come-and-get-me smile on her lips just for him.

Chapter Twenty

Y ou should go out there and shut her down. That's your man," Trinity declared.

Adria choked back a laugh. Trinity had a good heart and forgave Adria for keeping things with Drake on the down low. "He is mine. Which is why I'm fine letting him handle it. He needs closure just like she does."

"Who cares what she wants? She broke up with him when he was at his lowest."

"He pushed her away because she wasn't what he needed. She walked away because she didn't love him enough to hold on. They're better off without each other. He knows it. I bet she does, too." Adria knew that to be true even though anxiety tightened her gut seeing Drake with Melanie. She didn't know if old feelings would rise up between them. She squashed that idea and shared with Trinity the words that kept circling her mind. "I don't know what happened with you guys last night, but he thought it meant the end of us. He told me losing me matters more to him than Melanie ever did."

Trinity sucked in a gasp and covered her mouth, her eyes wide with shock. She dropped her hand. "He said that to you?"

"Right in front of Roxy and Noah after he shoved Noah away from me when he hugged me and Drake misunderstood the situation."

Worry filled Trinity's eyes, because she'd seen Drake lose it numerous times over the last few months. "He went into a jealous rage?"

"Kinda. He held it together and didn't hurt Noah. He really just wanted me to know he wasn't giving up without a fight."

Tears filled Trinity's eyes. "Really?"

Declan and Tate walked up behind them.

Declan stared over Adria's shoulder. "Is Trinity crying because Drake is getting back together with Melanie?"

"Please God, no." Tate rolled his eyes.

Adria didn't have to say anything to tell them what was really going on. Drake turned his back on Melanie, walked in the door, headed straight for her, wrapped his arms around her waist, picked her up, and kissed her socks off.

Trinity sniffled. "He loves her."

Adria kissed Drake right through that huge statement and laughed when Trinity hugged both of them, and then Declan and Tate joined in crushing her into Drake in this family circle of love.

Drake met her eyes. "Make them stop."

She laughed. "You love it."

Declan and Tate squeezed them all tighter.

Trinity squeaked.

Sunny bounced up and down around them, pawing at everyone's legs.

Drake had enough of all this closeness, let her loose with one hand, and socked Tate right in the side. He peeled off from them. Declan got a shove. Trinity stepped back with a huge smile for her and Drake and put her hands up before Drake went after her, too.

Instead, he set Adria on her feet and stared down at her. He traced the side of her face with his fingers. The unexpected and sweet gesture stirred up all the emotions she'd pushed to the back of her mind and heart. "Show me your place."

She took his hand and tugged him toward the back of the building. "Come see the kitchen. It's amazing."

"I thought you came to help with the shelves," Declan called.

"In a minute. I want to see what Adria does all day."

Adria turned into Drake, went up on tiptoe, and hugged him.

He rubbed his hands up and down her back. "What's this?"

"Thanks for caring. It means a lot." It really did. So much so, tears pricked her eyes and clogged her throat.

"I've been wondering about you, this place, all of it." Drake looked around the main space. "What are you going to put in the display cabinets along the main counter?"

She pulled herself together and stared at the beautiful marble-topped wood ten-foot counter with the glass cover. "That's where we'll keep the prepared food. Customers can grab something hot to eat here." She pointed to the wide area by the front windows where tables sat grouped together with chairs stacked nearby. "They can eat here at lunch or dinner or take it home."

"I thought this was shop-and-go. I didn't realize you were running a restaurant."

"We're not. Not really. But we wanted people to have the option to make their purchase and dine in instead of maybe sitting at their desk or eating in their car. They check out at the end of the counter. We set up another counter across the way by the refrigerated displays and rows of shelves for those who want to just shop and go."

"I love the vibe you've got going in here. The exposed brick makes it feel warm, but add in the rustic wood beams and the shelves made out of black metal and wood planks that match the tables and chairs you picked, and it's got a lot of charm."

Trinity came up next to them and hooked her arm through Adria's. "She designed the layout and came up with the brick, wood, metal concept for everything."

"Trinity had her own ideas. Like the free lending library in the dining area."

Trinity beamed. "Take a book. Leave a book. Sit and read your book."

"Lord knows you're always reading one," Drake pointed out.

Trinity eyed him. "Food and books, what more does a person need?"

"Sex," Tate called out.

"Beer," Declan added.

"Football," one of the workers installing the kitchen appliances yelled.

Because the space was so wide-open right now with high ceilings, voices carried.

Drake kept his mouth shut.

Trinity rolled her eyes.

Adria pulled Drake around the counter to the back room where they'd set up the kitchen.

Drake whistled. "Man, that's a lot of equipment."

Adria's heart fluttered with joy seeing the huge ovens and racks ready to hold trays of prepared food to go in the oven or cool after cooking. She pointed to the huge boxes of trays. "We'll use containers that are microwave and oven safe. Plus they're recyclable. We'll put the food together in single and double servings." She pulled out the separate lids. One read, "Just for me." The other read, "Plenty to share."

"Those are cool."

"If you're having a dinner party, you can buy multiple packs, or we'll have one that's family size." She grabbed the lid that read, "Family and Friends."

"You guys thought of everything."

"I hope so." She brushed her hand over the soup/chili containers in single and double sizes. "We have a professional photographer scheduled for the day after next to put together some displays for behind the counter and advertising. Trinity and I will cook up everything on the menu and put it together in the containers. I'd like some photos of the containers sitting empty between beautiful plates of food."

"Put you and Trinity at the table eating and you'll have guys coming in here wanting more than the food." Drake went quiet for a moment, frowned, then backtracked. "Never mind. I don't want anyone coming in here for you."

She chuckled. "The local paper is doing a feature story on us next week. We'll have our picture in the paper and online."

Drake looked around the massive kitchen and back into the main building space. "This is really something, Adria. You and Trinity took a great idea and turned it into reality."

"Well, we're close to reality. We open in two weeks. If it's successful, we hope to open more stores like this."

The appliance guy stood back from one of the four ovens. "They're all set up. Want to do the honors and test them out?"

"Trinity!" Adria walked over to one of the ovens.

Trinity walked in. "What's up?"

"They're ready."

Drake pulled out his phone and held it up.

Trinity took her place at the oven next to Adria's. They stood with their hands on the Start button and smiled at Drake. He took several pictures.

Trinity looked at her. They smiled and hit the buttons together. The ovens clicked and hummed to life. Adria celebrated this moment with a hug with Trinity. Drake took another picture of them.

Adria stepped back from Trinity. "I wish we had something to actually cook."

"We'll start getting supplies next week." Trinity hit the Start button on the other two ovens and smiled at the guy who installed them. "They're so pretty. Thank you."

"You can thank me with a free meal when you open."

Trinity pulled a postcard out of her apron pocket and handed it to the guy. "Half off seven meals. One week of food."

The guy took it. "Awesome. Does it come with your number?"

Trinity took it in stride. "You're sweet, but no. I'm working on this right now." She held her hands out to encompass the whole business.

"Maybe another time." He grabbed his huge tool bag and waved goodbye.

"How many of those cards have you handed out?" Adria had come up with the marketing idea and had the cards printed up a couple days ago.

"Almost all of them. I went around to the local business offices and asked if I could leave them in the lunchrooms. Most everyone said yes. I walked around at lunchtime yesterday and anyone eating their lunch outside got one."

"Genius."

"I received a lot of good feedback, and people seemed interested and anxious to try us out."

Drake touched her shoulder. "Show me the apartment upstairs." He nodded toward the stairs at the other end of the kitchen.

"It's kind of a mess right now. We haven't even started fixing it up." But she led Drake up the stairs to the open door.

"You're going to need a better lock on this door if you're going to live up here and have customers and employees in this place. Anyone could sneak up here."

"I don't know why they'd want to, but I'll put it on the list."

"Do you have a security system on that list? I haven't seen anything set up yet. Cameras. An alarm system."

"To tell you the truth, we hadn't thought of it."

"You need it. For your safety and to protect your assets here. Cameras and security signs are a great deterrent for anyone thinking of robbing the place."

"Do you think someone wants to steal our massive ovens?"

He narrowed his eyes. "No. But they may think you've got money in those registers or in a vault."

"The vault is in the office. I'm assured no one can move it or open it."

"Adria." The warning in Drake's tone cut off her resistance to adding security and another huge expense to her list.

She sighed. "I'll get on it."

"I can do it." Drake's enthusiasm surprised her.

"You can?"

"We used all kinds of surveillance equipment in the military. I can set up a simple security system for you."

One less thing for her to worry about. "You're hired."

"Just like that?"

"You're worried about me and Trinity and our safety. I've put a lot of money into this place. I want to protect it."

He swept the back of his fingers over her cheek. "I want to protect you."

"Which is why you're casing this place like you expect an ambush."

His eyes dropped to the floor.

She put her hand on his chest. "I know it's habit and ingrained in you. I'm not criticizing. I'm not trying to make you self-conscious. Hyper-vigilance is part of your PTSD. I see it when you come to my place and you're looking over your shoulder and locking the place up tight before we're falling into bed."

"I can't help it. If something happened to you . . ."

She went up on tiptoe and kissed him. "I feel the same way about you.

So tell me how much you need and I'll get you the money to buy a system and install it."

Drake nodded, then looked around the wide-open space. "This is more like a studio apartment."

"Yeah. It's not much, but it's got great views out the windows. It kind of feels like a loft. The kitchen needs a major upgrade." She slid her foot back and forth over the scarred wood floors. "I think I'll refinish the floors and maybe whitewash the red brick to brighten up the place." She glanced around the cluttered room. "Once the downstairs is complete, we can move all this stuff to the storage room. A couch, chair, and TV setup by the window and a bed over against the other wall with a dresser and that's all I'll really need. Oh, and a whole bottle of bleach to clean out the disgusting bathroom." She wrinkled her nose at the thought of what she'd seen in there.

"Or you could stay at the cabin?" He wanted her to stay.

Her belly fluttered with excitement. "That was never supposed to be permanent." But she really loved being with Drake.

"I don't see why you can't stay there. With me." Drake held up his hand. "I'm not saying we live together. Not exactly. But . . ." His shy delivery endeared him even more to her.

"You like the way things are now." So did she. No more sneaking around. The freedom they shared to be themselves with each other in front of everyone made it all the sweeter.

"With one small change. I don't want to have to leave you alone and naked in bed."

She gave him a sexy smile. "A dinner date tonight and a sleepover. I'm a lucky girl."

"Stop teasing and making this hard."

She slid her hand down his belly and over his fly. "I'm making you hard. Is that why you wanted to bring me up here to look at dusty floors and the leaking kitchen sink?"

He slid his fingers through her hair and held her head. "I can fix that for you."

"A guy who can fix things is really sexy." She rubbed her hand up and down the length of him as he swelled under her hand.

"Hey, I thought you were going to help with the shelves," Declan yelled up the stairs.

Drake jolted, then called over his shoulder, "I've got to fix Adria's leaking sink first."

"Is that what you two call it?" Unveiled mirth filled Declan's words.

Adria ran her hands up Drake's chest. "You and me. Later."

"All night."

She tapped her hand on his chest. "Well, that's quite a boast, big guy."

He smacked her on the ass. "You know I can make you fall to pieces with just a kiss."

"That's because of *where* you kiss me."

He leaned down and kissed her long and deep, then abruptly stopped before things got too hot.

She tilted her head and gave him a mock frown. "I was thinking of something lower."

"Me, too, which is why I stopped." He spun her around and smacked her bottom again to get her to go downstairs. Back in the kitchen, he touched her arm to get her to face him again. "I'm really proud of you and Trinity for what you've done here. It's amazing."

"Thank you, Drake. That means a lot." It did, because she'd worked hard in school and on this dream. And though Roxy and Sonya were proud of her, too, having him say it added something extra and boosted her confidence and made this a little more special.

But she had one big concern. "I hope Juliana likes it."

"Do you think she'll come work here with you once she's out?"

"That's the plan." One she hoped Juliana embraced. "A job. Stability. Support. She doesn't know what she wants to do with her life. I hope this place will give her a chance to figure it out."

His eyes brightened. "She can live upstairs."

Adria smiled and shook her head at Drake's blatant dismissal that Adria would move into the apartment. "That's a good plan." Because she'd already made up her mind to give in to temptation and happiness and stay in the cabin with Drake.

Chapter Twenty-One

Adria dropped everything and drove an hour to the rehab center. Once she got there, she paced the lobby, arms crossed over her chest, her mind whirling with what she wanted to say to Juliana and dreading what Juliana had to say to her.

"Sweetheart, you're going to wear out your boots."

Adria glanced down at her black leather ankle boots, jeans cuffed just above them, and sighed. "I'll buy new ones." She paced away from Drake. As soon as he heard her plans, he'd immediately said he'd come with her this morning and visit his Army buddy at the same time.

He didn't want her to do this alone.

She appreciated his support.

She hadn't seen or heard from her sister since she dropped her off here. Just hearing her voice this morning brought back the nightmare she'd finally stopped seeing every time she closed her eyes. But the whole way here, all she thought about was seeing her sister's blue lips as she lay lifeless on the bathroom floor.

She ran her hands up and down her arms over the soft blue shrug sweater she'd grabbed on her way out of the cabin. The ends waved out by her sides as she spun and walked back toward Drake, sitting in a chair, his arms over his chest, eyes locked on her.

"You're making me anxious." When she got within reach, he snagged her by the hips and pulled her into his lap. His arms banded around her and his chin rested on her shoulder. "Calm down. You're supposed to be the sane one in this relationship."

"Do you know how long it's been since I've seen her?"

"Longer than it's ever been before, but she needed this place, and maybe you needed to just be you for a while and not you and Juliana."

How did he know that's how it felt to be an identical twin? "I don't know how to be me without her."

"That's a lie. You were just you when you forced me to confront my demons and the lies I told myself and made me that deal. You wanted to be you when you walked out of that bedroom naked."

"That sounds like a story I'd like to hear." The deep voice drew both their stares.

Drake stood, pushing her up and off his lap in the process. He hugged the big, dark-haired man with a smack on the back and a smile. Drake held him by the shoulders. "Chase. Man, it's good to see you."

"You look better than the last time I saw you." Chase eyed her. "Is this your Melanie?"

Drake shook his head, pulled Adria close, and made the introduction. "This is Adria Holloway. She saved my life."

Adria shook her head. "All I did was make you see the truth behind the lies you told yourself. You did the work."

Chase looked Drake up and down. "Whatever you're doing, it's working. Keep it up." Chase glanced back at her, eyes narrowed. "You look just like . . ."

"Adria," Juliana called from behind Chase.

Both men turned to her.

Chase whistled. "They're twins."

Adria left the guys and ran to her sister. Her hug practically knocked Juliana down. Juliana held on and buried her face in Adria's hair. They held tight for a good long minute before Adria could pull herself together enough to release her sister and take a look at her.

She'd filled out a bit with regular meals at the facility. Her clear, not bloodshot, but still wary eyes studied Adria right back. "How are you?"

"Fine. Better. Ready to get out of here."

Adria didn't like the sound of that. "I know the month is almost up, but I thought you might want to stay and work on your issues."

"I'm clean, sober, and bored out of my mind." Juliana looked past her. "Who's the guy?"

Adria smiled as Drake and Chase stood talking in the sitting area. "Drake McGrath. Trinity's oldest brother. My boyfriend."

Juliana side-eyed her. "Well, well, well, sis. You took a page from my playbook. Big and dangerous. Just my type. I hope you put the little surprise I stashed in your bag to good use."

Adria ignored that because she didn't want to tell Juliana he'd torn up the nightie but used the condoms. "He's ex-military. He's been through a lot, so be nice."

"You like surrounding yourself with damaged people." That stinging accusation hurt.

"It started with Mom, then came Roxy and Sonya. Everyone who works at the Wild Rose Ranch is fucked-up in some way. It's no wonder you're drawn to people who are messed up. What happened to his face?" Juliana winced.

Anger flashed. "How can you be so callous? That man has two"— she held up two fingers—"two Purple Hearts. Be nice, or I'm out of here."

Juliana leaned back. "So it's like that. You don't need me anymore— you've got him." The seething tone made Adria clench her jaw.

Even though Juliana pissed her off, she understood her sister wanted to push her buttons and test her to see if Adria would back away. Never. "Juliana, I don't know what your problem is, but this isn't you."

"You're the one who left me here to get my brain fucked."

Adria stepped closer, looked Juliana dead in the eye, and pushed back. "You chose to stay. No one forced you. This place is voluntary. You can leave anytime you want."

"Right. But then I don't have my sisters, do I? Not much of a choice."

Adria resented the tone and the unwarranted anger. But at least Juliana valued them above her partying ways. "I saved your life. Do you get that? You were lying on the floor nearly dead." It took everything she had to get those shaky words out her clogged throat.

"Adria saves the day again." Sarcasm didn't mask the disdain or resentment.

She simply didn't get Juliana. It hurt her heart to feel this disconnected from her. "What the hell does that mean?"

"Let's discuss it in my office," a woman said from behind Juliana. "I'm Dr. Chen."

Adria shook the doctor's hand. "Adria. It's nice to meet you."

Drake came up to her, oblivious to the turmoil between her and Juliana. "Hey, Chase and I are going to be out on the back patio catching up."

"Okay. Drake, this is Juliana and Dr. Chen."

Drake nodded hello to both of them, but focused on Juliana. "Adria misses you. She talks about you all the time. She can't wait for you to come home."

"I'm not allowed to go home."

Drake took Juliana's snark in stride. "You're alive, thanks to her. Take your second chance and do something better with your life." Drake leaned over and kissed Adria on the head, gave her an encouraging nod, then left with Chase.

"Who the hell does he think he is?"

Adria wanted Juliana to see exactly what she'd shown Drake: she wasn't the only one who'd ever been hurt. "Someone who has found a way to deal with his problems and stop taking it out on everyone around him."

"You think that's what I'm doing?"

"Yes," she and Dr. Chen said in unison.

Juliana huffed out a frustrated sigh, spun on her heel, and walked down the hall.

Dr. Chen touched Adria's arm. "At least she's headed to my office. You two have a lot to discuss. I'd like to remind you that, while this may not seem fair, this is about *her* today."

Adria sighed, sucked it up like she always did, and readied herself mentally to face Juliana and her demons.

By the time Adria entered Dr. Chen's spacious office, Dr. Chen had taken a seat in one of the two armchairs facing the sofa where Juliana sat with her legs tucked up under her. In jeans and a plain white T, her hair down and face devoid of makeup, she looked young and vulnerable and angry all at the same time.

Adria sat in the opposite corner of the sofa, giving them both the space they needed to get through the hard stuff so they could be close again. Adria had to believe that would happen, because having her sister this angry at her shredded her heart and made it hard to breathe. She lived each day hoping she and Juliana found their way back to each other.

Juliana hugged herself. "It's always so cold in this place."

Adria pulled off her sweater and handed it to Jules, who slipped it on and rubbed her hands over the soft material. They'd shared clothes their whole life. They used to share everything, but Juliana had slowly closed up these last two years. Adria missed the days when she knew her sister's every thought.

"Are you sleeping with him?"

She expected Juliana to continue to be outrageous and say unexpected things for shock value and to get attention. She wished Juliana would calm down and talk about what was really bothering her. "We're not here to talk about me and Drake. I came so you could talk about what is upsetting you."

"I'm not upset."

Defensive much?

Adria eyed her, letting her know with a single eyebrow raise she didn't buy it. "What are you then?"

"You left me here."

"And that makes you feel . . ." Dr. Chen prompted.

"Angry. Hurt. Like you can't trust me to get my shit together on my own."

Adria tried to remain calm. "Well, you continue to prove that you can't keep your shit together."

"That's not true," Jules whined.

"You failed several classes and dropped out of school. You spend your days partying and going from one guy to the next without seeming to care about any of them."

"Two classes. I didn't drop out—I just didn't want to go anymore. It's a waste of time. And I like all those guys."

"Those are excuses for your irresponsibility."

"I don't need to be responsible. You take care of that for the both of us."

Adria half expected Juliana to stick out her tongue. She faced Juliana head-on. "You go about your life with no care in the world for yourself or those around you. Yes, I take care of you, because you don't take care of yourself."

Juliana folded her arms across her chest. "I don't need you to take care of me."

Adria drove her point home. "You overdosed. Twice. You nearly died. If not for me, you would be dead!" The words shook her to the core. The thought of losing her sister broke her soul.

"If not for you, I wouldn't be like this!" Bitterness filled Juliana's voice.

Why did her sister resent her for saving her?

Adria clutched her knees in both hands and tried to understand. She really didn't get it, but she wanted to for Juliana's sake. So she sucked in a breath and opened herself to listening. "Explain to me why you doing drugs and failing school is my fault."

Juliana pointed to the doctor. "Ask her."

Adria looked to Dr. Chen to explain. "I want to help my sister. I want her to get better. So tell me, what is it that I did that made her this way? Did I not love her enough? Did I protect her too much? Should I have let her fall and not tried to catch her? When she hit the bottom, should I have not tried to pick her up? What?"

Dr. Chen looked to Juliana. "Why did you sometimes pretend to be Adria?"

Juliana glared at the doctor for putting her on the spot instead of going after Adria, which seemed like what Juliana wanted her to do. "We're supposed to talk about what happened."

"You mentioned that you like to fool people into thinking you're her. I believe what happened to you girls when you were young has everything to do with why you do that."

"I like tricking people." That statement dismissed any notion that it was more than a trick. "We're identical. It's so easy to make them think I'm her. It's fun."

Dr. Chen pushed. "Why do you want to be her? Do you believe being Adria is easier than being you?"

"She carries around her damage in such a pretty way. Sad, lonely, poor broken Adria. Everyone wants to make her feel better." Juliana's unsympathetic words stung.

Taken aback, Adria tried to breathe through the pain those callous words inflicted. "Is that how you see me?"

"It's how everyone sees you."

She shook her head. "That's not how I see myself. I survived, Jules. I made it out and found a better life. I worked hard to understand what happened wasn't my fault."

"It was your fault."

Stunned by that accusation, Adria's heart slammed to a halt, then double-timed it in her chest.

Juliana sat up and leaned in close. "You left me there. Alone. Wondering what was happening to you. Not knowing if you'd come back. What would happen to me if you didn't come back?"

Adria sank into the corner of the couch, needing some space and a second to take that in. "You're angry that I . . ." It hit her then why Juliana pretended to be her all the time. "When he came for us, I pretended to be *you*. I made you be quiet and not say a word. I took your turn."

Juliana hugged herself tight and stared at her lap. "You'd come back and never say what happened. You'd be so quiet and look so hurt and haunted." Juliana picked at the end of the sweater. "It was my fault. I should have spoken up."

Adria shook her head, reached over, took her sister's chin, and made her look up. "No. There's no way I would have let him touch you. That was never going to happen. I'd have done anything to protect you from him. I did." Her body trembled as one horrible memory after another assaulted her.

"I wanted to protect you, but I was so scared." Jules's voice, though filled with remorse and regret, finally sounded more like the sister she remembered.

"I was, too. Jules, he took me first. I knew what he'd do to you. How it would make you feel . . ."

Dr. Chen broke in. "How, Adria? Explain to her."

She didn't know quite how to explain her nine-year-old confusion, humiliation, guilt, and the feeling that somehow she could have stopped him. "I was scared every time he took me. I didn't know what he'd do. It started off innocent but strange. He'd dress me up in pretty dresses and take pictures of me. He'd pose me in ways that didn't feel natural. When I got older and looked back at what happened, I understood. He wanted me to look provocative. Each time, the clothes got less and less and the pictures got worse. If I didn't do what he wanted, he hit me." Adria lost herself in the nightmares of all the horrible things that man made her do.

Juliana's hand covered hers. "Adria, was it only the pictures?"

Adria didn't like talking about it, but Juliana needed to know so she could stop imagining the worst. "Pictures and videos. It got to the point where I wasn't wearing any clothes anymore. He wanted me to touch myself. Pose. Smile for the ones who loved me and couldn't get enough of me." She sucked in a ragged breath. "He was grooming me. He made me touch him. He started touching me." She squeezed her legs together and concentrated on breathing in and out and not the echo of his horrendous touch or the images in her mind setting off an anxiety attack.

She tried to breathe through the adrenaline and panic rising inside her.

Juliana fell back into the couch and covered her face. "Mom found out he was selling the pictures and stuff online."

Adria tried to remain centered on the conversation and gave Juliana the cold hard truth. "They're still being circulated."

Juliana gasped and stared at her like she was crazy.

It was the sad reality Adria had to learn to live with. But she wanted Juliana to understand that the abuse Adria suffered ended. "Mom may have her own demons and faults, but the second she found out, she got us out of there. We ended up in a shelter."

"Then Big Mama found us and took us to Wild Rose Ranch." Juliana finished that chapter of their lives. "And things were better than they'd ever been for us."

Yet Juliana spiraled the last couple years.

Dr. Chen leaned forward. "Have you gone to the police?"

"The guy is behind bars for molesting another girl and child porn."
Adria regretted not doing something before another girl got hurt, but she
was just nine and didn't know anything except calling the cops meant
they'd take her mother away if they came. Then what would happen to
her and Juliana? They wouldn't have anyone. They could be split up in
foster care. Their mother always told them as bad as things were, they
could always get worse. They needed to stick together.

Their mother used fear to keep her and Juliana from speaking up
about just how bad things were for them.

"It's very frustrating to learn that once something is on the internet,
getting it off is near impossible. Pedophiles are prolific sharers. Once
you take it down in one place, someone else puts it up again."

Dr. Chen frowned. "I'm very sorry. That must be difficult and frustrating to live with."

"I try not to think about it. I don't recognize that scared, haunted little
girl anymore, all dressed up looking pretty but terrified. Even worse are
the images of her with nothing in her eyes." Adria had to think of that
little girl as someone else—another part of her—because she had to tuck
all that pain and the nightmares away, so they didn't take over her life
like they used to before she got the help she needed to unpack it and put
it away.

Juliana hugged her from the side. "So that's why you hate to shop for
clothes and play dress up."

A chill rippled up her spine. "It is not fun for me. You, Roxy, and
Sonya love it. I tried, but all I heard in my head was his voice telling me,
'Pose pretty. They want you.' I didn't know what he meant, but it didn't
sound good. Now I know what he was saying and it creeps me out even
more." Another cold shiver shook her.

"Did he . . ."

Adria gripped her sister's arm over her chest. "No. He didn't get that
far in grooming me. Mostly because he thought he was dealing with
two different girls. Sometimes I was me. Sometimes I was you. Or so
he thought." She didn't add that eventually he would have taken both
of them and put them together in his own sick twin fantasies for his
customers.

That disturbing thought soured her stomach. She swallowed back the bile rising to her throat.

She finally became aware of the tears streaming down her face and wiped them away, but more came. It had been a long time since she cried for the haunted, damaged little girl inside her.

Adria kissed Juliana's head. "I'd do it all over again to spare you. I love you. I can live with what happened. Stop blaming yourself because it happened to me. Stop blaming yourself because it didn't happen to you. We may have identical DNA, but we are not the same, Jules. And that's okay. I don't need you to hurt the way I hurt. I don't need you to punish yourself for what happened to me. I need you to be my sister and love me the way I love you. I need you to put this in the past and love yourself. You didn't do anything wrong. I don't blame you for what happened."

Jules covered her hand. "I want you to be happy."

Adria took that in and appreciated it so much. "Get well. Live your life without what happened dragging you down." She squeezed Jules's hand. "Be happy with me."

"Are you happy?"

"I feel bad saying this because of what you're going through, but these last weeks have been very happy for me. Drake is amazing. Trinity and I are almost ready to open the business. Things are coming together in my life, but I'm waiting for you to come and share it with me."

"No you're not." Hurt came back into Juliana's voice. "You made all these plans without me."

"Juliana, you weren't interested in culinary school or business. You didn't know what you wanted to do. That's okay. You've got plenty of time to figure it out. I couldn't put my life on hold and wait for you. You knew I intended to open my own business."

"With Trinity. Not me."

"Jules, you never expressed any interest in *Almost Homemade*."

"You never asked. You were so caught up in it that you moved ahead without a thought to it tearing us apart."

Dr. Chen intervened. "Juliana, do you feel that the closer your sister came to graduating and opening her business, the more you saw her life becoming separate from yours?"

"I knew it would. It's happened. She moved to Montana and opened a business. She intends to stay here. Now all of them live here."

"Jules, just because Roxy, Sonya, and I are here now doesn't mean we left you or don't want you with us. I thought we'd talk about it once you were out of here, but I'd love it if you came to work for me until you figure out what you want to do. I have a place for you and everything."

Juliana's eyes went wide. "You do?"

"Yes. Of course I do. There will always be a place for you with me."

Dr. Chen leaned in. "Do you see now, Juliana, how your fears have made you believe things that aren't true and separated you from Adria and your other sisters?"

Juliana scrunched her lips into a pout. "I guess so."

Dr. Chen continued. "You used Adria's past, pretended to be her, so that you could get the attention she received because of what happened to her. You wanted people to know you were hurting, too, and when they didn't understand that, you acted out even more. You saw her succeeding, got jealous, and acted out."

"You make me sound like a five-year-old."

If the shoe fits. Adria squashed the childish thought and tried to focus on Juliana. "When things don't go your way or you need something, speak up."

"Use my words, you mean." Juliana rolled her eyes, defaulting to being stubborn instead of trying to work things out.

"Stop being defensive. We're trying to help you."

Juliana rolled her head back and forth on the back of the couch. "I know. I just need time to let it sink in."

Juliana meant all they'd talked about today. It took Adria years to let the revelations come and sink in about what happened and how it affected her. Talking about it today brought it all up. She'd be dealing with the aftermath for some time to come, but at least she had Drake to distract her. And talk if she needed to later. He'd listen. He'd understand.

He wouldn't put the fault on her. He'd know she was the victim and that sometimes the hurt little girl inside her needed some love and care.

"Jules, just because I'm working on building a future for myself doesn't mean I'm leaving you behind. On the contrary. I want you to come along with me, just like we've always done. You're my sister, my other half. Nothing changes that."

"Not even your new boyfriend?"

"You may not understand this, but Drake is a symbol of progress for me. We're good together. I can be me with him. I don't think about the past when I'm with him. He lets me explore being a woman in my own way and in my own time. He knows what happened, but he doesn't treat me like I'm fragile or I'll break. I don't treat him like that because of what he's been through. We understand each other. I never thought I'd find that. Certainly not with a man."

Juliana's eyes softened. "Do you love him?"

She didn't think, just spoke the truth. "I love so many things about him. I tried so hard not to fall, but it just happened, and I was in his arms and his heart and I felt safe for the first time in my life. Not the kind of safe where I pretend everything is okay. Really safe, Jules."

"Careful. You let someone in that close, they can hurt you the worst." Ever skeptical. Juliana needed to smooth out her rough edges.

"Then stop punishing yourself because I made you stay quiet and hide when we were children. It hurts me to see you so reckless and in pain and pushing me away when all I want to do is help you."

"Maybe now that I know . . . well, I can help myself and stop disappointing you. I want things to be different. I want them to go back to the way they used to be."

Adria squeezed Juliana's thigh. "Me, too."

Dr. Chen took them both in. "You two have made a lot of progress today. You should be proud of yourselves for sharing so openly and honestly about this terrible thing you shared. I hope you both see that a shared event can be experienced in very different ways by the individuals involved. It doesn't make what happened to either of you any less traumatic because of how you experienced it. Juliana, you hurt for your sister and carried the guilt of feeling inadequate to stop it. You resented her for taking on the burden she did when you felt you deserved it more because you were spared. You thought you deserved to hurt as much as she did. Those are all valid responses. I hope we can work on accepting your new perspective of your sister's experience and forgiving yourself and letting this go."

Juliana nodded, accepting that one conversation didn't make everything better. She stood and raked her fingers through her hair. "I need some air." Juliana walked away.

Dr. Chen held a hand up to stop Adria from following her out. "I just want to say how brave it was for you to talk about what happened. She needed to hear it from you. Are you okay?"

She raked her fingers through her hair the identical way Juliana had done before she left. Some things never change. "It seems I've been confronted a lot about my past these last few weeks."

"Because of Juliana's overdose, or because of your new boyfriend?"

"Both. But just like this was good for Juliana, it's been good for me. I've dealt with many aspects of what happened, but I still had a few things to unpack. Like how I protected Jules and that it became a virus in her system lying dormant until she couldn't hold it off any longer."

"Nothing ever stays buried forever."

Adria nodded her agreement. "With Drake, I needed to confront the way I keep men at arm's length and think they're only out to use me."

"I see why you'd think that with a mother who is a prostitute and what happened with that disgusting pedophile. Not good examples of men acting admirably."

"And yet, Drake in his pain and rage and loneliness and desolation showed me a man who was good. He desperately wanted to love. His family. Himself."

"You?"

"Yes. Not at first. He wanted a partner in his life. Someone who saw the man he used to be, the one he is now, and the man he'd become as he learned to live and dream again."

"Has he?"

"It's been amazing to watch him work so hard and change so much. He's allowed me the space to do the same. We kept things casual until both of us realized we'd changed and wanted more from each other."

Dr. Chen reached out and Adria took her hand. "You've been through a lot of trauma. That man. Saving your sister. I hope you find happiness with Drake. Your sister needs time to heal. She's just beginning to understand how her past has affected her. Whatever you do, don't sacrifice the progress you've made or the happiness you've found for her. She may find it difficult to see your success is not her failure. You're twins. I imagine it's difficult to not compare yourselves, especially when others are bound to do that, too. You've done well, separating your life from hers. She needs time to do the same."

"Thank you for taking care of her. Today was hard, but if it helps her, I'm willing to come back and talk about it some more."

"I'm hoping now that she knows your part we can work on her part. The last thing I want to do is traumatize you again by asking you to relive it over and over."

"I'll be okay." In time. It always took a little more work to pack the past back up and tuck it away again.

"Take care of yourself. Treat yourself with something special."

"He's waiting outside." And just like every time she thought about Drake, she smiled.

Dr. Chen squeezed her hand. "Then go get him."

Chapter Twenty-Two

Drake slapped his hand down on Chase's shoulder. "I'm so glad you're doing better."

"Not as good as you. Your girlfriend"—he nodded, his lips drawn into an approving grin—"she's a knockout. Her sister though, that one is messed up. All she wants is attention."

"Adria's not like that. She loves her sister. She misses her. I hope for her sake, Juliana gets better."

Chase settled back into the patio chair. "How did you two get together?"

"Well, first I held her hostage during one of my blackouts."

Chase's eyes went wide. "Uh, that's one way to do it, I guess."

Drake chuckled. "She should have had my ass arrested. Instead, she surprised the hell out of me by deciphering what happened and why. She read me like a book. She called me out on all my shit and dared me to get better. She showed me that the lies I was telling myself weren't true at all."

"Yeah, we like to tell ourselves all kinds of lies. We repeat them over and over until we think they're the God's honest truth."

Drake nodded and said out loud what he knew Chase grappled with since returning home, too. "Yeah, like 'I should have died over there.'"

"If you did, who would have saved my life?" Chase held his gaze. "You saved me, man. You have no idea how low I was when you found me. I was ready to . . ." Chase glanced up at the sky.

"But you didn't." Drake had looked deeper into Chase's random texts and figured out that he was sinking fast. He went to Wyoming and confronted his friend. Drake may not have been able to save himself, but he'd been determined to save Chase from himself.

"I promised you and myself I'd give this place a shot. My sixty days is almost up and I'm looking forward to going home."

Juliana agreed to the thirty-day program. Chase knew he'd needed more to deal with his addiction and PTSD symptoms.

"Back to Wyoming and your brothers?"

"Back to real life." Chase had lost himself at the bottom of a prescription bottle. It started off innocently enough. A pill three or four times a day during his recovery to get through the worst of the pain. That turned into five, six, ten pills and more a day even after his injuries healed. He numbed the pain and drowned out the nightmares and, like Drake, put off dealing with his mental health. Because guys like them didn't have a problem. They just needed to suck it up and move on.

Easier said than done.

Just another lie you tell yourself to get by.

When you don't deal with your shit, it festers under the surface, infecting everything in your life whether you like it or not.

Now that Drake was finding his way out of the anger, grief, and pain, he saw possibilities that once seemed out of reach.

He hoped Chase had gotten to that point, too. If not now, then before he left this place for home.

"Here comes your girl." Chase notched his chin up.

Drake glanced over his shoulder, ready with a smile to greet Adria, but it died when he realized the woman walking toward him wasn't Adria. "She's not mine."

Juliana walked right up to them. "Let's get out of here."

"Nice try. Where's Adria?"

Juliana's eyes narrowed. "How did you know?" She held her hands up, showing him Adria's sweater.

"Adria is wearing black boots and a pink top."

Juliana glanced down at her canvas shoes and white shirt. "Are you always that observant?"

"No. I might have missed that if I hadn't seen your eyes. When she looks at me, they light up. You look a little desperate. You also don't have her I Love You tattoo on your hand."

Juliana shifted from one foot to the other and stared at the back of her hand. "Maybe I need one, too, to remind me to love myself more." She rubbed her hands together. "Adria's not very happy right now."

"Why?" He looked past Juliana, hoping to see Adria coming out of the building, but she still didn't appear.

"I made her talk about the past. I know what really happened now."

Drake pressed his lips tight. She'd go through hell for her sister. For him. That's just who she was, but he hated that she had to relive something so traumatic. "I'm sure that wasn't easy, but if it helped you, I know she thinks it's worth it."

Juliana's head tilted to the side the way Adria's did when she was thinking hard. "You really do know her."

"I'm working on it."

"Maybe you could do something for me. For her."

"I'd do anything for her."

"Cheer her up. Get her to stop worrying so much about me."

He nodded. "The first I can do, but she's never going to stop worrying about you. She loves you. Nothing is going to change that either."

Juliana locked eyes with him. "She's the best person I know. Don't *ever* hurt her."

Drake took the unspoken threat in stride. He wanted to make that promise, but knew it couldn't be kept. People hurt people without meaning to all the time. He would never hurt her on purpose. Because seeing her unhappy or upset killed him. "You want to make her happy, get better."

"I'm working on it. Today helped."

"Then take whatever progress you made and build on it instead of tearing down your life."

Her eyes narrowed. "You really don't mince words."

Drake leaned forward and gave it to her straight. "Get your shit together so Adria can have you back and you can be with her. How's that?"

Her lips tilted and scrunched into a lopsided frown. "I don't think I'm going to like you."

"Probably not, because I will always be on *her* side." He stood and went to meet Adria as she walked their way.

She ran into his arms and hugged him close, her hands fisted in his shirt at his back.

He cupped her face and made her look at him. "You okay?"

"Not really."

He loved that she went with honesty instead of simply saying she was fine when she wasn't. "What do you need?"

"You."

He hugged her close. "You've always got me."

They reluctantly pulled apart to go back to Juliana and Chase, who stood near the patio table he and Chase used earlier. Drake would take care of Adria later. Hold her. Feed her. Whatever she needed to shake off today.

Chase came forward and held out his hand to Adria. "Chase Wilde."

"Adria Holloway. My sister Juliana." Adria held her hand out to her twin. "It's nice to meet you. Drake told me you served together."

"We did. He looks like that because he saved my life."

Adria looked from Chase to him. "Really?"

Drake pressed his lips together and tried not to get lost in his own nightmare. "It's complicated."

Chase frowned at that. "Not really. People were shooting at us. I got hit." Chase tapped his shoulder, chest, then held up his arm, showing off the scar where a bullet went right through his forearm. "I went down. Drake came out of cover to drag my ass back to safety, but an IED went off nearby, nearly blowing us to bits. Somehow, Drake managed to get up and, using mostly his right leg, drag me another thirty feet to what was left of our team before he collapsed and bled all over the place." Chase gave him a halfhearted smirk, trying to make light of something dark. "Then another of our guys got hit. Drake found the strength to get up and go after him."

"Chappie." Adria put her hand on Drake's chest and locked eyes with

Chase so he'd know she understood. "I'm so sorry you lost him, but I'm so glad you both survived."

"Wow, you two have really been through it." Juliana had lost the attitude and found her sympathy.

Adria glanced up at Drake. "You're very brave."

"So are you. Juliana told me you opened up about what happened when you were a kid."

Adria stared at Juliana. "We have to face the past in order to move forward to a better future."

Juliana nodded and closed the distance to hug Adria.

Chase slapped him on the back. "I need to get back. I'd like to see you, say goodbye before I head back to Wyoming."

"Absolutely."

Chase put his hand on Drake's shoulder. "And thanks for saving my life."

"You thanked me in the hospital."

"That was for saving me on the battlefield. This one's for making me come here."

Drake hugged his buddy. "I hope you never need saving again. But if you do . . . I'm here anytime you need me."

Chase stepped back. "Same goes." Chase took off.

Juliana and Adria stood with their arms around each other.

"You two really do look exactly alike."

Juliana leaned her head against Adria's. "He knew I wasn't you when I came out wearing your sweater."

Adria's eyebrows shot up. "Really?"

"It must be love if he knows you so well I don't look like you to him." Juliana hugged Adria hard one last time, then let her go. "Be happy, sis. I'll see you soon." And just like that, Juliana walked back into the facility.

Adria watched her go. "She's scared. She's afraid she won't be able to do this and she'll disappoint me."

"I have that same fear." He hadn't really been aware of how much he meant that until he said it out loud. And deeper than that, he feared he'd lose her and his world would be even bleaker than when he met her.

"Let's just keep doing what we've been doing. It's worked for us so far."

"Where do you want to go to dinner?"

"The same place we spend most of our time."

He cocked his head, not understanding. "We haven't really gone any-where together. We spend most our time at the cabin."

"More specifically, our bed. Take me home, cowboy. I want a ride."

"I can't deny you anything." Especially that. He hooked his arm around her shoulders and hugged her close. "Dinner in bed it is."

"I'll be your dessert." She gave him a sexy smile that didn't reach her eyes.

He'd help her wipe out the bad memories from her mind when they got home.

He wanted to spend every day creating new, happy memories with her to take their place.

Chapter Twenty-Three

A week before they opened *Almost Homemade* Trinity and Adria set up a booth at the local farmer's market in hopes of enticing as many people as possible to try their food and come to the store for more. The market opened at eight. By ten, they'd nearly sold out of what they'd brought and called in reinforcements.

"There's Drake." Trinity pointed to her brother walking through the crowd ahead of a huge cooler and Declan carrying the other end behind him.

"I hope they brought more than that." Adria worried they'd start a riot if they didn't have enough for everyone. The line stretched twenty feet and never seemed to get any shorter.

"I told them to grab all of the prepacked food we put together over the last week."

They'd thought to get a head start on the dry ingredient kits. This would wipe them out. "We're going to have to hire more help at the shop if this is the kind of demand we can expect."

"Let's hope so." Trinity's eyes shone with delight as she rang up another customer and bagged up the last mac and cheese refrigerated entrée. Everything they'd put out to sample had been devoured.

Drake and Declan made it to the front of the line.

"Where do you want this, sweetheart?" Drake didn't even break a sweat carrying the heavy cooler. His physical therapy had made him stronger and steady on his bad leg.

"You shouldn't be carrying that. You have surgery tomorrow."

His mouth tilted in a lopsided grin. "I won't carry coolers after surgery, I promise. Now, where do you want it?"

"Do you have any more of the lasagna or chicken and fettucine Alfredo in there?" the woman Trinity rang up asked.

"There's a few of everything in here. We've got two more coolers and about five boxes of mixes coming."

"Really?" Adria asked.

"You said bring as much as we could. We grabbed all of it." Drake scoped out the line. "Looks like you'll need it."

Adria handed change to her customer, then held up her hand to stop the next person from coming forward. "Give me one second." She waved Drake and Declan around the booth to the back. "Put it there." She pointed to eight other coolers. "Those are empty. Mind taking them back to make room for what you brought?"

Declan gave her a quick kiss on the head. "You got it."

Of course, Drake shoved Declan away from her. It had become a thing, Declan and Tate being sweet to her just to get at Drake. All in fun. And it was so nice to see the guys all working and playing together again.

Trinity glanced over her shoulder with an affectionate smile. "Stop fooling around. We've got hungry people to feed."

Drake saluted her. "On it."

The guys made several trips back and forth to their truck to bring the much-needed supplies. As fast as they emptied the boxes of mixes, she and Trinity sold them. The guys finished unloading and helped fill orders. They sold out again before one o'clock when the market closed.

Trinity passed out postcards with the store location and a code for a discount for their first purchase.

"You guys better rethink how much stock you're going to need when you open the store." Declan wiped the back of his hand over his brow.

Adria hugged Trinity and laughed. "We sold out!"

Trinity hugged her back, her own joy overflowing in her laughter. "After the first hour, we didn't even have any samples to give out." She stood back. "That was unreal."

Adria beamed. "I told you people want fast and easy but healthy and fresh food."

"You guys knocked this out of the park." Drake folded up the last portable table they brought. "You should think about doing the farmer's market even after you open. There's twenty miles between here and your shop. A lot of people might not want to make the drive, but stock up here instead."

Adria glanced at Trinity. "It's a good idea. We could even do other farmer's markets in other towns. Test the waters. See where the demand is highest and consider opening more stores."

"Maybe you guys can turn this into a franchise," Declan suggested, hefting up his side of the stacked tables with Drake.

She and Trinity had carried them one at a time this morning. The guys took all four at once.

"Or sell to a grocery store chain." Trinity had dreams of seeing their products mass distributed throughout the country from the stores they'd strategically place across the States to create the high-quality food products and deliver them to the stores.

"Let's start with our first store and see what happens from there."

"What about doing a food truck?" Declan asked. "You could take it to the state fair or a corporate party. Cook the food you sell right there in the truck and serve it. People can come to the store and buy it after the event."

Trinity held her hand out to Declan. "We should hire him."

"I'm a rancher. I'll stick with being your beef supplier."

"At this rate, we're going to need a bigger herd to keep up with demand." Drake kissed Adria before walking off with Declan to put the tables in the truck.

Trinity bumped shoulders with her. "Can you believe today?"

After seeing Juliana the other day and with Drake's surgery coming up, she'd needed something really good to happen. She had faith in Drake's surgeons, but still worried that something could go wrong. What if he didn't get the results he wanted? What if they made things worse?

"It's okay to celebrate, Adria. We can worry about Drake's surgery tomorrow."

"You're starting to read my mind."

"We've spent the last many weeks together working on *our* shop. You're dating my brother. I think it's safe to say one day soon, you'll be my sister by law, but I think of you as my sister in my heart already."

"Oh, Trinity, that's sweet. I feel the same."

"I thought I'd go to culinary school and work in a restaurant in a big city. You had this dream and changed my mind about what I wanted. We own our own place. And today we sold out!"

Adria needed to stop worrying about everyone else and take a little time for herself. She needed to celebrate these victories.

Drake and Declan returned.

"We found a bar around the corner. Drinks are on us. Let's celebrate," Drake coaxed with a huge smile.

Trinity hooked her arm through Declan's. "Not exactly the date of my dreams, but for this, you'll do."

Declan rolled his eyes. "Thanks."

Drake hugged Adria close to his side. "You're my favorite date."

In that moment, Adria wished for more days like this. Family. Friends. Good times with the ones she cared about and loved.

The kind of life Roxy and Sonya found with their cowboys. Now she had one of her own.

With Juliana almost home, she hoped her sister found the kind of peace and happiness in herself that she'd found here.

"Let's go." Declan steered Trinity down the sidewalk toward the bar around the corner.

Drake noticed she'd gone quiet. "Stop worrying. I'm going to be fine."

She couldn't stop the feeling of dread that came over her. "I don't want to lose you."

"It's not that serious. It'll be over before you know it and I'll be able to move better." He nuzzled his nose into her ear and whispered, "You think I set you on fire now, just wait until I can actually move my hip. We'll burn the place down to the ground."

She squeezed his arm. "Don't do this because you think I want it."

Declan and Trinity walked into the bar ahead of them.

Drake stopped her on the sidewalk out front. "I'm doing this because it will relieve the pain. It will allow me to ride better and do more around the ranch. As it is now, I can't help as much as Declan and Tate need me to."

"They understand your limitations, but that doesn't mean you're not helping them."

"I know that, but I want to be able to do more. I want to be able to crawl around with our kids and run after them when they get big."

She tilted her head and stared up at him. "You think about us having kids?"

He held her gaze, his eyes alight with dreams. "A house. Sunny running around after the babies. Yes. All of it." He tilted his head and studied her. "Don't you?"

She'd been so busy with the business and waiting for Juliana to come back that she hadn't planned past any of that. Hearing Drake talk about their future, she realized that's exactly what she wanted with him. "I want it all."

"Let's start with celebrating your success today." He held the door open.

He'd opened a world of possibilities. A life she never thought she'd have with a man. He wanted to give her everything. He wanted to do everything with her.

When she raised a glass with Trinity, Declan, and Drake, it was with a heart full of hope.

She wished Juliana was here to celebrate with her. But there would be so much more to come, and Juliana would be with her for all of it. Because when she thought of her life with Drake, she saw Juliana still by her side.

Their lives had always been intertwined. They always would be.

Juliana just needed to get better and come home.

Chapter Twenty-Four

Drake floated on the numbing drugs. His leg, hip, and back ached, but not with the piercing pain he remembered the last time he woke up after surgery. His cheek and jaw felt swollen, the skin tight. He reached up and touched the line of stitches. The plastic surgeon had done what he asked and repaired the wide scars, closing them up to minimize the jagged lines.

He had no idea what he'd look like when they healed but it had to be better than the quick job they'd done in the field. Then they'd rightly prioritized saving his leg over prettying up his face.

The door to his room opened and Adria walked in, his brothers and Trinity behind her.

"You're awake." Nothing sounded better or eased him more than Adria's sweet voice.

"Barely." He still felt groggy from the anesthesia but he felt clearer by the minute. Seeing Adria at his bedside helped.

"The doctor spoke to us after the surgery. He said it went better than expected."

The doctor had said the same to him when he woke up in recovery. With all the drugs, his mind fuzzy, he feared he'd imagined it.

Adria leaned down and gave him a soft kiss. "How are you feeling?"

"Sore." He looked down at his bandaged leg and wiggled his toes. They moved, but he could barely feel them. "My foot and toes are numb." That worried him.

Adria rubbed her hand up and down his arm. "The doctor said that might happen because of the swelling. It's normal. It should go away over the next day or two."

"You're sure?"

"Yes," she assured him, her hands tight on his arm.

He stared down the bed to his two brothers.

Declan patted his foot. "You'll be up and walking again before you know it."

Tate nodded. "They're so sure things went well, they've scheduled the physical therapist to come by tomorrow afternoon."

Drake felt better about that. "Okay. That's good."

"You can't stand being stuck in that bed, can you?" Trinity asked.

Drake shifted, trying not to let it show. "It's bringing back all kinds of bad memories."

Adria lowered the bar on the bed, rested her hip next to his, and held his hand. "You're not alone. We're here."

He fought off memories of the attack he survived and seeing his gruesome hip and leg bloody and fearing he'd lose it if he even survived. "I just want to go home with you."

Adria held his hand to her chest. Her I Love You tattoo facing him. God, how he needed her. "As soon as you can walk out of here again."

"I'm going to be on crutches for a week or so."

"And then you won't be," Declan pointed out. "Stop worrying. Enjoy the drugs and everyone fussing over you."

Drake took a breath to calm his anxiety and stared up at Adria. "When's my sponge bath?"

She laughed and it eased his mind and heart even more. "Later. When we're alone."

He turned to his family. "Get out."

Trinity rolled her eyes. "He's going to be just fine. His mind is already on sleeping with my best friend." She patted his uninjured thigh. "I'm glad you're feeling better. I'm leaving you in Adria's capable hands. I'm heading back to the store to check on our new employees. If they followed directions and kept up with the pace, they should be just about done with what I left them." Trinity kissed him goodbye on the head. "Be good. Follow the doctor's orders."

"I will. Thanks for hanging out during the surgery. I know you're busy."

She patted his leg again. "Never too busy for you." Trinity headed for the door.

"Don't forget to stop by the printer and pick up the labels and packaging stickers," Adria called.

"I'll take care of work. You take care of him." With that, Trinity left the room as a nurse came in to fiddle with his IV and check the dressing on his leg.

"I'll be back with an ice pack for your face," the nurse said before she left.

He looked up at Adria. "Does it look really bad?"

She shook her head. "It's red and bruised right now. In a few days, it'll be markedly improved."

"Those were the doctor's words, weren't they?"

She gave him a placating smile. "Yes. But it's true, Drake."

"She liked you when you were mean and surly. I don't think a few scars are going to put her off," Tate pointed out.

Drake knew that, but he worried in trying to fix things he'd made them worse. He hadn't gotten a chance to see the doc's handiwork yet.

Adria took a compact from her purse and held it up in front of him.

It took him a second to look in the mirror. When he did, he was surprised by what he saw. "It's not that bad."

"We would have told you if it was," Declan pointed out. "You've gotten a lot better over the last month, Drake. It took time for you to come this far. Give your body time to heal again. You'll see—it will be better."

Tate slapped his hand on Declan's shoulder. "Time to head home and feed the critters."

"Don't forget to give Sunny his apple treat." He'd been reluctant to keep the puppy Jamie foisted on him, but now, Sunny had his heart. He loved the dog and wished Adria could sneak him into his hospital room.

"I won't," Tate promised.

"You have to make him sit and lie down first."

"I will. He's getting good at those."

Pride lit Drake's heart. "Training and discipline."

"Exercise some discipline and stay in this bed until they tell you, you can get up." Declan hugged him first.

Tate came next.

And moments later, he was alone with Adria. "I don't like the numbness in my leg and other parts," he confessed, because he could tell her anything.

"Seriously, Drake, you've been out of surgery for like an hour. Give it at least four before you start worrying."

"Only if you promise to help me make sure everything is working properly."

She leaned down and kissed him. "I promise, but not until you are fully recovered."

He leaned up and kissed her until the nurse cleared her throat and handed him the ice pack for his face.

Adria blushed and smiled down at him. "Be good."

"You know I'm better than good. As soon as I get out of here, I'll show you."

The nurse left with a chuckle.

Adria rolled her eyes, but she got it. Things had been going so well between him and Adria, he didn't want anything to come between them.

"Juliana is being released the day after tomorrow."

"So we're both coming home at the same time?"

She nodded. "I know we talked about her staying in the apartment over the shop."

"I take it you haven't had time to get that place in order."

"Not really. And I'd like Jules with me for a few days while she gets used to being out and free again."

"She wasn't in jail," he pointed out.

"They had a structure there that she wasn't used to going in but has learned to live by since she's been there. I want to give her some of that when she gets out."

He didn't like that they'd be apart for a few days, but he understood what she was trying to do for Juliana. "I'll miss having you next to me at night, but I understand you want to be with your sister."

"I'm sorry it comes at such a bad time. You need me right now, too."

He pressed her hand to his chest. "I always need you, but I know how important Juliana is to you. You've missed her. You want to spend time with her. I think it'll be good for you to get a gauge on just how well she's doing now."

"I'm worried. You said Chase stayed for sixty days. Juliana's only done thirty. Maybe she needs more time."

"You barely got her to stay that long. She agreed to weekly appointments with the counselor. Once she's home and you spend time with her, you'll know if she needs more." He rubbed his thumb over her hand. "Maybe she'll surprise you."

"I hope so."

He fell asleep thinking the same thing, because he didn't want anything, especially Adria's sister, to take her away from him and the life they were building together.

Chapter Twenty-Five

Adria set a plate in front of Juliana, who sat at the breakfast bar. She couldn't believe her sister was out of rehab, staying at the cabin with her, and looking so good.

"You didn't have to go through all this trouble."

"I wanted to do something nice for you." Which meant making Juliana her favorite mac and cheese with bacon and chives, fried chicken thighs, and broccoli with garlic butter.

Juliana took a bite of the cheesy noodles, hummed with satisfaction, but her eyes filled with remorse. "I'm the one who should do something nice for you." Juliana reached across the counter. Adria took her hand. "You saved my life."

Adria's heart pounded with the memory. If she'd come home from that rotten date even a few minutes later . . . Adria didn't want to think about it. "I can't live without you. So don't do that to me again."

Juliana squeezed her hand. "I take things too far. I do things without thinking. I try to make myself believe it's all for fun, but deep down I know I'm punishing myself. I thought I deserved to feel bad and worse." Juliana had lost the defensive edge she'd had at the rehab center. She was back to being Adria's sweet, loving sister, and it made her so happy.

Adria kept hold of Juliana's hand and walked around the counter to her side and looked her in the eye. "I know what that feels like." She brushed Juliana's hair back, needing the sweet contact. "You deserve to be happy. Just like I deserve to be happy. It took me a long time to get there. I know you will, too."

Juliana's gaze drifted to the counter. "Are you happy here?"

Adria rubbed her hand over Juliana's back, hoping to ease the sting. "Yes. I am. I thought Trinity and I would open the store in Las Vegas. But I love it here. It's an up-and-coming little town, close to Billings. I love the beautiful landscape, the weather, riding and working here. Trinity and I are great friends and business partners. It's the perfect fit."

Juliana stuffed another bite of mac and cheese in her mouth, chewed, then pointed the fork at her. "Nowhere in there did you mention Drake."

Adria went back around the counter and retrieved her plate, then took her seat next to Juliana, her mind full of happy memories of her time with Drake and her heart warm with love for him.

"Stalling?" Juliana asked. "Why?"

"Because I know Roxy and Sonya moving away from the Ranch is part of what set you off. They found love and made a life here instead of coming home." Adria had missed them, but she was happy for her sisters.

Juliana took it as abandonment. Just like Adria moving here.

"Is that what you found here? Love? A new home?"

Adria met Juliana's intense gaze and gave her the truth. "Yes."

Despite being initially upset, Juliana's smile was real and genuine. "I'm happy for you, sis. I mean that. I'm glad you found a way to put what happened behind you and move on with a guy who looks at you like you're everything he ever wanted." Juliana really had used her time at rehab to unpack the past and put it away.

Drake made Adria feel like she mattered more than anything in his world. "He changed my life. I don't know that any other man could have, or would have, done what he did for me."

Juliana raised an eyebrow and teased, "And what exactly was that?"

Adria stuck to a truth that had really changed her life. "He made me feel like a woman, not that scared little girl."

Juliana shifted uncomfortably, not wanting to talk about what happened again. "And so you're over it?"

She'd never truly be over it. "It doesn't rule my life anymore. It doesn't dictate how I look at a man anymore. It's not my every other thought. It's a memory." She squeezed her sister's hand. "Make it a memory, Juliana. It happened. It's done. Leave it alone. Stop looking at it and breathing life into it every time you do. Let it fade with every new experience and memory you make. Fill yourself up with so many happy, good things, you can't even remember that was ever part of you."

"How do you do it?"

"I choose, Jules. That ugly man took away my choices. I won't let him or anyone else do that to me again." It reminded her of how she took a chance, chose to take control of her sexual future, trusted in Drake, and herself, and made that deal that turned into the best choice of her life.

"I guess that's what I'm facing right now, to choose each and every day to live my life in a better way." Juliana sighed. "I did see how I was falling into Mom's patterns. I just couldn't seem to stop. It scared me sometimes, because I liked it a little too much."

"Find something else that excites you. You were always into drawing." Adria tugged down the shoulder of her shirt and showed off her tattoo. "We are all wearing your art."

Jules's shy smile surprised Adria. Her confident sister wasn't so confident when it came to what she considered just doodles. But to Adria, Roxy, and Sonya they looked like so much more. "When college seemed pointless. Math. English. All the rest. I didn't know what to do with all that. I drew pictures on my homework all the time. My teachers started commenting more on it than my poor grades."

Adria perked up. "Are you saying you want to go to art school?"

"I'm thinking about it. Soon. I need a minute to adjust right now." Juliana stuffed a huge piece of chicken in her mouth, set down her fork, and pulled a notebook out of her bag hanging on the back of her chair. "In rehab, they encouraged us to journal." Juliana flipped open the book. Adria marveled at page after page of Juliana's artwork. The view from her bedroom window. A gorgeous cherry tree in bloom. The Montana mountains at sunset.

Two hearts nestled up against each other like they were snuggling.

Adria tapped her finger on it. "I love this."

"I'm thinking of getting it as a tattoo."

Adria traced the lines with her finger. "I'll get it, too."

"You and me. We are forever connected."

Adria put her hand on Juliana's knee. "Yes, we are, even if we do different things." Adria tapped her finger on the notebook. "You can do this. You just have to want it and go after it with your whole heart, Jules."

"Like you did with Drake."

She'd been audacious and so unlike herself. She'd been afraid, but found her courage and leaped anyway. "I don't know what you call what I did with Drake."

"You wanted him. You went after him."

Adria shook her head. "It wasn't like that. I wanted him to see what I saw in him. He wasn't broken. I wanted to prove to myself that I wasn't either." Putting the focus on Drake in that moment had helped her to see the comparison but not make it all about her issues.

Juliana went quiet for a moment and stared at her half-eaten plate of food. "Do you think there's something broken inside me?" Those worried, whispered words hurt Adria's heart.

Adria shook her head. "No. There is nothing wrong with you."

"Addiction . . . it's hereditary. Maybe I got that gene and you didn't."

"We're identical. Exact same DNA. It's about choices, Jules."

Juliana looked away. "I make all the wrong ones."

"That's not true. We all make mistakes. We learn from them. Live today the best you can. And know that you're not alone. I'm here for you. Roxy and Sonya are here for you. Even Mom called regularly for an update."

"Yeah, but she didn't leave the Ranch to visit me." Disappointment filled Juliana's words, because some kinds of hope were eternal. Like wanting your mother to be there for you when you hurt. And Juliana could have benefited from an open and deep conversation with their mom about the past.

If only Mom were capable of such a thing.

Maybe she didn't give Mom enough credit. But history didn't bode well for her.

Adria spent her whole life wishing Mom was like the loving, kind, do-anything-for-their-children type she saw on TV. "Mom likes her life at Wild Rose." She didn't know what else to say. They'd been on their own since they were kids. Some moms weren't equipped to give their kids what they needed.

"I can't go back there. Not after I . . ." Juliana shook her head, her eyes downcast.

Juliana's wild nights included a few nights sneaking in and working at the Wild Rose Ranch to earn money to buy more drugs. And to punish herself for not saving Adria from her fate all those years ago.

Adria didn't blame her sister or judge her for what she'd done. Pain and hurt made people do strange and harmful things.

She squeezed Juliana's hand. "You don't have to go back. You can do anything you want."

"Thanks to Roxy and her deep pockets." Juliana stabbed a broccoli spear. "I don't know how I'll repay her."

"Stay clean and sober and be happy. That's all we want for you, Jules."

"I'm working on it."

They finished the rest of their meal, both of them lost in their thoughts about the conversation and what came next.

"Is Trinity okay with me coming to work at the shop?"

"Yes. We need the help." She pressed her hand to her fluttering belly. "I can't believe we open tomorrow." After the unexpected success at the farmer's market, they'd spent the last few days working their asses off to increase their inventory and make sure the online ordering system was up and running without any glitches.

"You should be excited."

"I am, but I'm also worried."

"You shouldn't be. You're an amazing chef." Juliana finished off the last of her fried chicken.

"I know working at the shop isn't what you want, but—"

"I want to see the store and be a part of what you built, sis." Juliana sighed and admitted, "Being with you makes things easier."

"Okay. Good. Because I want you with me right now, too. That's why I asked you to stay here and not move into the apartment above the store just yet."

"I don't know how long I'm staying."

"Take all the time you need."

"Does Drake mind sharing you with me?" Juliana's jealousy was showing, but Adria didn't mind. She hoped Juliana would settle in and see that Drake wasn't trying to take her away.

"Drake loves his siblings. He understands that you need me right now, and that I wanted to be with you tonight." True, but she kept it to herself that Drake had wanted her to come up to the house later tonight. They enjoyed their evenings together and had gotten used to sleeping with each other. She had to admit, she missed him. She wanted to share every part of her life with him and not split her time between Juliana and him.

But tonight was for her and Juliana to reconnect.

Though she did hope Drake was taking it easy and not overtaxing his leg. He needed to ice it. And rest. Something Drake had a hard time doing.

They cleaned up the dinner dishes and settled into bed with Adria's laptop, and their favorite childhood movie, *Aladdin*. Robin Williams as the Genie still made them laugh. Juliana snuggled close and rested her head on Adria's shoulder. She held Jules close, so grateful to have her home, safe and sound. The echo of fear she felt the night she almost lost her rippled through her, but she held on to Jules and swore that nothing like that would ever happen again, not if she had anything to say about it.

She loved Jules.

She needed her.

They'd grow old together.

And tomorrow when they opened the shop, it would be the first day of the next part of both their lives.

Chapter Twenty-Six

Adria voided another purchase and reset the register after showing Juliana how to use it. "Does that make sense?"

Juliana nodded. "It's easy enough. The computer does most of the work once I scan the bar code."

"Exactly. So you're okay working the register for those who want to shop and go?"

"I got it. If something goes wrong, I'll call you over."

"Okay. Trinity and I will work the other counter. If you need help—"

"I got this," Juliana assured her, a touch of resentment in her tone for being questioned.

Adria put her hand on her shoulder. "It's not you. I'm nervous."

Juliana hugged her. "Don't be." She stepped back and pointed to the door where customers were already lining up. "Once you open those doors and everyone smells this place, they'll buy everything in sight."

The hot food counter was filled with delicious takeout. The mac and cheese Juliana loved last night. Chicken broccoli fettucine Alfredo. Spaghetti. Meat loaf. Side dishes. Yummy desserts. The store looked exactly as she'd pictured it would with small vases of fresh flowers on the tables they'd set up by the windows. The shelves Declan, Tate, and Drake set up were stocked to capacity, along with the refrigerated cabinets. The guys helped box up and return the wrong chairs, then put together the new ones that arrived yesterday and set them around the wood tables.

Trinity walked over, checked her watch, then pressed her hand to her belly. "It's time."

"Let's open."

Juliana tapped her shoulder. "Check out who's at the front of the line."

Drake, Declan, and Tate stood in front of the double glass doors. Drake held a huge bouquet of red roses. Declan held another bouquet of mixed flowers.

Trinity took Adria's hand. "They're amazing."

They walked to the doors together. Trinity glanced over at her. They each reached for the sign hanging on the door and flipped it to Open. Adria turned the key in the lock and they both took a door handle and opened the doors wide.

Drake smiled. "Congratulations." He handed Adria the bouquet of roses, then kissed her. "I'm so proud of you."

Declan handed his bundle of mixed flowers over to Trinity. "You did it, sis." He kissed her cheek, then moved inside, so Tate could give Trinity a peck on the forehead, then move out of the way for their customers.

"Welcome," she and Trinity called out as people streamed in, helping themselves to the free samples they'd put out on the tables.

Drake whispered in her ear, "I missed you last night."

She leaned into him. "I missed you, too."

"How is Juliana?"

She appreciated that he asked and cared. "She's settling in and finding her footing."

"Good." Drake watched the customers milling around and checking out the shelves and filling their shopping baskets. "Listen, I wish I could stay for a while . . ."

She touched his arm. "I'm so glad you came. I know you've got physical therapy."

"I want to get rid of this cane again." He'd ditched the crutches after only a couple of days. Although the surgery was successful, it set him back a bit. But every day he got a little better and had settled his mind to the fact it would take time to heal and build his strength again.

She put her hand on his face. "The swelling is gone and the scar is fading." The plastic surgeon had delivered and minimized the scars on Drake's face. It didn't matter to her as much as it did to Drake. "You can actually bend at the hip now and lift your leg up. That's progress, Drake. It's only a matter of time before you can move even better."

He slipped his hand beneath her hair and held her head. "Don't worry about me, sweetheart. Not today. Enjoy this." He tilted his head toward the crowd at the back of the shop. "You did this. You're a success."

"If I want to keep it that way, I better get to work."

Drake leaned down and kissed her softly, then stared into her eyes. "I *really* missed you last night." He paused. "I'd like to talk about our living arrangements."

It did her heart good to know he wanted her with him all the time. "Juliana needs me right now, but eventually she'll want her own space."

"I know it's selfish, but I need you, too. And I don't mean the next few days or weeks. I'm talking about something more permanent."

She tilted her head, completely surprised, but also not, because they'd spent every day together since she made that deal with him. "Um, what are we talking about?"

"I think you know, but"—he checked his watch—"I don't have time to get into it right now. This isn't the time or place, but we need to talk about it." With that, he kissed her again, then said, "Knock 'em dead today. I'll see you tonight." He gave her a look that made it clear he wouldn't take no or any excuse not to see him tonight, then limped out.

It took her a second to process his abrupt departure. She stepped out onto the sidewalk and yelled down the street to where he'd parked his truck. "Thank you for the roses!"

"Those are just for you. I prefer benefiting from buying you pretty things."

He did so love to remove the underwear and nighties from her body— the ones he'd bought to replace what he'd ruined.

He winked, then climbed into the truck. As he drove away, he honked and waved to her. His easy, open smile made her stomach flutter and her heart warm.

How far they'd come.

Especially Drake. He had way more good days now than bad.

"Hey, I know you love my brother and all, but we've got customers." Trinity's teasing tone broke into her thoughts of Drake and plans for their future.

She turned to Trinity and beamed her a smile. "We have customers."

Trinity's smile amped up several notches. "Yes, we do."

As their workday started, so did the future they'd spent months dreaming about and setting up. Over the course of the day, the packed shelves thinned. Customers consumed all the samples they put out. As soon as one plate was finished, they'd have to set out another, with their customers waiting at the hot food counter for more food to come out of the ovens.

By the time Adria flipped the sign on the front door to Closed and locked up, they were all exhausted. Trinity disappeared in the back while Adria helped Juliana cash out her register. Pedro and Mike, the two guys Trinity hired to work in the kitchen, came out of the back with their dinner. Perks of the job. Susan, their other cashier and counter worker, had already finished her short shift and gone home.

Adria marveled that they had employees to pay and customers who wiped out their stock at a steady pace. This was the grand opening— things would slow down to a more even pace over the next days and weeks once the novelty wore off. But if they had half the customers they did today on a daily basis, they'd be busy and prosperous for a long time to come.

The customer feedback had been great. People loved the idea of good, wholesome food made with quality ingredients that was ready-made and just needed to be baked in the oven or dumped in a pan and heated.

A few customers had even used the online ordering system. Pedro had put together the orders, left them in the fridge behind Juliana's checkout station, and people had come in and picked up their food and left, happy about the ease of the service.

It all worked.

Yes, they needed to make some improvements and simply get used to the processes they put in place, but Adria couldn't be happier about how the day went. She had real hope they could make this business work and prosper.

Trinity came out of the back with a tray filled with glasses of champagne. She set them on the table in front of Pedro and Mike. "Come. Take a glass," she called to Adria and Juliana.

Juliana eyed her, unsure what to do.

Trinity caught the look. "This one is ginger ale." Trinity handed the glass to Juliana.

Adria took one of the champagnes. "I can't believe you did this."

Trinity held up her glass. "To *Almost Homemade* and my amazing business partner. I couldn't have done this without you. I wouldn't have wanted to. To many more days like today." Trinity clinked her glass to Adria's. Before they drank, she said, "To *Almost Homemade*."

"*Almost Homemade*," everyone said in unison, then drank to their success.

Adria couldn't remember ever feeling this good about anything and hoped this feeling stayed with her. Drake told her he was proud of her this morning. She appreciated it, but it was a much deeper feeling to be proud of herself. It filled her up and made all the things she hoped to have for her future seem even more possible. Like anything could happen.

Juliana clinked her glass. "You did it."

"You can do it, too." Adria believed that with her whole heart. She wanted Juliana to feel the way she felt right now. "I can't wait to celebrate at your gallery opening."

Juliana's eyes lit up and a soft smile tilted her lips.

Adria hoped Juliana believed that kind of amazing dream could come true. Adria saw it. She wanted it for Juliana.

All Juliana had to do was believe it, too. If she worked hard, she could have it.

Just like how Adria had opened *Almost Homemade*.

Just like she'd pushed herself to open her heart and found something amazing with Drake.

They'd put their dark past behind them. She wanted both of them to have the bright and happy futures they deserved.

Chapter Twenty-Seven

Drake limped into the stables looking for Declan. After physical therapy, his leg ached. He normally went up to the house to ice his hip and eat a late lunch, but Declan texted that they needed to talk. For whatever reason, that sounded ominous. He didn't know why, but things had been going so well for him lately, in the back of his mind he was waiting for the other shoe to drop.

Several horses, including Thor, poked their heads out of their stalls. He gave each one a pat as he made his way down the alleyway toward the office at the back. Declan sat behind the desk, reading glasses perched on his nose, a stack of paperwork in front of him.

"Hey, man. You wanted to talk." Drake took the seat in front of the desk and leaned his cane against the old wood chair arm.

Declan pulled his glasses off and tossed them on top of the paperwork. He took a minute to look at the stacks of papers and folders on the desk before he met Drake's steady gaze. "I need help."

"Sure thing. What do you want me to do?"

Declan shook his head. "That's not what I mean. After you joined the military, Dad expected me to pick up the slack."

Drake ran his hand over his head. He and Declan had never really talked about how things went down back in the day. He'd blindsided his family. He'd always loved life on the ranch, but he'd wanted something more. He'd wanted to serve his country, see something of the world, and find himself. Well, he'd done all three, but it hadn't turned out exactly as he hoped. He'd found himself, and then he'd discovered the limits of his body and mind. For all that he'd learned about what he didn't want his life to be, he discovered what really mattered.

"I know that wasn't fair."

"We always knew growing up that we were expected to help run the ranch. I just never thought I'd be the one responsible for carrying on the business and taking care of the land on my own."

"You're not alone. Tate and I are here to help."

"With the chores and the herd, but I'm the one who does everything else, including making the decisions. While I'm glad to have you home and finally doing well, it's clear the ranch isn't your priority."

"I've been trying to step up and help out more and more as I'm able."

Declan held up his hand. "I appreciate it. I really do. I'm happy that the three of us are working together again. I hope that doesn't change. But I want to ask you something, and I'd like you to be honest. Do you want to work here full-time?"

Drake hadn't expected the question. He'd been trying to focus on getting better, but in the back of his mind he'd been thinking about what came next. As the oldest, Drake had been expected to take over the ranch. Instead, he'd rebelled and gone another way.

He hadn't cared what his parents thought and never considered what it meant for Declan when he had to step up in his place.

"There's no right or wrong answer here, Drake. I'm asking what you want to do with the rest of your life."

Still, Drake felt obliged to acknowledge overlooking and dismissing any of Declan's resentments. "I never asked you before I left if you wanted to take over this place."

Declan shrugged that off. "Neither did Dad. It's just the way it went." Declan's nonchalance didn't cover his underlying resentment.

"I'm sorry, Declan. That wasn't fair."

"Fair or not, I run the ranch now. Unless you plan to take over." Declan sounded conflicted by which one of those he really wanted.

Drake would never take the job from Declan. He believed in his brother. The ranch had prospered under his watch.

"I have no intention of taking your place here. I've simply been trying to do what I can to help. I know it's not much. Not yet, but I'm working on getting better. I get stronger all the time."

Declan shook his head. "That's not what I'm concerned about. I'm happy you're making progress, of course, but what I'm trying to get at is—are you planning on working the ranch the rest of your life? Or, down the road, do you see yourself doing something else?"

Drake took a breath and thought about the one thing he knew for sure was in his future. Adria. While he loved working with his brothers on the ranch, he still wanted something different. And thanks to Adria, he'd found something else that appealed to him. "The truth is, I've been looking into buying my own business."

Surprise lit Declan's eyes. "Really? Doing what?"

"Security systems. I really enjoyed planning and installing the one at Adria and Trinity's shop. I'm good with the electronics and rigging everything up. The guy I bought the system from talked about retiring soon. He's got three good guys working for him. I've been looking at my finances, considering my options, and I'm thinking about making him an offer."

"Okay. Then, that makes this easier."

"What's that?"

"I'm going to hire someone full-time."

That stung. "I haven't bought the business yet, nor am I going to stop helping out around here."

"That's great. We always need the help, but I need someone who is dedicated to doing the job long-term." Declan held up his hand again. "That's not a dig at you. This is your home and ranch, too. That will never change. Your place is here, and there's work as long as you want it. But Tate and I needed help, even if you had decided to work with us full-time. If we're going to be supplying beef to the shop, we need to run more cattle. Trinity even asked about us getting some chickens."

News to him, but good business for the ranch.

He liked the idea of keeping business in the family.

Drake still felt the sting of not living up to his obligations. He didn't want to leave his brothers hanging.

"Drake, seriously, hiring on someone new has been on the back burner for a while. I'm spread too thin. I spend all my time working this place. The days are flying by and blend from one to the next. If I'm honest, it's because of you that I'm moving on this now." Declan held up his hand again. "Not because you can't help out the way I need, but because of seeing you with Adria. I barely have time to eat three meals a day, let alone head into town for a date. And being out here all the time, who would I meet?"

"Spend some more time at *Almost Homemade*. There were lots of good-looking women coming and going from that place."

"I'll tell Adria you said so." Declan's teasing smile annoyed Drake.

"Please don't. I barely see her anymore as it is."

"You mean that wasn't her sneaking into your room last night?" Declan's teasing tone made Drake's face turn a bit warm.

"Between the shop and her sister, we barely get a few hours together."

"I thought Juliana planned to move into the apartment above the shop soon."

"It's only been like ten days since the shop opened. They've been overrun with customers and the demand for their products keeps growing. They've signed up to do two other farmer's markets in the state, too. Adria hasn't had time to really work on setting up the apartment aside from having the contractor fix up the kitchen and bathroom. It's got a new bed, but nothing else."

"She got the most important thing for the two of you."

"That place is way too small for the two of us. The cabin is good for now, but I'm thinking about hiring a contractor to expand it by a room or two."

"Planning on adding on to you and Adria?"

It took Drake a second to catch on to Declan's meaning.

"Not anytime soon." But he wanted kids. He wanted everything with Adria.

Declan's mouth dropped open. "But someday? You're thinking about marrying her?"

"I can't see a single day ahead of me without her in it."

"Damn, man. I knew something sparked between you, but after Melanie, I thought you'd take your time or shy away from asking another woman to marry you."

"She's not any woman. She's *the* woman."

Declan sat back in his seat. "Wow. Okay. Congrats. I hope it all works out this time." Declan's sincerity touched him.

"It will." Because this time was different. *He* was different. If she wasn't ready now, he'd wait. If there was something she needed, he'd give it to her. He'd say or do whatever it took to make her happy and want to stay with him.

They had something special. They liked being with each other. And he'd never found it easier to open up and share everything with anyone.

Having her there in the hospital after his surgery showed how much she cared and supported him. She encouraged him every day with his physical therapy and working with Dr. Porter and Jamie to let go of the past.

He hoped he gave back to her as much as she gave to him.

"Hire some people to help out here. Find some free time for yourself. I'll keep pitching in while I work on turning my plans into reality. Thanks for understanding that I love this place, but I need something that doesn't wear on my body."

Declan rolled his shoulders and grinned. "I totally get it."

"I also want to be there for Adria while she helps Juliana get back on her feet."

Declan's smile faded. "How is Juliana doing?"

"Really good. Adria says she's enjoying working at the shop. The two of them have repaired the rift between them."

"Neither of them said what happened."

Drake didn't want to talk about Adria's horrible past, what happened to her, and how it affected her and Juliana. "They had a rough childhood. They both dealt with it in their own way. Juliana had a more difficult time putting it behind her than Adria did, though Adria had a hell of a lot more reason to fall apart. Juliana harbored a lot of guilt. It ate away at her."

"I guess she tried to numb it away."

"Believe me, that doesn't work. You only wake up hung over and hurting even more and you still have your shit and more to deal with because you've continued to hurt the ones around you."

Declan nodded. "You'd know that better than me, but yeah, I get it."

Drake didn't want to dredge up his problems. He'd put a lot of his stuff to rest and he wanted to keep it that way. "Juliana wants to hang out with Adria for a while."

"They've got a really close connection."

Drake didn't need the reminder. He saw it in the way they talked to each other, the way they stood close, finished each other's sentences, and anticipated the other in so many ways. He hated to admit it, but he sometimes felt jealous. He wanted that with Adria. He wanted to be the only one who knew her like that. They had years to get there, just like she and Juliana had built their relationship over time. He didn't share her life experiences the way Juliana did, but they were making memories of their own. Maybe what they shared was different, but it was theirs.

He didn't know why he thought about losing her all the time. Probably the thing with Melanie and his quick-trigger temper, though that had dissipated over the last many weeks. And he never directed it at her.

The fear that he'd lose the one thing in his life that worked and made him happy, yeah, that one worried him a lot.

It shouldn't.

When they were together, everything seemed great.

But he missed her and the time they used to spend together. He loved having her in his bed every night, but she spent far more time with Juliana these days.

That close connection they shared made it hard for him to squeeze in between them and get Adria to focus on him.

"Is Juliana planning on staying here? Because if you and Adria take the cabin and Juliana moves into the house, then Tate's going to live out his fantasy, where the two of you are dating twins."

Drake winced, not liking that idea at all. "Juliana's as big a flirt as Tate is, but Adria said Juliana wants to go to art school. She can't do that anywhere around here." Adria made it clear she and Juliana wanted to find their own separate lives. If Juliana stayed, she'd work for Adria in a job she didn't really want. Their lives would remain intertwined. Juliana might grow to resent Adria for having what she wanted while Juliana didn't have what she wanted.

They both seemed to need to find their own success. A healthy choice for both of them.

And he didn't mind the idea of having Adria mostly to himself again. Guilt over that thought burned in his gut. He didn't want to interfere in the sisters' relationship; he just wanted to be a bigger part of it.

Which meant he needed to get to know Juliana better. If they were friends, did more things as a group, he'd feel like less of the outsider between them.

"There's a lot going on around this place. I just wanted to know where you stand and what you're planning so I can make decisions for the ranch accordingly."

"I'm sorry if it feels like it's all your responsibility. If you want me to focus on the ranch, I will."

"I want you to do what makes you happy."

"I want the same for you, and it seems like you're restless here."

"Sometimes you choose your life, other times it chooses you." Declan sounded resigned to that fact. "This is my life. I've accepted that. I want this ranch to continue succeeding and growing. To do that, I need help. So I'm going to put out some feelers, see if I can find someone qualified, or at least crazy enough to take on me and Tate, and move forward with my plans for this place."

"You know I'll keep pitching in, doing my part."

"Drake, man, after all you've been through, I'm cool with you focusing on what you need to do and building the life you want. For what it's worth, I like Adria. I like you with her. She makes you smile. For a while there, I thought I'd never see you do that again."

"Me, too. I can't tell you what it's like to be that messed up and in a dark place."

"I saw it. I hope I never see it again. So buy that business, marry Adria, make me an uncle, and just be happy, man."

Drake stood and went around the desk. Declan stood. Drake wrapped him in a bear hug. "Thanks for understanding and backing me up."

Declan smacked him on the back. "Always, bro."

Drake released his brother and walked toward the door, thinking about what they'd talked about and why Declan wanted help. "You know, Adria walked into my life when I least expected her. Maybe the same thing will happen to you."

Declan deserved to have everything he wanted. The ranch might be his domain now, but it didn't have to be his whole life.

Drake had learned these last many weeks that you didn't have to stay stuck. One thing could turn your world upside down or right it.

Chapter Twenty-Eight

Drake walked into *Almost Homemade* at closing and took in the near-empty counter and shelves. The refrigerators looked full, but he bet someone had restocked them recently. Trinity waved to him, pulled the till out of the cash register, and walked into the back.

Juliana met him in the middle of the shop with a smile. "Hey there, handsome. Can I get you something?"

"I'm good. Would you like to go out to dinner?"

She scrunched her lips. "Um, I'm not Adria. She's in the office."

"I know that. I mean the three of us. Since you've been here, I've barely spent any time with you and I thought we could get to know each other better."

Surprise and suspicion lit her eyes. "Really? I kind of thought you didn't like me."

Drake didn't like that one bit. "I'm not always the easiest person to be around. I'm trying to change that. You're important to Adria, which means you're important to me. I get that you two are close. I'm close with my siblings."

"But being twins is a different kind of close. Lately, I've dominated Adria's time, and you want her back."

He shook his head. "I want to be part of her life, which means a part of your life. I don't want to take her from you. I want to be included." He hoped she understood that he really meant that.

Juliana's eyes took on a far-off look, then she focused on him again. "I'm sorry it seems like we've excluded you. That's my fault. She talks about you all the time. She misses you when you're not around. Especially when I try to keep her all to myself. I'm not very good at sharing. Ask her. She'll tell you I won all the fights over toys."

"She's too kind and giving not to let you have your way."

"Exactly. So whenever she said she was headed up to see you, I'd say stay. I wanted to be with my sister. I'm not good when I'm alone. I'll work on that, because I see how happy she is when she's with you. She's never been serious about anyone. I don't want to hold on so tight she loses you and I crush her."

"Not going to happen because nothing is going to keep me from her." He wanted that and something else to be clear. "But I don't want to take her away from you. Let's be friends and share her."

"Deal."

He chuckled at the way she said that, so much like Adria and how she dealt with him.

Juliana held her arms wide. "Can we hug it out?"

"Why not." They shared a quick hug that solidified this next step in their relationship.

"Juliana, you've got to stop pretending to be me." Adria stood behind Juliana, frowning.

Drake took a huge step away from Juliana, so Adria didn't get the wrong idea.

"Drake knows it's me. We were just coming to an understanding."

"What's that?" Skepticism filled Adria's words and eyes.

"That we both love you and want you to be happy. And Drake's buying dinner tonight."

Adria looked to him, her eyes narrowed with suspicion. Probably because he'd complained about Juliana more than he accepted her. He wanted her to see that changed now. "What's going on?"

"I'm taking you and Juliana out to dinner tonight."

"Are you sure? Trinity can probably drop Juliana at the cabin if you'd rather it just be us."

He appreciated how hard she tried to give both of them her undivided attention. But she shouldn't have to do it all the time. "I invited Juliana so we could get to know each other better."

A bright smile finally bloomed on Adria's lips. "You did?"

He should have shown Adria sooner that he wanted to get to know Juliana, the person she loved most. "Yes. Grab your stuff. Tell Trinity to close up. Let's go."

Juliana gave Adria a disgruntled look. "Does he always order you around like this?"

"I issue a lot of my own." Adria smiled up at him. "Kiss me hello."

He had no trouble following that order. He hooked his hand around her waist, hauled her body up close to his, and kissed her like he hadn't seen her all day because he hadn't. He broke the kiss and stared into her laughing eyes. "Hello."

"Hi. I missed you today."

"Then stop leaving me alone in bed at the crack of dawn."

"You two are too cute."

Drake glanced over at Juliana. "Go get your stuff. Give me a minute with her."

Juliana smiled. "Sure thing."

Adria focused on him. "Are you upset?"

"No. I had a talk with Declan before I came here to see you."

Her head tilted the way it did and her eyes filled with concern. "Is everything okay?"

"Yes and no." He loosened his hold on her.

She put her hands on his chest and stared up at him, ready to listen and offer him whatever he needed.

"Declan wants to hire someone to help at the ranch."

She immediately tried to soothe his ego. "That doesn't mean he thinks you aren't contributing."

Leave it to her to understand that's where his mind went, too. "I know. He got the vibe that I'm not all in at the ranch and making it my life's work."

Adria's head did that tilt thing again. "Okay. So what are you thinking about doing?" She seemed open to whatever he decided.

Juliana came back with her purse and Adria's draped over her shoulder.

"We'll talk about it later. Right now, I want to have dinner with you and your sister."

Mike rushed out of the kitchen. "Jules, where are you off to?"

Juliana handed Adria her purse and smiled over her shoulder. "Out to dinner with my sister and her boyfriend."

Drake liked the sound of that, but wanted to talk to Adria about his plans for the future and a much more permanent place in her life.

"Sounds good. I'll come with you—that way you're not the third wheel."

Not exactly what Drake had in mind, but he left it to Juliana to make the decision.

Juliana hedged. "Um, Drake and I were kinda working on getting to know each other better."

Mike blew that off. "We'll have fun. He knows your sister. You're pretty much the same."

Juliana and Adria exchanged identical eye rolls. They may look alike and have a lot of the same mannerisms, but they weren't exactly the same in personality. They were individuals. They deserved to be treated that way.

Mike didn't get it and steamrolled right over Juliana's attempt to be nice about turning him down. Mike took her hand and pulled her toward the door.

Juliana gave Drake a half frown and shoulder shrug as she passed.

Adria took his arm. "Looks like it's the four of us."

Drake went with it, because he got to spend the evening with Adria and her sister no matter what. He'd get to know Juliana in a much more casual way. Maybe it was better to have another person to keep things fun and easy.

An hour later, he wanted to plant his fist in Mike's face. Four beers in, all the guy did was dominate the conversation and talk about fixing up old cars.

"How come you're not a mechanic?" Juliana seemed happy to go along with Mike's jovial conversation, then try to include him and Adria, though Mike only had eyes for Juliana.

"Like I said, I used to work on cars with my dad and grandpa. I love it for fun, but doing it day in and day out . . . I like working in the shop. It's easy."

In other words, Mike didn't like to work hard or have to think too much.

"I get bored easily. That's why I tend to move from job to job every few years. Keeps things interesting."

Drake tried to engage Juliana again. "What do you plan to do after art school?"

"Art school? What a waste of time. You'll never make any money." If Mike liked Juliana and wanted to be with her, disparaging what she loved didn't seem like a great way to make her like him.

Juliana ignored Mike and answered Drake. "I'm not sure yet, but I've been thinking about doing book illustrations or getting into graphic arts and working in advertising. I know, they're very different things, but that's what art school is for, to learn and discover what I really like and what other options there may be for me and the kind of drawing I like to do."

Drake nodded, thinking that a great idea. Both jobs seemed like good options and viable ways to make a living.

Mike set his hand on Juliana's back and squeezed her neck. "Working in advertising will probably pay the most. You should do that. Then you'll have the money to go out, party, and have fun."

Juliana winced at the force of Mike's . . . affection? "My partying days are behind me."

"No way. You look like you know how to have fun."

"Oh, I do." Juliana gave Mike a mischievous smile. "But I'm looking for some tamer fun these days."

Mike's hand landed on Juliana's thigh. "Tame is for when you're old. Now is the time to have some real fun." Mike had to be closing in on thirty, yet didn't have a plan for his life and career. When did life get serious in Mike's mind?

None of Drake's business.

Juliana played along, but he bet Mike wasn't someone she'd want to keep for the long haul. She may not have the healthy dose of practicality Adria had, but she wasn't looking to repeat her past mistakes either.

Mike looked like a mistake waiting to happen.

Drake's phone rang. He checked caller ID just in case it was one of his siblings. He picked up after the first ring for his buddy. "Chase. How are you?"

Adria and Juliana started a discussion of their favorite children's books and which had the best illustrations.

Mike rolled his eyes and downed the last of his fifth beer.

"Hey, Drake, I'm glad you picked up. I'm kind of in a bind. I need your help." Chase's frazzled voice set off Drake's internal alarm.

Ready to assist, he assured Chase, "Anything I can do. What do you need?"

"A place to crash and lay low for a couple of days. I'd go to a hotel, but . . ."

"No way." Drake wouldn't leave a friend hanging. "I've got you. Hold on." He touched Adria's arm to get her attention.

She smiled and tilted her head, giving him her full attention. "How's Chase?"

"I'm not sure. He needs a place to stay for a couple of days. Mind if he uses the apartment?"

"Not at all. In fact, I've stored some things up there that I could use both your help setting up to make the place nicer."

Drake smiled, knowing Adria had probably bought everything Juliana would need to live there if she wanted to. "Chase, meet me at *Almost Homemade* downtown." He rattled off the address. "It's Adria's place. She'll let you have the apartment upstairs, but it's going to cost you a little muscle to move some stuff for her."

"Sounds good. I really appreciate this. I know it's last minute and all . . ."

"No worries. I've got your back." He meant it. He hoped Chase took it to heart.

"When can you meet me there?"

Drake didn't want to make Chase wait if he needed a friendly ear to go along with a place to crash. "We're about ten minutes away. Let me pay the check, then we're out of here. See you soon." Drake ended the call and waved to their waitress.

Mike shook his head and squinted his eyes. "It's early."

Juliana touched Mike's arm. "His friend needs help." Juliana looked at him. "I like Chase. He's intense. And so gorgeous."

Mike gave her a disgruntled look.

Juliana ignored it. "How long is he staying?"

"A few days, maybe more. I'm not sure what's going on. He was supposed to go home to Wyoming yesterday." Drake pulled out his wallet and dropped his credit card on the bill for the waitress.

Mike didn't blink an eye or offer to help with the bill. Mike clamped his hand on Juliana's arm. "Stay with me. We'll keep this party going."

Juliana put her hand over Mike's and patted it. "We'll head back to *Almost Homemade* with Drake and Adria. I'll drive you home in Adria's car and she can go home with Drake after they let Chase into the apartment." Juliana looked to Adria to be sure that plan worked.

Adria nodded, because none of them wanted Mike driving in his condition.

Drake filled out the tip amount on the check the waitress brought back, signed it, then dropped the pen on top and stood with Adria.

Mike reluctantly got up and draped his arm over Juliana's shoulder and they walked ahead.

Adria leaned in close. "I think I need to reevaluate Mike's employment. I had no idea he was like this. He works hard, but he loses focus when Juliana is around. I knew he liked her and thought it was nothing, but he seems to think it's more than it is."

"Juliana seems okay with the attention."

"She's been around a lot of guys like Mike. But that's not what she needs now. She needs someone who supports her recovery."

"I'm not impressed with him. Talk to her. See what she thinks. Maybe tonight showed her he's not the kind of guy she wants in her life anymore and that will be the end of it."

Adria looked skeptical, but kept her thoughts to herself as she climbed into the truck and he closed the door for her.

The short drive back to the shop made it easier to ignore Mike's ongoing campaign to get Juliana to stay out later.

"We could go to this pub down on Park Street. They sometimes have live music."

"I'm taking you home." Juliana tried to hide her exasperation, but even she couldn't say the same thing over and over again without letting her irritation show. "We both have to be at work early."

"Stay with me. We can drive in together."

Drake wondered if Mike even remembered he and Adria were in the truck with them.

He stepped in because he couldn't leave Juliana to fend for herself against Mike's relentless requests. "It's Juliana's turn to feed the horses in the morning so Tate can make breakfast."

Juliana's eyes met his in the rearview mirror. He read the "Thank you" in them.

"She works for her sister. She works for you. Give her a break."

Juliana spoke up for herself. "I help out at the ranch because I'm staying in the cabin for free. And Adria pays me to work at the shop. It's fair." Juliana didn't give Mike a chance to reply. The second the truck stopped in front of the shop, she jumped out and met Adria on the sidewalk and took the keys to Adria's car. She turned and walked to the Jeep. "Come on. Let's go. I need to get some sleep."

Mike narrowed his gaze at her clipped tone.

Drake stood beside Adria and watched Mike weave his way to the passenger side and get in. He slammed the car door.

They watched it drive away, then Drake had to know . . . "What did she say to you after she got out of the truck?"

"'I'll trade you Chase for Mike and a million dollars.'"

Drake busted up laughing. "I like your sister."

"I'm glad." She put her hand on his chest. "Thank you for tonight. It means a lot that you wanted to spend time with her."

"I finally figured out that our sisters spend more time with you than I do. I want to change that." He leaned down and kissed her.

Headlights swept over them as Chase drove into the lot and parked next to Drake's truck. He climbed out and pulled a duffel bag up on his shoulder. "Thanks for doing this."

Drake waved him over. "Not a problem. You remember Adria, right?"

Chase shook Adria's hand. "I appreciate the hospitality."

"Any friend of Drake's . . ." Adria unlocked the door and led them into the shop, through the kitchen, and up the stairs to the apartment.

At the top of the stairs, Drake glanced over his shoulder. "Why didn't you go home?"

"Long story. I'm not exactly welcome there right now."

Drake followed Adria into the apartment and stopped short when he saw the changes. "Wow. I didn't know you'd cleaned this place up this much."

Adria looked around. "I've spent several of my lunch breaks buying furniture and other stuff for up here and fixing it up."

Chase glanced at the queen mattresses. "All I need is a bed." He ran his hand over his head. "And some peace and quiet."

"You've got it tonight, but I'm not sure how quiet it will be tomorrow while the shop is open."

"In exchange for the bed, I'm happy to help out."

"Oh, that's not necessary. The shop is covered, but I could use both your help with a few things up here, if you don't mind."

Chase dropped his bag on the floor. "What do you need done?"

She pointed to the rolled-up rugs leaning against the wall. "Juliana and I got those up here, but they're really heavy and I'd like to roll them out. One in the living area, the other under the bed."

Drake and Chase did what she asked, shifting and moving the chair, sofa, and table she'd bought out of the way, rolling out the cream rug, and repositioning the furniture. Drake held the end of the white metal bed frame up so Chase could unroll the rug under it. He lifted the stained wood nightstand and set it back down on top of the navy-blue rug.

Adria stood back and looked around the open space. "It looks great." She ran into the bathroom and came back with a set of sheets for the bed. "There are towels in the linen cupboard in the bathroom. It's been completely gutted and redone. I think you'll find everything you need in there."

Drake helped her make the bed. "I can't believe you did all this on your lunch breaks."

"A little here. A little there. I'm only sorry I haven't gotten a TV yet."

"I've got my laptop and phone."

Adria beamed. "The Wi-Fi is all set up. The password is adriaandjules, all one word, no caps. There are sodas and iced teas in the fridge up here. Feel free to raid the kitchen and take whatever you want. There's a microwave to heat it up, dishes in the cupboard, utensils in the drawer."

"I'm good. I don't want to put you out any more than I already have."

"If I tell you there are brownies downstairs, would that change your mind?" Adria tried to tempt Chase.

"Maybe." Chase gave her a halfhearted smile.

"It's my business to feed people. Food makes everything better. Please help yourself. I really mean it."

"Don't hurt my girl's feelings by turning down her amazing food. Believe me, you won't regret it."

"I'll grab something to eat before I get some sleep."

Adria smiled and touched Chase's arm. "Make yourself at home." She handed Chase a spare set of keys and headed for the door. "I'll be downstairs. Take your time."

Drake appreciated that she gave him a moment alone with Chase. "Are you okay?"

Chase's eyes went from the door to him. "Yeah. I'm good. She's great. I'm happy for you."

"Thanks. Listen, if you're not adjusting to being out of rehab . . ."

Chase held up his hand. "It's nothing like that. My family is complicated. I planned to head straight home, but some shit went down, and I just need time to regroup and get my head straight before I face them again."

Drake wanted to believe him, but his gaze fell on the duffel bag and what could be in it.

"You can search it and me if it makes you feel better, but I'm not using. I've put that behind me. I swear it, Drake. I need you to believe me."

Drake looked his friend in the eyes, saw the pain and the need to have someone understand. "I believe you. You've got my number. Use it. Anytime." Drake gave Chase a hug and a slap on the back, then stepped back. "Take care of yourself."

"I'll start with the brownie. I don't want to hurt your girl's feelings."

"You will if you don't do what she says."

Chase's mouth tilted in a lopsided grin. "She's down there making me something right now, isn't she?"

Drake chuckled under his breath, because he knew she couldn't help herself. "Yes."

Chase slapped him on the shoulder. "You got lucky."

"Yes, I did."

"Don't let go of someone like that. I did. And I can tell you it sucks."

"You're not alone, Chase."

Chase planted his hands on his hips and hung his head. "I know, but sometimes it feels that way."

Drake tapped the back of his hand to Chase's chest to get his full attention. "That's when you call me. I've got your back. Always."

Chase nodded, and Drake figured that was as much as he was going to get out of Chase right now. Chase wasn't ready to talk about what was going on. The guy had a lot to deal with between rehab, the war, and whatever was going on back home.

Drake hoped he found the kind of peace Drake had, now that he'd turned a corner in his own recovery and had Adria in his life and a future that he never thought would be his because he should be dead.

After all they'd been through, he'd bet Chase felt the same way, too.

It wasn't easy to think of the rest of your life when you didn't plan to be here. Drake and Chase both should have died—more than once—and were living on borrowed time.

Drake found his way. Chase would, too, if he allowed himself to believe anything was possible.

Not so easy to do when you're living in the past. But Drake had a new future mapped out and it included the beautiful woman waiting for him downstairs.

Mike wasn't getting lucky tonight, but Drake planned to love Adria tonight and every night.

He thought about warning Chase that Juliana worked in the shop, but let it go. Juliana showed tonight that she wasn't the party girl she used to be. And although she showed an interest in Chase, she had her mind set on going to art school. And Chase needed to go home and face his demons. Drake didn't need to worry about them slipping up and getting into trouble.

Chapter Twenty-Nine

Adria woke up warm and happy in Drake's arms with her head on his chest. His fingers brushed up and down her arm, tracing the outline of her rose vine tattoo. "Juliana is the one who drew the original design. She and I have matching ones on our arms. Roxy's goes from her shoulder, across her back, to her hip. Sonya's twines around her hip and thigh."

"What made you guys get them?"

"Juliana wanted us all to have something the same. Something that tied us together. We grew up at the Wild Rose Ranch and lived with the stigma of that place. It is a part of us. In a way, that place saved us. We certainly saved each other. When we were teens, fed up with how people looked at us, Roxy decided we needed to make the name our own. So we got the tattoos and kicked ass at rodeos."

"You're a great rider."

"Roxy taught us all to barrel race. I loved the speed and danger. Roxy was the best, but the rest of us came in right behind her."

"And did people look at you differently?"

She laughed. "No. Most of those cowboys thought we were prostitutes. It didn't bother us. Much. We won. We showed them we could be something else."

"You proved it to yourselves."

"It helped. Roxy really needed to prove she wasn't her mother and was more like her father. Jules and I never wanted to be anything like our mom. Sonya is close to her mom. We all came from different circumstances but shared something most people can't understand, not unless you've lived it."

"Since you've been here, you haven't said anything about calling your mom."

"She likes to text. Avoids arguments and lectures. From me to her."

Drake's chuckle rumbled through his chest. "Do you have any plans to go back for a visit?"

She cocked up an eyebrow. "Why? Interested in visiting the Ranch?"

"No."

She didn't think so, but it made her smile to tease him.

"I wondered about your plans." He didn't drop the serious tone.

"For what?" She really didn't know where this was going.

"The rest of your life." The deadpan tone got her attention and made her stomach flutter with nerves.

She raised her head and set her chin on the back of her hand on his chest and looked up at him. "What are you talking about?"

He met her gaze, dead-on. "Me and you."

"And the rest of our lives."

He brushed his fingers through her hair. "I hope so."

"Me, too." Her happiness and excitement spread a smile across her face. "But where is this coming from all of a sudden? Is something wrong?" She searched his gaze for the answer.

"No. Sorry. I'm not saying this right." Normally direct, Drake actually evaded saying what he really meant.

She didn't like it. "Spill it, Drake."

"I'm thinking about buying a security business instead of working full-time on the ranch."

That unexpected revelation surprised her. "I think that's a great idea. You're better. You'll keep getting better, but the constant physical labor on the ranch will probably do more harm than good for your healing process. It might even set you back. Or make it so you don't heal as well as you should."

He stretched his leg. "I'm tired of being tired and sore all the time. I liked planning and setting up your security system."

He'd done an amazing job. It turned out better than she thought, even though she hadn't really put any consideration into what she needed in the first place. "I hope we never have to use it, but I'm glad we have it."

"I think I can take over the business and expand it with my knowledge and know-how from the military. I think customers will respect my military service and know they're working with someone they can trust to protect their property and safety."

"You don't need to sell me on the idea, Drake. I think you'd be great at it. You can use the shop as a reference for new business."

"Thanks. It's an established business, so I'm hoping customers won't mind the new ownership. But it's more than just getting your recommendation. I want you to know that I have plans for the future. A job. Security. Hopefully more money, so we can renovate the cabin or buy our own place in town if that's what you want."

Another surprise she didn't see coming. Not now anyway. "Really?"

"I'm tired of feeling like we're still sneaking into each other's beds. I want us to have our own place where we come home every night to each other."

She wanted that more than anything. "That sounds really good."

"Which one? The cabin or another place?"

"The cabin if you want to be close to your family and they don't need it, or maybe somewhere between here and town. A house with a few acres so we can still ride."

"I'll talk to the family about the cabin and their plans. Maybe Tate or Trinity wants it. I never really asked them. Declan should have the house since he runs the ranch."

"Maybe Tate will take the cabin. That way he and Declan have their own space but still work together."

Drake glanced at the clock. "We'll talk about it more later. Right now, you need to get to work and I need to head over to Rambling Range for my ride with Jamie."

She cocked up one eyebrow. "Should I be worried about your weekly dates with Jamie?"

"It's therapy. Of sorts. Besides, she's engaged and head over heels for her cowboy."

"Good, because you're mine."

He reached under her arms and dragged her up his body and kissed her. "I love it when you say things like that."

"I mean it." In all this time, they'd never said "I love you" to each other. Everyone saw it between them. They both knew it. They dived into their relationship but remained reserved when it came to declaring that to each other.

Some things were worth waiting for and taking your time.

She frowned at the clock. "I have to go. Trinity will be home early tonight. I'm closing with Juliana."

"Do you think she stayed with Mike last night?"

"She texted me when she got home ten minutes before us and said that Mike lives in a two-bedroom apartment with his mother." At nearly thirty. Not exactly the independent, I've-got-my-act-together guy Juliana needed in her life. "I don't think she'll be seeing him again outside of work."

"Thank God. I don't know if I can handle another double date all about cars."

Adria kissed his chin. "You were very sweet to invite my sister out to dinner. I appreciate the gesture and that you want to get to know her better."

Drake's gaze sharpened. "I do not want to know Mike better."

She brushed her fingers over the thinner scar lines that ran down his cheek and across his jaw. Maybe now they wouldn't remind Drake so much of what happened. Thinking about his service made her think of the others he served with. "I hope Chase had a good night."

"You left him with meat loaf, mac and cheese, and a brownie the size of Rhode Island and a brand-new bed. I think he had everything he needed. I'm pretty sure that first bite of meat loaf made him want to keep you."

That made her laugh again. "You're not worried about Trinity working alone with him there this morning?" They'd make a cute couple. She wanted her friend to be as happy as she was with Drake. But she didn't know if Chase's mental state now resembled Drake's when she first met him.

"Better Chase than Mike."

Adria poked him in the ribs and rolled out of bed. "You're bad."

"I'm right."

"You are, but poor Mike." She slipped out of the panties she'd slept in and stood next to the bed naked. Drake's gaze scanned her from head to toe and filled with heat. "Not now, cowboy, I've got to mosey."

Drake leaned up on his elbow, muscles flexing. "You're the boss. You can be a little late."

She stalled a second too long. He reached out, took her wrist, and pulled her down on top of him. She giggled and went willingly. She loved it when they were like this together. Since the beginning, their relationship had been easy. They enjoyed each other. They supported each other.

And thinking about a house on a little piece of land made her stomach flutter and her heart soar.

She pictured them there so easily. A simple, uncomplicated life filled with happiness.

Maybe her sisters weren't the only ones headed down the aisle soon.

Chapter Thirty

Another great day.

Adria racked them up with a sense that all the bad was behind her.

She hoped every day started off with her waking up in Drake's arms and that feeling of perfect contentment that stayed with her all day. She was where she was supposed to be. And with the man she loved.

The shop remained busy. Online lunch orders increased. The dinner rush wiped them out of several favorites. Everyone loved mac and cheese, but the demand for chicken pesto pasta with broccoli and kale surprised Adria and Trinity. Because of its success, they'd come up with a recipe for a similar vegetarian lasagna.

She thought the ready-made meal kits would appeal to a lot of people who were either too busy to cook or didn't have a lot of skill in the kitchen. She'd never imagined this kind of demand from the get-go.

Almost Homemade, her dream shop, was a success!

She wanted Juliana to have this same kind of accomplishment.

Adria glanced at the stack of art school printouts sitting on the passenger seat next to her purse. Juliana had done some research on her lunch breaks. Adria's heart swelled with pride and excitement for her sister. She was working hard to change her life and find a direction that made her happy.

Adria headed back to *Almost Homemade* after picking up the TV stand she bought earlier in the day at *Cute Clutter* for the apartment over the shop and picked up after closing. She spent her lunch browsing the store, trying not to be tempted by all the wonderful finds but imagining them in the home she and Drake would share.

She couldn't wait. The more she thought about their future together, the more she wanted it now.

Juliana was back at the shop finishing up closing for the night with Mike. Chase said he'd be happy to help Mike carry the console up to the apartment if she provided dinner again. She'd paid him up front with a tub of chili, a garden salad, and a thick slab of honey corn bread. Instead of thanking her, he'd asked her to dump Drake and marry him.

The memory made her smile. She liked Chase. He had the same lost and hurt look in his eyes she'd seen in Drake's. She hoped he found some peace and happiness the way Drake had with her.

Drake was so different now. Calm. Loving. Not so lost in the past and pain. He had his moments. PTSD didn't just vanish. But his nightmares had subsided and he hadn't blacked out again like he did when they first met. He wasn't so quick to anger anymore.

His anxiety sometimes got the better of him, but he used the tools he learned to calm and center himself.

Sunny helped with that, too.

It made her heart swell that she'd had a hand in making him happy.

She pulled around the building and parked the car with the back end toward the rear door. The overhead security light brightened the dark lot.

Thank you, Drake.

He'd done a great job making sure the building and perimeter were safe and secure. She appreciated it when she got out and didn't have to walk around in the dark back here where no one could see her from the street.

She grabbed her purse, slipped out of the car, and glanced up at the lights coming from the apartment windows. She'd call Chase down as soon as she made sure Mike and Juliana were done closing things up for the night.

An overwhelming sense of urgency came over her as she approached the door. Her heart raced and she couldn't take a breath.

Juliana!

She fumbled with her keys. Hands shaking, she unlocked the back door and ran through the kitchen to the front of the store where she heard a scuffle and shouting.

"Call a fucking ambulance. Stop stalling. Do it now!" The panic in Chase's voice chilled her heart.

"We have to get the fuck out of here." Mike's voice sounded high and desperate.

Adria's chest went tight. She couldn't breathe. The last time she felt this way . . . She dashed around the counter and out into the main part of the shop.

Chase leaned down and breathed into Juliana's mouth, rose up, then fell sideways onto his back. His eyes rolled back and he put his hand to his chest.

Mike paced back and forth next to Juliana's prone body, but stopped short when Chase went limp.

Adria rushed forward and dropped to her knees between Juliana and Chase. She looked from one to the other and back again, desperately hoping what she saw wasn't real, but knowing all too well that it was because she'd been here before with Juliana.

"No! No, no, no." She shook her head, trying to deny the obvious but seeing the devastating truth.

She dumped her purse on the floor, grabbed her phone, hit the speed dial that went straight to 911, hit the speaker button, and found the naloxone she still kept in her purse despite the fact she believed she'd never need to use it again.

"Nine-one-one, what is your emergency?"

"I have two people who have overdosed." Her hands shook so badly she had a hard time cracking open the ampoule. "I'm administering naloxone. I need an ambulance at *Almost Homemade*." She rattled off the address and used the first dose, hoping, praying she wasn't too late.

"Help is on the way. Are the patients breathing?"

Adria took in Juliana's blue lips and still body.

Mike paced behind her. "Fuck! This isn't happening."

Yes, it was. Again.

She didn't think her heart would survive this.

Adria checked Chase, didn't like what she saw, and administered the second dose.

"Ma'am, are the patients breathing?"

Adria couldn't—not right now. "Tell them to hurry." She curled up on the floor next to Juliana, held her close, buried her face in her sister's hair, let the tears fall, and prayed.

"No, no, no. No!" Mike ranted as he rushed one way and then the other in his pacing.

Red and blue lights swept the shop, but Adria didn't move. She held tight to Juliana, hoping the paramedics got here in time.

The officers banged on the locked front door.

Mike stopped in his tracks. "Fuck." He hesitated for another moment, but finally went to open it.

"What happened?" the arriving officer asked.

Mike scrambled to explain. "She had the heroin. She used it. Like ten seconds later, she passed out."

Adria hugged Juliana close, her tears too many to count, but managed to spit out the horrible truth. "Fentanyl." She avoided touching her sister's face because of the powdery residue dusting her nose and upper lip. Some of it coated her shirt, but Adria couldn't let her go.

"We've had six other overdoses in the last two days. There's a bad batch of heroin being distributed. Put your gloves on," one officer said to the other, knowing that getting it on their skin could cause them to absorb the deadly drug.

"What about him?" the officer asked Mike.

"He . . . I don't know. He OD'd, too."

The ambulance pulled in outside.

The officer crouched next to Juliana and looked down at Adria. "Let the paramedics check her out." His sympathetic tone undid her and she cried harder.

She wanted to hold on to her beautiful sister and never let her go. But she couldn't do that and reluctantly pushed herself up, stared down at Juliana, snatched her phone from the floor, and made the call she dreaded to make again.

"Adria, what's wrong?" Roxy asked.

This late at night, Roxy expected trouble. "Get Sonya. Meet me at the hospital. I need you."

"No. Not Juliana. Not again." Roxy's voice shook. "She was doing so well."

Adria couldn't speak the awful truth, so she simply pushed out the words for what she needed past her clogged throat. "Meet me there." She hung up, moved out of the paramedics' way so they could work, and made the second call she dreaded.

"Hey, sweetheart, I thought you'd be home by now."

Not even Drake's warm voice eased her shattered heart. "You need to call Chase's family, then meet me at the hospital. He and Juliana overdosed."

"What? No!" Rage filled that last word.

"I'm sorry." She couldn't say anything more. The paramedics had loaded her sister onto a gurney and were wheeling her out to the waiting ambulance. She needed to go with her.

The second set of paramedics took their time with Chase, who went in and out of consciousness.

"Miss, we need to get some information from you," the officer said and scooped up the scattered contents from her purse off the floor and put them back in the bag. She took her purse from the helpful cop and pointed at Mike. "Ask him what happened. I came in, saw Chase giving Juliana mouth-to-mouth before he collapsed, administered the naloxone, and called 911 because Mike wouldn't." She glared at Mike, wondering how much critical time passed while Mike freaked out, afraid to get into trouble instead of helping a friend. Her sister. "Check the security footage." With that, she ran for the ambulance carrying her sister, her throat clogged tight, and her heart in a million jagged pieces.

Chapter Thirty-One

Drake had gotten ahold of Chase's brothers at home in Wyoming and delivered the bad news, though he knew very little about what happened. He'd called and texted Adria numerous times, but hadn't heard back from her. No one in the hospital would tell him anything about Juliana. He only got updates on Chase because he'd woken up enough to give consent.

He sat in the waiting room going out of his mind with worry, his anxiety off the charts, and his heart pounding despite how hard he tried to convince himself Chase and Juliana would be okay.

He needed to talk to Adria. He needed to know what happened. He had no idea what would possess Chase and Juliana to use again.

His thoughts spun out to a hundred different scenarios, none of them good.

"Drake. There you are." Trinity walked into the waiting room ahead of a police officer. She'd gone to the shop to close up after the cops finished their investigation there. "Where's Adria? I thought she'd be with you. The officer needs to talk to her about what happened."

"I haven't seen her. She must be with Juliana."

Trinity shared a look with the policeman.

Drake needed answers. "What happened at the shop? How did this happen?"

The officer glanced at Trinity again, then explained. "Chase Wilde and Juliana Holloway overdosed on heroin laced with a very high dose of Fentanyl. We've had several deaths the last few days that we believe are linked to the same supply."

Drake didn't want to believe it. "You're saying Chase took a deadly dose."

"The drug came from Juliana—"

Drake shoved past the officer midsentence the second he saw Adria walking down the hall toward him.

She looked pale and wrecked, her eyes puffy, red, and swollen.

He took all that in, but the officer's words replayed in his head and he let his anger fly. "Your sister gave Chase drugs. You said she was better. How could you let this happen?"

Adria stopped short and took a step back. Her eyes widened a second before they narrowed. "Is he alive?"

"Yes, no thanks to you!"

What little color she had drained from her face.

It should have warned him to take a breath and get his anger under control. But the thought of all Chase had been through surviving the war, the surgeries to fix his injuries, the PTSD, and getting hooked on the prescription pills that were supposed to help him get better, not worse. He spent sixty long days in rehab working on getting clean. A day with Juliana, and he ended up in the hospital again. All his progress lost.

He'd nearly lost his life. Again.

Drake couldn't take it. "Because of Juliana, he nearly died. When I get my hands on her, she'll pay for hurting him."

"She's dead!" Adria's rage dwarfed his. "Is that enough for you?"

A gasp went up from Roxy, Noah, Sonya, and the other man with them.

Tears streamed down Adria's face, but the hurt and pain in her eyes undid him.

His anger vanished, replaced by remorse and a need to comfort her so strong nothing else mattered. "No. Oh God, sweetheart, no."

He'd let his anger get the better of him instead of seeing the pain that stole her smile, joy, and everything about her that lit up his world. He recognized the hurt and wanted to erase it. What she felt, he felt. His heart ached for her. Everything in him wanted to hold her and take away the misery from her eyes and heart.

He took a step toward her. He needed to make up for the horrible things he'd said, but she held up her hand and shook her head. "Stop. I can't. Not now."

She'd always said go. She'd always come to him.

This time, she turned her back and ran into her sisters' arms. Noah and the other man—Austin, if he remembered the stories Adria told him about her family—stood in front of the three crying sisters.

Trinity grabbed his arm. "Drake, wait. You need to know what really happened."

He shook off his sister and tried to go after Adria, but she walked away, hugged between Roxy and Sonya. "Adria, wait. I'm sorry."

Noah didn't budge. "Leave her alone. They need to be together right now."

"I didn't mean what I said."

"I don't think she cares right now." Noah turned to his friend. "Let's go, Austin."

The cop followed them to get Adria's statement.

"Mr. McGrath, Chase is asking for you." The doctor he spoke to earlier waited at the nearby nurse's station.

Trinity took his arm. "Adria needs to say goodbye to Juliana. Go see Chase. Make sure he's okay."

"I can't leave her like that."

"She's not thinking about anything, except that Juliana is gone. They were twins. Closer than close. They could look at each other and not say anything, but say so much. Adria told me they could even feel what the other felt sometimes."

"Juliana is part of her. I know how much this hurts her."

"I don't think you do. It's more than Juliana dying. Adria saved Juliana once. She couldn't save her this time."

He'd seen the devastation of that in her eyes.

He knew exactly how guilt, remorse, anger, and failure devastated him. He didn't want to see it destroy his beautiful, kind, loving, strong, and resilient Adria. She'd been through so much.

"I need to find her and be with her."

Trinity grabbed his wrist. "Adria has her family with her. Chase is alone and asking for you. Go see him. Give Adria time to calm down and sort out what happened tonight."

"I yelled at her."

"You were upset and angry. She'll understand."

He hoped so. But he didn't wholly believe it. As he walked away from Trinity and headed down the hall to Chase's room, that seed of doubt took root and tightened his stomach into a knot.

But he had to set that aside for his friend. For now.

He pushed open the door to Chase's room and his stomach dropped. Chase sat up in the bed, his face pale, a lost look in his eyes that punctuated the desolate vibe coming off him.

"Drake. They won't tell me anything. What happened? Her lips . . . they were blue. Her eyes . . . Did Juliana make it?" Chase's eyes went wide. His intense gaze bored into Drake, imploring him to fill in the blanks and tell him everything was okay.

But it wasn't. For Adria, it would never be.

He wished he could make this right for both of them.

He stood beside Chase and gave him the brutal truth. "Juliana died."

Chase fisted his hands and pressed the heels to his forehead and shook his head. "No. No. It can't be. She can't be gone."

Drake put his hand on Chase's shoulder. "She is."

Chase broke down. "I tried to save her. That fuck wouldn't call an ambulance." Chase slammed his hands down on the mattress. "And then I lost it. I couldn't . . ." He slammed his hands down on the bed again. "Fuck!"

Drake took him by the shoulders. "Calm down."

Chase knocked his hands away. "She's dead. I should be, too." He sank into the bed, covered his face with his arms, and let loose all the wild emotions he couldn't contain anymore.

Drake rubbed his hand up and down Chase's arm and tried to comfort him. "It's going to be okay. You tried to help her. That's all you could do. I'm glad you lived. You've got another chance to change your life."

Chase knocked him away again. "I don't have a fucking life anymore."

He hated to see his friend so broken.

Unable to comfort him, he let Chase ride it out, but stayed close.

Drake turned off the overhead lights, leaving just one light burning next to the bed. He'd had his share of bad nights, where he just wanted to be left alone. But not.

Drake dropped into the chair and let the hospital noises outside the room and Chase's sobs wash over him. Chase didn't want to talk. He didn't want to listen. He wanted to wallow. So Drake let him. But he wouldn't leave him alone. Not in his condition. Drake feared what he might do given a chance and too much time alone.

So Drake settled in for the night, because Chase's brothers wouldn't be here for hours still. He wouldn't leave a fallen soldier behind.

He wouldn't let him face the nightmares in the dark alone.

But his heart was also with Adria.

Everything in him wanted to go to her. He wanted to comfort her.

He wanted to know how this happened.

And that it wasn't the end of them.

He pulled out his phone, pulled up his texts, and thought about what he wanted to say, though nothing would take away her grief.

DRAKE: I'm so sorry about Juliana
DRAKE: I'm sorry for what I said
DRAKE: I'm with Chase. He's in a bad place.
DRAKE: If you need me, I'll come to you
DRAKE: Where are you
DRAKE: I miss you
DRAKE: I'm thinking about you

Chase fell into a fitful sleep.

Drake's phone remained silent. When he woke up stiff and aching sitting in the chair in the early morning, she hadn't responded.

Her silence killed him.

Chapter Thirty-Two

Adria had let Roxy and Sonya walk her back down the hall to where Juliana lay, silent, still, and gone. It broke her heart all over again. She didn't know how she managed to take the emotionally jarring hit and slap of reality. Her mind denied what she saw, but the agonizing pain in her heart made it all too real.

"What happened?" Roxy wiped away tears, but they just kept coming.

Adria tried to catch her breath. "I . . . I don't know." She didn't believe what seemed so obvious.

"You said she'd turned a corner." Sonya hugged her to her side.

"She did. This makes no sense."

"You didn't see any signs?" Roxy's question set her off. It reminded her too much of what Drake said to her.

"This isn't my fault! If I thought she was using, or going to, I'd have done something about it." She stepped away from Sonya and brushed her hand over Juliana's soft hair. "You gave me the papers for the art schools. You were happy and excited about going. Why? Why would you do this?"

Juliana had no more answers. Her dreams of art school and using this second chance at life to find happiness vanished with her last breath.

Adria could ask all the questions, but none of them mattered now. Juliana was gone. Adria couldn't bring her back no matter how hard she prayed for this to all be some bad dream.

She had to live without Juliana.

She didn't know if she could do that.

Because nothing mattered right now. Not even the text messages coming in on her phone. She knew Drake wanted to talk, but she had nothing left. No words. No thoughts other than she missed her sister with every cell of her being. So much so that she felt like her soul had torn in two and a part of her was missing.

The eerie absence of her twin deep inside her stunned her.

They'd had that connection. Adria had felt Juliana her whole life.

And now it was gone.

She didn't know if she could live like this, feeling this empty.

Roxy, Noah, Sonya, and Austin helped her make the final decisions for Juliana before they left the hospital. Adria didn't remember how she ended up in Noah's truck or at their house, tucked into a bed that felt cold and lonely in a house that was unfamiliar and a world that felt empty.

She didn't remember sleeping. One minute she'd been in the dark and then the light came but nothing had changed.

She wanted to scream. She wanted to rage. But she couldn't manage to do anything but mechanically move from one minute to the next.

"Adria, Trinity called. She wanted you to know that Chase is doing well this morning. His brothers arrived. They're taking him home. The shop is covered. Sonya will help Trinity for as long as you need her there." Roxy's voice barely penetrated her mind as she sat at the dining room table, a cup of coffee in front of her, a plate of untouched eggs and pancakes.

She didn't remember coming downstairs.

She vaguely recalled crying her eyes out in the shower.

Roxy touched her arm. "Mike is missing. The police are looking for him. They want to question him about what happened."

That should matter to her. Mike was her employee. He was there when Juliana died. But she just couldn't seem to care.

"Drake is worried about you. Trinity let him know you're here with us, but he's going crazy wanting to talk to you."

She didn't want to talk to anyone. She wanted to get away. Escape the thoughts in her head and the pain eating her alive from the inside out.

"Do you want to talk about what happened at the shop?"

Juliana lying on the floor . . . Chase passing out . . . The fear that she was too late, that the naloxone wouldn't work . . . She stood and stared at Roxy. "Can I take one of the horses?"

"Let's ride." Roxy glanced down. "You'll need your shoes."

Adria looked down at her bare toes sticking out of the jeans she'd worn yesterday to work.

Yesterday. It seemed like a lifetime ago.

"We'll go by your place and get you some clothes later today when you feel like it. Or I can send Noah. You can stay here as long as you want."

She didn't feel like doing anything but getting on a horse and riding away, but the practical part of her brain kicked in for a moment. "I need to pack up Juliana's stuff at the cabin. We'll need to clean out the house back at Wild Rose." She thought about the three-bedroom cottage they grew up in and how they'd all left that place. Well, Juliana planned to go back there once she had her bearings and until she decided on an art school. She'd liked working at the shop, but that was just for now. Not forever. They wanted to take a few weeks, reconnect, make sure Juliana had a plan and the support she needed.

But none of that mattered now.

Forever ended when Juliana took her last breath and her beautiful heart stopped.

"That's not home anymore, is it?"

Roxy stood and hugged her. "Home is with us. Sonya and I are still here. We love you. We are and will always be your sisters."

"I can't go back to Wild Rose and see the life we had there. I can't go back to Trinity's because Juliana's there, too. I can't stay here. I don't know where to go. I don't know what to do."

"You don't have to do anything right now, except put your shoes on and ride."

"The horses are waiting outside," Noah said from the doorway.

Of course Roxy had him saddle them. She knew Adria liked a nice long ride to clear her head when things got tough. She shared that with Roxy.

And right now, Adria clung to the fact that someone still knew her enough to know what she needed.

She met Roxy out front with her shoes on and her head still fogged with grief. Noah kissed her on the head before she mounted the beautiful Appaloosa he held for her.

Roxy didn't say anything, just kicked her mount and off they went, leaving the ranch behind and riding out into the vast land, losing themselves in the quiet, the wind, the pounding of the horses' hooves, and the big blue sky.

She didn't have to think about Juliana. About Drake. About anything as she tried to outrun the pain.

Chapter Thirty-Three

After his shower, Drake dragged his haggard ass down the stairs to the kitchen for some much-needed coffee. Before he pulled the carafe out, he checked his phone again. Nothing from Adria.

His heart sank and throbbed with the pain that would only go away when he got Adria back.

He left Chase early this morning after his brothers arrived to take him home. Chase didn't want to go, but he needed to go home and face what happened.

Drake tried to get him to talk about it. He'd asked him half a dozen times if he wanted to go back to rehab. Nothing. Not one word out of Chase. He just sat there staring into space. The doctor even sent in a psychiatrist to evaluate him. He didn't know what Chase said, but it was enough for the doctors to release him once the cops talked to him.

Drake wished they'd let him sit in on the interview. He wanted to hear the details from Chase, but he'd been kicked out of the room for that as well.

He poured himself a mug and took a sip, thinking about what to do next. His first priority was to drive over to Roxy and Noah's place and see Adria. He didn't like the silence between them. Maybe she didn't want to talk right now, but he had to see for himself that she was okay.

The front door slammed ten seconds before Trinity walked into the kitchen. "We need to talk."

"I thought you went to the shop to open it."

"Sonya is there with Declan and Tate."

"Why are the guys working there today?"

"Because Mike is missing and I needed to come here and tell you what really happened last night." She slipped her bag off her shoulder, set it on the counter, and pulled out her laptop. "What you said to Adria last night, it was completely out of line and unfair." It took a lot to piss off his sweet, easygoing sister, but she was riled this morning.

He agreed with what she said, but she needed to remember a lot of shit happened last night. "Tell that to Chase. He nearly died last night because—"

"Adria saved him! She sacrificed trying to save her sister to save his life!"

Drake's hands shook with the burst of adrenaline. Coffee sloshed over the rim of the mug and burned his skin but he barely felt it. He dropped the mug on the counter, spilling more, and stared at Trinity. "How do you know that?"

"Because I gave the evidence to the police last night."

It hit him all at once. "The cameras recorded what happened."

Trinity opened her laptop. It came to life with the video paused on the screen showing the main room of the shop with Juliana and Mike sitting on the sofa in the reading corner.

"Chase didn't take any drugs. Neither did Juliana. At least, neither of them meant to."

He pinned Trinity in his sharp gaze. "What does that mean?"

"Watch." Trinity hit Enter and played the recording.

Juliana sat on the sofa, her purse next to her, a notebook open on her lap, and a pencil in her hand as she sketched something. She and Mike conversed. Everything looked normal.

"I wish there was sound."

Trinity frowned. "You don't need to hear anything to understand what comes next."

Mike pulled something out of his front pocket. He said something to Juliana. She shook her head. Mike spoke again. Juliana shook her head again and said something back. She tucked her notepad back in her purse with her back to Mike, who tapped out something onto the back of his hand.

"He didn't just—"

"Watch," Trinity snapped.

Juliana pulled the strap of her bag up her arm and scooted forward on the couch, but before she stood up, Mike took her shoulder and turned her toward him. He said something that looked suspiciously like, "You know you want it," if Drake read his lips right, then shoved his hand into Juliana's face.

"Holy shit."

Juliana instinctively licked her lips and brushed at her face.

"The police believe she inhaled and ingested the drugs. The concentration of Fentanyl had already caused six deaths in the surrounding community. It only took a few minutes to . . ." Trinity choked up and couldn't finish that sentence.

Drake couldn't take his eyes from the screen. Juliana shoved Mike away and stood up. With her back to the camera, he could only guess at the tirade she unleashed on him for doing something so vicious and underhanded when he knew she'd just gotten out of rehab and wanted to change her life.

Mike stood up and got in Juliana's face.

"If you read his lips, it's clear she threatened to call the cops on him."

Juliana suddenly grabbed her chest.

"She can't get a breath," Trinity whispered.

Juliana fell to the floor.

Drawn by the argument, Chase walked out of the kitchen, looking pissed and rushing to Juliana. He and Mike exchanged words while Chase tried to comfort Juliana. Seeing the dire situation for what it was, Chase's military training kicked in and he started CPR.

"Juliana must have still had the Fentanyl-laced heroin on her face. Enough that he overdosed, too."

Chase kept breathing for Juliana, unaware of the danger.

Drake was so proud of his friend for stepping in to help.

Chase yelled at Mike several times in between pumping her chest and breathing for Juliana, who never moved or responded.

"I know it's hard to watch, but it gets worse."

Chase touched his hand to his chest, the effects of the drug taking hold and making his breathing labored. He yelled at Mike again, gave Juliana one more breath, then fell to his side just as Adria came out of nowhere.

She stood over Juliana, staring down at her for one long moment, then glanced at Chase, dumped her purse, and grabbed her phone.

"Mike has been standing there all this time, too damn concerned about what he did instead of calling an ambulance." Trinity narrated what Drake just couldn't grasp.

Why didn't he help?

Mike kept wiping his hand on his pants. If Drake remembered correctly from news reports about the rise of Fentanyl use, it could be absorbed through the skin and cause an overdose.

Drake didn't say anything. Couldn't. Because he watched Adria break open a vial of some sort, fill the syringe she unwrapped with her teeth, then plunge it into Chase's shoulder muscle. She glanced over at her sister, then back to Chase. She waited. Drake waited, but Chase didn't wake up. He didn't move. So Adria filled the syringe again and gave Chase a second dose. She put her hand on his chest. And Drake saw what she felt. He breathed on his own. Deep and even.

Adria turned from Chase and curled up on the floor next to Juliana, who never moved. He didn't need the video to know the pain Adria felt with every racking sob that shook her body.

Trinity slammed the computer shut. "She saw Juliana lying on that floor with Chase and knew she couldn't save her sister, so she used both doses of naloxone she had to save Chase. If she'd tried to save her sister, knowing she was already too far gone to bring back, Chase would have died. That's the devastating decision she had to make in a split second despite how much she must have wanted to *at least* try to save Juliana." Trinity took a calming breath, then let him have it. "Then you blamed her and Juliana for what happened."

Drake closed his eyes and heard the angry words that had come out of his mouth at the hospital. "I didn't mean it. I didn't know the circumstances. I only knew that a man I served with, a man who had been struggling like me just to survive, nearly died again."

"I know." Trinity put her hand on his shoulder. "I hope for your sake and Adria's that she comes to that conclusion as well. You two are so great together. I want you to be happy. But I don't know if Adria will ever get over having to make that choice and wondering what might have happened if she'd given both those doses to Juliana. Could she have saved her? Probably not. But living with not even trying, that's got to be hard, especially when she saved her sister the last time."

He couldn't even fathom how Adria felt right now. "Does she know that Mike dosed Juliana like this?"

"I told Roxy this morning on the phone about what happened and that the cops are trying to find Mike. She said Adria is in a state. She's there, but not there. Roxy and the rest of them are scared what Adria might do. They're keeping a very close eye on her."

"What about a service for Juliana? Adria needs to say goodbye."

"I don't think Adria will ever be able to say goodbye to the person who not only looked exactly like her but knew her best. Can you imagine what it will feel like every time she looks in the mirror and sees Juliana staring back at her?"

No. He couldn't imagine it. But he'd seen the bond between them. Adria called Juliana her other half. He'd wanted to be that for her, too, but it hadn't been clear until now how deep that truth went for Adria and Juliana. Adria would always know what was missing in her life every time she saw herself. Everything she did, Juliana would never do from this point on. Because of their unique bond, they'd shared every little thing right down to the way they tilted their heads when they listened and finished each other's sentences.

Every accomplishment and setback in their lives, they'd been there for each other. They'd understood each other in a way no one else could.

He thought he understood. Roxy and Sonya would probably say the same, but how could any of them really know what it was like to be with someone who came from the very same cells that made you?

"Drake."

"I've lost her."

"Only if you give up and let her go. She needs you right now. She is in a dark, dangerous place. You know what that feels like. You know how to help her." Trinity touched his arm. "Can you imagine how alone she must feel right now?"

Yes, he could. He'd felt as alone as someone could be before she walked into his life with her light and beautiful heart and understanding and compassion.

"You needed her. Now she needs you."

Drake kissed his sister on the head, pulled his keys out of his pocket, and headed for the front door. He didn't know what he'd say to Adria, but he had the whole drive over to Roxy and Noah's place to figure it out.

Right now, Adria didn't think she could live without her sister. It wouldn't be easy, but she'd find a way. He'd help her find a new normal. The way she'd helped him find his.

And his life wasn't complete without her.

Maybe knowing that would be enough for her to forgive him for letting his anger get the best of him and lean on him during this difficult time, the way he'd leaned on her.

That's what made them so good together.

All those thoughts and more went through his mind on the long drive. Ready to say his piece and do whatever Adria needed to feel better, he slammed on the brakes in the driveway, hopped out of the truck, and headed up the path to the front door.

Noah opened it before he hit the steps. "She's not here."

"What? Where is she?"

"Roxy and Adria went for a long ride this morning. Adria wasn't really talking, or even engaging with anyone, but when they got back she insisted she wanted to go back to Wild Rose Ranch."

That shocked him. "Why?"

"Because she wanted to tell her mother in person that Juliana died."

Drake swore. He'd missed her. "No one's told her yet?"

Noah sighed. "I don't know how much you know about the girls and their moms."

"I know that Adria's mom was a drug addict who left her daughter alone with a child pornographer and pedophile."

"I thought Roxy's mom was the worst, but that one surprised me." Noah stuffed his hands in his front pockets. "Crystal cleaned up her act, but there are times she goes off the rails again, so the girls decided to wait to tell her until Adria could deal with her mom."

"You can't tell me that Adria is in her right mind right now."

"That's why Roxy went with her. They'll be back tomorrow night."

Which meant Drake had to wait.

Noah notched his chin up. "So I guess you found out what really happened."

Drake dropped his gaze to his boots. "Trinity showed me the video right before I came here."

"You had to see it to believe it?" Noah's question leveled an accusation at the same time.

His head snapped up. "No. No one told me anything before I saw that video. Trinity went for maximum impact. She wanted me to see what Juliana and Adria went through so I'd know the choice Adria faced and that she made an impossibly difficult decision."

"Not so impossible."

"What?"

"Adria spoke to the police last night. I was there. She told the officer she gave Chase both doses because she knew Juliana was already dead. What she doesn't know is that Mike dosed Juliana."

"Why didn't anyone tell her that? Why let her think Juliana and Chase purposely took the drugs?"

"Because thinking her sister used again seemed a bit easier for her to take last night instead of telling her Mike killed Juliana." Noah raked his fingers over his head. "We wanted to tell her today, but then she wanted to go back to the Ranch."

"She needs to know her sister didn't start using on her own again."

"I assume Roxy will tell her before they speak to Crystal."

Drake sighed out his frustration. "I wish I was with her."

Noah seemed to understand that, although he'd messed up with Adria last night, Drake cared deeply about her.

He loved her.

He should have told her by now.

It shouldn't have taken him this long to say the words. Maybe if he had, she couldn't have walked away from him last night.

Noah clamped his hand on Drake's shoulder. "How is your friend?"

"A mess. His brothers took him home to Wyoming this afternoon." Drake hoped Chase's brothers kept an eye on him. He hoped Chase found the strength to overcome this latest setback.

"I don't know where Adria's head is at right now, but I hope you two work things out. Roxy does, too. She said she's never seen Adria as happy as she is with you."

Drake was glad Noah didn't say, "*was* with you." He needed to believe there was still a chance to make this right. "I'm not giving up on us. Maybe she saved me so I could save her now."

"I'll let her know you came to see her."

"Thanks, man. I appreciate it." Drake left dejected, missing Adria even more, but hopeful that he'd get her back.

He wanted a future with her, because without her, his future looked bleak.

Chapter Thirty-Four

Adria stood outside her mother's door with Roxy's revelation ringing in her head. She came here to tell her mom the devastating news, but she could hardly believe the truth herself. She read the scene all wrong last night.

If she'd known Mike purposely dosed her sister, she'd have killed him.

If she got her hands on him before the cops, God help him.

The door opened and her beautiful mother stood there shocked. "I thought I heard someone lurking out here. Adria, what are you doing back? I thought you and Juliana were too busy to visit. I'm so proud of you both."

She appreciated that unexpected sentiment, but grabbed her mom's arm to make her listen. "Mom, stop."

Crystal finally took a good look at her. "You're working too much, baby. Look at you."

She'd seen her bloodshot, swollen eyes in the mirror a split second before she'd turned away because she couldn't stand to look at herself and see Juliana staring back at her.

It wasn't fair.

She loved her sister desperately, but the reminder of her made Adria so sad she wasn't sure her heart could take it.

"Mom, I came because I have something important to tell you."

Crystal looked both ways down the hall. "Did Juliana come with you? I spoke to her the other day. She raved about your store. She texted me a picture she drew of the cabin. She said she loves it there, but can't wait to go back to school. I'm so happy she's moving on with her life."

"Mom! Please. I need to talk to you."

Crystal hooked her arm around Adria's shoulder and pulled her inside the room. The bed was made with a navy cover. Hardwood floors gave way to a cream rug with a faded navy pattern that gave it an antique feel. Adria went for the two velvet navy chairs by the window and fell into one, trying not to think about what her mother did in this room.

"Seriously, baby, you're starting to worry me."

She stared up at her mom and took in the lines at the corners of her eyes and around her lips. She'd recently cut her hair short but a little longer on top. The soft waves gave her kind of a rock vibe. It went with the tight black tank dress that ended at her toned thighs, inches above the black leather thigh-high boots with the four-inch heels. Diamonds the size of dimes at her ears, around her neck, and on her fingers.

Crystal liked the good stuff.

She could afford it working here.

She and Juliana had Mom's soft curves and lithe frame. They always wondered if they had their father's face—a more feminine version of it anyway.

They'd never know. Could be any number of men their mother slept with back in the day when she worked the street, making money for her next fix.

"Baby, you need to start talking, because the longer you sit there staring at me the more I think you don't want me to know whatever it is you came here to say."

Adria took her mom's hand and tugged. "Sit down."

Crystal took the seat across from hers. "It can't be that bad, baby. Whatever it is, you can tell me. I'll help you any way I can. Though Roxy's been the go-to girl these days, what with all her money."

"Money can't fix this. Nothing can fix this."

"Are you pregnant, baby? Did that cowboy knock you up and leave you? Don't you worry about him. You don't need a man to take care of you. You're strong and independent and you've got your sisters."

"Mom! I'm not pregnant."

Crystal sat back and slouched, dejected that Adria snapped at her. "Okay then. Did your cowboy up and leave?"

"No. Drake is . . ." She didn't know how to finish that sentence. He was angry Chase got hurt. She didn't blame him for that. She felt bad for walking away, but she couldn't deal with him and losing her sister all at once. It hurt that he thought Juliana deceived them, went back to doing drugs, and roped Chase into it with her.

Juliana wasn't like that. Yes, she'd liked a good time, but she'd never, ever, coax someone into doing something they didn't want to. She'd simply go find someone else who wanted to join in her fun. "Drake is home with his family and visiting with his friend in the hospital."

"Was there an accident?"

"Yes." She sucked in a breath. "Chase, Drake's friend, accidentally overdosed giving Juliana mouth-to-mouth."

Crystal sat forward, her body straight and rigid. "Wait. What?"

Adria's eyes filled with tears and her heart overflowed with grief and guilt. "I couldn't save her this time. Juliana didn't make it."

Crystal shook her head, denying the truth. "You're lying. That's not true." Tears filled her mother's eyes.

Adria understood her initial shock and disbelief. She felt the same way. Her brain refused to hold on to the belief that Juliana was truly gone.

Crystal leaned in. "She finished rehab. You guys talked about what happened and why she was upset." Bitter feelings rose up that her mother reduced what happened to them as children as her and Juliana being upset. They'd been traumatized. Not in the same way, but they'd both suffered because of Crystal's drug addiction.

Because of what their mother allowed to happen.

Because she didn't protect them until it was too late.

Though those memories assaulted her again, she set aside her anger over that and tried to focus on Juliana.

"Jules wanted to go to school. She was with you, working at your store. Everything was right again."

Adria's heart pinched at all those truths. "That is the hardest part of all of this. Jules had a bright outlook on life and a real desire to take her second chance and live her life, happy and exploring a future full of possibilities, free of past hurts. But that was stolen from her." Anger, all-encompassing, washed through her.

She wanted to rail at the unfairness and unjust way her sister died.

She wanted to find Mike and make him hurt the way she hurt.

She wanted to kill him for taking her beautiful sister from her.

"Stolen? You said she overdosed."

"Someone forced her to take the drugs."

Her mother shot up from her seat. "What? Someone killed my baby. Who?" She paced away, then turned back. "Why?"

"I wasn't there when it happened. Mike liked Juliana. She liked working with him, but she wasn't interested in dating him."

"This man worked for *you*." That sounded a lot like blame and it stung. But it also rang true because she did blame herself.

"Yes. That's how they knew each other. I don't know the exact circumstances, but based on the initial investigation, Mike offered her drugs. She said no. She tried to get up and leave, but Mike shoved the drugs into her face. She inhaled and ingested them. It is believed that Mike didn't know the drugs were heavily laced with Fentanyl."

Having used drugs in varying degrees and at various times in her life, Mom knew exactly what Juliana was forced to take.

"He killed her." Finally, reality hit her mom and the devastation reflected in her eyes and the lines in her forehead. The tears streamed down her cheeks but her mom seemed frozen in place.

Adria rose, went to her mom, and wrapped her in a hug.

Crystal pushed her away. "I should have never let you take her there. She should have stayed here."

Adria lost it. "With you! You never took care of us. *You* taught her that the way you deal with a problem is with a drink or drugs. Numb the pain. You don't face it and do the work to come to terms with it. If I left her here with you, she probably would have overdosed again. And who would be there to save her? You?"

"I love her."

"*I* love her. I wanted her to have a better and different kind of life than you bore us into."

"I did the best I could." And that's all her mom had for her defense. Adria had always found it lacking and self-serving. For her twins, she could have tried harder.

"*I* did everything I could think of to help her. I miss her more with every breath I take. I can't stand that she's not here. I spent nearly every day of my life with her. I can't imagine spending the rest of my life without her."

Her mother's hands shot down to her sides in fists. "Then you should have protected her."

"No one could have predicted this would happen. If I'd seen signs that Juliana was slipping into old bad habits, I would have stepped in. If I'd seen any hint that Juliana wasn't happy and looking forward to the future, I would have stepped in. If I thought for one second that rehab hadn't been effective in getting Juliana clean and helping her find better ways to cope with adversity, I would have sent her back or found something, anything else to help her."

But Adria could have never predicted this or spent every second with Juliana.

Mike's horrible behavior and impulsive actions killed Juliana.

Adria could play the what-if game all day. What if she'd taken Juliana to pick up the TV stand? What if she'd sent Mike home instead of letting them hang out in the shop after hours? What if she'd gone with her gut and warned Juliana to stay clear of Mike? Juliana didn't seem to be interested, but what if a warning would have made Juliana decide not to be alone with him?

What if she'd gotten back to the store just a few minutes earlier?

What if she'd given one of the naloxone doses to Juliana and administered CPR until paramedics arrived?

What if? What if?

"*I* was there for Juliana every day. She knew that. You knew that because you separated yourself from us and left us to raise ourselves. If I could change what happened, I would. I would take her place in a heartbeat, I love her that much. But what happened, happened, and I can't change it. I flew here to tell you this in person, hoping we could share this pain and come together for Juliana. I don't want to fight with you. I don't want to play the blame game. I wanted you to hear what happened from me. I wanted you to know that Juliana had changed her life and someone else ruined that for her. *He* took that from her."

"He better pay for taking her from us."

"The police are looking for him."

"And what about Juliana? What happens now?"

"I've made the arrangements for her to be cremated."

"Why? Why not bury her? Someplace I can visit her." Crystal barely visited them over the last few years since they graduated high school. In her eyes, they were capable adults who didn't need a mother anymore. They'd done better on their own than with her anyway.

"Because Juliana would want to be free, and I expect to do that for her by spreading her ashes."

"So I don't get a say in that either."

Adria held her hands out wide. "What do you want me to do?"

"I want you to remember that I'm her mother." Crystal wrapped one arm around her middle and pointed to her chest with her other hand. "I grieve for her."

"Then remember that I was closer to her than you ever were. I knew her better than you ever did. I'm doing what I believe and know in my heart is what she would want, including coming here to see you when all I want to do is crawl in bed, pull the covers over my head, and cry until it doesn't hurt anymore."

Adria tried to suck in a breath around the emotions clogged in her throat and tightening her chest. "I fear nothing will make this pain go away."

Mom did the unexpected. She pulled Adria into a tight hug. "I'm sorry, baby. I'm angry. I'm hurt. And I'm taking it out on you when all I want to do is kill that man who killed my sweet baby girl."

Adria hugged her mom tighter. "I miss her so much."

For the life of her, she couldn't remember the last time her mother held her. It had always been Juliana who comforted her. They'd clung to each other physically and emotionally their whole lives. Juliana had been her heart. Her home. The soft place she fell when life got to be too much.

The overwhelming urge to see Drake mixed in with her desperate need to have Jules back.

But he was in Montana. She was here. And she didn't really want to be anywhere right now.

She wanted to lose herself in oblivion and not feel anything anymore.

She recognized on some level how dangerous that was, but it didn't change how she felt.

She stayed and talked to her mom about the mundane. At least everything felt that way now. The store's success, Roxy's and Sonya's upcoming weddings, her life in Montana—none of it seemed consequential.

But it settled her mom.

Roxy arrived with the brothel's Madam, Big Mama, who was clearly wrecked by Juliana's death.

Big Mama pulled Adria into her ample bosom and hugged her close. "I'm so sorry, honey. I can't imagine how difficult and heartbreaking it was for you to see your sister like that again and be unable to save her. You are brave and strong and you will survive this."

Right now, Adria wasn't so sure about that.

Not when she'd been faced with an impossible choice and second-guessed whether she'd made the right decision.

Roxy pulled her from Big Mama's arms. "Come with me. We've got some things to do before we head back."

Her mother wiped her eyes, smearing black mascara and making her look like a woman scorned. The anger was still there in her bloodshot eyes. Adria didn't want to be here when her mother's grief took over and she fell back on old behaviors.

Adria couldn't deal with that right now. Breathing seemed like a monumental task.

She'd leave Crystal in Big Mama's capable hands.

Crystal shook her head side to side, her arms wrapped tight around her middle. "How did all of you end up in Montana?"

Adria had wanted to get Juliana away from here, where she faced temptation at the Wild Rose Ranch and when she went out partying in Vegas.

But drugs infested every community.

She hadn't been able to keep them away from Juliana even in her own shop.

Mike did this, but she'd hired him. She'd brought him into Juliana's life.

Roxy cupped her face. "This is not your fault."

"I'm not so sure about that. My decisions led us here."

Roxy swept her thumbs over Adria's damp cheeks. "All you ever did was love her and want the best for her."

"Stay here," Crystal pleaded. "This is your home."

She didn't want to hurt her mom more by pointing out a brothel wasn't home. Not for her. The cottage she lived in with her sisters used to be her sanctuary, but now it held too many memories of her and Juliana's best days together. She had a business in Montana but she lived at the McGrath ranch.

She may not have her own place, but she'd felt like she finally found herself with Drake.

Her phone rang in her pocket. She let it go to voice mail, but her heart beat a little faster and lighter knowing it was Drake.

She wasn't with him, but he wanted her to know he hadn't left her.

He was just a phone call away.

But she didn't reach out.

If she heard his voice, saw him, she'd break.

Right now, she had something she needed to do.

"Let's go, Roxy." That feeling of needing to escape, get away, intensified again.

By the time they got out of the mansion and walked halfway across the wide pasture separating the cottage from the big house, she couldn't stand not listening to Drake's message. She pulled her phone out and hit the voice mail button.

"I know you feel lost right now. You and me, we belong together. Come back. I miss you so damn bad." Her tough talking cowboy's words were gruff and filled with emotion. He meant every word. He understood that she didn't really know where she belonged right now. And he was leading her right back to him.

Chapter Thirty-Five

Drake thought going for a ride and talking to Jamie would help him sort out his jumbled thoughts and maybe improve his mood. Instead, he'd said nothing and felt even further away from Adria.

"I can't help you if you don't tell me what's wrong."

Dr. Porter said the same thing during their last session, but he didn't know how to put into words everything swirling inside him. Didn't know how to do it then; didn't know how to do it now.

"Are the flashbacks back? Did you lose your shit again? What?" Jamie didn't mince words.

"I lost Adria." He wanted her back so damn bad he couldn't stand it.

She was due home late this afternoon, but that didn't mean she wanted to see him. She hadn't answered a single text or voice mail.

She grieved for Juliana. He got that. He couldn't believe what happened and that she was gone. He liked her. He missed seeing her and Adria together and finding the little things that made them different. Everyone saw how alike they were, but he'd always been looking for what made Adria special. And he guessed in some way also made Juliana special.

"I heard about the murder at *Almost Homemade* on the news. They're still looking for the suspect. Adria must be devastated."

She and Dr. Porter probably already talked about all this and how it might affect him. "She left. She won't speak to me."

"Why? I'd expect after what happened she'd lean on you."

"She might have if I hadn't blamed her sister for almost killing Chase and blamed her for not keeping Juliana under control."

Jamie frowned. "Oh, Drake."

"I didn't know what really happened at the time. None of us did. But I was angry and spoke without thinking."

Jamie held his gaze. "Don't you think she knows that?"

"If she does, she doesn't care."

"Don't go there. You haven't spoken to her. You don't know where her head is at. She lost her sister. She's grieving. Maybe she just needs time."

"Maybe. Until then, every second feels like an eternity without her."

"Tell her that."

His anger flashed again. "She won't answer the damn phone."

"Find a way." Jamie pinned him in her sharp gaze. "Words sting. They hurt. We say things we don't mean all the time. Actions speak volumes. Show her how you really feel."

He needed to get out of his head and do something. What he'd wanted to do was go find her and make her listen, but what he really needed to do was remind her what they had together and what they could have for their future.

Jamie broke into his thoughts. "Does she know you love her?"

"Everyone knows I love her." It hadn't been a secret. His family and hers pointed it out more than once.

He knew she loved him. At least she used to. Now he didn't know how she felt.

"So she's just supposed to know what you're thinking and how you feel because someone else said it's so? You talk about how solid you and Adria are, how she knows you and you know her. Yet you both hold back the one thing you both want the most. What are you afraid of, Drake? How can you expect her to forgive and stick by you when you're still protecting your heart from her? You keep holding part of yourself back, so she does the same."

Why are women always right?

"Tell her exactly how you feel."

He'd wanted to say it in every message he left her, but he told himself that wasn't something you left on voice mail. It needed to be said face-to-face.

He needed to show her they weren't just words.

She needed to see it in him.

Jamie persisted. "Imagine how it will feel to hear her say it back to you."

It would mean everything. His heart kind of floated in his chest with just the thought of it.

He reined his horse around and galloped back to her ranch.

Jamie followed and took the reins for his horse when he dismounted just outside the stables and headed for his truck. Jamie called out, "Go get her, Drake."

He wished he could right this minute, but she wasn't due back for a few more hours. Until then, he needed to prepare for her homecoming.

Chapter Thirty-Six

$\mathfrak{D}$rake spent the rest of the day checking things off the list in his head. He called a Realtor on his way home and stopped at the property he thought Adria would love. He wanted to buy it for her. For them. When he got home, he crunched the numbers and decided a life with Adria was worth the initial debt to buy both the house *and* the business he wanted.

He hated going to the cabin and not finding Adria there, but found himself choked up for a whole other reason. Seeing Juliana's things brought home that she wasn't coming back. So he saved Adria more heartache and cleaned the cabin, packing up Juliana's things. He couldn't imagine how it felt for Adria to go back home and see where she and Juliana grew up together and know she wasn't coming home.

That unpleasant chore done, he headed back to the house to get ready to go see Adria, but his phone delivered the bad news right when he got out of the shower.

NOAH: They're back
NOAH: She's exhausted
NOAH: Better to come tomorrow morning
NOAH: Sorry know that's not what you want to hear but she's not doing well

Drake swore. He wanted to ignore Noah's texts and go over there and demand to see her. But he also didn't want to make a bad day worse for

her either. He wanted to hold and comfort her, but right now he didn't
know if she wanted anything from him.

Waiting sucked, but he'd do it for her if that's what she needed. He had
to believe Noah knew Adria well enough to know what she wanted and
needed because he was there with her.

Drake skipped dinner and hunkered down in his quiet room on his
lonely bed with his laptop and Sunny, who lay along his thigh and hip
and whined.

"I miss her, too."

Sunny looked up at him, hope in his eyes.

"Tomorrow. I promise."

Sunny laid his head back on his paws and whined again.

He felt the same way. All he could do was distract himself from the
pain and loneliness, so he got back to researching available security systems. If the owner accepted his offer, he wanted to hit the ground running.

Lost in the types of motion sensors on the market and the best types
for different situations, it took him a minute to decipher the alarm going
off on his phone.

Sunny lifted his head and barked a split second before Trinity burst
into his room.

"She's at the shop."

Drake snagged his phone off the bed and swiped the screen to be sure.
He'd reprogrammed the system so that even if she shut off the alarm and
reset it, an alert would come to his and Trinity's phones the second the
motion-activated cameras were triggered after store hours.

Drake jumped out of bed, knocking his laptop to the floor. He didn't
even bother to stop and pick it up. He pulled on his boots without lacing
them and hustled to the door. Sunny barked and pounced up and down
on the bed. Trinity barely got out of his way before he rammed into her.
He took the stairs down two at a time, dangerously putting himself at
risk of falling if his left leg gave out, but his need to get to the store and
see Adria overrode good sense.

Adrenaline pumped through his system. It probably gave him the
strength he needed to avoid a bad fall.

Why was she there this late?

He jumped into his truck and leaned back so Sunny could jump into his lap and leap across the seat. He'd gotten so big these last couple months.

Trinity ran down the porch steps. "Drake. Wait. I want to go with you."

He slammed the truck door and hit the window button, making it go down. "I need to make things right. I'll call you after I talk to her." He pushed the gas pedal to the floor and peeled out of the driveway.

Sunny barked, then sat on the seat, his head straight ahead as if he knew exactly where they were going and who they were going to see.

Drake disobeyed every speed law on his way into town. He kept his eyes straight ahead except for that couple seconds when he passed the property he checked out today.

A second alert chimed on his phone. He assumed she left the shop, then went back in. Why? He didn't know. Didn't care. He just wanted to see her. So on the straightaway into town, he did what he didn't take the time to do when he got the first alert and went through the steps to view the secure live stream.

And there she was standing in the main part of the shop near the reading corner, staring at the floor. She collapsed to her knees and covered her face. Her shoulders shook with her sobs.

"I'm coming, sweetheart."

He wanted to push the gas pedal to the floor, but as a concession to being in town, he slowed to only ten miles above the speed limit. When he spotted the shop, he breathed a sigh of relief that he'd finally made it.

He parked next to her Jeep by the back door, barely put the truck in Park and shut it off before he jumped out with Sunny right behind him, and slammed the truck door. His hands shook as he tried to find the right key to open the locked door. Sunny barked and pawed at the door, ready to get in and find Adria, too.

Drake pulled the door open, noted the alarm wasn't set, and ran through the kitchen and out into the shop.

Sunny beat him to Adria.

She broke his heart, sobbing her heart out, lying on her back on the floor, knees bent, arms covering her face.

In the exact spot Juliana died.

Chapter Thirty-Seven

Adria collapsed under her grief. She couldn't hold it in. She couldn't make it go away. So she let it wash over her, knowing that it just might kill her.

She couldn't stand to stay one more second at Roxy and Noah's with them watching her every move. She missed Juliana, so she came back here to where it all ended, hoping to feel her sister.

But she only felt empty.

The high-pitched whine didn't register until a heavy furry body draped over her belly.

Sunny. Her sweet pup. Here to comfort her.

Which meant Drake was here.

Her desperate need to see him only made her cry harder.

She didn't resist when Drake put his hands under her arms, lifted her, slipped down behind her, and pulled her and Sunny into his chest, held her close with his legs out straight on both sides of her, and wrapped her in his warmth and strength.

"I've got you, sweetheart." Drake squeezed her close and buried his face in her hair. "Let it out. I won't let you go."

Those words only made her cry harder, because that's what she'd had with Juliana. Someone who would never let her go, who'd never let her cry alone, who would always be there for her no matter what.

"I can't stand to see you hurting like this. Don't let this pain devour you. I need you. I love you."

She turned in his arms, knocking Sunny off her lap, and hugged him tight. "I don't want to fight with you."

"No one is fighting. I'm sorry for what I said, sweetheart. I didn't know what really happened. You saved Chase." He squeezed her tighter. "I know you miss Juliana with your whole heart and that is a loss greater than you can bear, but hold on to the fact that Chase is alive because of you."

Her grief had made her completely lose sight of that one amazing fact. She wiped at her eyes, tried to catch her breath, and leaned back and looked at Drake for the first time in days. Just the sight of him eased her heart. "He's really okay?"

"A little messed up in the head—"

"Who isn't." She managed a scoffing laugh.

"I've been a wreck without you. But Chase is home with his family and they want you to know how grateful they are for what you did."

"I hated it, but it was the only choice to make. I'm just glad I got two more naloxone injections or they'd both be dead." She wiped her tears and found that sitting in Drake's arms, she could breathe again.

"Why did you have it? Didn't you believe Juliana had put that behind her?" No sense or suspicion that she held something back came with that question.

"My mom has put it behind her about twenty-something times. As much as I believed in Juliana and that she wanted to be better, I couldn't take a chance that she'd . . ." She buried her face in Drake's neck because her worst fear had come to pass, but not in the way she thought it would happen.

Juliana had wanted to live. She'd worked hard to turn her life around and find a new direction.

Drake rubbed her back, up and down, trying so hard to soothe her. "I'm sorry, sweetheart. For what it's worth, I saw the way she settled in here with you. Every day she seemed a little stronger. I wanted to get to know her better."

"She liked you. She liked me with you. It surprised her. You seemed the least likely man I'd choose, but then she saw what I saw—you're perfect for me."

He leaned back and stared down at her. "Do you mean that?"

She sat up but didn't move away. "That night in the hospital, I didn't know what to do. I didn't want to think or feel anymore. I wanted to get away from everything and everyone. But after I told my mom what happened and I was done doing the things I felt had to be done, I realized I was trying to find something. I listened to your message and I knew. I wasn't running away from something, I was trying to get back to the way I feel when I'm with you. Here you are making me feel better."

"I went to Noah's but you were already gone. I wanted to go after you but I knew you needed to see your mom and take whatever time you needed. I wanted you to know I was here waiting for you to come home."

"That's the other thing I realized. When Juliana died, it felt like I didn't know where I belonged because home was always where she was. Without her, I felt lost. Without you, there was no hope anything would be right again."

"All you had to do was call me. I'd have come to you no matter how far away you went."

"I know. Leaving didn't make sense. Being here with you does. Because I love you, too."

She leaned in and kissed him. The second her lips touched his, her whole body went warm and she felt something wonderful instead of all the emptiness and sadness.

Sunny, his body pressed up behind her, growled, low and deep.

She'd never heard the young pup growl at anyone or anything.

Alerted to danger, she and Drake broke apart.

Adria spotted Mike, his eyes bloodshot, red rimmed, narrowed, and dazed. High, he stumbled to a stop when he locked eyes with her.

She saw red, rose, and ran right for him.

"You killed my sister." She slammed into him, shoving him back a few steps, then she pummeled her fists into his chest.

He tried to grab her, but she dodged his grasp. "I didn't think she'd die. I was just having some fun."

She slapped him and left the imprint of her hand on his ruddy cheek. "You killed her!"

Mike pressed his hand to his face, then his eyes went wide, and he lunged for her. He pulled her close, spun her, and wrapped his arm around her throat, choking her.

Drake didn't stop. He kept coming, his eyes narrowed and filled with fury. "You will not get away with this."

"Back off!" Mike's high-pitched words rang in her ear. The fear in those words set off the trembling in his body pressed to her back.

Drake stalked Mike as he dragged her backward.

Mike, rightfully so, feared Drake getting his hands on him.

She wasn't going along with Mike willingly.

She wouldn't be anyone's victim. Never again.

She played dirty, reached back behind her rump, took his balls in a viselike grip, and twisted.

"Fuck!" He released her and shoved her toward Drake, who had no trouble catching her before she fell.

Sunny raced past them.

Mike leaned over, both hands on his balls.

Sunny sank his teeth into Mike's arm. When he stood, Drake planted his fist right in Mike's face, busting his nose and sending him falling backward like a felled tree. He hit the floor, his head thumping against the hardwood. Sunny barked and danced around him, making sure he didn't get up again.

Mike curled into a ball, one hand on his bleeding nose, the other on his busted balls. "Fuck. You broke my nose. Call an ambulance," he wailed.

"Why the fuck would I do that for you when you couldn't do it for my sister!"

"Help me, you bitch." Mike took a swat at Sunny, but missed. "Get him away."

Drake whistled at Sunny. "Heel." Sunny ran back and sat at Drake's side, but gave one last warning growl.

Drake pulled out his phone to call the cops, but the sound of sirens grew louder outside until a patrol car pulled into the lot. Adria ran to the front and unlocked the door.

Drake stood over Mike. "You ever fucking touch someone I love again, you're dead."

"You can't let them take me to jail."

"It's better than dead."

"I didn't mean to do it." Mike's whiny voice reinforced what an annoying, juvenile man-boy he turned out to be.

Drake stood over Mike and gave him the cold hard truth. "You shoved drugs into Juliana's face."

"I just wanted to party with her."

Drake gave Mike a disgusted look. "You wanted her doped up so you could take advantage of her because you knew she'd never sleep with a shithead like you."

"She was so beautiful."

Drake leaned over, grabbed Mike by the shirt, pulled him up, and got in his face. "And now she's dead because of you. You killed her. Because of you, my friend overdosed and nearly died, too. You took away someone precious from the woman I love. You deserve a hell of a lot worse than jail and I hope you get it." Drake shoved Mike back onto the floor. He thumped his head on the hardwood again. Mike yelped and grabbed his busted nose. As Drake turned, he got a nut-shot in with his big, booted foot.

Mike grabbed his junk again and wailed in pain just as the cops walked in the door, missing the exchange between Drake and Mike.

Drake pulled Adria into his arms and hugged her close.

She held tight, letting the adrenaline wane and the trembling in her body fade. "How did the cops know?"

"Trinity. She's probably watching the live feed from the cameras." He tightened his grip. "I should have realized what happened. I set up an alarm to let me know if the motion-activated cameras went on after hours."

"You thought I'd come here."

"If you decided you didn't want me anymore, you'd come to the apartment instead of the ranch."

She looked up at him. "I never stopped wanting you."

He kissed her on the forehead, but he wasn't done being angry at himself. "The alert came through, so I thought it was you. I didn't even look to see who set it off. I just jumped in my truck and came after you. But on the way, the alert went off again. I thought you went out, then came back in. I checked the feed then and saw you in here."

"Crying over my sister."

He brushed his hand over her hair. "I never considered that Mike or someone else came in first."

"He must have been up in the apartment or hiding in the kitchen when I came in. You arrived shortly after I got here."

"Pure coincidence we all ended up here at the same time."

Adria took great satisfaction in watching the cops forcibly roll Mike to his stomach, pull his arms behind his back, and cuff him. When one of the cops read him his rights, Mike repeated, "I didn't mean to kill her," over and over again.

She stepped in front of him as they walked him toward the door. "Maybe you didn't mean it, but you did kill her. Now you're going to pay for it. And I'll be there, every step of the way, making sure you get what's coming."

Mike stared down at her, tears streaming down his cheeks. "You look just like her."

Drake wrapped his arm around her before she could attack Mike again.

The cops pulled Mike back, too, eyed her, but walked Mike out as Drake held her back.

"I know you want to, but don't give the cops a reason to take you, too. I can't go another night without you."

Those words and how much he meant them made her stop struggling and turn to the man who loved her. He wrapped her in all his strength and love and let her cry out her anger, frustration, and grief while he answered the cop's questions. She barely managed to nod her agreement.

Sunny settled in at her feet, his body pressed against her leg.

The cops searched the shop and apartment and found what was left of his stash of drugs and bagged it as evidence. They'd been looking everywhere for Mike, but he couldn't go home, so he must have come here to crash. That or his guilt brought him back here to face what he'd done.

Drake spoke to Trinity on the phone to let her know they were okay and planned to stay at the apartment. He left Adria on the sofa in the

reading nook with a hot cup of herbal tea and went up to the apartment
to pack up Chase's things so they could get them back to him.

She let the quiet surround her and stared at the floor where her sister
died and Mike got a little taste of what he deserved.

I miss you, Jules.

I wish you were here.

She pulled her shirtsleeve up and tore off the bandage on the back of
her wrist. She swept her fingers over the brand-new tattoo. She traced her
finger over the nestled hearts and thought of what Juliana told her.

*Two joined hearts filled with love. When you have that, you can get
through anything.*

"When did you get that?"

"I made Roxy take me before we came back. Juliana drew it."

Juliana had been talking about them when she described what the tattoo meant to her. Why she wanted it. Because it reminded her that she'd
always have Adria to get through anything. They had each other.

She looked up at Drake and Juliana's voice whispered in her heart,
You have him now.

"I love you."

He squatted in front of her. "I love you, too." He slipped his hand under her arm and stared at the tattoo. "You've got one for your sisters. One
for Juliana. You think you'll ever get a tattoo for me?"

"Someday. I'll have to figure out what that would be." She leaned
forward and put her hand on his face and looked deep into his blue-gray
eyes. "Until then, right now, and forever, you're tattooed on my heart."

Drake leaned forward on his knees, drew her close with his hand at
the back of her head, and kissed her. Softly at first. Then he took the kiss
deeper, and she felt just how much those words meant to him.

He pressed his forehead to hers. "God, I love you."

"Show me."

He took her hand, stood, and helped her up. "You sure?"

"You are the only thing I'm sure about right now."

He led her out of the shop, through the kitchen, and up the stairs to the
apartment. He opened the door and let her go in ahead of him.

She gasped and put her hand over her mouth, then settled it on her chest, surprised and amazed by what he'd done for her. "Drake. It's so pretty."

Drake had stripped and remade the bed and strung white holiday lights over the metal headboard. They lent the otherwise dark room a bright, cheery feel. "Trinity bought a whole bunch of them for the shop. I stole one of the boxes out of the office." He took her by the hips and walked her toward the bed. "I don't know about you, but I can't sleep without you." He pulled her shirt up and over her head and tossed it. The lace bra surprised him. "That's new."

"I borrowed it from Jules."

He looked up to the ceiling. "Thank you, Jules." He meant it. More than that, he loved that Adria had put the past behind her and didn't shy away from wearing pretty things.

Adria caught her breath, not believing he'd be so casual about speaking about Juliana.

"Just because she's gone doesn't mean we have to stop talking about her." To get them back on track, he dipped his head and kissed the swell of her breast. "And I like her taste."

Adria slipped her fingers through his short hair and held him to her breast.

"But this has to go because I want your skin against mine." He unhooked the bra and slipped it down her shoulders. Out of respect, he didn't toss it, but set it on the dresser.

Her hands went over his head, down his neck to his shoulders, gripped his shirt, and pulled it off. He hated to let her go for even that long, but then she pulled him to her and his chest met hers and the searing kiss they shared didn't come close to the heat that rushed through him feeling her body pressed to his.

The rest of their clothes disappeared in record time. It had been too long. Too much had happened. They needed to be as close as two people could be. Right now.

So he laid his body over hers, kissed her long and deep, and slipped his hand between her warm thighs and found her slick heat against his fingers. He slipped one deep inside her and stroked it in and out as her hips rocked against his palm.

"Drake." She hooked her hands around his sides, fingers splayed on his back, and held on tight.

"I'm here. I'm not going anywhere."

"Promise me." She kissed her way up his neck.

"I swear." Before he could move, think, or grab for the condom, she took him in deep. He stilled, locked tight in her body. One with her. His chest pressed to hers.

"Two hearts filled with love. Nothing between us. You and me." Those words, the image of her tattoo in his mind, and then she moved and he forgot everything but the sheer pleasure that washed through him.

If she wanted him this way, he was all in, because he meant what he said. He wasn't going anywhere.

Ever.

He wanted a life with her. And if they made a new life, well, that would be a gift from someone who had already given him so much.

So he poured everything into showing her how much he loved her. He gave himself over to the pleasure and the love they shared. And when they reached the height of ecstasy and he held her in his arms, safe and loved and his, he found peace.

She slept snuggled to his side, her hand over his heart, I Love You tattooed on the back of it and on his heart, too. In the quiet, her breath a whisper across his skin, he sent up a silent pledge to Juliana. *I will love and protect her always.*

Maybe his eyes tricked him, but he thought the lights flickered right before he gave in to sleep.

HE WOKE UP with Adria staring up at him, tears swimming in her eyes and a soft smile on her lips.

"I dreamed of her. She was holding a pink-and-blue flower." She pressed a kiss to his chest. "I don't know why. But I woke up happy and sad."

He hugged her close. "It's going to take time to get used to missing her."

Her smile dipped into a lopsided half frown. "Thank you for understanding that I will always miss her."

"And when you miss her most, just look in the mirror and there she'll be. No matter what, she'll always be in your heart."

"My tough talking cowboy is a poet this morning."

He chuckled. "Hardly. But I get your pain and loss. Maybe not in the same way because she was your twin, but I miss the guys we lost overseas. They're a part of me, just like Jules is a part of you."

She pressed another kiss to his chest, then looked at him, and in her eyes he saw that same lost look as yesterday. "I'm so glad to be here with you, but I have no idea what to do now that she's gone."

"Get dressed. I have an idea about that."

Chapter Thirty-Eight

Adria stood in front of the house and took in the overgrown front yard, wide front porch with the weathered and probably rotten boards, the gorgeous but in need of sanding and staining wood front door, and a roof that had seen all the weather it could handle and probably leaked.

"Four bedrooms. Two baths. Twenty-eight hundred square feet on five acres. The outside needs work, but inside, they've remodeled. Kinda."

That didn't sound encouraging.

"It's only twenty, twenty-five minutes outside of town. We can have a couple of horses here, or go up to the ranch to ride whenever you want. The ranch is only about another fifteen minutes away. It'll be tough at first financially, since my offer was accepted on the business, but I think we can swing it."

"Um, two questions."

He looked down at her, waiting.

"What business? And are you asking me to move in here with you?"

"The security company I told you about. I bought it. Once the paperwork goes through, it'll be mine. So I have a job, a steady income, a way to take care of you."

"You know I make good money at the shop."

He glanced back at the house. "It'll come in handy if we want to fix this place up. It needs it." He turned back to her and answered her second question. "We can stay at the cabin for a while, but for the long run, and having a family, I think this place will suit us."

She thought about how she'd just wanted to be close to him, feel all of him, and the impulsive thing she'd done last night and what it could mean. "Four rooms, you said?"

He nodded and gave her a sexy smile. "Four."

"You and me?"

"Always."

She swept her hand out toward the house. "Let's see it."

He took her hand and pulled her into his chest and wrapped her up tight against him. "I can already see it." He kissed her softly, drawing it out until she melted against him, then pressed his forehead to hers and looked deep into her eyes. "Do you see it, Adria?"

She woke up these last few days not knowing how to go on without Juliana. But standing here with Drake, in his arms, in front of the house he wanted them to share, she saw a bright, happy, loving, family-filled future.

Tears pricked her eyes and clogged her throat. "I see it."

He kissed her quickly. "Good." He stepped back, took her hand, and pulled her toward the house. "We can redo the garden and porch, put on a new roof, and a fresh coat of paint. That will fix the front." He unlocked the door and pushed it open wide. "The hardwood floors are gorgeous, but the whole place needs to be painted."

"You think?" Standing in the entry, she saw three rooms. One dark green, one a pale peach, and the kitchen in a deep, dark blue that made it look like a cave.

"Imagine it with a light, neutral color. With all the windows off the back, this place will be bright and cheerful."

She loved the windows off the spacious living area. "Do you think we can knock down that wall between the kitchen and living room?"

"It's probably load bearing, but I think a contractor can put a header from the entry wall across to the other side of the breakfast nook." He pulled her into the kitchen.

"This has to be gutted." The old, outdated cabinets had been painted white but still looked shabby. The appliances were cheap and white, not stainless steel. The porcelain sink was chipped and stained.

"If we get rid of the wall, the entire kitchen has to be reconfigured.

And since you're a chef, we need top-of-the-line appliances. I'm thinking we nix the breakfast nook altogether and expand the kitchen across the whole back wall and add a huge island with stools as part of the expanded living space. We'll still have plenty of room for a good-sized table in the dining area for when your sisters and brothers-in-law come over. If we have my family over at the same time, we'll have to bring in another table, but I think there will be plenty of space."

She saw his vision and loved it. Even more, she appreciated so much that he wanted this place to be theirs. A place for them to make memories together and with their families.

She'd never been to such a family gathering, but she wanted to fill the house and her life with their loved ones.

"Let's buy it."

"You haven't seen the rest of it."

"I already know I want it. I have some of the money left over that Roxy gave me to start the business, plus what I've saved from my earnings at the shop, so I can help with the down payment and renovation costs."

He scooped her up and off her feet and held her against his chest and stared up at her. "You mean it. Yes?"

"Yes." She cupped his face and kissed him. "But I get to pick everything for the kitchen."

"Deal." He kissed her again. "Just keep in mind we own two businesses, so have mercy on my wallet."

She nodded, knowing that eventually she'd have to convince him to accept that being Roxy's sister meant never having to worry about money because her sister insisted on using the Wild Rose Ranch profits to benefit all of them.

She couldn't believe how alone she felt when Juliana died.

But she wasn't alone.

She had Drake.

She had Roxy and Sonya.

Two brothers when Noah and Austin married her sisters. Trinity, Declan, and Tate.

And a family with Drake in her future in their new house.

Chapter Thirty-Nine

Everything can change in six weeks.

Adria and Drake took a trip to Wyoming to visit Chase. He'd let grief and guilt over what happened with Juliana drag him back into a dark place. Adria helped him see the light again when she assured him Juliana's death wasn't his fault.

Mike was the only one who needed to pay the price. He took a five-year deal and pleaded guilty to negligent homicide. In her opinion, he got off easy. The district attorney had to take into account it was his first offense. But Adria fought to get those five years because Mike forced the drugs on her sister, failed to call an ambulance, left the scene, and evaded police.

Justice had been served and Mike had five long years behind bars to think about the life he took. He'd get a second chance, but Juliana's life ended because of what he did.

Adria and Drake closed on the house and started renovations using the same contractor Sonya used at Austin's ranch. Drake balked at the price of the renovation. He wanted to pull back on the extensive plans. He'd rigorously fought Roxy on paying for all of it. But in the end, he put up the white flag and surrendered when Roxy bypassed him and paid the contractor directly.

Adria loved watching him try to win against Roxy.

Noah told him a dozen times to give up.

Sonya and Austin simply said, "You can't win."

Drake took the defeat in stride and without any animosity because coming up with the plans, discussing the details, and picking colors and appliances and furniture had brought them all closer together.

Sonya and Roxy helped more than necessary, but they'd wanted Adria to know they were still a family. They'd always do things together.

She'd needed that. It helped her grieve and let go and live her life with joy again.

Almost Homemade doubled profits from opening month, and they were looking to do the same over the next two months.

McGrath Security took off. Customers liked the idea of a trained soldier assessing their security and setting up protection for their homes and businesses. When the owner sold, two of the workers retired, too, so Drake hired a couple of ex-soldiers Dr. Porter referred to him, who had similar PTSD issues to Drake's. They now had jobs and the support of their fellow soldiers. Drake even got them to join him on his rides and talks with Jamie. They formed their own support group.

Drake's injuries healed. The surgery gave him more mobility. He didn't need his cane. In fact, he realized the night he came racing to the shop to see her that he'd relied too much on it. His hip ached sometimes, but he wasn't in constant pain anymore, so long as he was careful.

The scars on his face faded just like the plastic surgeon promised. Drake didn't seem to care one way or the other anymore when people stared.

It did her heart good to see him happy and living a productive life, free of pain and anger. He woke up happy. She liked to think most of that was because they woke up together every day.

This morning Drake woke her up in the nicest way. Making love to him always made her day better and made the connection they shared even stronger.

She stood on the brand-new back terrace of the home they bought together. The renovations weren't quite finished, but they couldn't wait to move in.

She put her hands on the railing and stared out at the beautiful trees and bright blue sky overhead while she waited for Drake to finish getting ready.

Roxy and Sonya couldn't have asked for a better day to get married.

They deserved a perfect day.

And that thought reminded her that Juliana wasn't here to witness their happy union.

Drake's hand settled on her shoulder a second before he kissed her on the head. "You're absolutely beautiful in that dress."

She glanced over her shoulder and smiled up at him. "Thank you. It's the dress Roxy picked for Juliana. The one Sonya picked for her to wear during her ceremony is hanging by the front door." Adria would wear both of them to honor their sister.

"I know today is very special for Roxy and Sonya, so I thought I'd make it special for you, too."

"Oh, you did. And I appreciate it." Reminded of their morning together, she gave him a sexy smile.

He returned it, but looked a little unsettled. She tried to turn to him, but he pressed his chest to her back, leaned over her, and set his chin on her shoulder.

"This is your favorite spot."

True. She came out here every morning for the view and the quiet. They ate dinner out here and enjoyed the stars. She loved the quiet moments and talks about their day and their future they shared out here.

Drake kissed her neck. "You and me, we've made a few deals."

"That first deal we made led us here."

He softly kissed her again. "Yes, it did. And at the heart of everything we do and say to each other is honesty."

Nervous and unsure about what he was talking about, she gripped the black railing tighter.

"We needed something from each other to find a way to be whole. You healed me. I healed you." He swept his fingers over the double heart tattoo above the back of her wrist. "Two joined hearts filled with love. We have that, and we've been able to get through the rough times." Those words were very close to what Juliana said about the tattoo. "We are joined forever, Adria." She leaned her cheek against his. "Read your hand, then mine."

She glanced down at her hand on the railing. "I love you." He set his hand on the railing next to hers and she read what he'd written on the back. "Marry me."

Tears filled her eyes and spilled over, making it difficult to see the diamond ring he held in front of her.

Instead of taking the ring, she turned to him.

He cupped her face. The ring on the tip of his finger pressed against her wet cheek. "Say yes. Be my wife and I will spend the rest of my life making you happy and loving you."

"You already do. Yes. Yes, I'll marry you."

Drake kissed her and it was like the sun brightened just for them. Fireworks burst in her heart, lighting it up with a rush of love. She didn't think she'd ever be this happy.

He broke the kiss, took her hand, slipped on the ring, held her hands in his, then stared down into her eyes. His shone with love and happiness. "I wanted you the moment I set eyes on you. I never thought I'd ever be happy again. I never thought I'd get married and have a family, but you make everything possible."

She smiled up at him and narrowed her eyes with suspicion. "You know."

He tilted his head and feigned ignorance. "Know what?"

For a split second she thought maybe her secret prompted the proposal, but she dismissed it immediately. The proposal was inevitable no matter what because they loved each other and wanted to be together forever.

Drake gave her another silly grin. "Are you talking about the fact you're pregnant with my baby and have kept it to yourself for weeks?"

"You've known for weeks?"

"I may not know a lot about women, but I do know how their bodies work." He gave hers an appreciative sweep with his hot gaze. He put his big hand on her belly. "We didn't exactly talk about it." No, they'd silently agreed to accept the possibility the night they made love at the apartment. "Are you happy about it?"

She put her hand over his and stared at the diamond ring winking up at her. "I am over the moon excited." She looked up at him. "You may have figured it out, but I still have a secret."

He tilted his head. "What's that?"

She put her other hand over his. "Twins."

Drake gasped. "Really?"

"I'll show you the ultrasound when we go back into the house."

"Why didn't you tell me?"

"I planned to tell you tonight after the weddings. Something special that is just for us."

"We think alike." Drake kissed her softly. "And you needed to hold on to it for a little while and let it settle because of Juliana."

She nodded, appreciating that he understood she wasn't keeping it from him, but needed time to reconcile losing something dear and being given something so precious at the same time. Something that brought back all the wonderful memories she shared with her twin.

Her children would have that.

"I miss her. She would have loved this. Twins. Two souls forever connected from the moment we created them."

Drake didn't drop to one knee when he proposed, but he did so now and planted one, then two kisses on her belly. "You guys are so lucky." He looked up at her. "I am, too."

She leaned down and kissed him. "I'm pretty sure I'm the lucky one to have found you."

He wrapped his arm around her thighs, stood, and lifted her in his arms. "When do you want to get married?"

"As soon as possible. Here, at our home, in our backyard." That made him smile. "But for today, let's keep this between us and let my sisters have their day."

"Deal." He let her body slide down his until she was face-to-face with him. "I love you."

"I love you, too."

This time, the kiss was soft and sweet to seal the deal. She'd be his wife. He'd be her husband. Soon, they'd be Mom and Dad to twins.

Life had a way of giving and taking. Today, it gave her everything she'd ever wanted.

Chapter Forty

Adria turned her face up to the sky and let the sun warm her skin and fill her heart.

Today had been a long time coming. For all of them.

Roxy stood arm in arm with Noah watching Sonya marry the man she loved more than anything. Roxy was already Noah's wife.

"I now pronounce you husband and wife." And now Sonya was Austin's wife.

"You may kiss your bride."

Austin didn't hesitate to pull Sonya close and kiss her like his life depended on it.

Everyone cheered for the happily married couple.

They belonged together.

So did Roxy and Noah.

And her and Drake.

As happy as she was for her sisters today, it was hard to stand up for each of them without Juliana beside her.

Roxy and Sonya didn't forget that. So they gave her a wedding present inspired by Juliana's joined hearts. She touched her finger to the twin sapphire heart pendants made from stones mined on Austin and Sonya's land. Perfectly matched sapphires. One for her and Juliana on separate chains. Because Adria and Juliana were the same but separate, too.

One day, they'd be together again. She believed that.

But for now, she had to live her life. And it looked brilliantly bright.

She caught Drake's eye. It seemed everyone else disappeared when she looked at him. He looked back and made her feel like she was his whole world, too. She pressed her hand flat against her melting heart, showing him the I Love You and double heart tattoos.

He mouthed, *I love you*, back.

The joy that brought washed out her grief and her hand dropped to her belly and their two little secrets. She'd taken off her engagement ring so as not to overshadow the brides. Drake promised to put it back on her finger tonight.

Today was about her sisters. So she smiled for all the pictures. She was nice to her mom, who flew in from Vegas with Big Mama and Roxy's mom, Candy. June, Sonya's mom, sat with all of them.

After dinner, Adria, with Trinity beside her, graciously accepted the round of applause for catering the event from *Almost Homemade*.

And then it was Adria's turn to give the toast. All day she dreaded and anticipated this moment.

"You can do it." Drake sat beside her at the wedding party's table, encouraging her, then clinked his butter knife against his champagne glass to get everyone's attention.

She stood and held her glass in her hand. Everyone stared back. All but one face that matched her own. Her heart pinched again with the pain of Juliana's absence.

"Hi, everyone. I'm Adria." She took a deep breath and spoke from the heart. "Roxy, Sonya, and I are sisters. Not by blood, but something much deeper." Most of the guests, if not all, knew that. "Our souls are connected. When we found each other, we knew we were better together." Tears gathered in her eyes. "Roxy was our fearless leader. Tough. Strong. Independent. Noah had his work cut out for him winning her heart. She protected it well. But Noah saw Roxy's true beauty and captured her heart." Roxy wiped away a tear. Noah raised his glass and gave her a nod. "Sonya likes her numbers. She didn't think she and Austin added up at first, but it soon became clear she and he equaled a perfect couple. Austin liked her spitfire, get-it-done attitude. It matched his own. Her compassion made him want to hold on to her when he thought he had nothing. She turned out to be the most precious jewel in his life." Austin, sitting next to Adria, took her hand and kissed the back of it. Sonya smiled up at Adria, tears streaming down her cheeks.

Adria barely held it together.

"When Roxy and Sonya moved to Montana, I was jealous of the life they'd found and the men they loved. I wanted what they had. And when I came here, I found it for myself." She glanced down at Drake and smiled because he always made her smile. "Roxy, Sonya, and I brought our sister Juliana here to heal. And she did. Because, like I said, we have always been better together." She looked from Roxy to Sonya. "She dreamed of the life and love we found here. But she was taken from us before she found it." Adria let the tears fall and spoke through her clogged throat. "I know with everything I am that she is here with us. Today. Tomorrow. Always. We are together. We will always be together. We are a family. And I wish you"—she pointed her glass toward Roxy and Noah—"and you"—she pointed her glass to Sonya and Austin—"a long and happy life. Together." She held her glass high and everyone gathered stood. "To love and family."

"Love and family," the small, intimate crowd said in unison, then sipped champagne.

Drake stood and wrapped his arm around her, pulling her back into his chest and kissing her on the head. "You amaze me. That was perfect. I love you."

She turned in Drake's arms and hugged him close, needing his support and comfort to get her through this moment. Roxy, Noah, Sonya, and Austin closed in and swamped her in love in one big group hug that made her tears dry up with her laughter. "You guys are squishing me."

They stepped back, but all of them stood close.

Roxy spoke for the group. "I know you're supposed to cry at weddings, but, Adria, that was beautiful."

"I meant it. We all deserve to be happy. We are a family. All of us."

Sonya glanced up at Austin, who nodded down at her. "Austin and I brought a plus-one to our wedding," she whispered, not letting the rest of the guests overhear.

Her sister, pregnant, too.

She glanced at Drake, who nodded at her. "I'm surprised you held out this long."

Adria laughed and turned to her sisters. "I hate to show you up on your wedding day, but Drake and I are expecting two."

Her sisters gasped.

Drake pulled the ultrasound photo from his jacket pocket and held it up.

"And I do mean two." She pointed to the two little beans in the picture. "Twins."

That set off another round of tears for her and Sonya along with back slaps and bear hugs between the guys. Noah and Austin had no trouble including Drake. They'd all gotten quite close.

When the congratulations faded, Drake took her hand and slipped the diamond engagement ring on her finger for all of them to see. "He asked me this morning." She looked up at the man she loved more than anything in this world. "I said yes."

Yes to love.

Yes to happiness.

Yes to a beautiful life.

She accepted all the congratulations, then took both of her sisters' hands. "Juliana would have loved this. She would have been a great aunt."

Roxy smiled. "She'd be the one sneaking them candy and letting them stay up all night by the time they're two."

Adria laughed. "They'd be tattooed by the time they're twelve."

"Hey, I still haven't been allowed to get mine," Annabelle, who'd become Roxy's "little sister," grumbled. When Roxy's father passed away he made Roxy Annabelle's guardian.

Sonya tried to appease Annabelle. "We'll all go together when you get yours so we can have a fifth rose added to ours."

"Just promise us you'll finish high school and college before you get married and have little ones of your own." Adria hugged Annabelle to her side, understanding all too well the need to connect with others and be included.

She looked around at their group, felt the close bond between all of them, and knew none of them would ever be alone. They were what family should be.

The celebration went on into the night long after the cakes were cut and the happy couples left for their honeymoons.

Drake took her home and showed her just how much he loved her and how much he wanted to make her his wife.

Which he did a month later in front of much the same crowd of friends and family who attended Roxy's and Sonya's weddings. They held the ceremony at their completed home in their backyard just like she wanted. And though she missed Juliana even more that day, she celebrated what she did have in her life.

A month after that, Adria, Roxy, and Sonya did what Juliana would have wanted. They spread her ashes and let her fly. They went up in a helicopter and spread her ashes over Roxy and Noah's ranch, Sonya and Austin's ranch, and Adria and Drake's place. Now she would always be with them.

That night she and Drake hosted their first of many family dinners.

Roxy and Noah hosted dinner a month after that and announced that they were expecting.

Soon enough they found out Sonya was expecting a boy, Roxy a little girl.

Adria and Drake wanted to be surprised.

On the morning Adria went into labor, Adria woke up from the recurring dream she'd had of Juliana for months. Her sister standing in the sunlight with a blue flower in one hand and a pink one in the other.

Hours of labor later, Adria and Drake held their twins in their arms. Their son, James. And their daughter, Juliana.

Author's Note

Dear Readers and Friends,

I'm excited to bring you a brand-new Wild Rose Ranch book and a story fans of His Cowboy Heart have asked for ever since I introduced Drake McGrath in the Montana Men series.

My husband was an Army Ranger. He earned a Purple Heart while serving. He came home a better and different man in many ways, but suffered PTSD symptoms for years. He still looks for snipers on roofs and has nightmares sometimes, even though he's turned into an engineering geek (I say with love and pride).

Brody McBride (The Return of Brody McBride), Jamie Keller (His Cowboy Heart), and Drake McGrath are loosely based on my husband's experience and my research into soldiers who suffer from PTSD.

Drake's story is a raw and difficult look into a man suffering and trying to escape his past and find a way to live with his new reality. Though Drake makes it (of course he does, it's a romance), other soldiers/veterans suffer in silence or lose their battle with PTSD. If you or someone you love needs help and support, contact the Military Crisis Line at 1 (888) 362-4217 or the National Suicide Prevention Lifeline at 1 (800) 273-8255.

Drake is supported by his family, psychiatrist, and a woman who changes everything for him. But Adria is dealing with trying to help her sister Juliana overcome her drug problem. She gets

Juliana into a drug treatment program. *If you or someone you know needs help, contact the National Drug Helpline at 1 (888) 633-3239 for treatment and recovery.*

I hope everyone out there knows recovery is possible. Hold on. Ask for help. You are worth it.

You deserve your own happy ending.

I hope Drake and Adria's happy ending inspires you!

With Love,
Jennifer Ryan

Keep reading for a sneak peek at

Waiting on a Cowboy

the first book in Jennifer Ryan's new series

The McGraths

Coming August 2020 from Avon Books!

Prologue

Back in the day
Kindergarten Playground

"Hey, Lizard, I'll trade you my grapes for one of your chocolate chip cookies."

"Stop calling me that."

Tate sat next to Liz, rolled his eyes, and stuck his tongue out at her because she told him that *all* the time. And he ignored her *all* the time.

Liz handed over the cookie and popped one of the grapes into her mouth. She'd rather have the cookie but didn't mind sharing with Tate— even if he did call her names. He didn't mean it.

He's weird.

But she liked him. He always picked her first to play a game, let her ride the pony at his birthday party before anyone else, and always sat with her to paint during free time and at lunch. She liked that. Daddy picked Mama to do everything with him, too.

Tate stuffed the whole cookie in his mouth and she announced, "I'm going marry you."

Tate stopped chewing and stared at her. "Na-uh."

"Yes, I am."

He shook his head. "Na-uh."

She smiled, confident she knew better. "You'll see."

Chapter One

Tate walked into the Backroads bar ahead of his brother Declan and spotted the woman who'd been dodging him for weeks. A you-done-me-wrong country song blasted through the overhead speakers as he closed the distance, his eyes locked on the girl he'd known since pre-school but who couldn't be bothered to call him lately. It used to be all he had to do was think about her and the phone rang. But ever since her parting "you just don't get it" shot weeks ago, he'd heard nothing from her. And he wanted to know why.

He wanted things to go back to the way they used to be.

"What the hell, Lizard?"

She turned on the stool, her head tilting to look up at him, fiery dark red hair falling over one shoulder, down her arm, and brushing the table-top. "What do you want?" Not an ounce of welcome tinged those words or filled her annoyed green eyes.

"I want to know why you haven't called or come by the ranch in weeks."

Her head fell back in exasperation and those green eyes that always saw everything about him so easily narrowed. "Have you missed me?"

The question set off an alarm in his head, but he didn't know why. Answering her question seemed like stepping on a landmine, so he avoided it. "Why are you avoiding me?"

"After our last conversation, I thought that'd be clear."

He tried to remember what they'd talked about, but he'd been distracted by what happened with Drake and Adria and her sister Juliana. The whole thing had been a traumatizing mess. He'd been so happy and relieved for his brother when Drake and Adria worked things out, got back together, and ended up engaged that everything else in his life faded to the background.

"Lizard, I was in the middle of helping Trinity and Adria get their business up and running. I was building shelves or some shit when you called and then all that stuff happened with Juliana. Sorry, I've been distracted."

Sadness and regret filled her eyes. "That's just it, Tate, you unloaded all that on me at the time, yet you can't remember what I said to you."

He thought back and recalled the thing that stuck with him. "You told me that if things were meant to work out, Drake and Adria would make it happen. They did. They're married and expecting and Drake's happier than I've ever seen him."

For the first time since he walked in, a soft smile tilted her lips. "I'm happy for him."

Of course she was. Their lives had been intertwined forever. She knew everything that happened in his life and with his family.

"So what's the problem?"

"You," she snapped. She never raised her voice to him. "And me for hoping for something that is never going to happen because you're *you.*"

He held his hands out wide, then let them fall and slap the sides of his thighs. "What the hell does that even mean?"

Before he got an answer, some dude with dark hair and a fuck-off look in his eyes walked up and inserted himself between him and Liz.

Tate immediately hated the guy.

"She's with me."

That's what you think.

Liz was *his* best friend and no one got in between them.

Tate glared at the guy and took a step closer, but the guy stood his ground and didn't move out of Tate's way.

Liz slipped off the stool, stood next to the guy in a tie, button-down shirt, and slacks in a honky-tonk bar, linked her fingers with his, and leaned into him. "Clint, it's okay. Tate's an old friend."

One of the uptight dude's eyebrows shot up at that. Liz looked a little sheepish.

Tate refocused on *Clint*. "I'm her best friend."

Clint's stance relaxed even if he didn't back down. "Ah. She told me about you." Whatever Liz told him obviously didn't impress the guy.

Tate could not care less. "Then you'll excuse us while I have a word with her."

Liz spoke before Clint said anything. "I said what I wanted to say the last time we spoke."

"And you haven't said anything since," he pointed out, his gut tight. Obviously, he'd missed something big. From the sound of things, it just might cost him the person who knew him better than anyone and had always been there for him.

"It's not like you called or came to see me in the last six weeks."

"It hasn't been that long." They never went more than a few days without talking or seeing each other. Maybe it had been a couple weeks this time, but not six. Right?

"You're busy doing your thing. It's time I did mine. If you'll excuse us, we'd like to get back to our date."

What the fuck?

Liz dismissed him and turned to take her seat again.

Tate couldn't let things go on this way. They definitely didn't end this way. "Wait."

Clint put his hand on Tate's chest to stop him from touching Liz's shoulder.

Tate went still and pointedly looked at that hand on him. "You want to keep it, you'll take it back. Now."

They locked eyes and the energy around them became charged with animosity.

Clint dropped his hand but still didn't get the hell out of Tate's way. "You didn't want a shot with her, so I took it. Back off. She wants to be with me."

Like she didn't want to be Tate's friend anymore. *What the fuck was going on?*

Tate felt Declan come up behind him before Declan's hand settled on his shoulder. "Come on, bro, let's get a beer and leave Liz and her date alone to enjoy their evening."

Tate glared at the back of Liz's head. She sat there, not saying a word. She wouldn't even look at him.

"We'll talk later, Lizard."

Clint shook his head. "She hates that silly nickname."

No, she didn't. Though she'd never admit it. It had become a thing between *them*. It didn't have anything to do with Clint. "What the hell do you know?"

"From what I've heard, I know a hell of a lot more about her than you do."

Declan grabbed Tate's arm before he decked the guy and pulled Tate back a step. "Let's go."

Tate had known Liz practically his whole damn life. "You don't know anything about me and Liz."

"I know she wants a man who appreciates her and doesn't take her for granted."

Tate cocked his fist back and was about to plant it right in smug Clint's jutted chin when Liz jumped in between them and planted both hands on his chest and shoved him back into Declan. "Don't you dare ruin this for me!"

He had no idea what she meant.

She held up her hand. "Just go." The plea in her eyes killed him.

His gut went tight and his heart had trouble beating against the tightness around his chest. "Liz?"

Her lips tilted in a half frown. "Go get a beer with Declan. Flirt with the waitresses, pick up one of the dozen women staring at you right now. Do what you do and let me be."

That almost sounded like goodbye.

It couldn't be.

But Liz turned her back on him again.

Clint took her hand, pulled her close, then walked her to the dance floor where he took Liz in his arms and swayed to the slow song with her head resting on his shoulder.

Declan smacked his hand on Tate's shoulder. "It was only a matter of time."

Tate couldn't take his eyes off Liz in that asshole's arms. "What the hell are you talking about?"

"She's a beautiful woman. You had to know that at some point she'd want a serious relationship with someone who wants to make her his wife and have a family. He seems decent enough."

Tate turned on Declan. "You don't know anything about him."

"He'd have to be a good guy for Liz to like him so much."

"How do you know she likes him?"

"He stepped in to get you away from her because he wants her all to himself. She let him."

She picked *Clint* over him.

She never chose anyone over him.

What the hell is going on?

The crack about flirting with waitresses and picking up a woman hinted that she didn't like him choosing others over her either.

He knew that. He wasn't blind or an idiot.

But she was Liz. Hands-off had always been his rule.

"It's unusual for women and men to be friends." Declan headed for the bar.

Tate followed. "We've been friends since we were finger painting and eating Play-Doh."

Declan took one of the open stools and held up two fingers to Tami behind the bar, who nodded that she'd get them their usual. "Liz has been in love with you since then, but you can't expect her to love you, and only you, for the rest of her life when you dismiss her feelings the way you do."

"What are you talking about?" Tate didn't want to go there.

Declan glanced over and laughed. "Oh come on, you can't tell me that you don't revel in the fact that she loves you and puts up with all your shit while you treat her like your favorite pet."

That pissed him off. "I do not." Did he? That sinking feeling in his gut intensified.

Declan shoved his shoulder so he'd turn in his stool. "Look at her. Do you want to strip her bare and get your hands on her?"

"That's Liz." He didn't dare think such things about her. They were friends.

Or they used to be.

"Exactly. How long did you expect her to wait for you to stop seeing her as pigtailed Lizzy Lizard? She's a woman grown now, Tate, with hopes and dreams of love and marriage and a relationship that isn't all about you."

"Our relationship isn't all about me."

Declan laughed in his face. "Keep telling yourself that, bro, but you're the one who has no idea what happened six weeks ago that made her take a huge step back until she fell right into Clint's arms."

Fucking Clint.

"*He* made her dump me."

Declan saluted Tami with his beer bottle in thanks for filling their order. "Dumped? Is that how it feels?"

Kinda. But he denied, denied, denied.

"It's not like that. We've only ever been friends."

"And it's been clear for years she wanted more." Declan frowned. "Don't shake your head at me. You know I'm right. Everyone can see it. She settled for friends because you mean that much to her, but you can't expect her to settle for that for the rest of her life. You can't expect her to watch you date other women, listen to you tell her all about how it's going, and cry on her shoulder when it doesn't work out, and think she doesn't feel jealous and left out."

"She dates."

"And nothing ever comes of it because you've got her heart." Declan took a sip of his beer. "Were you even a little happy when those relationships ended?"

His stomach clenched. "Of course not." As soon as the words left his mouth, he heard the lie. He'd never been jealous of her relationships. He was just happier when she was focused on him.

I'm an asshole.

And a terrible friend.

He should be happy for her. He should want her to find someone special. He wanted to see her as happy as Drake and Adria looked when they were together.

He glanced at Liz on the dance floor smiling and clapping her hands as she spun and swayed her hips in the line dance, Clint trying to keep up with her.

He just didn't want her happy with Clint. "Something about that guy bugs me."

"Mom always told us we have to share our toys."

Tate smacked Declan upside the head. "She's my best friend, not a Hot Wheels."

"Maybe she'll make you her maid of honor at her wedding."

Tate fumed and downed half his beer. "Fuck you."

"Nice comeback." Declan turned and leaned back against the bar, sitting like Tate, watching Liz on the dance floor. "You ate up all her attention. Are you upset that she's giving it to someone else or pissed that she might be falling in love with him and you want to be that guy for the rest of her life?" Declan held up his hand to stop Tate from spitting out another expletive. "Don't answer. Think about it. Because she deserves to find someone who treats her the way she's treated you all these years. Don't take this chance away from her just because you want her to love you and no one else when you don't really want her."

"Fuck you." Tate slammed his beer down on the counter, stood, and walked out of the bar without looking at Declan or Liz because he didn't know what to do with Declan's question or how Declan's words made him feel.

This was *Liz*. Liz! The girl who played in the rain with him and raced him on horseback and never won but always took it in stride. They double-dated to all the school dances. She warned him when one of his girlfriends did something behind his back and always consoled him after a breakup. She had no problem pointing out all his faults and where he'd gone wrong but in a humorous way that made him smile and laugh and somehow feel better despite the fact she was probably right.

Honest. Dependable. Smart. Kind. Generous. The list went on of all the good things he liked about her. Her sweetness was what drew him to her when they were kids.

She was a part of his life. A piece of him.

And with that thought, he went back to what Declan asked.

Did he want to keep her from falling for some other guy just because he didn't want to lose her as a friend?

He wanted her to be happy. She deserved to have everything she wanted.

What really got to him was that it wasn't that he hadn't ever looked at her as a woman he wanted, but that he always stopped himself from crossing that line because he didn't want to lose what they already had together.

But if he lost her to some other guy, would he forever wonder what might have been if he took a chance on them?

What if he'd waited too long?

What if she really was done with him?